CHAPTER ONE

"It's okay. You will be alright." The words tumble out, soothing but hollow. My tears betray the lie even as I hold them back. Across the green expanse, stone cairns rise in uneven clusters, the irregular protrusions and dolmens reaching ever upward. I've seen this place before—felt its shadow wrap around my throat. I almost died here. No…she… she almost died here. That's the aspect, not me… and not yet.

Lost in thought, I trip over a root, nearly dropping the soulstone cradled in my arms. Its massive form quivers with light, swirling colors flaring and then settling as I steady it.

"No," I whisper fiercely, clutching it tighter. *"I won't let you fall."* But she feels heavier with every step, her weight pressing into my chest like an iron shackle. The burden of destiny grows with every pulse.

The twilight world around me hums with life, its beauty both a balm and a torment. In the aspect's thoughts, I feel it as well, a sense of alien comfort. Beneath an unfamiliar sky of three luminous orbs, blue flowers bloom in the soft glow of perpetual dusk. A warm breeze plays across my skin, stirring the grasses where strange, sleek mice dart in and out of sight. Above, ravens wheel in the fading light. In the distance, Umbryss roars. I will miss the ancient dragon.

Lesser Fae stand silent, hiding at the edge of the forest, their

1

luminous eyes watching. One flickers into focus—vermillion wings unfurled against the dark backdrop of trees. Their stillness unnerves me. They feel the fracture in my heart, the rift that widens with each faltering step. Run, I call mentally. Run to the nearest gate. Escape. I have no faith in Nemhain's plan. Of course, she doesn't either. Why else open so many gates?

The soulstone pulses in my arms, its rhythm matching my own faltering heartbeat. Each thrum is a reminder of the weight not just on my body but on my very soul. I tried to warn my sister. I tried to stop this. But she wouldn't listen. And now, I carry her, my child—both of us staggering toward an end I cannot see.

"We're not alone," her voice whispers, soft and childlike, echoing from within the crystal.

"No," I reply, my voice trembling.

Her fear leaks through the connection between us, sharp and jagged. "Is it her? She will destroy me."

I clutch the stone tighter, suppressing the sob rising in my throat. "No. She will not. I won't let her."

"She will," she insists, panic fraying her words. "She will destroy us both."

I've seen it, too—glimpses of what she fears. The looming shadow, the hunger. But futures twist like vines; their paths are never clear.

"Destiny is strange," I murmur, trying to soothe her. "It's never what we expect. We can't see it all. Not yet." My words feel empty, even to me. There's so much I'm holding back, truths she isn't ready to hear.

Her panic subsides, her presence fracturing into fragments of thought. It's a good sign. And yet, it wounds me, this unspooling of her mind, so necessary but so hard to endure.

"How can your aspect be here?" she asks, her voice faint now, more curiosity than fear. "She's not even born yet."

"The soul is timeless," I say, my tone softer now. "It's a thread that winds through all things, tethered to itself beyond the limits of time. And a part of me lives within her; it binds us."

A pause. Then, in that questioning voice I know so well: "Mother?"

"Yes, daughter?" I answer, my voice a shadow of a smile. She always saves this tone for her most unanswerable questions.

"Will she love me?"

The ache in my chest sharpens, the weight of the soulstone crushing me in ways it shouldn't, as if I were the one trapped within.

"I don't know," I admit finally, my voice breaking. "But I'll make sure she remembers how—and why. When she understands, she will go to her grave to save you."

Her voice fades, and I'm grateful for the silence. It gives me a moment of peace as I tread through the garden, careful not to disturb the blossoms. I chose to walk this path even though I could have flown. She is my most precious child, and today, I wanted to carry her. I wanted as much time as I could have.

Lindon Danu passes beneath me. Despite the surface calm, its currents are alive with an urgency that feels almost sentient. It's as if it knows the pain and worry in my heart.

I carry her across the vast expanse, my massive boots just brushing the surface with a lightness that shouldn't belong to me, not today. My heart should send me to the bottom. And yet, I leave only the barest ripples in the lake's stillness, until finally, I reach Féagharach, a solitary refuge nestled at the heart of the immense crater lake. Here, she will rest, hidden and safe. If all goes well, her father will come to find her, and we will strike in this place where our power is greatest. It's not much of a plan, but it's all we've got. I cradle the soulstone one last time, voice choked with guilt. "I should have fought for you."

"You would've died," my daughter says softly. "And I don't want that. I love you."

"I know," I whisper. "And I love you more than life itself." With a mournful wail and burning tears, I set the soulstone on the stump of Crann Bethad.

Only moments pass before the ground trembles. In the distance, the mountains convulse, their peaks shattering as they belch ash and molten rock into the sky. Rivers of fire carve relentless paths down their flanks, devouring everything in their wake. Hot winds blow in the stench of sulfur and the roar of the land tearing itself apart. My worst fears crystallize into reality, undeniable and merciless. Our world is unraveling before my eyes. We are ruined—our lives, our plans, our very future—all slipping into the abyss.

I try to grab the soulstone, but it's already sinking into the stump, beyond my reach. "Please, Mother Danu, help me!" There's no answer, even as my fingers slip from the crystal, and it sinks from view. "Mother of Waters! Where are you?" The words are a roar of pain and rage.

"Run, Mother! You must run!" Her voice tears through my panicked thoughts, sharp and desperate.

I still scrabble at the stubborn stump of ancient wood, tearing away bits. If I can just get to her. But for every splinter I rip loose, more form. The old stump remains, ancient and defiant, the last remnant of our connection to the Light Fae, and now, it is her prison. Every instinct screams at me to free her—to fight, to rescue my child—but I can already feel the frothing water boiling, rising, lapping at my boots. The storm of ash and flame closes in from every side.

She's right. I can't stay.

My throat tightens as I lift off. I take to the sky. I push myself faster, higher, the wind dragging at me as I flee. My chest burns with the horror of what comes next, what I must do. But even as I race against the end of the world, a weight claws at me.

I know what awaits her. She will remain, bound to the stone, trapped in darkness for what will feel like an eternity.

And no one—no one—can remain sane, alone in a box, for thousands of years.

I stayed in bed for quite a while, the blackout curtains still drawn. Liz lay awake, her stillness a silent comfort, and I adored her for that, her patience. It allowed me time to wrestle my feelings into some semblance of order, to push back the wellspring of tears.

I drew myself from the warmth of the bed and pushed open the curtains. The moon hung outside, bright and full, casting a soft glow. The power outage had snuffed out the orange haze of the city, and the stars gleamed, each a frozen point in the endless black—sparkling reminders of the Akkorokamui's wrath. And yet, their beauty calmed the knots in my chest, clearing my head.

Liz rose and slid up behind me, wrapping her arms around

my waist. "What are you thinking?" she whispered, her warm breath tickling my neck.

Smiling, I relaxed and felt the tension ease. "Just the dream again. I'll be fine." I didn't want to talk about it. "By the way, Leah's talking again. She asked for eggs this morning and wants to return to school tomorrow. I think the routine would be good for her."

Liz sighed, her relief palpable. "I'm glad. I was starting to worry."

"I didn't expect Anne's death to hit her so hard," I murmured, a knot of guilt twisting inside.

"It was still her mother," Liz stated, just a fact, not an accusation. "And the wound is not so deep as you imagine. Anne was already gone, and it wasn't as if she wanted to go back to her. Leah will recover. She has us."

"Us." The word hung in my thoughts. For the first time, I had a proper family. I'd never really known how much I wanted or needed it: a daughter who was growing up so quickly, another who was happy to take her sweet time, and a partner who loved us all and whom I respected and loved back. It really was my own little slice of heaven, solidifying my resolve around something.

"Liz?" I whispered.

"Mmhmm?" She said as she nuzzled my neck and then ran her tongue over my ear, raising gooseflesh on my arms. The soft scent of dragon's blood, which the Romans called dracaena, played about my nose and tongue.

"Do vampires get married?"

She stilled. With her face still tucked against my neck, she gave a muffled, "I'm sorry?"

"I said—"

She pulled back, resting her chin on my shoulder. "I heard you. I'm just wondering why you're asking."

"Answer the question, love," I said, reaching back, my fingers tracing gentle paths through her hair.

She tugged me around to look at her, eyes intent under a scalloped brow. "Not that I've ever confirmed myself, but there's nothing against it. Now, again, why do you ask?"

I grinned, pulling away to retrieve something from the wardrobe. Then I dragged Liz back over to the bed. "Let me tell you a story. A true story."

She raised an eyebrow, her grin widening, eyes narrowing. "Another goddess in your family tree I should know about?"

I barked a laugh. "Not quite. But then again, who knows? Anyway, my parents didn't have much at first. My dad was a new cop, and he did something crazy. He bought a diamond, far below retail, from a guy who used to move jewelry." I pressed the side of my nose. "Know what I mean?"

Liz chuckled. "I do."

"He had it set and used it to propose to my mother."

"So, You're saying Mike proposed to your mother with a stolen diamond?"

"So Ma says," I replied. "Of course, my mother said yes, and then they got married."

Liz just looked at me, her face a mask of checked amusement, waiting for either the punchline or, perhaps, what was actually coming. I twisted off the bed to one knee on the floor and opened the box between us. Inside was a platinum ring set with a two-carat diamond.

"Liz Medlyn, will you marry me?"

Liz blinked at me, wide-eyed, her mouth opening and closing. Then she drew a hand to her face as her eyes glistened. The silence lasted a long time—*a long time.*

"Umm, hoping for an answer here, babe," I said, giving her a questioning look.

Finally, she whispered, "Yes. Yes, I'll marry you." She laughed, tears streaming down her cheeks as I slipped the ring onto her finger. She admired it for a moment before glancing up at me. "Now, please, tell me you didn't just propose with a diamond that fell off the back of a truck."

I shook my head, grinning. "You're too easy. This was supposed to be my mother's anniversary ring. She insisted you have it." Liz's tears came harder, and I brushed them away with my thumb. "I love you, Liz. I don't want anyone else."

She smiled through the tears. "Eternity is a long time, Cait. Will you still love me in a hundred years?"

"I'm sure I will. The real question is, will *you*?"

She looked me over, smirking. "Maybe. Though, this model is a little dated already."

"Hey!" I protested, laughing.

She pulled me onto the bed, and we lay there for a long time, just staring at each other. Finally, she said, "You know, I've never known two vampires to get married, but I think that had more to do with religious convictions. As I said, there's no rule against it, and I did know a pair once, Françoise and Sabrina. They were together for five hundred years, and they were so in love, even after all that time."

"Did they die in the fire?"

She nodded solemnly. "Not long before that, though, Sabrina had told me that Françoise was her soulmate and that her only desire was to die when he did, whenever that day came." Her expression turned wistful. "Sad as it was at the time, she got her wish. I suspect that if the two of them hadn't both been pretty firm deists, they might have gotten married. Of course, they always presented themselves as husband and wife, so they may have for all I know."

"Well then, let's see what the next five hundred years bring," I said, my grin making my cheeks ache.

She kissed me, her warmth filling every corner of my soul. For the first time in a long time, I felt like everything would be okay. It was fleeting, though, and my impending journey began to weigh on me.

Mother Lamia had convinced Aoife to let Bian place Úmbra's lehos in her when she died. The intention had been simple—Úmbra's essence would take over Aoife's lifeless body, reshaping it to bring Úmbra back to life. But something had gone wrong. Instead of just reviving Úmbra, the ritual brought them both back, trapped in a single body. Now they lingered in a strange stasis, the body alive but their souls locked in conflict. Now, it was on me to unravel it all and, hopefully, save them both.

"I'm afraid, Liz. Right now, I have everything I want, and this trip is a risk. What if I don't come back? I feel like I have no control. When do I get a choice? When does fate stop deciding my life?"

Liz cupped my face, her gaze unwavering. "You do have a choice, Cait. You have a family that loves you, that wants you here. You don't have to do this if you don't want to. It's okay to choose us. But I know you. You will do it. You can't not. I accept that about you. I also know that you will survive this."

Tears spilled down my cheeks. "I don't deserve you."

"Yes, you do," she murmured, brushing my tears away. "You saved me, and together we saved Katie and Leah. For that alone, you deserve everything. I'll take care of them while you're gone."

Jabba nuzzled Liz at that moment, and she laughed, petting him. "Yes, you too, you big Hutt."

I smiled, clutching her hand. "Just one more time," I whispered to myself.

CHAPTER TWO

"Liz, I have a job for you," Marcella said, slipping another heavy leather-bound book onto the library shelf. The tone of her voice sent a ripple of unease down my spine.

A flicker of tension tightened Liz's mouth as her eyes narrowed. "Okay," she replied, arms crossed. I could feel her tension, coiled like a spring.

"Grace is stuck in D.C., but she has a plane. I need you to convince her to loan it to us."

Liz's expression hardened, and she pressed her lips into a thin line. She rolled her eyes to the ceiling, her fingers tapping a steady, impatient rhythm against her arm. "It's not like she wants to see me, M." A faint edge colored her voice.

"She'll see you," Marcella replied.

I caught a hint of something unsaid and turned to Liz, raising an eyebrow. "It's you she wants to see, specifically?" It wasn't so much a question as a statement expecting confirmation.

Liz gave a stiff, dismissive shrug, shifting her weight with clear reluctance. "An old ex." She brushed a hand through her hair as if wanting to shake off the thought. "We didn't exactly part on the best terms." Jaw and eyes tight, she turned to Marcella, voice sharp. "Fine. But maybe I'll pay Senator Kim a visit while I'm there. That woman deserves what's coming to her."

Marcella turned, a hand on her hip, the other loosely gripping a worn book as she leveled a stern gaze at Liz. "Absolutely not. One wrong move, and things spiral out of control. That would mean war with the humans. I won't risk that, not unless there's no other recourse."

"Whatever, but I'm taking Cait with me on this one. We've been apart long enough, and there's been something I've been meaning to do while we're down there."

Marcella glanced my way with a questioning gaze.

Taking a half step back, I raised my hands defensively. "Don't look at me. This is the first I've heard of it."

"You know what," Marcella said, placing the book on the shelf and turning back to us. "I don't want to know. But, I need you both back here in seventy-two hours. We're going to start packing up the camps, and I need help with coordination. How do you plan to get past the cordon?"

"They're looking for preternatural creatures, not two women on a girl's trip," Liz answered. "Should be no problem."

Like clockwork, my anxiety flared. "Is this our only option for a plane? They may not last three more days. They could die in that time." In truth, I was pretty certain Aoife was far more powerful than Úmbra, simply by her very nature. Aoife would likely survive, but Úmbra certainly wouldn't. No one wanted that, least of all Aoife.

Closing her eyes, Marcella pinched the bridge of her nose and sighed. "There's nothing else I can do. Logan's closed for repairs. We've exhausted every avenue at this point. Nastasia is down to calling in favors from Russian oligarchs, but she doesn't expect much. I'll do everything I can to step up the repairs to the jet I bought, but it needs far more work than I expected. So, we're stuck with a minimum of three days unless, by some miracle, the Light Fae let the Irish turn their fucking electricity back on. If that isn't irony, I have no idea what is."

I went to say something else, but Liz touched my forearm. "Let it go, Cait. We've got three days minimum, and I need you on this trip."

I spun sharply and stalked from the Library. We were getting nowhere.

Liz caught up and pulled me to a halt before placing a hand on one of my shoulders and cupping my cheek. "There's nothing to be done about it, so let's make the best of the next three days."

I sighed and nodded, then gave her a chaste kiss. "I know. It just sucks." I shot a heated glare back toward the library entrance. "If she didn't have you around to keep her organized, she'd be fucked. I had no idea how much Ninetta and Caldwell must have been doing. She's a mess."

"I heard that," Marcella called from the library.

"Good, you pain in the ass," I muttered.

"I heard that, too," she shot back, stomping to the doorway. "Cait, try to understand. Just like you have duties as a cop, I have duties to all of us. Time's running short. I have to get the camps ready for evacuation and find a place for the occupants, and I still have no idea exactly what to do about Senator Kim. We can't risk the wrath of the entire US government. She can still out us, you know."

I nodded and gave a resigned sigh. "I know." The whole situation was a cluster fuck. And we still had no idea how Senator Kim, formerly a second-rate mayor from Boston, kept outmaneuvering us. So far, Kim had kept mum about vampires, but that didn't matter much. When Aoife woke up, she would be a target, what with her shimmering skin and silver hair. And then people would start looking very closely at her twin, which was, as Déra would say, 'no bueno.'

When we returned to our room, Liz packed a small travel bag. Then, she picked up my duffel as I grumbled further about Marcella and where she could shove her duty.

"Where are we going?" I inquired as she stalked toward the door to her—well, our room.

"First, we're going to sign the papers on a building in the north end. Unfortunately, it looks like a dungeon, so we'll have to renovate it."

"You don't mean…" I said as she stopped in the doorway.

She grinned. "I bought the building. We're going to renovate it back into a four-story single-family home. The leases all end between now and the end of June."

"What about Rebecca?" I asked, referring to my old upstairs neighbor, and it suddenly occurred to me that I probably should have checked in before now.

"I checked on that. She had a stroke a couple of months ago and is in an assisted living home. As for the building, I got it for a pittance. The tsunami wrecked the first floor, but after we renovate it, it'll be as nice as this place and private. No more sudden visits from unwanted guests." At my skeptical expression, she added. "It's walking distance to your precious cannolis and coffee. Though, I still don't understand why you put yourself through that every single Wednesday."

I laughed. "Because, darling, it's how I start my week. Besides, I like cannolis, and they're no good without coffee. I can accept the consequences."

She shook her head in disbelief and changed the subject. "I hope you don't mind that I lined this up while you were asleep."

I blinked and looked around, not meeting her eyes.

"You're upset," Liz said, reading my expression.

"It's not that. I mean, it's great that we'll have a place of our own. I'm just a little torn. I like it here, and it's nice having all the help with the kids. It feels comfortable."

She twisted her pursed lips. "Let's talk about it on the way."

"You still haven't told me what we're doing," I said as we walked toward the elevator.

"You'll see," Liz said. "I have a few surprises in store."

In the garage sat a jet-black jeep with a new wench, an LED light bar, and some serious trail tires. It even had a snorkel. Liz held the fob out toward me. "Here."

"Rental?" I asked, taking the fob from her hand.

"No." She replied, her expression cool and neutral.

"You bought a new Jeep? I really thought you were more the Land Rover type or maybe Audi, like Marcella."

"First of all," Liz replied, her tone half amused, half exasperated. "I'm a Jaguar type. I've got a '99 XJR tucked away in storage, practically showroom condition." She gave a little shrug. "Secondly, I didn't spend a dime on this Jeep. Nas bought it."

My hand froze on the rear gate handle as I looked over my shoulder at her, suspicion prickling at the back of my mind. "So… why are we taking it? I mean, sure, it serves her right after what happened to my car, but…" I trailed off, turning to Liz, eyes wide. "She didn't," I whispered, breathless.

"She did," Liz confirmed, grinning from ear to ear. "I helped her pick it out, just for you."

My mouth dropped open, and I spun back to the Jeep, taking it in like I hadn't even seen it until now. "You're telling me this is mine?" My voice squeaked with excitement, and I half-laughed, half-gasped. "No way." I threw my arms around Liz, laughing.

Stalking around the jeep with giddy abandon, I examined it inside and out. Mother of Waters, she was gorgeous.

I dropped in our bags and closed the back. I checked every inch and took a moment to finger the seventy-centimeter antenna attached to the driver's side A-pillar. "I almost don't want to take it, not knowing where we're going. What if it gets blown up again."

Liz laughed. "That won't happen. Here, it's all in the file. " She handed me a thick dossier. I went to flip it open, but Liz stopped me. "If you want, I can drive us out of the city, and you can read those on the way."

I looked at the car, then at the files, torn. I sighed and handed her the fob.

Liz winked. "Good girl," she said, and we climbed in.

The Jeep was perfect. The seats were cloth, with not a hint of leather anywhere. The radio was nice but not top-of-the-line. No point in buying high-end crap that was just going to get ruined the first time I took her off-road or if she got wet. A police band radio hung from the forward header. "I have a stereo," I whispered in awe.

"Yes, you do. Now read," Liz said and started the car. It didn't make a sound.

"Is this a hybrid?"

"Yes. Three hundred seventy-five horses and four hundred seventy-five foot-pounds of torque."

I blinked. That was more than the gas Jeeps. "Sweet," I murmured. "I owe Nas a thank you fuck for this."

Liz gave me a wry look.

"Kidding, dear," I said with a grin and kissed her on the cheek.

"I said, read, love," she answered with a smirk and drove us out of the garage.

The dossier was a new recruit write-up on a woman named Catherine Sanford, with tabbed sections for work, family, psych evaluations, and personal connections. I thumbed through it and whistled. The work that had gone into this would have made a CIA analyst blush. It had everything about the target, and halfway through, my eyes went wide as a giddy excitement filled me. "Oh, Goddess, really?"

"I thought you might appreciate that," she said with a grin. And for the first time since the gate chamber, I was reminded that Liz did have a nasty streak when push came to shove.

CHAPTER THREE

The trip to D.C. was uneventful. The only indications that anything might be amiss in Boston were the few police roadblocks we'd had to navigate in the city. At the one Army checkpoint on 95 South near the 93 junction, we were all but waved through. That had been a worry but turned out to be nothing. I could only hope it stayed that way.

Marcella put us up at the Sterling, a luxury affair with high thread count sheets, a garden tub, and an amazing view. We were meeting with Grace at sundown, which gave us a few hours to snooze in the super-soft sheets. She probably figured anyone Liz brought would be stuck, still asleep, or struggling. *Surprise, I'm an early riser.*

It was funny. As a human, I'd hated mornings, so much so, it seemed, that I literally had to die to appreciate waking up without at least eight hours. Unfortunately, the early meeting meant no long soak in the tub. Neither of us wanted to get up that early. We did, however, manage to catch a few gropes and kisses in the shower, which was nice and seemed to brighten Liz's mood some.

Liz dressed in business attire. I selected a slick black women's polo and a pair of black cargo pants—typical nondescript bodyguard attire, but comfortable. Finally, sundown arrived, and it was time to go meet this Grace person, whoever she was. We stepped into the elevator, and Liz tapped the lobby button.

"Where are we meeting her?" I asked as the elevator descended.

"Top floor, but we have to go down to go up." Liz shifted on her feet and fidgeted with the room key.

"You know," I said in hushed tones, stepping a bit closer. "I've never seen you nervous before, not ever."

"I'm not nervous," Liz lied as the lobby doors opened. At the express elevator to the penthouse suite, she swiped the key card, but the light on the reader stayed red. She swiped it again. Still, it stayed red. "Damnit," she squeaked, a white-knuckle grip on the key.

I reached out, plucked the room key from her fingers, and took her hand. "That's our room key, dear, not hers."

Liz turned toward me, her expression flush with panic. It caught me off guard, and I pulled her away from the suite elevator into the lobby, sitting her down on one of the sofas.

"What is it?" I asked as I sat next to her.

"I'm sorry, Cait. It's just…" She broke off and looked down, fiddling with the gold bracelet that matched my own.

"You look as nervous as I felt when I went to dinner with Morgan. So what don't I know?"

Liz sighed in resignation. "Grace and I were together for maybe ten years. It was beyond horrendous. She's older than me by over a century, and at the time, that was a significant difference. When we first met, she was sweet and charming, but she turned controlling almost overnight, to the point of keeping me housebound."

"Housebound?" There was only one way to keep a vampire housebound.

"Chained up," Liz muttered, confirming my suspicions.

I pulled one of my handkerchiefs and handed it to her. "We don't have to do this. I'll find another way."

She set her hand on my thigh, applying the barest reassuring pressure. "First of all, no, we need to get this done. It's your sister we're talking about. Secondly, I have to face her at some point. She needs to know that I'll fight tooth and nail.

What I wanted you to know is that I was kept, for all intents, as her prisoner for all that time, and it was Marcella who helped me escape. Eventually, she paid Grace a small fortune to leave me be."

"But Marcella is the oldest."

"As I've said many times," Liz interrupted, continuing her explanation. "Marcella's not invincible, and Grace was one of the rebels who tried to take the throne. She brought down the monarchy. She helped force the council on everyone. It was a bad time for all of us." She looked down at our joined hands despondently. "Honestly, I wish she'd just died in the fire."

I stroked a thumb across her knuckles. "Listen to me. You're not alone." I spoke in comforting tones, but inside, I was seething with an almost unassailable rage. Just the idea that someone could do that to Liz was all I needed to know to end them. And the idea that Liz might still be afraid of her burned me even more. Liz was never afraid. Cautious? Yes. Careful? Certainly. But afraid? Never. "She can't hurt you anymore," I said, mashing on the angry, gut-wrenching feeling. I needed to stay cool.

She squeezed my hand. "I know. But, please, let's not turn this into a bloodbath. We need that plane, Cait."

I grinned and laughed with a mirth I didn't feel. "Come on, now. It's me. I can be subtle."

Liz rolled her eyes, and we stood, heading back to the elevators. On the way, I mentioned casually, "Just remember this when I'm all shaken by our next stop."

She gave me a warm smile that lit up my entire night. "Somehow, I don't think it'll go the same way."

"Do come in," a voice called from the room ahead of us as we stepped off the elevator.

Liz and I stared down a long hallway to a picture window that looked out across the city. The Capitol building rotunda sparkled in the distance, a pretty white reminder of all things wrong with this city and the country. I took Liz's hand, and we strode confidently down the hallway.

A female vampire greeted us. If I'd had to guess her age at turning, I'd have said forty-five, but it was hard to tell. Her plain Irish face was framed in wavy red hair and green eyes, not unlike my own. She wore black trousers, low heels, and a black shirt that plunged all the way down, revealing a scandalous amount of cleavage. *She had it in the tit department but not much else.*

I decided then and there that she was ugly and that Liz could do so much better. Had done better, actually, with me. My mother would have said that was the green monster talking, but I certainly wasn't jealous, that much I knew. *Absolutely not—no, no way am I jealous.*

"Hello, Elizabeth," she purred in her Irish brogue. "And who is this you've brought with you? Is this the famous Cait Reagan that I've heard so much about? I saw your handiwork at the Liberty Hotel on the news. Rather impressive. You can call me Gráinne Ó Máille of Clew Bay."

I nodded and took her offered hand, keeping my face neutral. In my head, it was another matter entirely. *Holy shit. This is Grace O'Malley, the fucking pirate queen of Ireland?* She'd been a hero of Aoife's and mine growing up. I tried to keep the total letdown of finding out she was an evil narcissistic skeeze from coloring my nostalgia too much.

She was an amazing woman who came of age in a difficult time I could only imagine, but I shouldn't have been surprised by her nature. She never kept a single promise to the English crown, and when the Brits came for Connacht, she turned on her own people. She was an opportunist. They always say, 'never meet your heroes.'

"So, Elizabeth, I finally get you before me. What has it been, now?"

"Two hundred fifty years, three hundred eighteen days, and roughly six hours," Liz said smartly. "Obviously, you don't need me around to vouch for Marcella, so why am I here?"

Grace moved forward, and I almost stepped between her and Liz, but Liz placed the back of her hand on my midsection before stepping up and giving the other woman a polite cheek kiss.

"I missed you, of course," Grace said and sat down on the wide, plush couch with the air of a panther perching on a branch, waiting for its meal. "And I missed our time together. With Marcella so busy, I thought perhaps I might spend some time in Boston. I might be of use to her, and we could be friends again."

"I don't think that's a good idea," Liz said firmly. "Boston is fast becoming an unwelcoming city for our kind."

"Perhaps, but, as you know, an unwelcome port never stopped me."

I almost snorted at the crude innuendo. Grace's disrespect, haughty manner, and predatory smile were starting to grate on me. It also might have been the way she kept looking Liz up and down like she was a piece of meat.

I caught a twitch of Liz's fingers; it was subtle, but it was there. The veiled threats of petty torments were actually bothering her. And because of me and what I needed, Liz was taking it from her.

Grace's fangs were on full display as she smiled at us. "Honestly, though, Elizabeth, I want you back. It's as simple as that. We had something once."

I raised an eyebrow at the brazen comment.

"That will never happen," Liz growled. "I came here because you wanted to see me, and we need the jet. But that's as far as it goes. And we had nothing. I was your prisoner and your victim. But that was a long time ago. I'm not afraid of you anymore."

Grace stood swiftly and moved into Liz's space until I put a hand on her chest. "That's close enough," I said.

The older vampire glanced at me and donned an oozy smile. "I wouldn't hurt Elizabeth. Besides, you know, she'll tire of you, too. I bet she never told you about me or what we had."

I narrowed my eyes. "Back up," I demanded, pressing firmly against her sternum.

Grace did, indeed, back up, returning to her seat on the sofa. "Come, sit," she said, patting the cushion next to her and clearly nodding toward Liz. When Liz balked, she added, "You must not want that jet."

Liz started to move, but I dropped into the seat instead. "You know, I don't mind if I do. Do you happen to have any A-negative here? Would you be a dear and fetch me some?"

Liz's jaw dropped. Grace looked taken aback, but she stood and headed into the kitchen.

"What are you doing?" Liz mouthed, but I put a hand up and gave her a dismissive shake of my head.

Grace returned a moment later and handed me a glass. "Sit," I said, putting the force of command into it, but Grace only shifted slightly. "Please," I added when it didn't work. Marcella could probably control her, but I couldn't, but that was okay. I could always go back to the old-fashioned way: threats.

"Liz is only here because I need something," I said and took a sip of the blood. It was cold and goopy and had that anti-coagulant taste to it. I grimaced slightly, but it went down okay. "And frankly, I don't need it so badly that I'll let you make her feel uncomfortable." The room seemed to darken slightly as I continued, a bit of the rage I felt filtering into my voice. "And even though she's old enough to take care of herself, I feel obliged to tell you that if you pester her or bother her in any way, I will kill you, and you will never hear the shot that blows your head clean off your shoulders. Don't let my youth fool you. I'm perfectly capable of handling someone twice your age. You may not be a refined woman, but she is, and she deserves more respect than I'm seeing from you right now."

Liz gaped at me, but Grace's reaction was the most surprising. There was real fear in her eyes. Something I'd said or done had gotten to her. She continued to look at me, her eyes searching until she finally looked away, taking her own glass from the table.

"I like you, Cait Reagan," she said as she turned back and held up her glass for a toast. "You're direct and loyal. I couldn't ask for anyone better to protect my Elizabeth."

I raised an eyebrow at her choice of words but didn't argue;

it was pointless. Besides, she needed to save face now. If I wanted the plane, I needed to let her get back on top of the conversation.

"Well, I've enjoyed this trip down memory lane, as it were, but I have other business this evening." We all stood, and Grace stepped forward, taking Elizabeth's hand and kissing it. "It was good to see you, Elizabeth."

"And the plane?" Liz mentioned.

"With my compliments," Grace said. "I'm sure we'll see each other again soon."

That can't be good, I thought. *Just what we needed, a four-hundred-year-old pirate screwing with our lives.*

We left quietly before she could change her mind, or I finally lost my temper and destroyed the suite in an effort to murder her.

Once in the elevator and several floors down, Liz finally spoke. "You didn't have to do that," she murmured.

"Yes, I did," I said coolly. "She doesn't respect you. You're a lot stronger now and a lot more capable than you probably were two hundred fifty years ago, but she doesn't see that. She just sees her victim, and while I'm sure you can handle yourself, that woman is an underhanded pirate, literally. Speaking of, you could have told me that we were going to meet the Grace O'Malley. Fuck me, Liz. Really?"

Liz just pursed her lips.

"Anyway," I continued. "She needed to know that you aren't alone. I'm sorry if I spoke out of turn, but I was trying to save us both a long, fraught battle to keep her from pestering us with petty bullshit."

"I'm not upset, darling," Liz said as we exited the express elevator and headed back to the room so she could change into more casual clothes. "It was sexy as hell. I was just afraid she might keep the plane if we didn't at least give her some deference."

"Maybe, but I wasn't going to let her fuck with you like that. Sorry, babe, it's just the way I'm wired. If she's not careful, I'll sick Katie on her."

Liz chuckled. "You know, I don't think I want to see what

Katie would do to her."

I laughed. "It wouldn't be too bad. Katie doesn't really have a nasty streak. She's just too practical. She'd just kill her and be done with it."

"True. Well, enough of that. Now let's go have some actual fun."

CHAPTER FOUR

Liz and I sat at the bar top of the tacky seventies-themed diner, pretending to drink two cups of coffee. Angelique, the waitress, wore a pink throwback uniform straight out of *Alice Doesn't Live Here Anymore,* and the old, hard-backed, laminate booths sported surfaces in obnoxious orange. The foul harvest gold paint that covered the walls was relatively fresh and adorned with ugly floral prints in a few spots.

"Van Gough's sunflowers are apparently pop art," Liz muttered dryly. "Shame. He was really a good guy, if a bit sad."

I rolled my eyes at the namedrop. I was pretty sure Liz was fucking with me, but then again.

"That's her," Liz whispered when the door opened, letting in the steamy night air and a cute brunette in a mid-length brown skirt and white blouse. She exuded the precise air of a professional, albeit stereotypical, librarian, all the way down to the tight bun and black, square-rimmed glasses.

"Hey, Catherine, your usual?" Angelique, called as the petit brunette dropped into the empty booth by the door.

Catherine Sanford looked every bit of her twenty-seven years and then some. Soft eyes, filled with disappointment and pain, sat cradled inside dark circles and cast a forlorn gaze into her coffee mug. She had been pretty once, but now she looked used up. Her drawn, tired expression seemed to hang on her cheeks, more out of fatigue and misery than anything physical. One side of the woman's face was dark with a fat, blotchy bruise.

I turned away before she looked our way, and molten rage crushed my breast. I did my best to keep my face neutral, but I just couldn't. So, instead, I let my eyes trail Angelique in her starched pink as she marched around the countertop. I'd glamoured her at Liz's insistence, despite my misgivings of glamour in general. I'd helped her understand we were here to save Catherine. Fortunately, that was all the push she needed to help us, letting me keep it simple.

Angelique stopped at Catherine's booth, a coffee pot in one hand. Catherine gazed up at Angelique with haunted eyes and set a buck fifty on the table. Angelique filled the upturned mug and pushed the money back.

"The redhead at the bar already paid for it," Angelique whispered. Catherine's expression softened as her eyes flicked up to Liz and me. I tilted my head and raised my mug, trying to control my trembling hand. I wasn't nervous, just angry. Okay, I was a little nervous. Recruiting was all new to me.

The soft expression didn't linger long, and Catherine returned her gaze to the mug, absently touching her cheek. She didn't like being pitied, but she didn't refuse the free coffee. Battered and miserable, she didn't want to go home. Liz's estimation had been dead on, proud but practical with just a touch of dreamy.

I couldn't blame her. I knew what awaited her: an old, grizzled army vet with a chip on his shoulder, a bad attitude, and a violent streak. I knew the marks that people like that left, especially that particular person. I might not be able to save her from herself, but I would definitely save her from him.

After all, hadn't we saved Leah and Katie from the Finchers? That had been easier, though. I didn't have any feelings for Anne either way to be tied up when she died. What I'd done had been more mercy than murder.

I paused for a second, wondering why I was thinking about Katie and Leah now, in the midst of this trip. It was

Catherine's grey eyes. They were listless and sad, just like Leah's had been when I'd first met her.

"Well, shall we get to it?" Liz prompted and stood.

I nodded.

Liz gave me an encouraging glance, and I followed her toward Catherine's booth. We weren't hunting, and neither of us used glamour, but Catherine's eyes never left us as we padded toward her. She glanced us both up and down, appraising each of us in turn. When her eyes swept to Liz, a bit of color heated Catherine's cheeks. I suppressed a smirk. *Yeah, my girl is stunning. I don't blame you for gawking.*

The closer we got, though, the more Catherine's face showed hints of panic. She snatched up her purse, but I dropped into the booth before she could scoot out, rudely hemming her in. We needed her to sit tight for the pitch. She was trapped and looked the part. Liz took the seat across from her.

"Hello," Liz purred, sending gooseflesh over Catherine's bare arms. "I am Elizabeth. You can call me Liz, and this is my friend Cait. You are Cathy, yes?"

"Umm, Catherine," she answered, looking down at the table, her voice soft and low. Her left leg trembled against mine beneath her wringing hands. "I'd like you to leave, please. You're scaring me."

I withdrew my badge, all polished and plated in red chrome, and set it in front of Catherine. She picked it up. She turned it over once, and her mouth turned downward. She ran a finger over the bright gold number. "You're part of that new supernatural task force," she said.

I kept my voice soft, afraid she might just shatter or panic. "Yes. You don't have to be afraid. I just want to talk to you for a moment. Then we'll leave. But you should know that I'm a friend, and we won't mistreat you in any way." I peeked around a lock of hair that had fallen loose and caught her wide, skittish eyes. "I promise I'm a friend."

The trembling in her leg ceased, and her hands drifted back to her coffee.

I reached up toward the angry black bruise under her left

eye. "Did John do that?"

She flinched back. "It was an accident," she lied. "I bumped into the door when he was opening it. It was my fault."

My tone was a touch reproving but still calm and coaxing, almost motherly. "Catherine, I know John Holley. I served with him in the war. You don't have to lie to us. We already know."

Her bottom lip quivered. She batted at tears, furiously pushing them aside as if they were little betrayals. She almost leaned into me but fought off the urge to lay her head on my shoulder and cry.

I saw the war of emotion in her expression. She hurt, and she could see that I understood, but she was afraid. I knew that feeling all too well. Catherine wanted comfort. She needed it desperately, but she was terrified to trust anyone.

She looked over at Liz, then glanced up at the ceiling and used the edges of her fingers to wipe away the tears, now stained in mascara. She sniffed and dabbed at her eyes with one of the paper napkins. "I'm sorry. I don't know what's wrong with me."

"It's okay. It's not your fault. It never was."

Catherine's grief exploded like a vase dropped to the floor. Every bit of rage, fear, and hurt just hurled out of her as loud sobs bubbled from her lips, and I pulled her into me, letting her lean on my shoulder.

Angelique walked past, shooting Catherine a sympathetic look, before drawing the blinds next to the booth. Then, with a soft thump, she locked the door and flipped the open sign to closed. Liz mouthed her a quick "Thank you."

Angelique nodded.

I felt for Catherine, but even as my heart went out to her, part of it turned frost-bitten and cold as I thought about just how many Catherines there were out there. I wanted to—

My thoughts jumbled and stalled as I couldn't decide what I wanted. I wanted to murder Holley, slowly, or perhaps shoot him at a thousand yards with one of his rifles, or maybe stick him in a cage and torture him with glamour until his mind broke. Nothing seemed satisfying. Nothing felt like enough. There was no punishment fit for him.

Liz reached out and touched my arm. Her expression was filled with compassion, not just for Catherine but for me, too. The ache in my chest was unbearable, and I couldn't help thinking that vampires shouldn't hurt like this. But the tears still came.

Catherine stayed there, cradled in the arms of a stranger, sobbing her heart out into my shirt, her hot forehead against the cool skin of my collar. All I could do was run my hand across her back and shush her as I fought furiously at my own tears.

"Shh," I whispered. "It's okay. It'll all be okay."

After a while, her sobs slowed, and I wiped my own eyes. When I next spoke, my voice was thick with emotion. "We think you're very brave and very strong. After all that you've suffered, it's a miracle that you haven't come apart."

She unwrapped her arms from my midsection and dropped them desolately to the table with a thump. "What would you call this? I'm a mess."

"You hold down a stable job at the library," Liz said. "You manage your finances well. Your credit is good. You even have your own car. That all takes effort. You're hurt, and you need to be someplace safe so you can heal. But you're not broken, despite how it feels."

"And where would that be? Johnny was a scout sniper. He has friends. He'd find me."

I slipped a soft, pale finger under Catherine's chin and lifted it upward, staring back into those pretty, gray eyes so full of hurt. "We can protect you," I said with absolute confidence. "What's more, we can make it so that you never, ever have to worry about anyone hurting you ever again."

Catherine's brows knitted together skeptically, but her curiosity was clearly piqued. "How?" She asked, then blew her nose on the napkin. "Sorry."

Liz filled in the gaps as I wiped my tears with a handkerchief. "We can give you something you've never had before: power, more than you ever thought possible."

"I'm leaving, Cait. I'll be back in an hour," Angelique called from the kitchen. "Come on, Larry. I'm closing up early. I'll take care of the cleaning when I come back." A few minutes later, a door slammed as Angelique and her grumbling cook exited through the back.

"Tell me, Catherine," I said. "If you could be anything you ever wanted to be in your life, what would it be?" I already knew the answer. Liz had been extremely thorough in her interviews, even talking to old friends from high school.

Catherine gave a mirthless chuckle full of misery. "When I was a kid, I wanted to be like Star in The Lost Boys. That way, no one could hurt me."

"But Star was a victim," Liz said, watching her from beneath a raised eyebrow.

"Star was written as stupid and weak," she retorted, a touch of anger coloring her voice. "She had all this strength. She could fly. And all she did was hang out, be scared of David, and basically be his bitch. It was dumb. I would have staked his ass and headed to another city, someplace bigger, where I could really get lost."

I gave Catherine a warm smile. "It's like this was destiny."

Liz chuckled and then fixed Catherine with a steady gaze. "I'm going to show you something, but I want you to know that you're in no danger, and if you want us to leave, we'll let you go unharmed, okay?"

She nodded, but fear clouded her face again, and her hands started to shake.

Liz opened her mouth, giving Catherine the full show as her fangs lengthened. Strangely, Catherine didn't react with terror. Instead, she looked at Liz, then back to me, then back to Liz, then back to me. Finally, recognition lit her face. "You're Cait Reagan. The cop from the video everyone said was a hoax."

One corner of my mouth quirked into a crooked smile. "It wasn't a hoax."

"How do you know Johnny?" she asked.

My face was impassive, but Catherine saw the burning rage in my eyes. "You may not want to know this, but John raped me on my first deployment to Iraq."

Catherine didn't defend him, argue that I was lying, or blurt out that he'd never do such a thing. She just nodded and whispered, "John's violent." She took a shaking sip of her coffee and twisted the cup on the table. "I wouldn't have believed that four years ago when we first started dating. He was charming, always with an easy joke. He even held doors for me. Over the following year, though, he began to get worse and worse. Looking back, I realized now that it was insidious. First, it was screaming fights. Then, he stopped going to A.A. and started drinking all the time. And he's a mean drunk." She touched her face again.

"You can't imagine the number of women who've been there," I whispered. "There's no way you could have defended yourself from him, but we can fix that."

She looked up at me then with an expression of self-loathing that stabbed into my very soul. "I don't deserve that. I'm an awful person."

I frowned. "Being abused doesn't make you an awful—"

"I gave him an alibi," she interrupted and looked away, trying to hide her eyes under a mop of locks that had loosed from her bun.

"I don't understand," I said softly.

"One night, a couple of years ago, Johnny came home from the auto shop, beaten and bloody. The cops showed up the next day, asking after him. A young girl—she was maybe twenty— had accused him of sexually assaulting her. The cops had been trying to figure out who he was, but the girl's brother and his friends had found him first." She hiccuped a sob. "Johnny swore to me that it wasn't him, that they had the wrong guy, but I knew better. And still, I stayed. I gave him an alibi." She looked away, the heat of shame a creeping red in her cheeks. "I helped him get away with it."

I held her shoulders and tilted her face up to mine again. "Now, you listen to me. It is very hard to stand up when you've been terrorized all of your life. You were protecting yourself the only way you knew how. But we're going to give you the strength to put all of that to an end. Are you ready?" I placed my hand on hers.

"What?" she breathed, voice mousy and small.

I gave her a kind smile, then let my fangs descend, almost as an afterthought. "Are you ready to be one of us? To have a world that you can scarcely imagine? I won't lie. It's not easy. But it's a damn sight better than what you're dealing with now. And we could use someone with your skills."

"But what about the sun and—"

"The sun is a myth," I giggled, cutting her off. "We don't go poof. And if anyone gets close enough to you with a wooden stake, you kind of have it coming."

"And if I say no?" she asked, watching me carefully.

"Then we leave. Angelique will return, and it will be like we were never here."

"And Johnny?"

My hard expression returned. "I'm not going to lie to you. John Holly will not live out the night, no matter what you decide. We will both understand if you don't want to do this."

"You want me to kill John," Catherine gasped. "I can't do that."

Liz shook her head. "No. We're not asking you to kill John, but he's a rapist. The things he's done to you are just the tip of a very large iceberg. We're not recruiting you because of John. You are very intelligent, and you have skills that we need, Catherine. We also see the strength inside you that you likely don't. The offer still stands despite what you wish to do about John. But I'll ask you this. What has a man ever done for you?"

She lifted my arm from around her shoulders and moved away. Staring at the table, eyes downcast, she said, "You're not wrong. No man has ever treated me right, the way they were supposed to, not my father, not John, or the men before him. They've all been difficult to deal with, mostly lazy or broken with a mean streak. I would like to say that I have a type that I gravitate to, but that's only partially true. They pick me. And each time, I hope it will be different, but it never is, probably because I'm easy prey, quiet, and reserved. I've always felt like I was lucky to have them, no matter how bad they were. I've always believed that." She looked up at Liz. "You're the older one." It wasn't a question.

Liz nodded and smiled approvingly. "By about four hundred years. That kind of perceptive nature, Catherine, is part of the reason we came to you. We don't just select women for their skills. Vampires live a very long time, and with effort, we can learn to do almost anything. We pick women for their temperament, courage, and the things they can't learn."

Catherine blinked, and then her expression turned firm. Her eyes were clear and bright. "What do I do?"

Liz stood and lowered the rest of the blinds before shutting off the lights.

I also moved out of the booth and held my hand out in invitation. "You need to be sure about this, and you should know that we can't fly. And there are rules. Loose lips sink ships, things like that."

She stayed firmly planted in her seat. "I do have a few questions."

I withdrew my hand and crossed my arms, nodding to her. "Ask us anything."

"Can I keep my job at the library?" She asked. "I like my work. I'm good at it."

"We'll arrange a job at the library in Boston if you like, one that suits the hours you'll need to keep. But I think the opportunity we're offering will entice you much more than a job at an ordinary library."

She tilted her head at that, and I thought she would ask about it, but she didn't. Instead, she asked, "Sunlight doesn't kill you?"

"It just makes us sleepy," Liz answered.

"A stake through the heart?"

"It paralyzes us," I said. "Only decapitation or cremation will kill us. I grew back an arm once in a pinch, though I don't recommend that."

"Do you have enemies?"

"Just a few pesky humans. Though they're making themselves quite the nuisance at the moment," Liz replied.

"And we leave them be if they don't fuck with us," I added.

"Do I have to kill to feed?"

"No," Liz said flatly.

"No coffins?"

I laughed. "Not unless you want to."

"Will it hurt?" She asked, brushing past the joke.

"Less than getting a vaccination," I replied with a barely suppressed grin. "All in all, I think you'll find the entire experience… um… pleasant."

"Last question," Catherine said, clearly weighing the pros and cons. "Can I still eat human food?"

Liz shrugged. "If you don't mind vomiting it up later. We can eat it. We just can't digest it."

"Is there anything else I should know?" Catherine asked finally, though I could tell she had already made her decision.

Now that we were here at this moment, I suddenly felt a little uncertain. I had never turned anyone except Katie, and that had been in desperation. This was different. I wanted to be dead certain that we were doing the right thing. Liz nodded at me supportively, clearly reading my expression.

"You have to stay with us for a time," I said. "At least until you know the ropes. You'll be expected to contribute. In your case, we need an archivist who can sort, collate, and manage information for us and handle research. You'll be working for the queen, not for us. She is relatively nice and reasonably fair. But she's also very strict about the rules."

"And what are the rules?" Catherine's demeanor had shifted, and I could almost see the wheels turning.

"No turning other vampires without The Queen's permission," I quoted. "No turning men into vampires, period. Ever. You never let anyone know you are a vampire except at her discretion. And no killing if at all possible, except in certain cases, again, at her discretion."

"And Johnny is one of those exceptions?" She asked.

I nodded. It was a lie. Marcella had no idea that we were even here, but Catherine didn't need to know that.

Catherine took a deep breath through her nose and pressed her lips into a thin line. "Okay," she said softly. "I'll do it."

I gave her a kind smile. "Now I have a question?"

She looked at me, her brows knitting back together.

"Do you prefer blondes or redheads?" I asked, and she actually laughed.

CHAPTER FIVE

"Where the fuck have you been? You're three hours late!" John hollered from the other room as we walked in the door.

Catherine flinched at his tone but then seemed to remember what we had told her. Absently, she scratched at her arm, and I felt more than a bit of anxiety over turning her. I hoped she was ready for this. If she went off the rails like Caldwell, it would be on me to fix it—to kill her. I could do it, I knew, but it would hurt like nothing else. I knew that, too.

"We'll get you fed after this," I whispered, and she nodded.

"I stopped for coffee at the diner," Catherine said from the kitchen. The iron in her voice surprised me. Then she spotted the half-empty fifth of Jack Daniels sitting on the counter and dropped her head with a sigh. "Oh, Johnny."

I placed a hand on her shoulder, but she shrugged it off.

"You know," she called into the living room. "I ran into one of your old army buddies there. She came with me to say hello."

"What the fuck? I'm barely dressed!" John pulled himself off the couch and started toward the tiny kitchen but stopped cold when he saw us.

"Hello, Johnny," I said, and there was something horrible and sly in my voice, a low, sultry, almost predatory purr. I hadn't meant to do it. It nearly made *me* shiver. I glanced at

Catherine, but she was all smiles. She was getting off on this. Maybe she would be okay.

"Reagan?" John barked. "What the fuck are you doing here?" He spun on his heel and headed toward the back of the little apartment.

I smirked and blood-stepped, dissolving into a puff of red mist and coalescing in front of him. Catherine gasped at the display of power.

My smile widened. "Now, now, Johnny, none of that." My voice was almost motherly but filled with a wickedness that matched my fang-laden grin. "We don't need any gunfire in the apartment."

His hand shot out, grabbing me by the throat. I laughed as I yanked it away, almost jerking his arm from the socket. With sickening ease, I twisted his right thumb until it popped. He screamed.

"Have a seat." I shoved and watched him careen onto the sofa.

Catherine's gaze was predatory and excited. A bright, intense glee sparkled in her eyes. She might have loved him once, but she didn't anymore.

"Sergeant John Holley," I said as I stalked toward him. "For aggravated rape in the first degree, how do you plead?"

"Cat, call the cops!"

"No, John," Catherine said softly as she entered the living room and stopped beside the couch. "I don't think I will."

"You bitch. What did she tell you? That I raped her? She was askin' for it. You shoulda seen the way she was lookin' at me."

I had a flash of memory: the Fae scouts who'd let Boudka die while they had been raping a poor farmer's wife. I wanted to end him right there, but I just smirked. "And that cute little blonde thing at the bar? Sandy? What about her?"

Catherine's eyes went wide, then flashed with anger. "You knew?"

I just shrugged. "You needed to get it out," I said, surprised at how flip my tone was, but I was having way too much fun with this. My regrets and anxiety had fled. I'd turned Holley's girl. And now it was playtime.

The brief irritation in Catherine's expression passed, and she put a hand on my shoulder. "Hold on, Cait. I have a few questions I'd like to ask my man here." The way she said 'my man' rang with sadistic delight. I giggled at the irony. The little librarian, it seemed, was a latent psycho-top from hell.

Good for you, Catherine. Good for you. My worries about Catherine instantly evaporated. She wasn't looking at John with anything more than abject disdain. He had become prey.

She dropped casually onto the sofa and pulled his other hand into hers. He flinched and yanked his arm, straining to resist, but he might as well have been a toddler for all the good it did. And that's when it appeared. Fear. Of me. Of Catherine.

Sweat broke out across his forehead, and his eyes were brimming with horror. If they grew any wider, they'd pop out of his skull. For all of his training, for all of his toxically hyper-masculine bullshit, he was helpless, and it terrified him. The taste of it was like honey.

"Tell me, John," Catherine cooed softly, stroking his fingers with her free hand. "How many?"

"Wha…what?" His voice squeaked, and his nostrils flared with a flight response as his body tensed. I stepped a bit closer, glaring down imperiously.

"How many women did you rape?" Catherine clarified. "How many?"

"Oh, come on, baby," he started, but Catherine twisted his left pinky finger. It snapped with a sickening sound, and he screamed again. His right hand swung around and slapped her. She snapped her eyes back to his and grinned.

"How many?" She demanded again, more forcefully this time, grabbing his ring finger.

He swallowed. "I don't know. Some of 'em wanted it."

She snorted and shook her head. "Let's try another question. One you should be able to answer honestly. How many women did you stick your dick in while we've been together?"

"Please, Cat, don't," he wailed as Catherine flexed slightly, pulling on his finger. "Okay, okay. At least, I don't know, eight or nine."

She looked up at me. I shrugged. She turned back at John, growling at him."Not that it matters anymore, but my name is Catherine, Johnny. It's not Cat, or Cate, or Cathy. Don't you ever call me anything but Catherine." Her fangs were down, and I thought for sure she was going to bite him, but she didn't.

"Okay, okay," Johnny said through gritted teeth. "Catherine. Please. I don't deserve to die for what I've done. Please stop. I don't know what this bitch did to you, but I love you baby."

She let go of his hand and put her palm to his cheek. He flinched away, and Catherine cackled. "No one needs your kind of love, Johnny. The kind that comes with broken bones and bruises. I should have left a long time ago and called the police."

"You still can," I said, touching her shoulder. I was giving her an out, a way to retain some semblance of who she was, but I could see it. She didn't want to be that woman anymore. This was the new Catherine; if it weren't good enough, she would burn the world. *Perfect*, I thought. *She's my perfect creation.*

"No," Catherine said softly. "It's too late for that. He's a rapist. And only a man would think that rape doesn't deserve death, given the damage it does." She lifted from the sofa. "But I can't do it. His life isn't mine to take, and it won't help me." With that, she walked out the front door and closed it behind her. I had to admire her level of self-awareness. I, on the other hand, had other plans.

John tried to rise, but I pushed him back on the couch. "I've been waiting for this for a long time."

"Fuck you," he shot back, regaining some sense of composure. "I should have—"

I slapped him, whipping his head around. The lights dimmed slightly as my voice seemed to take on an eerie tone, reminding me of my mother's when The Morrigan took her. "Mind your manners, boy. As I was saying, I have been waiting for this for a long time. And, honestly, you should probably be grateful that my sister didn't get you first."

"What? What sister?"

"She's the quiet one, you know. And, well, she would probably torture you in ways even I couldn't imagine, and I've had twelve years to think about it. It seems that Aoife's not as forgiving as I am. Honestly, I was shocked." It wasn't a total lie. She had shared some seriously fucked up ideations with Morgan. Mother of Waters, our relationship was complicated. "Though, I wonder, which of us you should fear more, little boy in a man's body."

"I need help," he whispered. "I was doing okay for a while. I was going to A.A. I knew I had a mean streak when I drank. I lose control. I—" He broke off, and he started crying.

"Look at you," I laughed as I drove his nightmarish dread. His heart banged in his chest, and amid the rhythm, there sounded a barely perceptible click followed by a bit of a whoosh. My lips curled into a malignant smile. "You're so sad, John. You know, there was a time when you scared me. When I trembled at the thought of seeing you again. Every time your stink came anywhere near me, I was afraid. But not anymore. You see, I have this friend; her name is Nastasia," my voice took on a playfully seductive tenor. I swiped my thumb down his jawline and tapped his nose with each word. "She taught me…" I broadened my grin, revealing my fangs. "…how to handle little boys like you who forget their place."

His heart fired at a jackrabbit pace, and he grabbed his arm. I spoke slowly, my voice rising from a whisper to a crescendo. "Oh, does it hurt, John? Do we have an undiagnosed heart condition? Is that your little ticker going boom… boom… BOOM!?"

He squeezed his eyes shut, and his breathing turned shallow. I dropped an anvil on his will, calming him. "Oh, don't worry, John. I'm going to kill you, but I really want you to feel it." He was still in pain, but some of the tension eased from his body as his blood pressure dropped. He would still die, just not quite yet.

"Call me a doctor," he wheezed raggedly.

I chuckled incredulously. "A doctor? Whatever for? How would I savor this moment?" I dropped to the floor, straddled his body, and ran a thumb over the fear-stinking sweat that poured from his forehead. "How does it feel, John?" I drove another spike of fear into him, so powerful it would have made Nastasia jealous. "To be helpless? To be afraid? To believe that the person on top of you will kill you?" I whacked his forehead, causing his skull to bounce off the floor. Not hard enough to do more than break the skin and make him see stars for a moment. He tried to move, but his heart was exploding on him.

I stood, watching the veins bulge on the side of his head and his face twist in agony.

"Please," he ground out, a tight whimper between his gritted teeth.

I looked down at him and growled. "That's right, John. Beg."

He looked up with a pitiful expression. "I just need to get help."

I pursed my lips, and then one corner of my mouth pulled crookedly in triumph. The room was almost pitch black now, an inky, syrupy darkness shrouding the television and the single shitty lamp.

I was getting off on this, torturing him. When I'd tortured Matt Churdin, when he'd threatened to rape my child, something had snapped. And that something would never be put back again.

Most of all, I wanted to drink him dry, but I couldn't. Natural causes or suicide, that was all I could do and still protect my protégé, my new daughter. Abruptly, John's heart stuttered, gave a feeble contraction, and stopped. His expression turned hollow. His breath ebbed away, and he died, terror still painted on his features.

I kicked lightly at his corpse, just for my own benefit. "Good." I checked for a pulse and breath. There was nothing. John Holley, the man who'd stolen the last of my innocence both on and off the battlefield, was dead.

I stared at him for long moments. Nastasia and I were actually so much alike. It was an odd realization at that moment, but it was so clear. Nastasia killed the men who raped her to avenge herself upon them. I had just done the same, and despite what everyone else said, it felt good. In a weird way, I realized that this wasn't his story after all. It was mine. It was my life and I'd reclaimed the last of it from monsters like him. And if I'd had to be a monster to do it, so be it.

Liz's voice filtered in from outside, just a whisper. "It's done."

Holley's dead eyes gazed sightlessly upward. I was amazed at how well she knew me. As she had once said, I was an open book to her. Bringing me here and letting me recruit Catherine had been her way of giving me permission, telling me that it was okay to let the demon off the leash. It reminded me of two things. As loving as she was, Liz was still the creature that lurked in the shadows of humanity's most terrifying nightmares. And so was I.

"Even this was more mercy than you deserved," I whispered to his corpse, my voice low. "Hell is where you belong." As far as I was concerned, it was fitting that the last thing he laid eyes on was me, smiling in malicious glee as he died a painful death.

Of course, it still wasn't quite satisfying, but no amount of torture would have given me that, I realized. It was good enough, though.

I wiped down everything we'd touched with a dishtowel I'd found in the kitchen and took it with me as I exited the apartment. Catherine still stood on the landing, waiting.

"What did you decide?" It was simply a question. It was as if becoming a vampire had knocked the humanity right out of her, but still, I was afraid she might one day suffer for her part. It was probably a silly idea, but there it was.

"He had a heart attack. Maybe it was the fangs." I stalked to the car and opened the passenger door. "You want to ride shotgun?"

"I'll sit in the back, I think," Catherine said, and it sounded almost imperious, like she was stepping into a limousine. She paused, the door still open, one leg in the car. "What about the police? They'll come looking, won't they?"

Liz shook her head. "No. You'll get a phone call, and it will be over. It's handled. You're free."

She took a last look at the apartment window. "I very much doubt that," she whispered and got in.

CHAPTER SIX

Liz and I returned home a day later than anticipated but still within the three-day window. We'd taken an evening to teach Catherine the basics and get her some new clothes. Her first feeding had been almost like clockwork, and again, I was mesmerized by how suddenly different she was: cold, heartless. The only correction we'd made was that she shouldn't spend so much time toying with her food. She really enjoyed making the man she had selected suffer first, keeping him so terrified of her that he couldn't move.

"Where have you two been?" Marcella demanded as soon as we stepped in the door.

I rolled my eyes. "We're not your kids or at your beck and call, queen or no queen. We brought a new recruit. Catherine, come in."

Catherine walked in the door. She dressed professionally: a white blouse buttoned up, a black, mid-length pencil skirt, her feet stuffed into black patent leather heels. "I'm Catherine Sanford, ma'am," she said confidently. "I'm your new administrative assistant and archivist."

Marcella blinked in astonishment, and for only the second time since I'd met her, she was speechless. I had to bite my lip to keep from laughing at her discomfort. However, she regained her composure quickly.

"Welcome to the family, Catherine," Marcella said, gesturing to the oak double doors opposite the sitting room. "The library is through there. Would you mind waiting for us? Then we'll get you settled. It will only be a moment." Catherine vanished into the library, and I heard an audible gasp. She'd found the books.

Marcella stalked toward the marble staircase and up, then she stopped. "Well, come on," she demanded impatiently. Liz and I about fell over each other in our eagerness to follow, stifling giggles.

When we reached her office, Marcella sat down behind her desk. "Close the door, won't you, please, Caitlin?"

I was still suppressing a grin as I did so. Oh, but Marcella was ragin', as Aoife would say. I could tell by the way she called me Caitlin. We were in the principal's office now. It was funny how I reverted to old high-school habits, slouching in one of the chairs—very passive-aggressive. By contrast, Liz remained standing, arms crossed, appropriately defiant.

"I thought I expressly told you that we would vet every new vampire across my desk," Marcella said quietly, leaning forward and steepling her fingers directly in front of her.

Liz and I waited.

"Well?" Marcella said in irritation.

Liz tugged at one ear a bit, then grinned. "You need an assistant, M. I'm not your bitch, you know. So, I took it upon myself to find you one since you absolutely refused to do it yourself." She tossed the dossier on the table.

Marcella raised an eyebrow and then opened it, leafing through the materials. "Library sciences. Organized. Capable. And, oh, ladies, honestly?" She must have gotten to the part about Holley.

"I did not kill him," I said defensively, my hands up. "He had a heart attack. Bum ticker."

Marcella looked at me askance. "And I imagine there was no glamour involved."

I looked over and studiously examined her bookshelves.

"Uh huh," Marcella muttered. "Is anyone looking for her?"

I crossed my arms and stared down at her. "Of course not.

We're not sloppy. It was natural causes, open and shut."

"And you think she's up to the work we do, why?" Marcella asked as Liz finally sat down. I stood and moved to lean against the wall.

"Just read the dossier, M.," Liz answered, leaning back. "Trust me, she'll do whatever you need done. She's already had her first feed. She's a natural. No problems whatsoever. Now that she's in the know, she will need some visits with Jennifer."

My brows knitted together. "You outed us to my therapist? That's a little over the line, don't you think?"

Marcella shook her head. "No. It's about time. We deal with death every day, and many of our recruits come from broken homes, abusive relationships, and harsh backgrounds, much like yours, Cait. I wanted someone they could go to. And we didn't just out ourselves. I turned her."

I jerked as if I'd been slapped. "You what?" I whispered.

Marcella looked at me. "Let's get something straight. I don't answer to you either, young lady. You both get wider latitude because we're friends, but don't be confused. I decide what's best for us as needed. When I need input, I'll ask. And this little stunt needs to be your last. What you do in your day job is your business, but I need to know about it when it affects us. Is that clear?"

I opened my mouth to argue, but Marcella gave me a vicious glare. "I said, Is. That. Clear?"

"Yes, ma'am," we both replied like a couple of scolded schoolgirls.

"Good, now get out and send Ms. Sanford up. I need to arrange for a place for her to sleep. Your room, Liz. That should suffice."

"My room?" Liz asked reflexively.

"Yes, your room. You're always sleeping in Cait's room, anyway."

"But why not Cait's room? I have the bigger bed."

"If you want a bigger bed, Liz, buy one. Besides, didn't you just sign paperwork on an entire building?"

"But it's not ready yet," Liz muttered, sulking.

"I don't have time for this. Now go." She waved us out with a shooing gesture before adding, "Cait, Grace's plane will be ready tomorrow afternoon at a small airport in Maine, so get yourself packed."

"Haven't you forgotten something?" I said from the doorway.

"What?" Marcella snapped.

"Pilot?"

"I already have one. She'll be here tomorrow when you leave. Now, out!"

I nodded and closed the door. As soon as we were in the hallway, we looked at each other and burst into laughter.

"That went better than I expected," Liz said with a haughty smile. "I told you."

"You know I can hear you," Marcella called. "Now stop fucking with me and send Ms. Sanford in." Her words were harsh, but her light tone made Liz and I grin.

We trotted downstairs and found Catherine mentally cataloging the books in the library. "This collection," she said. "It's unbelievable."

I barked a laugh. "Wait until you see the sub-basement." I stopped for a moment and watched as she walked around, entirely enthralled by the sheer extravagance of the library. She ran a finger over a half dozen first editions before settling on one of the lesser-known and lesser-valued volumes.

She spoke in a hushed tone, her voice thick with memory and wistfulness, and her eyes sparkled with unshed tears. "This is a first-edition copy of The Brown Fairy Book. Have you read it?"

I shook my head as I walked over, smiling at her. If I was honest, I decided I was going to like Catherine. Despite everything she had been through, there was a childlike awe in her. In some ways, she reminded me of Maki. And maybe that was why I had initially looked at Maki like she was a kid. Maki's child-like exuberance over all things supernatural was endearing. And Catherine's awe of the books here similarly struck me, almost infectious in its subdued glee.

I held my arm out as if to pull her toward me. Catherine

looked at me for a moment, a bit bemused, but then her need for belonging got the better of her, and she leaned in close, allowing my arm to settle around her shoulders. "You are among sisters here," I whispered and then added, almost as an afterthought, "my daughter."

Liz padded over to Catherine's other side, arms crossed but standing close. "I've read it," she said in that gentle way she had, so soft but full of such strength. "I've read most of these."

Catherine didn't look at either of us, eyes still on Andrew Lang's ninth fairy work. "My mother had one before…" She trailed off and sniffed, blinking back her tears. Then she stepped away and turned to us. "Thank you for this."

I smiled back at her, saying, "You're so very welcome." She nodded at me and tugged a finger beneath one eye.

Turning her towards the door, I said, "Marcella wants to get you settled. She's upstairs. Turn right, second door on the left, and Catherine, welcome to the family. I know you'll like it here. And I'm sure Marcella will like you, too."

Catherine quirked a sly, crooked grin. "Until she gets my salary requirements."

"Oh, my," Liz said, clutching imaginary pearls and making me laugh. We both grinned wildly, thoroughly pleased with ourselves, watching Catherine clack away in her heels and ascend the stairs.

"Are those seamed stockings?" Liz asked as she disappeared down the hall of the second floor.

"She insisted," I whispered. "It's always the quiet ones. Five gets you ten that she has Marcella eating out of the palm of her hand by morning."

Liz snorted. "I'm not taking that bet. A far cry from the battered girlfriend we found two days ago."

"Give it time. She's on the upswing right now. It'll all hit her in a few days."

"Well," Liz said. "That's why we have a therapist among us."

Moments later, the front door opened, and a cute brunette with shoulder-length hair and startling brown eyes walked in. She wore her usual skinny jeans and an oversized sweatshirt, sporting her alma mater, Bryn Mawr College.

"Speak of the devil," I said as Jennifer, my erstwhile therapist, hauled a large cooler over the threshold.

"Oh, Cait! Hi! Haven't seen you in a while," she admonished lightly.

I gave her a quick hug. "Hi. Yeah, I've got a good excuse: vampire coma and all. I promise we'll get back together at some point."

She nodded. "Be a dear, won't you, and help me load this stuff into the refrigerator."

I picked up the cooler and carried it into the kitchen. Inside, I found it full of blood bags and started loading them into the Traulsen, which was nearly empty.

"How'd we get so low?" I asked, forgetting whatever I was about to say to Jennifer for the moment.

"Blame our daughter," Liz replied. "She acts like their drink boxes instead of a last resort. Please talk to her. She's not paying attention to me."

I nodded. "I will. With so many vampires coming in and out, we can't have her snacking all the time." I looked pointedly at Jennifer. "So, joined the family, I hear."

Jennifer looked up. "Yes. It's the opportunity of a lifetime. Working with vampires on deep-seated issues they've had for centuries. It's fascinating."

I raised an eyebrow. "Well, I hope it's the opportunity of an eternity because that's what you've got."

She just shrugged and helped me load the fridge while Liz snatched a bag and opened it, drinking from it just like Katie did.

"Hmm, and you wonder where Katie gets it?" I asked wryly.

Liz just shot me two fingers. "Do as I say, not as I do. Besides, I haven't fed in a few days."

I shook my head in disbelief. "You just fed at the rest stop with Catherine. You nearly drank that pudgy guy down to nothing."

"So?" Liz responded.

I arched an eyebrow.

"Oh, shut up, Cait," Liz finally said and grabbed my arm. "It's bedtime for us anyway."

I looked at my watch. "It's only midnight." Then I looked back at her and caught the gleam in her eye. "Oh! Why yes, it is!"

We vacated the first floor and headed up to my room, still whispering conspiratorially about Catherine and giggling all the way.

CHAPTER SEVEN

Once she had me completely naked, Liz slid my duffel from the bed and pulled something from her skirt pocket: handcuffs. No, not just cuffs, but vampire shackles designed specifically to restrain us. They were thick chromium steel. I raised an eyebrow. "What are you up to?"

"Do you trust me?" She asked as she drew my hands over my head.

I nodded vigorously, liking where this was going, and then relaxed as she cuffed me not to the frame but to a chain running under the mattress. Then she went to the lower corners of the bed and pulled a set of manacles from underneath, one from each corner and likewise attached to chains.

I pulled on the chains, and something beneath me ticked, drawing the chains taut. The more I tugged, the tighter it got, spreading my legs and pulling my wrists painfully. I stopped struggling as the mattress began to creak from the tension. She'd done a number on me, which was extremely exciting. I couldn't lie.

"Uh… honey," I said, grinning in anticipation and maybe a touch of fear. It was thrilling. "I can't move."

Liz said nothing. She disappeared into the bathroom and returned a few minutes later. I had thought she was going to change, but she returned in the same black blouse and skirt. I was very confused—until she began to disrobe. First, she undid her shirt, and I raised an eyebrow as I realized she was wearing a leather corseted bustier that gave her ample cleavage. Then she undid her skirt, and it slid down to her feet. As she stepped out, I gasped. She was in a full-on domme outfit. The vertical zipper on the latex panties was already open.

"Oh, shit," I whispered.

"How about a little playtime, darling?" she asked solicitously. She sat on the bed, and my feet moved slightly. Another tick of the mechanism between the mattress and boxed springs spread my legs a little wider and pulled my arms taut. "Are we comfortable?"

"Not really," I said flatly. "Don't we need a safe word or something?"

Liz laughed. "Why would we need a safe word? You're a vampire, and so am I? It's not like I can permanently hurt you."

"Yes, but…"

She tilted her head and gave me a "hmmm," as if she were thinking about it. "Okay, our safe word will be—Oh, wait, how will you be able to say it?" She stuffed a scarf in my mouth. "What a shame."

My eyes went wide. I trusted Liz with my life, but this was new, and it had gone from cute and fun to a little scary in seconds. "Mmmph…mmmph."

"Shut up," she ordered and reached over, pressing a button on a black box lying on the nightstand. The ticking restraint thingy finally stopped.

She returned her attention to me, slowly dragging her fingertips and manicured nails across my abdomen. I closed my eyes and gave a light gasp.

Liz slid further onto the bed, pushed my hair from my face, and drew right up to me, our lips barely touching. I could taste her intoxicating breath in my lungs. "Now, tell me, love. How much did you miss me? You were gone such a long time."

I made a few muffled grunts, but she just laughed. "What's

the matter, Detective? Cat got you're tongue?" Liz tilted her head, ran her hand across my cheek, and then down my chest, stopping to palm a breast. Her silken fingers were soft and cool. My belly jumped with her featherlight touch. Finally, she splayed her fingers, running them to either side of my clit, teasing and yet promising.

"Lift," she said, drawing her hands up to hover just over me. I arched my back but had almost no leverage, and my body was already taught against the chains. She scraped her nails across my thighs. "Lift!"

I tried again, pulling painfully on the chains, lifting my hips, and hearing the mattress creek beneath my efforts. Just as I was about to give up, I felt the touch of her fingers on my wetness. Then she drew them away.

I groaned and dropped back to the bed. Liz removed the scarf from my mouth and twisted around, her crotch hovering above my face as she dipped her head between my legs. I moaned lasciviously as she began lapping at my wetness slowly.

"Oh," I sighed as she continued her ministrations and lowered fully to my mouth. I found her clit and began to lick and suck at it, eliciting soft whimpers of pleasure. Bound as I was, I couldn't do much else

She found small places to lick at or bite at or kiss, drawing out the experience, while I just did my best. Liz nibbled at my thigh, allowing one of her fangs to play along it.

A humming, not unpleasant, almost delicate, set itself up in my head, somewhat like the feeling one gets in a head rush. It took a moment for me to realize that it was her thoughts, her mind touching my own. It wasn't glamour or command; this was something else, something closer, something deeper. And the expression of affection we shared now seemed to make it more powerful.

My core burned with need, and I begged her. "Liz," I said through a heavy breath.

Her body pressed down, and she began to work me toward orgasm in earnest. Then she bit into my leg, drawing blood from it. I felt the pull within me even as her hands began massaging me, continuing where her mouth had left off.

I moaned loudly and turned my head, trying to get at the artery in her thigh. The mattress groaned. Frustrated, I flexed at the cuffs and returned to work at her soft folds, finally driving my tongue to its furthest penetration.

Liz released my leg and arched, moaning loudly. "Oh, Goddess!" she breathed before pressing her lips to me once more. She squeezed my clit between her tongue and the roof of her mouth, massaging it with long, wet strokes. It was heaven. I could feel the tension between us, drawing taught like a bowstring until finally it snapped, and we both groaned in ecstasy.

Liz turned herself around and pressed her bloodied lips to mine. We lay there for a long time, kissing, our tongues intertwined, and our breath suddenly hot. And in the air mingled the scent of dragon's blood and cinnamon and burnt embers.

"I love you," she said softly and gazed into my eyes.

"And I love you," I replied.

She tensed and then drew up, sitting back.

"What is it?" I asked.

Liz's expression turned serious, and she undid the restraints. Her voice was low and tremulous. "I hope you mean that because—and maybe this isn't the best time—there is something you should know."

My brow furrowed with worry as I sat up. "Is it bad?"

"Yes," Liz said with a solemn nod. "I did something and need to tell you before you leave. There should be no lies between us."

I leaned away, and my brows knitted. I had suspicions about things she'd done, one thing in particular. No, I had known, hadn't I? It was the only logical way it could have happened. Marcella and I had been on Boston Common that day. "Gabe," I whispered, my voice breaking.

Liz nodded in confirmation before dropping her eyes.

I was sure Marcella had ordered it. She'd wanted me isolated and pliable, and Gabe was a complication. She didn't kill him because there was a good chance I would have dug deeper into how he died. But him losing his shit, attacking me? She could blame that on Blackman. It was plausible, and it drove me right to her.

"Why?" I asked finally after a long silence.

"Marcella wanted—"

"No," I said as gently as I could. "Why did you do it at all?"

She sniffed and looked down, picking at a loose thread on the blanket. "I was tired of being alone. I wanted a companion, and Schmidt promised me that I could make one once the gate was open. We were all so sick of being alone. So, I played along with Marcella, doing her bidding. Besides, you met Grace. Marcella protected me from her for over a hundred years. I owed her for that. And, at the time, Gabe was no one to me, just another worthless human."

I was struck by how she didn't try to soften the blow. Hell, she could have kept it to herself, and I would have probably kept on without another thought for it, which showed just how much I'd actually cared about Gabe. But I did care a little, so I asked, "Is there a way to help him?"

"I don't know. Nastasia might be able to do something, but we've never been successful at curing glamour-induced psychosis. Trying has only ever made it worse. Sometimes, it works itself out if the person is strong enough, but I did a number on him. I won't lie. And I wasn't gentle about it."

I shook my head, finally gathering my resolve. "Gabe's not strong by any measure, but it's over now. We can't change it, and I won't give up what we have. What's done is done."

She looked up at me then. "But it hurt you."

I noted that she didn't say she regretted it, but then again, that's what we were: vampires.

"Yes. It did, but I'm okay now." I touched her cheek and gave her a soft, chaste kiss. "We're okay."

Her expression softened as I gazed into her eyes and she realized I was sincere. I certainly cared, but there was nothing for it. Gabe hadn't deserved that, and I felt a tinge of sympathy for him and Deborah, but again, the past couldn't be changed.

"I'm grateful for you," she whispered. "For every day we have together, you and Katie and Leah and me. If someone had asked me just six months ago if I'd ever have a family, I'd have laughed. But then, you came into my life. And you have such courage of spirit."

I snorted, but she continued.

"No, I mean it. You are the bravest person I know. And you love people that others might think unlovable. It's a gift."

It was my turn to blush, and my instinct was to deflect, but instead, I just murmured, "Thank you."

She leaned in and kissed me. I shoved the cuffs off the bed and curled up with her, pressing closer as if I could crush away the niggling pain of her admission between our bodies. It still hurt, though, and it would take time before that feeling faded, but I hadn't been lying. I loved Liz. And I wasn't going to give up what we had.

As the sun rose, we fell fast asleep in each other's arms with my stupid cat lying deflated across us like some kind of furry blanket.

CHAPTER EIGHT

I open my eyes and feel a familiar comfort that I haven't felt in a long time. A long hallway, more a gallery, really, crafted of dour gray stone runs maybe thirty-five feet in either direction. From a nearby doorway, muffled feminine voices chatter and giggle. The voices don't carry. I would have expected more echo in this vast space, but it's relatively quiet. Even my impressive vampiric hearing seems subdued.

I glance down, a little startled at my appearance. My pajamas have been replaced by an odd side-slit skirt and a top of soft cottony black with purple trim. It's not Shaddani, nor is it quite of earth. I think it's Óşenic; it certainly looks like their style. The skirt is a simple mid-length A-line affair, but it's the accompanying top that's so eye-catching. It's a kimono-style wrap with long black sleeves and a wide view of my cleavage, which might be more flattering if I weren't so muscle-heavy. As it is, my chest isn't exactly impressive. I stick out one of my legs, well-toned and milky white. My feet are shod in a pair of fashionable black slippers. It's not what I'd have picked, but okay. I gingerly step forward, intentionally keeping my steps quiet.

"So, you say your sister plays one of these?" a voice says from the room ahead.

"Oh, for sure," another voice, accented in Irish, replies. "She's a dab hand, too. Maybe when she sorts us out, you can play with her."

A grin spreads across my face, and I quicken my steps. I know that voice. Rounding the doorway, I spot my sister relaxing in a large conservatory on an elegant chaise lounge in one corner, next to a small tea table and a few plush chairs.

Instead of Óṣení finery, she is dressed casually in a pair of brown cargos and a black Boston Police Department t-shirt. A pair of Timberland boots that look suspiciously familiar lay casually strewn next to the chaise, socks loosely stuffed inside.

Úmbra, I assume, sits at a large harp-like instrument. She has her hands on the strings, poised to play. She wears a beautiful midnight-blue dress similar in fashion to my own but much more intricately designed and ornate.

"I'm a little rusty, to be honest," I say flippantly as I enter the room, startling them both.

"Sis? What are ya doin' here?" Aoife asks with a wide grin. "More importantly, how did you get here?"

"No clue," I answer. "But I'm glad to see you."

"You're not supposed to be here," Úmbra says somewhat demurely.

"Says who?" I ask, striking a defiant pose.

Úmbra purses her lips, showing her irritation. "You're supposed to be off finding a way to help us."

I blink. "Wait, this isn't just a dream?"

Úmbra shakes her head. "No. This is how Aoife and I are passing the time. You're inside our head."

"My head," Aoife corrects. "You're an interloper."

Úmbra snickers at some inside joke. "If you wanted it, you shouldn't have given it away, remember?"

Aoife gives her a dry look. "I'm not having this conversation again. We're stuck with it, and we're not going to argue and end up walking around in the desert for three days again."

At my bemused expression, she adds, "When we fight, the scenery becomes a lot less comfortable. The worst was a desolate portion of Shaddan, where we were chased by the freaky spiders. So, we have a truce at the moment."

I arch an eyebrow and cross my arms, glaring at both of them. "Well, you need to keep it and stay as calm as possible." I look pointedly at Úmbrá. "I'm sorry you're in this fix, and I'll get you out, but we've been having problems getting what we need."

It is her turn to raise an eyebrow. "And what do you need?"

"A soulstone. One of those," I point to a crystal hanging in the corner. "In one piece," I add, as this one had been drilled out to make a lamp. What a waste, I think.

Úmbra scowls and stomps one foot. "You are not putting me in one of those. My soul isn't disconnected from my thoughts. I'll go mad."

It's all I can do to keep a straight face. She looks like a kid having a temper tantrum. "It's my plan to move you to another body quickly," I argue. "It would only be for a few minutes."

"And my lehos?" Úmbra narrows her eyes. "I'm Kylr. I don't want to be human."

I pursed my lips and sighed. "Look, I'm trying all I can, but I don't know what else to do. I'm sorry."

Úmbra turns her back with a dejected look, and her shoulders begin to shake.

"Nice one, Cait," Aoife says and walks over to comfort Úmbra, shushing her softly. "Did you just come here to let us know how bollocksed we are? Thanks for that."

"Me?" I scoffed. "This isn't my fault. I wasn't even there." I drop my head in a mixture of irritation and resignation. Finally, I walk around them both and kneel, ducking my head to meet Úmbra's eyes. "I promise, if there's a way to do this right, I'll make it happen. I'm not giving up."

"My people could help," Úmbra said, wiping her nose on the back of her hand. "But we have no way to reach them."

"Do they have any relations with the Bethadi?" I ask, not daring to hope.

Úmbra furiously wipes her eyes, which turn wide. "The Bethadi? You can't go to them. They're insane."

I pull them both over to the tea table and guide Úmbra into a seat. "Okay, so tell me what you know. I haven't seen the Bethadi in two thousand years. Though that's maybe only fifty of theirs, so I can't imagine they've changed that much."

"It's not first-hand knowledge," Úmbra tells us. "But it was my understanding from travelers that something is wrong in Bethad. No one seems to know what, but no one who goes there returns anymore,

and the gate in Centrus is heavily guarded."

I frowned at that. "No one?"

She shook her head, and Aoife gave me a grave look. "What was your plan?"

"We used a soulstone to hold Boudka's soul when Nemhain, our other mother, made her a vampire. I had planned to do the same thing to one of you."

Úmbra gasped, and Aoife shook her head. "No," Aoife says. "No way. You're not making me a vampire."

"Wait," Úmbra interrupts. "That might actually work." At Aoife's incredulous stare, she continues. "If my soul was extracted, my lehos might exit your body, Aoife."

"What would that do to me?" Aoife asks. "It's what keeps me alive."

Úmbra chuckles. "No, not exactly. I mean, it shouldn't kill you. Most likely, you'd revert to our original form. At least, I think."

I don't like all of the qualifications like 'most likely' or 'not exactly.' "You think? You're not exactly giving me the warm and fuzzies here, Úmbra."

"Yeah," Aoife agrees, a wry look on her face.

"It's uncharted territory. The Kylr weren't always this way," Úmbra continued. "Once, we were just like you. Well, a lot like you, anyway. We're not indigenous to the Kylr plain. We were refugees from some massive catastrophe. There were forty thousand of us. In those first few years, one in four died."

"How do you know all this," I ask. "I've never heard any of this."

"My people are secretive, Cait, ridiculously so. They're also a little on the primitive side. Anyway, wait here." Úmbra stands and hustles out the door.

"Sorry, Sis, I didn't know what else to do," I say, suddenly feeling as if she were watching me with judging eyes.

Aoife takes my hand. "Look, I don't judge you for being a vampire. How could I? But I just don't want that. I like all of the things that come with being alive: working out, eating pizza until I pop, pints of Guinness 'til I'm bollocksed, you know?"

I nod. "I can understand and respect that. I still have my cannoli and coffee every Wednesday. It's just that—" I pause as the house gives a little rumble, like a minor tremor, and I hear a sound like the *tinking of a glass chandelier as it shakes somewhere nearby.* "What was that?"

"This place is from Úmbra's memory. It's getting unstable," Aoife says. "Úmbra thinks she's dying and that the tremors are like the precursor to all of this coming apart."

I nod. "That makes sense. You're the more powerful soul. The most likely outcome, if I don't find a way to extract one of you, is that your soul consumes the energy of hers."

"And what happens to her?" *Aoife asks, horrified.*

I shook my head gravely. "We don't exist without our souls, Aoife."

"You can't let that happen. Please, Cait."

I sigh. "I'm trying not to. I'm just scared, Aoife. The Light Fae are scary enough, and if they've somehow gone off their rocker, I'm not sure how I can do this, but I'm going to try."

"Okay," *Úmbra says as she returns to the table with a thick book and opens it.* "Look here."

I stare at her. "So this place is built from your memories?"

Úmbra glances up from the book, obviously confused. "Yes."

"And every page of the book is in here?" *I ask, and she catches on.* "I'm Kylr. Our lehos record everything we say and do."

Aoife flushes a deep silvery-gray. "Umm. . .everything?"

With a smirk, Úmbra looks back at the page. "Everything," *she says flatly, and I chuckle, then press my lips together to suppress a grin.*

"What are you laughing about, Cait?" *Úmbra says, still smirking tartly.* "I have your memories, too, at least up until I was extracted."

My eyes grow a little wider, and I put my hand to my mouth in mortification. At least I wasn't fed enough to blush. "Moving on. What does the book say?"

"So," *Úmbra says.* "There's a reason that the Kylr are all women. My people arrived on the Kylr Plain maybe fifteen thousand Shaddani years ago, about the time that Ósen was settled. Anyway, the refugees who settled there were all women, and about a quarter of them died before they made a rather interesting discovery. Here, read this bit."

I look at the page. "The Kylr discovered the existence of the kwedwyrm." *I pause and glance up, shocked.* "Kwed is a Shaddani *word."*

"It's old Óṣenic, too. Keep reading," Úmbra said.

"Through a complicated ritual, the high priestess of Mehter Korwo bound the souls and knowledge of each Kylr to a lehos, the larva of the kwedwyrm."

"Mother of Waters," I swear. "They're Shaddani, and not just Shaddani, they're high-Shaddani."

Úmbra nods. "Yes. And, from what I can tell, the Óṣení are, too."

I look at her askance. "Why do you say that?"

Aoife chimed in then, quite proud of herself. "Think about it, Cait. Linguistically, Óṣenic is clearly a daughter language of Shaddani, and the Medhen use Shaddani magic."

"Hang on," Úmbra says and stands, running out of the room again. She returns much quicker this time, a little out of breath. In her arms, she holds a much larger tome. "I read this one years ago. It's not complete, though. I didn't have a chance to finish it."

I look at the spine. The title reads 'On the Óṣení People and Culture.' Úmbra opens it to a page and points at a short section. "It says here that the original name for the Óṣení people was Argos Alv."

I gasp. "That means gray elf in Shaddani."

Úmbra nods again. "We're all one people, Cait." The house gives another rumble, and Úmbra clutches at her head. Her form seems to shimmer momentarily, losing cohesion at the edges before she solidifies once more. "Ow," she brays. "That one hurt."

"How long?" I ask.

"Not long, a few weeks at best," Aoife says. "It's accelerating. You have to do something, Cait."

"I will. I promise. I'll figure something out." Honestly, though, I have no idea what I can do. The soulstone is a long shot as it is.

"I'm sorry," Úmbra says abruptly, and I look at her, forehead creased with a mix of confusion and concern.

"For what?"

"I never meant for this to happen. I thought I could get help from Mother Darkness in stopping the attacks on Óṣen."

I chuckle. "Let me guess. You discovered she was the reason they were attacking."

Úmbra gives a wan smile. "Yes. I'll never understand why my

people worship her. She's insane."

With a mental start, I realize I have a wealth of knowledge in front of me. "What can you tell me about her?"

"Not a lot, really. Ask me about Óşen or Kylr or magic, and I can tell you a great deal, but about her, I know almost nothing. Just a few legends."

"Anything might help," I say, trying to temper my excitement and sense of urgency.

"Her body is karanite crystal. Shadowsteel will scratch it but won't destroy it; that requires magic. The Book of Darkness, my people's bible, says that she created the Kylr in her image, but I'm pretty sure that's just your typical creation myth. There is a bit, though. Hang on a second."

She gets up again and takes off, returning a few minutes later with another much smaller, less ornate book. It is bound in black leather and bears only a dark blue circle on its cover.

When she returns, I ask, "If this is your head, why do you keep getting up to get books?"

Úmbra gives a childish giggle. "Aoife asked that, too. There's very little room in Aoife's noggin for much more than my consciousness. So, I have to access what I know in pieces from the lehos. I'd say Aoife studies too much, but I'm not one to talk. In any event, that's just how my subconscious represents it, I'm sure. So look here." She points at a passage in the book. "This is our legend of the end times."

"I can't read that," I state, staring at the odd symbols. The symbology is odd. There doesn't seem to be enough differentiation in the script to support more than a handful of sounds.

"I know," Úmbra says with an arch smile. "With the exception of prayers, all Kyliri religious texts are written in a musical script." She snatches up the book from the table and steps back to the harp. "This one is in Swadis. It is, I think, what you'd call a minor key."

I sit down. Déra says that Úmbra is a prodigious talent with the instrument, so I listen intently.

"Kassí Glaurwin was my teacher," she says, plucking one string and setting up a wild resonance among several of the others that sound like the distant wailing of a horn. Then she adds, "He was a racist clod but competent."

I bark a laugh, and Úmbra winks at me as she begins to play.

She plucks at the strings, and the music flows from the instrument like the burgeoning light of a universe. It takes me a moment to realize that the ambient sounds I hear, the crashing of waves, the rumbling of molten rock, and the hiss of the surf are all coming from the instrument itself, timed sympathetically with the music. The tones of the strings are themselves like no instrument I've ever heard.

The Field of Heroes stretches out before me—endless, windswept, silent. The ground is a barren landscape of forgotten tombs, its soil gray with ash. At the far edge, where the land simply gives up, the ground falls away into the yawning void of what was once Lindon Danu.

And there, rising from its center, looms Mother Darkness.

She is immense, shadow and crystal. She stands alone. There is no army. No vast hoard of Fomori. Nothing but the silence of her dominion.

I can feel it—the weight of her loneliness. The wind no longer howls here; it whispers, soft and sorrowful, a funeral song no one is left to hear.

As I watch, cracks begin to bloom across her crystalline body.

The scene shifts. A ball of tarzhi, the colors of Shaddan, floats in a sea of blackness. It is swallowed up by a blasted world, Shaddan, as it might be seen from space. The vision within a vision is like nothing I've experienced. I am tiny amid the images, insignificant.

The scene shifts again.

A man stands there, salt and pepper hair swept back like a storm has been through it. His shoulders are rigid, his back turned—always turned—toward the girl who stands just a few steps behind him. She's beautiful, black-haired, so still in the quiet of the moment. Her face, though… it's ours. Aoife's and mine, as we were at maybe twenty. Before the weight of the world touched our features.

She reaches out—tentatively—as if to speak, as if to touch, as if to matter. But the man doesn't move. Doesn't see.

He's staring into something ahead: a swirling portal that devours the air, a wound torn into the world. Beyond it lies a wasteland of shattered towers and skies the color of sickness, where the sun itself seems to have given up. The landscape is cracked, twisted, broken. Ruined.

And still, he stares. Into everything else. Anywhere but her.

The girl lowers her hand, fingers curling against her palm like a secret she's ashamed to keep. A flicker of understanding crosses her face—soft, fragile—and then it's gone, like dust swept from a windowsill.

Finally, the vision fades. The crystalline form of Mother Darkness rises one last time, radiant and solemn, before her body fractures. Cracks race through her glassy surface like spiderwebs, until—

Shatter.

The sound rings out, sharp as grief.

There is no one to grieve her. No one to remember.

Black. It floods the world—thick, tar-like fluid swallowing everything. I am drowning in it. It seeps into my mouth, my nose, clinging to my skin like living oil. I can't breathe. Where's the surface? I flail, desperate, limbs cutting through the molasses-like dark, but there's no up, no light, no air. My lungs burn. My chest screams.

I paddle harder—harder—until my fingers strike something coarse. Sand. Sand. I went the wrong way. I am swimming deeper.

I can't turn around. I can't—

The weight of it crushes me, pushes me down, deeper into silence, and something coils in my chest: the certainty that I'm going to die here. Alone. Drowning.

I snap awake with a gasp. Air slams into my lungs, cold, feeling jagged and sharp. I choke on it, trembling, the song's echo pounding in my skull. I sit up—heart racing, breath ragged—clawing at the sweat-dampness as though it might still swallow me whole.

"Mother of Waters!" *I whisper hoarsely.*

I look over. Aoife is trembling.

Úmbra's hands hover. Her eyes are wide, body sweat-soaked. "I've never played it before. Good gods."

The house shakes violently, and Úmbra cries out, clutching her head. The house, Úmbra, and Aoife disintegrate before my eyes, leaving me in blackness.

CHAPTER NINE

After I'd awoken, I called Bian. Her voice was tight. "Aoife's vitals crashed, but… she's stable now." Stable. The word that felt more like bare hope than anything real. Stable until… when? Tomorrow? The next day? My chest squeezed. We were out of time.

I was loading several cold packs into a cooler to hold spare blood when Nastasia strode into the kitchen, Jess in tow, and dropped her duffel on the floor. She was dressed in black fatigue pants, combat boots, and a black tank top. Jess was in jeans, hiking boots, and a t-shirt.

Nastasia crossed her arms and stared at me skeptically. "Okay, so tell me your plan."

"I believe there's a soulstone in Ireland. I'm going to go get it and use it to house Úmbra's soul briefly until we can find a long-term solution."

"Do you even know where?" Nastasia asked.

"Where the soulstone is? No. Where to find Áine, who probably does? Yes."

She looked even more skeptical. "And who is this person?"

"Áine is The Summer Queen, leader of the Light Fae."

Nastasia screwed up her face in disbelief. "You're insane, dorogaya. You can't trust them."

"No," I responded hotly. "I can't. But I don't have a choice.

Úmbra and Aoife are dying."

She leveled narrowed eyes at me, leaning against the doorframe, arms crossed. "Have you ever been to Camp Five?"

"The Bethadi… uh… Light Fae camp? No."

"There are two-hundred-fifty of the most capricious and obnoxious little posers right under Hyde Park. They could all pass for human, apart from their ears, and not one of them deigns to do a day of labor on their own behalf. But that's not the point. One day, about five years ago, there was a massive power outage in that part of town."

"I remember. I had to assist with traffic duty that night. What's your point?"

"My point is that Marcella pissed them off, and the first thing they did was threaten to take out power across half the country. To prove it, their leader, a woman named Doirend, snapped her fingers and put out the lights across half the city. What's worse, they tried to glamour the hell out of us, too. On Marcella, it worked. She was a blubbering mess, believing she was alone in a desolate, empty world." Nastasia raised an eyebrow and gave me an arch smile. "I saw right through it. Fae glamour doesn't often work on me. I know myself too well."

I paused from loading thermoses of blood and noticed for the first time that Jess was holding a duffel of her own. I frowned at that and jerked a thumb at the duffel. "What's this about?"

"Where Nas goes, I go," Jess said with her usual bouncy demeanor.

"Jess, I don't think that's a good idea," I argued, thinking of all the bad things that could happen to her.

"It doesn't matter," Nastasia interjected, her voice flat and firm. "She's coming. You'll need us to watch your back. Besides, I'm eight hundred years old, and unlike your paramour, wife, or whatever you're calling Elizabeth these days, I am a fighter. I spent years providing services of a different sort to various covert organizations around the world. You may need—how did Liam Neeson put it?—the particular set of skills that I have gained through a very long career." To emphasize the point, she pulled out a lovely ninjato, twirled it a bit, and re-sheathed it smoothly before holding it out to me.

"You were an assassin?" I asked, eyes wide as I slid the beautiful, well-balanced blade from its scabbard, giving it a few swings.

"She was," Liz confirmed from the hallway entrance. "I came to tell you that Marcella has confirmed that the plane is ready."

Then I rolled my eyes as it hit me. "You're the pilot," I said to Nastasia, and she nodded. I shook my head. "Of course you are. Can you tap dance, too?"

In response, Nastasia performed a little shuffle step and gave me a crooked smile.

I gave her the finger and a wry smirk.

"Focus," Liz said, shaking me gently. "Once you have what you need, you need to convince them to open a portal to Camp Two. Barring that, you need to get to Cardiff by hook or by crook. The Brits are patrolling the Irish Sea, so you'll have to be careful. Once you're in Wales, Robert will be waiting to bring you back." She handed me a folded piece of paper. "This is the address and phone number where he's staying."

She turned toward Nastasia. "You better watch out for her, Nas. I mean it."

Nastasia donned what was probably supposed to be an innocent smile, but it just looked maliciously delighted. "Not to worry, Elizabeth, I will save the day."

"Fuck me," I muttered. "I never thought I'd put my life in your hands again." And yet, the thought sent a dark, almost erotic thrill through me. I pressed my lips together, suppressing the shiver that threatened.

Nastasia was evil, a bully to her core, but she'd shown me a part of myself I hadn't known existed—ruthless, unrepentant, and utterly devoid of forgiveness. A place I could retreat to when emotions became too much. And damn, if that still wasn't sexy as hell. The fact that she'd once been a legendary assassin only made it worse, or better, depending on how you looked at it.

But I mourned the shift in our power dynamic. I wasn't the helpless mortal she'd once toyed with. I was a vampire now, damn strong in my own right. She couldn't feed my fear or force me to bed. Oh, she still scared me, just enough to make my anxiety spike—not that I'd admit it—but it was different now.

Not quite enough.

Liz placed a finger under my chin and pulled my gaze upward and away from Nastasia. "I need you to listen to me. I have no idea what you'll face over there, but if the Fae in Ireland are anything like the ones here, then let me leave you with this. Trust Nastasia. She knows herself better than anyone. She's not prone to self-delusion. You, on the other hand, are very young. They'll take advantage of that."

At my incredulous stare, she continued, her tone more forceful. "I'm serious, Cait. I love you, but you sometimes struggle with guilt and what you are. You're getting better, but still."

I lowered my eyes. She wasn't wrong. The most powerful glamours used the victim's own emotional hangups against them. I wasn't a fool. I had more hangups than I could count. "I'll keep Nas close," I said solemnly.

She nodded and gave me a quick hug. "Not too close," she said with a smirk, then added with a quick, chaste kiss and watering eyes. "Come back, safe."

Katie and Leah appeared in the doorway, still in their school clothes. Leah fingered a piece of paper in her hand.

"You leaving, mama?" Katie asked.

"In a little bit," I answered and bent down to Leah. "Are you going to be okay while I'm gone?"

Leah threw her arms around my neck and squeezed tightly. "Please don't go, mama."

Tears welled in my eyes as I hugged her. *Damn. This is fucking hard.* "I'll be back before you know it," I whispered. "I promise."

"I had a dream last night," she said. "We were watching someone have a baby, and you were really upset."

I hugged her a little closer. "Well, I don't know anyone who's going to have a baby, but I'll keep that in mind. Sometimes dreams are just dreams."

"I know, but sometimes they're not. You have dreams that aren't dreams. It's how you found Katie and Auntie Liz. I was afraid this was one of those, and I thought you should know."

I gave her a loving smile and stroked her head. "It could be. There's a lot of magic floating around. Thank you so much for telling me." I offered an arm to Katie, who knelt into us and hugged us both. Liz joined in.

"Don't worry, Mama," Katie said. "I'll keep her safe. I promise."

I sniffed and swallowed hard, unable to contain my tears. "I know you will. Now, Leah, you mind your sister and Auntie Liz."

Leah locked her hands at the back of my neck. "I will, Mama, but I don't want you to go. I'm scared of the mean lady."

My brow furrowed, and I looked at her. "What do you mean?"

"She was in my dream," she said and held out the paper she'd been holding. "I drew her."

I took the drawing from her. For a twelve-year-old, it was damn good. She had talent; that much was certain. In the drawing, a woman stood, dressed all in black, with black hair and green eyes. She looked like she might be snarling or growling. I pressed my lips together and looked back at Leah, searching her face. I didn't know exactly what I was looking for, though.

"You saw her in your dream?" I asked, finally.

Leah nodded. "I don't want you to go. I'm afraid she'll hurt you."

"I'm sure it was just a dream, honey," I lied. "And I have to. Auntie Aoife is in trouble, and I have to help her."

She nodded silently and let go. I thumbed a tear off her face and stood. "Okay, you two. Have you done your homework?"

"I did mine already," Katie said, but Leah shook her head.

"Katie, take her upstairs and make sure she gets hers done."

With a last hug, I sent them off. I looked back at the picture, tracing the huge black wings on the woman with a finger.

"What is it?" Liz asked.

"Badb," I said and handed it to her. Without another word, I headed upstairs, thoroughly disturbed.

When I returned with my bollóm, I found Déra in the middle of the foyer, tapping her foot. She greeted me with a quick hug and held out a sheathed dagger. "Here. Take this. It's all I have, but it might help."

I looked down. "A nisís. Thank you."

Her eyes went wide.

I smirked and bumped her shoulder playfully with my own. "I told you. I'm Valtárí." I pulled the dagger from its sheath. Inscribed in Óṣenic were the words 'Saya ca Afruné.' I gasped and brought my hand to my mouth before brushing away an unbidden tear. "Saya," I whispered.

"She was an ancestor. It has been in my family for twenty generations, almost five hundred cycles."

I searched her face, looking for any resemblance to the woman I had known, but there was none apart from how all Óṣení shared certain features. "How much do you know about her?"

"Not a lot. I know she disappeared defending this world against Mother Darkness, and I know she was an honorable woman and had a reputation for being, as you say, a hard ass."

I laughed. "She had a softer side, too. When I return, let's chat. There are some things you'd probably like to know. I really wish you were coming with us."

Déra nodded. "I do as well, but given the military cordon, you stand a better chance of getting out of the city without me. I stand out like a sore thumb."

That she did. I gave her a quick hug and put the nisís in my bag. "I'll take good care of it, I promise."

"I know you will. You are a warrior through and through. Though, I was surprised that Morgan isn't joining you."

"She offered, but it's not a risk I'm willing to take. I want Aoife to have someone to come home to." I saw a pain in Déra's normally stoic gaze that I knew all too well. "Listen, you might want to talk to Morgan about Caileigh. She's just sitting there frozen at the compound, not doing anyone any good."

"You know our ways, Cait. I can't do that. It was hard enough to accept when Aoife offered."

I gave her a nod, and with a quick hug, we said our goodbyes. She wished me good hunting. A half-hour later, Nastasia, Jess, and I sat in an armored Chevy Suburban. I turned and looked at each of them. "You don't have to do this."

They just glared at me.

"Okay, then," I said and started the car.

Our destination was Carver-Branford Airport in Maine. It was further than some of the others, but it was the only place where Marcella could quietly arrange our exit. The airport also had a skydiving school, whose services we would need. I hadn't told Jess that part. *Maybe she'd grow wings,* I thought wryly as we pulled away from the house.

CHAPTER TEN

Getting through town had been relatively easy. Patrol had started setting up checkpoints along heavily traveled routes, which, to my mind, was stupid. But then again, the light nature of the in-town checkpoints was likely Sesi's doing. She had made it clear she wasn't thrilled about President James' order. Anyone not in a hurry to leave could take any of a dozen un-covered routes. I was able to badge my way past patrol and the one Massachusetts National Guard unit we found along the way. We thought we were in the clear, but then, just south of the Lynnfield junction with I-95 North, we ran into trouble. The US Army had set up a checkpoint complete with a fucking Abrams tank sitting on the road.

They had left only one lane open, which snaked to the right, past the tank, and then to the left around the sandbag and sawhorse barricade beyond. Fortunately, there was no traffic at three in the morning, so whatever happened next hopefully wouldn't be caught on someone's cellphone. I had the distinct feeling that things were about to get ugly, well, uglier.

"I need identification for all occupants, please," the first soldier, a young, fresh 2nd lieutenant, said curtly as we pulled up.

I opened the door a crack since the windows didn't roll

down and slid my badge through to him. "Detective Reagan, Boston PIU. I'm on assignment."

The soldier backed away from the door. "Please step out of the car, ma'am." He shifted his grip on his M4.

Shit. I thought. *This is going to suck.*

I turned back to Jess in the back seat. "When the shit starts, get down." Jess crossed her arms and nodded, sort of.

Nastasia looked at me, her eyes holding not a small amount of glee in them. I shook my head. Then we got out of the car. I hoped we wouldn't be bothered too much, maybe just questioned, but the tension level suggested that they'd known to look for us. How? I had no idea, but it didn't matter.

Fuck 'em, I thought. *I'm on mission, and this is the enemy.* I couldn't muster one bit of empathy for them.

"What's the problem?" I demanded, snatching my badge out of his hands and putting it back on my hip. "I have work to do, and you're in the way."

He didn't answer, but two more men jerked up their rifles. *Oh, so it was like that. Okay.*

I scanned the group, counting twelve infantry: eleven men and one woman. With the tankers, that would be probably sixteen. One guy, a staff sergeant, stood in the tank hatch, and there were likely three more enlisted guys inside.

Two men stood beyond the barricade, weapons down, and three others stood foolishly close to Nastasia. There was also a dude in the Humvee next to the barricade. He manned the fifty caliber. I'd leave those six to her.

On my side were the butter-bar who'd asked for my ID, two guys with M4s up, and two standing casually, looking bored.

A dark-skinned young woman, a medic by her arm patch, stood with a small kit leaning against the tank. She looked irritated as she swatted at a wisp of brunette hair sticking from under her helmet. I felt bad for her, being the only woman in this sausage fest. More than that, though, there was something about her that caught my attention and held it fast for a second. I felt that same tug that I felt with Jess, an irrational protectiveness. I brushed it aside.

It was obvious to me that whoever had warned them hadn't

really told them what they were up against. Or, if they had, these guys didn't understand or didn't believe them. I felt the cool, reassuring metal of the bóllom against my back, giving me comfort as I eyed the tank. With my strength, it would cut through the top armor like butter.

"Corporal," the first man called, and the woman stepped forward. She looked no more than twenty. From the medical kit, she extracted a forehead thermometer.

I pressed my lips into a thin line and adopted a warning tone. "Lieutenant, you don't want to do this. It won't go well for everyone. Just let us go, and no one will get hurt."

The corporal wavered for a moment and looked back at the Lieutenant, who said, "Just get on with it, corporal."

She raised the thermometer to my head. I looked down. She was unarmed. Her nametape read 'Sobrai.'

"Please hold still, ma'am." Her soft southern accent was similar to Carlos' but with a little less twang.

I looked up. "For what it's worth, Corporal, I'm sorry about this."

"Eighty-six point three," she read from the thermometer with a shaking voice. So they had definitely been warned, and she was about to piss herself. The others may not have understood what they were facing, but somehow, she did.

The men started raising their weapons and stepping toward us, and then it was on. Compared to us, they might as well have been moving through peanut butter. Nastasia moved first, dashing between the men next to her, slugging each one so hard that they fell like dolls, almost certainly dead. Then she went after the two men behind the barricade.

I shoved the corporal aside, knocking her to the ground, and then kicked the lieutenant so hard he flew through the air and smacked into the side of the tank, where he lay unmoving. Then I blood-stepped behind the other four men who were closest as they pulled their triggers, their rounds leaving deep divots in the rear driver-side window near where Jess sat. She was playing a game on her phone, not even paying attention to the carnage outside.

I drew my bóllom and cut down the four men who'd shot at

me. Before the guy in the Humvee had time to swing the fifty in our direction, I switched the sword to my left hand and pulled my weapon, shooting him in the throat.

That delay, though, did give the tanker time to close the hatch on the tank, but it didn't matter. I leaped on top of the tank as Nastasia flashed through the remaining two soldiers, now shooting them with a weapon she'd snatched off of one of the first four she'd downed. My blade cut through the hatch hinges and locking mechanism with a few whacks that left not a scratch on the weapon. I loved karanite blades, the next best thing to a fucking lightsaber.

I tossed the hatch aside and yanked the staff sergeant from the tank, throwing him hard to the ground down in front of Nastasia, who rag-dolled him and broke his neck. Then, I dropped in and killed the other three tankers with swift strokes. One of them got off a shot that hit me in the chest somewhere, but I ignored it as I stabbed each one in turn.

Pulling myself out of the tank, I noticed something that shouldn't be there. It was just a little nub on the turret, but I'd seen more tanks in my time than I cared to. That little nub didn't belong there. Someone had painted it and tried to disguise it. They'd done a good job, but I suspected they hadn't planned on one of us having been around an Abrams before.

I used my nisís to cut away the plastic housing. Underneath sat a wide-angle camera. For a moment, a spike of fear ran through me. They'd caught the entire attack on camera. I tore the camera out of its bracket and examined it. There were no antennae, and it looked too small to have cell service. I looked around for a Wi-Fi or Bluetooth receiver, but I didn't see anything. There was a slot for an SD card, but it was screwed shut. I stuffed the camera in my pocket. I'd look at it later.

"Hey, Nas," I called. "They had a camera mounted on here."

"There's one on the Humvee as well," Nastasia replied a few moments later. It's attached to the bumper and well hidden."

Someone was trying to catch this on video. "Look around and see if there are any others, and grab cell phones from the soldiers."

While Nastasia collected several cameras, I walked the exterior of the tank to see if there were more. There weren't, so I dropped back inside. I literally tore apart the commander's and driver's workstations until I found the solid-state drives and pulled them. I didn't know if they'd been recording anything when we rolled up, but I couldn't chance it. The commander's station had been easy to get at; the driver's station had been a bit more difficult as I'd had to work around his body.

A picture of a woman fell out of his pocket onto the floor. It looked recent. I sighed and shook my head. I hated this. He probably didn't have kids, given that there were none in the photo, but that was little comfort. Some of these guys probably did.

A few minutes later, drives in hand, I stood in front of the corporal, the only one left alive. She trembled mercilessly, and urine stained her pants, poor kid.

"We can't leave her alive," Nastasia said, holding a couple of cameras and four cell phones.

"I'm not killing her," I stated flatly, and Nastasia rolled her eyes. It would have been the prudent thing, to eliminate the witness, but for some reason, I just couldn't. The very idea felt repugnant, and some part of me was sure that she wouldn't be safe anywhere but with us. So, instead, I pulled her off the ground and frisked her. She was in way too much shock to resist.

"Into the back, if you want to live," I ordered and opened the door. "Move over, Jess." Jessica slid sideways, and Sobrai got in, a dumbstruck look on her face.

Jess just smirked. "It's just not your day, is it? By the way, I'm Jess."

Okay, Jess had gone insane, I decided. More likely, she'd always been insane and just hid it better than most of us. Not that I could say anything. Nastasia and I had just cut down over a dozen soldiers without blinking. I thought I should feel bad, but this was war now. It wasn't my fault that no one told them how powerful we were or how brutally efficient we'd be in defending ourselves.

We hopped back in the SUV, and I stepped on the gas, burning rubber out of the checkpoint. It wouldn't be long before those guys were missed, and the Army came looking. We needed to be long gone, and we still had an hour of driving. This was going to be touch and go. I just hoped Otis Air Force Base didn't send anyone after us once we got in the air, or we'd be totally fucked.

CHAPTER ELEVEN

The army hadn't had time to spread out their cordon of Boston any further, so we managed to get to the airport with little difficulty. A Challenger CL-600 private jet that looked at least thirty years old sat on the tarmac waiting for us.

"Wow, cutting it close, M.," Nastasia commented when we exited the SUV.

"What do you mean?" Jess asked, looking at the jet.

"It's around 2800 miles to Ireland from here," Nastasia explained. "That plane has a maximum range of about 3200 miles, give or take a few for shitty weather or other issues. That doesn't leave much room for, well, other issues. So we're pushing beyond the edge of safety."

I sighed and turned to Jess. "If we have to ditch over the ocean, you're getting turned. No questions or arguments, you hear me?" I didn't know if I'd have time or if I could even turn her, but I'd try.

She swallowed but nodded. Damn, she was a trooper.

Nastasia turned to look at Sobrai. "And what do we do with you?"

Corporal Sobrai was under Nastasia's glamour, so she just followed her around like a lovesick puppy dog. She could have just made her obedient or something, but no, Nastasia had to make it weird. For a minute, I'd forgotten who I was dealing with.

"You know what?" Nastasia muttered. "It's not my problem. Oh, Cait?"

I looked up from digging our stuff out of the back of the SUV. "What?"

"What are you going to do with your little lamb here?"

I looked over. "Sobrai? You ever jump out of a plane before?"

"Sure," she said cheerily. "I love skydiving."

Jess's eyes went wide. "Jump?"

I snickered and nodded. "Yeah, we may not be able to land that thing once we're over the island. It'll have no power. So we might have to dive in."

"Dive in, as in skydive?" Jess's face was deathly pale.

Nastasia walked over and put a hand on Jess's shoulder. "Don't worry. You're with me. We're not just throwing you out of the plane."

"But how fast will we be going? I'm not sure I can do this. I'm terrified of heights."

Nastasia looked her in the eye. "Trust me, Jess. You won't be when we get there. If you let me."

She shook her head and donned a firm expression. "No. If this is what it takes, I'll do it."

For a moment, I was reminded of myself, well, of Weyna, unwilling to quit as she hobbled on her battered feet after the Óșení women in the early days of her training. "Attagirl, Jess," I said and turned back to Sobrai. "How many jumps have you had?"

"One hundred thirty-eight."

I stopped. I couldn't do this to this poor woman. She'd be UA, and the Army would most definitely not understand. I sighed heavily. "Turn her loose, Nas."

Nastasia didn't even blink. Sobrai just started backing away, a horrified look on her face. "What did I do? Why did I go with you?"

My arm shot out and grabbed her before she could bolt. "Look at me. Tell me, where are you from?"

"Texas, ma'am," she replied shakily. "Houston."

How about that? I thought and almost laughed. *Ma'am.* The new recruit smell wasn't even off her. "Do you know what we are?"

"They said you were monsters looking to escape the quarantine, but I could tell right off. You're vampires. You and her."

I nodded and turned to Nastasia. "What's the likelihood that she'll crack if we try to make her forget?"

Nastasia snorted. "Something this traumatic? It's hard to say. It really depends more on her than on me. You survived Marcella's glamour just fine, and she took away half your life, but the Medical Examiner I glamoured was on the edge of insanity. I'd rather not chance it if we can avoid it."

I rubbed my forehead in exasperation and sighed. "You know what, we're wasting time. Fuck it. Get on the plane, kid. Welcome to the club. You're a hostage." Nastasia laughed and grabbed Maggie's arm, dragging her forcefully to the plane while I checked with Marcella's man. "Are you Grierson?"

"Yes, Ma'am. She's all fueled up with reserve, and there are two chutes plus a tandem harness. I'm assuming you're gonna need this one." He held up an extra chute.

"Great, thanks, man."

His face remained cool and professional. "No need to thank me. I'm being well paid, but you know that jumping out of one of these is suicide, right?"

"Thanks, I'm well aware. I'm hoping it won't be necessary."

I climbed into the plane and pulled up the stairs. He wasn't wrong, and I worried for Jess. I could only hope that those "missing" British aircraft had just lost power rather than being destroyed mid-flight. Bringing her was an awful risk.

"Cait, get up here," Nastasia called from the flight deck shortly after wheels up. "We have a problem."

I made my way to the cockpit and slid into the co-pilot's seat. "I hope you're not looking for me to fly this—"

"Shut up and put on the headset. I need you to respond to

these guys," she snapped and pointed to a headset hanging from a loop next to me. "I feel like a Russian accent might not be welcome."

"What guys?" I asked as I grabbed the headset and slid it over my ears, adjusting the mic.

"We've been intercepted." Nastasia gestured casually to either side of the cockpit.

I looked out the window, and my stomach sank like a stone. "Oh, shit," I whispered. Two F-35 fighters flew in escort position on either side of the plane. The one on the left had rolled, exposing its open weapons bay and giving us a prime view of four missiles.

As if that threat wasn't perfectly clear, a crisp, professional female voice spoke over the radio. "White and Brown Challenger, This is U.S. Air Force fighter Frost Queen. You are instructed to immediately change course to zero-three-zero and follow us to Bangor for detention. Please acknowledge and comply. We have authorization to fire." The calm in the pilot's voice was beyond chilling, and while call signs were typically earned from embarrassing moments, I wondered if hers was more deliberate than the usual inside joke. Everything about her said she was not the woman with whom to fuck, at least not in the air.

I glanced at the GPS. We were beyond the three-mile mark from the coast. I flipped on my microphone. "Frost Queen, this is Challenger. We are a passenger jet in international airspace. We have a properly filed flight plan for London. We are not a threat to anyone. What is the basis for detention?"

"Challenger, Frost Queen, this is a direct order. Turn to heading zero-three-zero degrees now. Non-compliance will be treated as a hostile act. This is your final warning."

It had been worth a shot, but I hadn't expected that to work anyway. I hated what I had to do next, but I had no other choice. "Frost Queen, there is an active duty US service member on board. If you fire, you will kill her."

On the one hand, I was happy that Sobrai was here as a bargaining chip. On the other, I had just tipped our hand that we were the ones who'd slaughtered Sobrai's unit. "Corporal

Sobrai is alive and on board this aircraft. I repeat. If you fire, she will die with us." I flipped my microphone over to the cabin. "Corporal, get up here if you don't want to die."

There was about a nine-month pregnant pause, and then, "Challenger, Frost Queen, have the corporal state her full name, rank, and service number."

Sobrai opened the door to the cabin and peeked in. "What is it?" She asked, and I pointed out the window. Sobrai's eyes turned into saucers. "Oh, shit."

"Challenger, respond." One of the fighters dropped back while the other moved wide to our right. A red light at the top control panel marked RWR lit up.

"What's that?" I asked, nodding at the light.

"Radar warning receiver. They've locked on with a guided missile," she said, chuckling. "I will say, though, we're about to die in a very nice aircraft. My compliments to Ms. O'Malley."

"Frost Queen," I barked into the mic. "I'm working on it."

I held out the headset to Sobrai. "We are not going to hurt you," I said carefully. "You will live through this, I promise. I will even get you back home, but you need to tell them what they want to know. Otherwise, they'll shoot us down. It's that simple."

"Hey," Jess called over Sobrai's shoulder. "Did you see the fighters outside?"

"Yes, Jess, we see them. Go strap in!" I called back. Not that it would do any good, but Jess was a distraction right now. As soon as Sobrai had the headset in place, I keyed the mic and gestured for her to speak, praying silently to Mother Danu that they wouldn't just kill us anyway.

"This is Corporal Margarida Fernanda Sobrai," the corporal said frantically, her voice a bit shrill.

"Serial number and unit, Corporal," Frost Queen responded.

"Serial Number 9993785610. I'm assigned to the Massachusetts National Guard, 126th Support Battalion. For God's sake, please let them go. They promise not to hurt me, and I believe them." There was a long pause. "Hello? Please, don't kill me, ma'am!"

"Standby, Corporal," Frost Queen answered coolly.

I took the headset from her and waited. Several minutes passed, with Sobrai's murmur of Hail Marys and the engine noise the only sounds. I didn't have the heart to tell Sobrai that her God was buried somewhere in a karanite crystal; she didn't deserve to have her faith crushed right then. Finally, the RWR light went dark, and Frost Queen spoke.

"Challenger, this is Frost Queen. You are cleared to continue on your own navigation." There wasn't even a hint of frustration—just another day at the office.

I sighed in relief. "Thank you, Frost Queen. Safe Travels."

There was no reply, not that I'd expected one. We were murderers who had just escaped from the US Military. Frost Queen, no doubt, wanted to knock us out of the sky. With that thought, doubt and guilt gnawed at my gut for the first time. What else would happen? What more danger would Jess be in? I realized that I really had no idea. Everything I knew about the Bethadi was either theoretical, from my mother's lectures and lessons, or the tidbit of experience that Weyna had had with them. In all truth, I had no idea what we were walking into, but I didn't expect a warm welcome.

"Go sit down," I told Sobrai, but she didn't move.

"Were you telling the truth?" She asked, giving me a firm glare.

"Yes," Nastasia answered for me. "Now go sit, Corporal. There'll be time for questions later."

Finally, she left the cockpit.

"She's going to be a handful," Nastasia said. "You really should have let me glamour her anyway and have her get lost."

"I didn't want to risk it," I said, trying and failing to get comfortable in the co-pilot seat. "Besides, we'd be dead." On that pleasant thought, I changed the subject. "So, you gonna teach me the basics here or what?"

Nastasia chuckled. "Sure, why not? We have time."

CHAPTER TWELVE

After my impromptu flying lesson, which had been amazing, I returned to the cabin. I dropped into a seat across from a very meek-looking Sobrai. Several emotions played in her expression, flickering between discomfort and abject terror.

"I'm Cait," I said casually.

"M-Maggie," she stammered. "My real name is Margarida, but I got tired of boys joking about tasting the Margherita in high school, so I just go by Maggie." She turned shy then, reminding me, for all the world, of Katie when she overshared. "So, what are you gonna do with me?"

I started rifling through my backpack. "Well, first, how tall are you?"

"Five-foot-eight," she answered, craning her neck to see what I was doing.

I pulled a pair of jeans, a shirt, sox, and a pair of panties from my bag. "First, we get you out of those pants." Jess snorted loudly in amusement, and I shot her an annoyed glare. "Here are some clean clothes, Maggie. The sweater might be a little big, but the cargos should fit you fine. The panties are mine, so that's optional if you're icked out by wearing someone else's, but they're fresh from the wash. There's a latrine in the back of the cabin with a pod shower you can use."

She grabbed all of it and stood. "My foster mother worked in a sweatshop where they made underwear. If a pair fell on the ground, they'd use their dirty feet sometimes to pick them up from under the sewing table. After that, washed and unstained is all I've ever cared about."

"Wow," Jess cackled. "You got her out of her panties and into yours in less than four hours. That's like a record."

"Really, Jess?" I said lightly as the door to the latrine pulled shut. "Honestly. Grow up."

She laughed again and smirked at me sidelong. "Never."

I rolled my eyes and shook my head, but the truth was, I had missed them all. To everyone else, I'd been out for a couple of months. For me, it had been a lifetime. As Weyna, I hadn't remembered them, hadn't felt their absence. But when I woke up and the two lives collided in my mind, it hit me. It felt like I'd been gone forever.

"Seriously though," Jess said. "What are we going to do with her? She's got no passport. When we get back, they'll put her in Leavenworth."

"They won't put her in prison for UA, Jess," I said. "If they charge her at all, she'll spend some time in the stockade and probably be discharged. I promised to get her back alive. After that, it's her problem."

Jess raised her eyebrows. "Wow, you have changed."

"I suppose. I've spent half of my life so far whining about every bad thing that's ever happened to me. I've died twice. I'm done complaining. And it's probably high time I accept what I am."

Jess looked at me askance. "And what are you?"

"A killer, Jess. A vampire. And I'm not going to be anyone's prey animal. So Senator Kim and her pack of nutballs are going to get more than they bargained for. I tried to straddle the line between vampire and human, but it's impossible, so fuck that. I'm all in." The normally gregarious forensic tech just nodded and grew quiet.

About fifteen minutes later, Maggie emerged from the latrine. She tossed her neatly folded stack of fatigues on the floor behind her seat and sat back down in front of me.

"Thanks for that," she said, then whispered, "I'm sorry."

"For what?" I asked, confused.

"I don't know. Pissing myself, I guess."

I gave a mirthless laugh. "It's okay. I've done it myself. As an adult, I mean. You had every right to be scared." My tone was calm, even detached. Maggie's gaze softened for just a moment, but then, her eyes burned with resentment, and her jaw tensed as she bit back the harsh thoughts undoubtedly swirling in her head, likely conjured by the memory of just who she was talking to, just what we had done.

I switched subjects. "So tell me, how long were you in foster care?"

She looked up, face hardening again, shock mingling with a flicker of rage. "Look, we're not friends. I'm your hostage, so I don't think you've earned an answer to that."

"Okay, then." I let my face remain neutral, studying her tightly clenched fists, the taut line of her mouth. "I'm sorry about your unit. I didn't have a choice." I wasn't sorry, not really, but I let the words fall as if I were.

Her lips thinned, and she looked away, staring out the window. "They were American soldiers," she said through gritted teeth. Her voice wavered, her fingers twisting into her shirt in agony like a lost child, angry and hurt. "They had families. Lieutenant Sipian has two kids."

As I watched, her jaw trembled, and despite her eyes flaring with barely contained anger, they flickered, hinting at something else—an understanding, maybe a kinship she didn't want to acknowledge. I paused, speaking slowly, each word careful, controlled. "Corporal—" I paused for a second, then I leaned in, softening my tone as I addressed her by name. "Maggie, I have kids, too, and Jess isn't a vampire. What were they going to do with her?"

Jess flipped a page in an old fashion magazine left lying around. Her voice was casual, and one eyebrow popped up with disdain. "That's a good question. What were they going to do to me?"

Maggie's mouth tightened, and she looked away, her face hardening. But her eyes betrayed her, glistening as tears threatened. She blinked furiously, her shoulders rising defensively as she swiped a hand beneath a bottom lid. *Poor kid,* I thought. *This broke her.*

"I thought so," I said, letting the words linger, my voice barely above a whisper. "I'm only thirty-two, Maggie. I was born in Boston in 1996, not the fifth century. There's nothing in the Constitution or federal law that says the US Military can arbitrarily exterminate US citizens. I'm not an enemy of the US government and have done nothing wrong. On top of that, I'm a cop and a damn good one. Not some trigger-happy asshole."

Her jaw set, teeth gritted as she stared back at me, defiance flaring in her eyes only to flicker and die as the fight seemed to drain from her shoulders. "We had our orders," she said quietly, her voice hollow, but her gaze slipped away as if she knew how it would sound.

"Yes, that's what Eichmann said," the words landed like stones in the ensuing silence.

Maggie's gaze dropped to her hands, her fingers tightening until her knuckles turned white. She looked back out the window, her face unreadable, but I watched in real-time as the dark hand of despair swept across her expression like an ashen gray cloud. "This sucks," she muttered finally, so softly I could barely hear it, her hand trembling as she swatted tears off her cheeks.

I gave her a moment of silence, sliding one of my handkerchiefs across the table. She needed to digest the truth, dark as it was. When she finally looked back at me, dark circles had appeared under her red, tear-filled eyes. She looked gutted, hollowed out. My right hand still rested on the table, one finger on the handkerchief she still hadn't taken. She stared at the fabric, the embroidered CGR in light grey, gothic letters adorning the cloth. Slowly, she reached for it, but her hand didn't stop, landing instead on mine. Confusion washed across her face, as if she hadn't meant to do it but couldn't help herself.

I felt it—a distant, dim awareness, like the faint static of an old television. Maggie's lost expression said she felt it, too, an unintended brush of consciousness. Normally, I would have shut out such an intrusion immediately, but this time, I didn't. Unsettled, I leaned back, withdrawing my hand, trying to get some distance. The feeling stayed, though.

"Let me tell you a story," I said, seeing the weight of our connection still lingering in her head as surely as if it were strapped around her neck. "My sister saved Boston from a monster. Without her, the whole city would've been gone, drowned completely. And because of her, instead of two hundred thousand, we lost a tenth that many." I stopped, letting the gravity of those numbers settle over us both. "Small comfort, maybe, but it's something. She did her part, even though it almost killed her. Now I'm out here trying to save her life, risking everything." I could feel my throat tightening. "So tell me, Maggie Sobrai, how am I supposed to weigh that kind of hero against the lives of a dozen people?"

"Find another way," she whispered, but her eyes were downcast, fixed somewhere around my collar, like even looking at me was too much. Her pat, thoughtless answer made me want to shake her, but I reminded myself that she was a child. She didn't have anything but pat answers. Life's complexities still eluded her.

Maggie's head dropped, and she fidgeted. "Do you have any water?" Her voice sounded weak. It was a deflection and a poor one at that, but it was all she had left. She was desperate to save her own fragile world. It had already crumbled, though. She just hadn't realized it yet. And strangely, I hurt for her. The memory of Morgan at the door, suitcase in hand, came to mind. That had been my moment. Not Holley, or the grenade, or, well, any of that. They were things that just hurt. But when Morgan had left, that's when my world turned to ash—for the first time.

I stood, grabbed a bottle from the wet bar, and, more out of emotional fatigue than frustration, dropped it in front of her with a hard thud. "Here."

I sat back down, folding my arms. "The question still stands. What was I supposed to do? Let them take a clean shot? Lay down and die? Let them report back who we were? We have lives, too. I don't want my daughters to lose their mother over this." I leaned forward, lowering my voice. "So tell me, Maggie, what exactly were your orders? Be honest."

She stayed quiet, gripping that bottle of water so hard I was sure it would burst. She was shrinking under the weight of it all, of what she couldn't bring herself to say.

I pursed my lips and sighed. "If I had to guess. Just a stab in the dark. They probably went something like this: We're watching for a group of people leaving Boston. They're monsters, and you can find them by checking their body temperature. They should be eliminated before leaving the cordon area. Really dangerous—blah, blah, blah."

Maggie didn't answer, but I saw her shoulders shudder, her breath catching as she fought back whatever emotion she didn't want me to see. But then she gave it voice, finally, through a horrified choking sob. "They didn't even warn us."

"No, they didn't," I affirmed softly. "Now, did they tell you about the cameras?"

She froze. This time, she did look at me. Horror bloomed in her expression, drawing her eyes wide, even as she fell to pieces. "The...the what?"

She must have been in shock when we found them. I reached into my pack and pulled out the crushed remains of one. "This camera," I said coldly as I practically slapped it onto the table between us.

She picked it up and turned it over. "Where was this?"

"There were several," I said, digging the rest of them from the backpack and laying them down. "They were on the vehicles, including the tank. You were supposed to die horribly on camera, from multiple angles, for the glory of politics."

"How do I know you're telling the truth?" She argued with zero conviction. I gave her a wry look anyway, though.

"I just so happened to run into your checkpoint, and I just so happened to save you so that I could confuse you with bogus cameras in my pack? As my ex keeps telling me, I'm not that smart."

"Fuck," she whispered through her tears. "I don't want to die, Cait. If whoever did this found out that I know..." She trailed off. "Did my CO just send me into a meat grinder on purpose?"

I placed my hand on hers, and that weird sense of connection returned. "I don't know, but someone up the chain of command had to know."

"Someone knows what you are," Maggie reasoned, anger now replacing her despondency. "They were looking for you specifically."

"I know, but I'm less worried about who might know what we are than how they knew we were coming." It was the truth. I had my suspicions that this was Senator Kim's handiwork, but I still didn't know how she was always two steps ahead of us.

Assuming she did engineer the attack on the Liberty Hotel, which was still a long shot at best, it didn't explain how she seemed to know right where we were all the time. I did understand why she might want to have us on camera doing the dirty, though. If she exposed us herself, it would eventually come out that she'd known for quite a while despite any denials, and that would in no way endear her to her chosen base. This way, she could just ride the wave of rage. It was bad enough that she would probably blame this largely on the innocents in the camps, anyway. It was frustrating, and when Marcella found out, it would really be war.

"Huh?" I grunted as I realized Maggie had said something.

"Six years," she repeated softly. "I was in the system for six years. I never knew my father, not really. He died in a car accident when I was little. And Mama was shot in a supermarket in El Paso when I was twelve by some guy who just didn't like Mexicans. I'm not even Mexican. My parents were Brazilian. The guy just didn't like brown people."

I let go of her hand and nodded in sympathy. "How many homes?"

"Seven."

"And how did you come through it?"

"Is this a psych eval? Because it feels like a psych eval."

"No. It's just that I'm no stranger to abuse, and it helps me to know how others deal with it." It was a lie. I wanted to fix her. It was clearly an Achilles heel of mine, and I knew it, but there it was.

"Okay, I guess. A few of them were abusive, some of them, all the way." She looked down as she said this, and I closed my eyes, thinking about Holley.

"What do you think of men?"

She shrugged. "They're okay, I guess. I like men, if that's what you mean. It wasn't only men that abused me."

I shook my head. "There's no right answer. Just curious. So, what about women?"

She shrugged again. "I like them, too. Your friend is hotter than hell."

"Hey," Jess protested from her seat. "She's taken."

"What's your MOS?"

"Sixty-eight Whiskey," she replied automatically, with no small amount of pride.

"You're perfect," I said with a seductive smile. "So, do you want to be a vampire?"

Jess choked on her bottled water.

CHAPTER THIRTEEN

Maggie turned me down flat, but I still discussed it with her for quite a while. I didn't go into our weaknesses and was a little vague about our strengths, except our hearing, and I did point out that we didn't go poof in the daylight. She'd already witnessed how fast, strong, and ruthless we could be.

I'd like to say that her being a combat medic had been why I'd offered, but I knew better. Still, though, she liked helping people, and she had no aversion to action. I tried convincing her by pointing out that once we sorted the details of getting her out of the army, the sky would be the limit if she wanted to have a job in medicine. But she didn't care too much about that other than saying she'd rather be a paramedic and didn't like the night shift.

I didn't blame her. Ten years was a long time in school, even for the undead. How Liz had managed it, I'd never know, though back in the 1800s, I didn't think it took that long. It was also possible that I was just too young to appreciate how short a time that was for us. The conversation finally dried up, and we all rested for a bit before Nastasia's sultry voice drifted over the speakers a few hours later.

"This is your captain speaking. We are roughly thirty minutes from Irish airspace at an altitude of ten thousand feet. I want to remind all of you to stow your tray tables and unbuckle your seatbelts. Parachutes are located in the forward portion of the passenger cabin.

"It's a beautiful sunny day over the Emerald Isle, so we should have great weather for our drop. Also, a reminder for our human passengers: the chutes do not have a floatation device, not that it would matter. The water temperature is a chilly seven degrees Celsius. In the event of a water landing, I would suggest using the minute or two you have before hypothermia sets in to kiss your ass goodbye."

Jess and I laughed. Maggie didn't. Instead, she asked, "Does she always sound like she's trying to seduce the mic?" We laughed even harder.

Nastasia came out of the cockpit and strapped into her parachute, looking more cocky than usual. It probably had to do with the fact that I struggled to get into my chute properly, and Maggie had to help me. Jess was positively grey and looked as if she might puke, pass out, or both. She had been adamant that she had to be here. I didn't know why, but of all of this, that, strangely, was something I trusted. It was just a feeling.

Nastasia returned to the cockpit, set the autopilot for just over one hundred ten knots, about one hundred thirty miles per hour, and shut down the left engine.

"Looks like someone upgraded the avionics suite," Nastasia said as she exited the cockpit. "I was afraid the autopilot wouldn't engage at this speed with an engine out. Lucky us."

I turned slowly and looked at Nastasia, incredulous. "And you're just mentioning this now?"

She shrugged nonchalantly. "Hey, it's been a while since I've flown."

Maggie put on her chute and then helped Jess into her tandem harness. With my pack attached to some nylon webbing at my waist, I glanced out the window and figured we'd lose power in a few minutes if our expectations held. It never occurred to me that our expectations might be exceeded. I had just attached Jess's pack to her waist when the most amazing, albeit terrifying, thing happened. The airplane exploded into a million little daisy flowers.

We were falling.

Maggie acted like the pro she apparently was, looking around to figure out what the fuck just happened but not panicking. She had her equipment on and knew how to use it. The kid was starting to grow on me.

Nastasia was curled up, tugging at a strap on her chute.

I was fine. I had no clue what I was doing, but I was a vampire, so fuck it. It was unlikely I'd die. Marcella had once fallen from twenty-eight thousand feet and survived, so there was that, though it had been into a snowbank. And a few years before I met Marcella, I'd gone on a skydiving trip and chickened out, but I did get the basic rundown of how to do it. So, I knew where the ripcord was, at least.

The problem was Jess, who was screaming and not having a good morning at all. It was all I could do to keep myself from spinning, not that I could help her anyway, but Maggie glided effortlessly over to Jess.

Maggie righted her and pointed up to Nastasia, who had finally uncurled and sailed right over me to the pair. Jess immediately calmed.

I glanced at my watch, which sent me spinning again. We'd only been falling for a few seconds, but it seemed like forever, and the ground seemed to be coming up really fast.

With Nastasia clipping into Jess's tandem harness, Maggie floated back over to me. "You've never done this before, have you?" She shouted.

I grinned and shook my head.

"Okay, you nut job, here's the deal. When your chute opens, there will be two steering toggles. If you need to change direction, pull gently. You won't be falling straight down. These chutes glide. Try to stay close to Nastasia and me. When you get to around one hundred feet, lift your legs. And watch out for trees or other obstructions. You will get some ground effect at the end, but not much. Pull down on both toggles to slow the chute. I sure hope your legs can take a hard landing."

With that, she reached out and unceremoniously pulled my ripcord. I watched her shoot away from me toward the ground. Moments later, she and Nastasia opened their chutes and started to glide in slow, lazy circles, falling softly toward a golf course. I did my best to follow their lead.

Over my left shoulder was Galway and the bay, and to the south, I could see the northern end of the Burren. Nastasia had threaded the needle over Galway Bay. Goddess, we had been lucky. If the plane had vanished a few minutes sooner, we'd have ended up in the North Atlantic. Jess and Maggie would have died for sure.

The parachute steered more readily than I'd thought, and as long as I took it easy, it moved gently. And I did take it easy, very easy, doing my best not to oversteer and stay close to the other two. They landed a few seconds before I did, somewhere off to my north.

Drifting in over a long stretch of low green grass, I yanked down on both steering toggles before I hit. I still landed hard, and it hurt like a son of a bitch. Fortunately, nothing broke, and I was thrilled when my rump kissed soft earth on what turned out to be the fifth fairway of the Galway Bay Golf Resort.

What a fucking rush, I thought. *I need to do that again sometime.*

I unclipped my harness with some effort and pulled in my chute, wrapping it up as best I could before tossing it aside. I looked around. The course was completely empty. The only sound was the crows and other birds. I glanced at my watch. It was dead. My phone was dead, too. If I needed any proof that the Bethadi were here, I had it: no power and a plane that poofed into flowers—capricious assholes.

It was a weird feeling being back here after so long, a little like coming home to a place I didn't belong anymore. Not that I didn't love Ireland; of course I did. But I was a Boston girl, born and bred, and it had been over sixteen years since I'd been here.. So much had changed. Even from the air, I saw Galway was different, with a few new buildings and a little more spread out.

I pushed aside the wave of nostalgia and weird feelings and

hoisted my pack. I needed to find the others. With a last glance at the sun to get my bearings, I started through the trees to the north, calling for Nastasia, Maggie, and Jess.

It didn't take long to find them. They had seen me come down and were walking right toward me, meeting me at the tree line as soon as I'd cleared the fairway.

"Wow, that was something," I hooted, a shit-eating grin on my face.

"Yeah, it was something," Jess muttered shakily. She had a bit of something on her lips, and it took me a minute to realize it was vomit.

"Oh, Jess, honey, are you alright?" I asked, in genuine concern.

"I'll be fine. It just scared me. That's all."

"So you glamoured her after all?" I asked Nastasia, who shook her head.

"Nope, she's seriously fucking courageous, Cait."

"I wouldn't say that," Jess said, spitting into the bushes. "I was fucking terrified the whole way down."

"Courage isn't the absence of fear, ma'am," Maggie said firmly. "It's doing what you need to in the face of it. So, good job."

That seemed to perk Jess right up. "Thanks for that." Then she stuck her tongue out at me. I returned the favor, wriggling my forked tongue.

Maggie's eyes almost popped out of her head. "You know what, Jess?" She said as we started for the clubhouse. "I may have to reconsider my interest in men."

Nastasia looked at me from behind both their backs and rolled her eyes.

I smirked. Now, things felt normal.

CHAPTER FOURTEEN

Even at the clubhouse, there was no one around—no one working, no one inside the building, nothing. There were easily a dozen cars in the car park, but they looked like they'd just been left. It was fucking eerie, like something out of a zombie apocalypse movie. In a country of five million souls, the lack of people was starting to disturb us all. Maggie was the first to say something.

"Where is everyone?"

I shook my head, "I don't know. I feel like we've stepped into an episode of the Twilight Zone."

"The what?" Maggie asked.

"A Stephen King Novel is probably a better approximation," Nastasia said, rescuing me from the Gen-Z baby who was making me feel all kinds of old at the moment.

"Salem's Lot, maybe," Maggie retorted with a grin. I was liking this kid more and more.

"How old are you, Maggie?" I asked as we walked down the road away from the building.

"I turn twenty-three in August."

My eyes bulged. She was only twenty-two? Shit.

"Wow, Cait, I didn't think you liked them this young," Nastasia joked as her eyes searched the landscape. "Cradle robber."

My head was also on a swivel. Nothing about this felt right, but I couldn't sense any kind of threat anywhere. Everything smelled pretty normal, too, at least as far as I could tell. All we heard were animal sounds—bleating sheep and birds in the distance—and, of course, the waves kicking against the shore to our north and east.

It wasn't until we entered Renville Village proper, just about two klicks down the road, that we saw the first signs of actual human habitation. A man in a police sergeant's uniform rode toward us on a bicycle from the opposite direction.

"Oi!" I called when he got closer, and he veered toward us.

"Now, where did you come from?" the man asked. He was probably in his early thirties, with short brown hair. "Were those your chutes I saw?"

I donned my Tourmekeady brogue. "Yeah, our plane just vanished in mid fuckin' air. Would ya believe it?"

He looked at me with wide eyes. "Aoife? Aoife Reagan?"

I relaxed slightly and dropped the accent. "Nope. I'm Cait, her sister. We're trying to get to Galway and find a place to sleep for the night. These are some of my friends. This is Jess, Maggie, and Nastasia. How do you know my sister?" The others nodded in turn at the man but said nothing.

He looked at me, the wheels obviously turning. "Aoife? All of us in Galway know her. For a while, she and I patrolled together in the city. Well, we did until she got promoted. Aren't you supposed to be in America?"

"I was, hence the parachutes. Where is everyone?"

"Indoors. The country's on lockdown because of the lootin' and the other things. It's not really safe out here, though there's not much left to loot."

I put my hands on my hips. "What do you mean, other things?"

"You really came here in a plane with parachutes?"

"Yes," Nastasia interjected. "Now, could you please kindly answer the question? What other things are you referring to?"

"You probably won't believe this," he said, leaning forward on the handlebars.

"Try us," Maggie responded.

I was amazed at how well Maggie was suddenly finding her place with us. It was probably a survival mechanism. Be one with the group, and you might just make it. She really had no way to know that I'd die to protect her now that she was here.

"Well, at night, there's been reports of banshees, leannan sidhe, and wee folk. They say that Gentle Annie's returned, too. Everything's dead, cell, power, all of it. It's as if the laws of physics don't apply anymore."

I shared a glance with Nastasia. How right he was, in a manner of speaking. Of course, he didn't know that the 'leannan sidhe' were standing right in front of him. Despite the fact that most Irish weren't a truly superstitious lot, this guy looked spooked with a capital S.

"So far, not shocked," Nastasia said. "We've come from Boston."

"Well, you won't find many places open. There are some coffee shops in Galway serving warm sodas and drips made with boiled water from portable stoves. Most of the pubs open around five, and you can get a warm beer, but food is hard to come by. The country is in trouble, for sure. No milk on the shelves. The army, or what's left of 'em, is handin' out clean water." He paused for a moment and looked us up and down. "Well, ladies, you should probably be on your way to Galway if that's where you're goin'. You'll want to get inside before dark."

He moved away from us and got back on his bike without so much as a backward glance, white as a sheet.

"Well, that was informative," Jess said, absentmindedly tugging at the gold collar around her neck.

"And a little disconcerting," I replied. "Let's keep going."

"Gentle Annie?" Maggie asked as we continued onward.

"My aunt Badb, the Goddess of Battle," I replied casually. "I was afraid of that." It would be just my luck to run into her, and I thought briefly about Leah's dream. I couldn't help but think that it was Carol all over again. No one had seen Carol since she'd taken off with Janelle over the Liberty Hotel incident. I prayed Leah's visions were something transitory. I didn't need Mother Darkness after her, too.

The walk into Galway would take almost three hours. The cop had been right. A few cafes were open, and we even stopped at one with plywood-covered broken windows. There, we were able to get a couple of pour-over coffees for Jess and Maggie, which were predatorily priced at ten euros per. After a bit of haggling, I gave the girl behind the bar ten euros for two day-old scones. The girls had to eat something.

The barista was cute—short—but cute, with strawberry blonde hair blended in warm and vibrant hues, exuding a delicate mix of golden blondes and a heavy cast of soft reddish undertones, like *all* the reddish undertones. Her skin was pale, almost as pale as mine, but she had that healthy color, human-looking—definitely not a vampire. And when she looked at me, a flush ran to her cheeks. At the last minute, she threw in a couple of pats of half-melted butter.

As I walked away, though, I looked back at her. There was definitely something familiar about her. The way she moved or maybe her hair, I wasn't sure, but I felt like I'd seen her before.

"This is actually pretty good," Jess said as she bit into her scone. "Better than Starbucks."

"It should be," I commented. "It was made here, not shipped from Goddess knows where."

A few patrons walked in and ordered, most looking at us strangely as they left.

Another of the Gardaí walked in as well and eyeballed us. He had dark hair, too, but where the other fellow had been clean-shaven, this bloke had a short black beard. It was my guess he didn't know my sister, or if he did, not well enough to recognize me—or her—on sight. Maggie watched him closely as he headed up to the bar.

"He's cute," she whispered.

I nodded with a smile. "Yeah, I suppose so. If you're into that sort of thing."

Jess snorted. "We are. At least sometimes."

I looked at Nastasia, who gave me a half-shrug. "To each their own."

"Where's Mike?" The cop asked, nonchalantly leaning against the bar.

"He's off today, Key. What'll you have?" She answered, her brogue sounding a bit forced, and I suspected it was an affectation for the locals.

"Just my usual, Rowan. You catch the chutes coming in over the bay?"

"I did. Strange indeed. Now, aren't ya supposed to be patrolling the streets, not sitting in here for chit-chat?"

The cop smiled. "Still just wondering why you won' go out with me."

"Ya know why, Key. You're not my type. She threw me another glance."

"What is it with you?" Nastasia hissed.

I gave Nastasia a haughty smirk. "Just my natural allure, I guess."

The more people that came in, the more uncomfortable I became. The locals were starting to give us more hostile looks. I realized that it was our pale skin, Nastasia's and mine. Pale skin was the standard here, but Nastasia and I were something else entirely. We had to be careful, or we would eventually be fighting our way around the country. These people were terrified, and they knew what was happening wasn't natural.

I ordered two more coffees for Nastasia and me. "Time to play human," I whispered, not thrilled with the looks we were getting. "We best get on to Galway after we're done."

Nastasia played at drinking it, but I shook my head surreptitiously. "Drink it. We can't leave full cups. This is terra incognita for us."

Nastasia gave me an irritated look and a low hiss. "I have done this before, you know."

"Yes, but I'm sure it's been a while. And I know this populace."

Jess's eyes were darting around. "Do you smell that?"

I nodded almost imperceptibly. "I do, the smell of burning leaves in autumn with a hint of pressed apple in the undertones."

Jess's eyes grew wide. "Where are they?"

"I don't know. Nas?"

Nastasia frowned. "I don't see them either. But they're here.

I can feel it."

Maggie looked perplexed. "Who?"

"Unknown vampire," I said softly. "And they're close by."

We all finished our drinks. Nastasia seemed fine, but my stomach was starting to feel none too well. I stepped up to the counter and asked the coffee girl, "Is there a Dunnes or maybe a Tesco superstore around? I need a coat."

"O'er on Orannmoor, the Lidl is all that's open. They might have somethin'. And Miss Tess's, it's just down the street, but all she sells is posh stuff, Barbour 'n' such. Cost a fair bob, but worth it."

"Thanks," I said, and we left. Once we were out of sight—easy enough with so few people around—Nastasia and I both emptied our stomachs and turned to our supply of cold, goopy, but drinkable blood. The hunger was still just a faint jitter in the background, and the blood pushed it away.

We did stop at Miss Tess's. Most of the stuff there was gaudy as hell or cost way more than I was carrying. I did find two Barbour wax canvas coats and wool hats for Maggie and Jess and two long wool coats for Nastasia and Me. I also spent about half of my remaining euro on the lot of it. Not good, but it was going to rain, and we still wanted to blend in. We could have gone to the Lidl and found something much cheaper, but that was still a half-hour walk, and a mist was already starting to fall. I didn't need Jess or Maggie getting sick because it was a fair bet the chemists were empty of over-the-counter medicines. At least the walk would be scenic.

CHAPTER FIFTEEN

We followed the road around the bay for about half an hour before we saw anything other than a desolate, terrified village. Not for the first time, it struck me how dependent humans had become on their technology. It also occurred to me that I could do nothing, just stay here, and I'd never have to worry about being found out or scooped up by the government to be slaughtered or experimented on like those poor people that Reese had mangled. That thought bothered me, not in its logic; it was flawless, but in that I'd had it at all. I frowned and brushed it away. It wasn't like me.

The walk did turn out to be scenic, just not in the way I'd expected.

To the east, no more than a hundred yards away, a vast thicket choked the land that just weeks ago had been nothing but open pasture. The trees shouldn't exist—couldn't exist—their gnarled trunks and twisted branches looked like they'd grown decades in days. The way they blocked our view felt deliberate, like a curtain drawn to hide something dark and malicious.

The hair on my neck rose and stayed rigid as though electrified. A million invisible eyes seemed to track our every movement from within those twisted branches, their hungry gazes crawling across my skin like insects. They were there; I could feel it, yet there was nothing when I looked.

My body warred with itself. Every instinct I possessed urged me to flee, while something older, something buried deep in my blood, pulled me toward those watching shadows. I shivered.

"Do you feel that?" Jess said, her eyes darting back and forth across the darkened forest as she strained to see anything.

"Yes," I whispered in terror and shivered again. "There is something in there. We're being watched."

Jess nodded. "It feels..." Her voice trailed away for a moment. "It feels wrong, and yet..."

"Like you want to rush in and disappear?" I finished, placing hands on the shoulders of both Jess and Maggie, just in case.

Yes, protect your children. The voice slid through my head like silk before turning dark with a knowing tinkle of laughter. *Until they're needed, that is.*

"Yes," she answered. "Just like that. It's nerve-racking."

"I don't feel anything," Maggie said. "It just looks like trees."

"Trees that shouldn't be there," I told her. "All of this land was clear just two weeks ago, filled with homes, farms, and sheep. This—" I waved my hand at the woods in a wide arc. "This is madness incarnate."

"Yes and no," Nastasia said. "The trees and the glow are real enough, but I don't feel any foreboding or like we're being watched. I'm sure that's just some kind of static glamour to entice the kids and keep the adults at bay."

I wasn't so sure. "Maybe," I said finally. "But we should pick up the pace anyway."

"It's not like you to be nervous like this, Cait," Nastasia said as the walk turned brisk. "What is it?"

I shrugged. "Just a feeling..." I began, but my steps stuttered to a halt. My lips parted slightly. My face fell slack as the world vanished.

In its place, my vision filled with ash—so much ash, falling like gray snow, coating my hands and getting in my hair and clothes as I knelt in a great chamber. The floor beneath my knees was black marble shot through with veins of dark red, polished to a mirror shine. The ash wasn't just ash, though—it was the remnants of someone I loved, someone precious who had been consumed utterly. My chest collapsed in on itself as soul-crushing grief overwhelmed me.

My voice emerged as a raw, animal shriek of loss as I clawed at my hair and face, smearing the ash across my skin. The wailing echoed off unseen walls, a sound of such primal anguish it barely seemed human. Broken sobs wracked my body as I tried desperately to gather the ash, to hold onto these last traces of someone now forever lost. But it kept slipping through my fingers, floating away no matter how I tried to contain it.

Hands shook my shoulders. Voices called my name. But I couldn't get free. "No," I whimpered in tears. "No."

The vision hit me with such force that when it released me, I staggered, nearly falling. The ash was gone, but the soul-deep agony lingered, the certainty that I would fail someone I loved, that I would be forced to watch them burn to nothing while I remained helpless to prevent it. The echo of that grief squeezed my chest like a vise.

"Cait?" Nastasia prodded.

"Ashes. Ashes of a person," I whispered in horror as I struggled to hold the vision and see more. But it was like a ghost in fog, the details fading—all except one. I could taste it, the ash, like a viscous thing clinging in my throat, making me gag.

As fleeting as it had been, I knew it was important—no, vital—to decipher it, but it drifted away like smoke. I clutched my chest as if that might release the tightness inside.

"What did you see?" Jess asked, her gaze keen and piercing. "You saw something, like Carol does."

I glanced up at her, my voice full of shocked disbelief. "How…"

Jess pressed her hand to her diaphragm, her fingers pressing just so, like she could trap whatever was sinking in there. "I felt it here," she murmured, almost to herself. Her eyes clouded over, and for a moment, she seemed lost, drifting in the weight of it. "It was this... ache," she said, voice soft and almost searching, like she could barely put it into words. "... something precious slipping through my hands, fading..."

She bent forward, and for the first time, I realized I was on my knees as her body settled over me and her arms wrapped around my shoulders. She sagged slightly as if the touch grounded her, or maybe me.

Confused, I turned my head slowly, catching a glance at her face. Jess had a horrified, vacant expression, as if she watched something abominable taking place that she couldn't fathom, something that left her hollowed out and open. A breath caught somewhere in her throat, and then she exhaled slowly. "I'm...I can't...Let me help you," she said, her voice a thin squeak reverberating with cold desolation. "Love you."

Jess's voice seemed to come from everywhere around me. It took a moment to realize that her lips hadn't moved.

I blinked, but instead of pushing away, I leaned into the comforting gesture. It felt intimate, like a lover's comfort.

Nastasia cleared her throat. "Khhm."

I looked up and found her staring at us, an eyebrow raised. Behind that arch gaze, I detected the dark emotions swirling— possessive and jealous. I swiped at a tear on my cheek and slowly stood before gently pushing Jess back. "I'm alright. What brought that on?" I kept the question neutral and unaccusing.

It was Jess's turn to blink, this time in confusion. "You needed me," she said flatly. "I could just tell."

Nastasia took Jess by the shoulders. "Are you okay?"

"I'm fine," Jess responded, brushing her hands away. But she wasn't. None of us were fine. Despite the protestations, we all felt it.

"We're going to have to go through that," I conceded, jerking a thumb toward the trees, even as I fought not to look at them. My voice grew cold and harsh, quietly enraged. "We're not all coming back."

That stopped everyone.

"What do you mean?" Jess breathed, her voice taking on a

cautious edge.

"I think someone is going to die, someone close to me, but I don't know who."

"Could it be someone from your past?" Nastasia asked, her eyes hawkish and shrewd. "I don't think I need to remind you that visions are always tainted by our own perspective."

I considered her words. The dreams at home—the ones that woke me gasping—were certainly of someone else. Weren't they? This had to be the same. It just had to be, even though something about it felt closer. It was as if a shadow clutched my heart—owned a part of my soul.

I forced a lightness into my voice, brushing it off with a shrug. "You're probably right, Nas."

"Of course I am, dorogaya. Now, let's get out of this accursed rain." Still, though, I heard the jangled nerves in her tone. She had felt it, too. She was just better at hiding it.

We started moving again, but then I noticed that Maggie wasn't following. Turning back, I saw her standing in the middle of the road, staring into the woods. Her eyes looked vacant.

"Maggie?" I called, and she blinked before running to catch up.

"I'm sorry. I was lost in thought for a moment," she said, but her eyes looked haunted.

"Did you see something?" I asked, watching her expression closely.

"No…" Maggie said, but she trailed off, still squinting into the tree line. "It's just trees." A lie.

"Are you sure?"

Maggie didn't answer, still staring.

I followed her gaze. The trees moved rhythmically, hypnotically like…like breathing. I placed a hand on her shoulder and pulled her around to face me. "We need to get out of here."

She blinked and looked at the ground with a deep breath. Belatedly, as if she hadn't heard my urging, she answered the question. "Just a weird feeling, that's all. I think ya'll spooked me with all that talk of glamour and people watching us."

I raised an eyebrow at that but kept my thoughts to myself as we pressed on.

CHAPTER SIXTEEN

We made pretty good time to Galway, just over two hours, and, just as I had hoped, Carrie, one of my mother's old friends, still had a place there. She offered to put us up for the night, avoiding us having to search for an empty flat or braving a hotel. Most importantly, she had a fireplace, and it was roaring when we walked in.

"Thank you so much for letting us crash here," I said as we walked into the place. It wasn't tiny by Irish standards, but that just meant it wasn't a postage stamp. It had three small bedrooms, a single room that served as a common room, dining room, and kitchen. The bay was visible through a picture window, which was currently obscured by two thick tapestries that kept out the cold air.

"This is a really nice place," Maggie said as Carrie made us some tea. "Cozy."

"Thanks, love. It's been home since my dear old George died almost six years ago. We used to have a larger place further into town, but I couldn't stay there, not after he died."

"So, what do you think of what's going on?" Nastasia asked, clearly trying to get the lay of the land in town.

"Faeries and wee folk? Oh, that's ridiculous. It's probably some government screwup they don't want to admit to, or maybe some foreigners thinking we'll be easy prey if they knock out the power. Obviously, it isn't the Brits; they'd know better. Maybe whoever did this should have talked to them first. We're not pushovers, you know."

Jess and Maggie engaged Carrie in conversation over tea. Both listened intently as Carrie detailed her many complaints, mostly about her failing health. Carrie was almost seventy and mostly blind.

With the three so engaged, Nastasia and I excused ourselves. I had to attend to the now painful stabbing in my skin before it got worse, and I started to lose focus.

"We're going outside for a breath of fresh air," I said.

"Be careful the hooligans about," Carrie said. "With the power out, they've been making trouble."

I nodded. "Not to worry, ma'am. We'll be careful." Under my breath, I added, "Eating the hooligans."

Nastasia just smirked, thoroughly amused that the human thought she should be careful.

"Split up?" Nastasia asked.

"Nah, let's stay together. We could actually run into something worse than us, and I know the town, you don't. When was the last time you were here, anyway?"

Nastasia laughed. "Not for many, many years. Lead on McDuff."

"That's Scottish," I remarked.

"Whatever."

"So, where to?" Nastasia asked after we'd wandered a bit with no luck.

I looked around, getting my bearings. "Well, there's Nova. It's a gay bar across the river. We could go there, but with the shutdown, it's probably closed, as are most of the pubs, though some will undoubtedly be open. Most places are probably running out of booze if they're not out already. The riots will start soon." I sighed heavily at the state of things, and we started walking toward the Latin Quarter.

We passed a few empty stores that had been looted. One in

particular caught my attention: an old bread shop that had been in business for ages, the windows and interior empty of product. It reminded me that if something wasn't done, all of these people were going to starve. Back home, I'd probably have felt like it was justice. Here, though, in the country so close to my heart, it felt like the edge of tragedy. "We can't let this stay the way it is, Nas."

"Stay on mission, Cait," Nastasia warned. "We're not here to fight with a group of deranged Fae."

"But I know those Fae," I insisted. "I might be able to get them to turn the power back on at least."

Nastasia glanced at me sternly. "Cait, you're not Weyna. They won't know you."

"No, but Áine respected Weyna and the Óṣení. If I can convince her of the truth, I might be able to get her to change her mind."

"What do we have here?" A young man in his late twenties called from an alleyway, interrupting our conversation. "Two lovely lasses out for a stroll?" The man was accompanied by two others lurking deeper in the darkness.

Nastasia and I came to a halt, and I looked at her.

She just shrugged and glanced about. "No one around, dark alleyway, convenient."

"Well, it's Irish for dinner then," I quipped. "Who do you want?"

She tapped a finger to her lips. "I'll take the tall one. You can have the scrawny duo."

"Why do I get the skinny ones?" I grumbled half-heartedly.

"Seniority," she said impassively. "Apologies, my dear, but I'm older."

"Fine," I sighed.

Pleased, it seemed, by our banter, two of the three men started moving forward, obviously having no idea we were dividing them up as victims. However, the short fellow in the back, with thick glasses and mussy black hair, started to back away, looking ready to bolt. Apparently, he was the smart one or the superstitious one, and he turned to run. But I was right there, having blood-stepped behind him.

"Relax," I said softly, letting my glamour flow over him. "I'm not going to hurt you." I didn't really want to drag this out. I'd never fed on a man before and didn't relish the thought. But, any port in a storm and all that, so I simply bit him. He squeaked at first, then sighed with my pulls.

"Let me go, you mental cunt," the leader said, jerking at Nastasia's iron grip. She had one in each hand.

"I don't think so," Nastasia replied with a wicked smile, then aimed her sarcastic wit at me. "Take your time, dorogaya! I have all night."

The feeding was over in moments, and I used the man's shirt to wipe my chin. I didn't even bother to give him changed blood, just letting him die in the alleyway. *Next*, I thought, and approached the leader, letting my will settle over his. He went slack-jawed, and Nastasia released his arm, turning to her own victim.

"So," I asked, tucking a finger under his chin and lifting his gaze to mine. "What were you planning to do with us?"

Under my glamour, he gave a monotone response, "Yeah, for sure, you know, have sex with ya."

"Rape us, you mean." It wasn't really a question.

"If you want to call it that. But you'd have enjoyed it. All women have that fantasy."

I shook my head, disgusted. Nastasia had already started feeding on the other man, so I didn't waste any more time taking this one as well.

When we'd finished, I stumbled a little, woozy from all the blood, and Nastasia had to help me clean up. At least I'd had the presence of mind to grab some alcohol pads from my pack before we left.

A sneering voice sliced through my thoughts, dripping with derision. *Sloppy work, Cait dear. Surely you're not so weak from a single drink?* I blinked and shook my head, feeling my temples pulse. I was imagining things. Just the blood making me lightheaded.

"You're blood drunk, dear," Nastasia said as we dragged the men further into the alley and darkness.

"Yeah," I chuckled. "I am. Well, maybe more blood tipsy."

Then I fell over my own feet and giggled. "Oops."

"We should walk a bit more until you regain your senses. Why'd you drain them both? You should have just disposed of the little one."

I whirled on her but almost fell, grabbing her chest for support. I giggled again. "Sorry. Because they were planning to rape us."

"Of course they were. But does that deserve a death sentence?" Her voice was laced with curiosity.

"Yes!" I answered, probably a little loudly, because a light turned on in an upstairs window in one of the buildings.

Nastasia gave me a thoughtful look, quietly watching me. "You're sure."

"Yes," I hissed, a strange, righteous fury flaring in my chest. "I'm bloody well sure."

"My, Ms. Reagan, you have changed so much," Nastasia observed and started walking again.

"You have no idea," I said with a laugh and twirled down the street, my arms out, feeling that strange warmth curl tighter, like something dark nestled just under my skin, delighting in the mayhem.

CHAPTER SEVENTEEN

A little while later, as we wandered back toward the bay, I reached down to pick up a coin on the ground and noticed Nastasia's footwear for the first time. "Did you skydive in Louboutin sneakers?" I asked. "For that matter, did you just risk getting them all bloody?"

Nastasia just laughed. "You just now noticed? Some detective you are. No, I wore a pair of tactical boots on the plane. I put these on at Carrie's. And, yes, I did risk getting a bit on them. But I didn't. I'm not a messy eater like you."

"Ha," I shot back lightheartedly. "That's bullshit. You always leave a horror show in bed."

She grinned wickedly. "That's different. And tell me you didn't enjoy it like the vampire tramp you are."

I laughed. She wasn't wrong, but somewhere dimly, part of me couldn't believe we were joking around like this. Where was my conflict? Where was my agony over killing people? I looked into Nastasia's deep brown eyes, searching for an answer.

"You were once afraid of becoming like me," she whispered, placing a hand on my cheek. "And now, you are." Her voice was gentle and yet full of a deep desire that made my chest feel light with anticipation. She leaned in and pressed her lips to mine, placing her rapidly warming hand on the back of my neck. I stepped into her, pulling her closer. *Goddess,* I thought. *Why can't I stop this?*

We stood like that for what seemed a long time, our tongues brushing, my mouth and lungs filling with the breath of her deep moan. Finally, she broke the kiss and drew from my arms.

"I know that you love Liz. But I promise you, Cait, true long-term happiness for vampires is hard to come by. You told us that Boudka glamoured herself out of Skaja's life. That's because your mother taught her the one thing she needed most to know. All things are transitory for the immortal."

My expression hardened. I hadn't expected her to go after my engagement. "I shouldn't have done that. I'm sorry," I whispered, turning to walk away. "I love Liz, and she loves me."

"But I love you, too," Nastasia whispered, sounding almost forlorn.

I stuttered to a halt and turned back to face her, pressure building at the back of my eyes. The tenderness I felt in my chest turned to anger, and I clenched my hands into fists to keep them from shaking. I wanted to lash out at her, rail against her shitty timing, but the hurt in her expression left me flummoxed and wordless. I gawped like a fish. I couldn't think of anything to say.

Nastasia rushed forward and slammed me to the nearest wall, causing dust and bits of plaster to fall. I grabbed the lapels of her jacket, wadding the leather under my fingers, and crushed my lips to hers.

She braced her legs, pinning me. A soft moan escaped my mouth as I released her and pressed my hands flat against the stucco.

Her lips passed across my cheek, moving to my jaw, then to my throat. I opened myself to her mentally as she drove her fangs into the blood vessel. The writhing blackness of her dark gift mingled with mine, driving an orgasmic flood of pleasure at her first draw. It wasn't glamour; she wasn't transmuting my pain; I was feeling her need and the burst of lust and love that consumed her.

Fire burned inside me as I dug my fingers deep into her hair and held her tight. "Oh, God," I breathed raggedly.

My head spun, drowning in the waves of dark ecstasy, but then Liz's voice whispered like a ghost, brushing against my mind, threaded with her soft, sardonic laugh. "Not too close."

Reality slammed back in, my instincts snapping like a whip, and I pushed Nastasia away, my breath coming in shaky gulps, more from anguish and longing than need.

"No," I choked out, feeling tears gathering, blurring the edges of my vision. "Nas, I just—I'm sorry—I can't. We're a disaster waiting to happen." I turned away, the words lacerating my heart even as they left my lips.

I heard her breath hitch, her cool exterior fracturing like stabbed glass. She hissed, anger and heartbreak edging her voice. "Say it. Say you don't love me, Cait. Tell me that lie, and I'll leave. Just give me a reason to walk away."

I glanced up, my face streaked with tears, my heart battling itself. I tried to find some escape, my gaze darting from the ground to the shadows behind her, even to the star-filled sky—anywhere but her eyes.

"I—" My voice broke, my thoughts shattered. "Fuck," I muttered, clenching my jaw against the agony clawing through me. Finally, I squeezed my eyes shut, steeling myself. I wouldn't say it. I wouldn't betray Liz. But I had, hadn't I? I had already betrayed her in my heart.

Her hand found my face again, gentle but unyielding. I tried to pull away, but her hands held me fast, framing my jaw, forcing me to face her. "Look at me," she murmured, her voice thick with desperation. When I resisted—tried to pull away with an anguished whimper—she spoke again, more forcefully, "Look. At. Me." My eyes met hers, and the fierce resolve in her expression was as brittle as it was unbreakable. "Say it, Cait."

"I love you, Anya." The words tumbled out, breaking free from the prison of my heart, each one a knife twisting deeper. I shook my head, a slow, broken movement, then let it drop in weary resignation. "I do. Goddess help me, I do."

Her finger traced up to my chin, crooking beneath and

tilting my face toward her. Her leg slid between mine in a sandy whisper of fabric, the presence both torment and solace. "That's all I wanted," she said, her voice a fragile echo.

She pressed her lips to mine, and the kiss was fire, raw and endless. I wanted to fall into her, let myself drown in the intensity of her. I wanted to feel her love, dark and consuming, possessive and needful, but I drew away. The flames flickered, still blazing in the wake of her touch. When her lips left mine, searing me with the ache of unfinished fire, I let my hair fall over my face, hiding the damning tears streaming down my cheeks. I didn't brush them away.

I understood. Goddess, did I understand. Beneath her layers of feigned indifference, cruelty, and calculated bitterness, she was just like me—or like I had once been. Nastasia believed herself unwanted, so deeply tainted that love couldn't possibly reach her. And in that moment, I knew no one—not even Jess —had ever seen her laid bare like this. We were afraid, both of us terrified.

My chest clenched for her, my ribs like iron bands. She wanted to be loved. She'd found someone who loved her, but she couldn't have her—couldn't have *me*. And it hurt like hell, knowing I could take away that pain but wouldn't. That ache still simmered in me, a dark, unquenchable need. I'd seen it in my own reflection—the cruelty, the coldness, the unrestrained power. I'd felt it with Holley, with Matt Churdin, and even with Catherine.

I hadn't saved her from Holley; I'd taken her like some twisted prize, something to use and discard in the name of my own vengeance. Catherine hadn't been a person to me—she'd been a tool, a plaything in my plan to drive him to his darkest depths. I wanted to shatter him, to see him undone before I finished him off. And I had. Worse, I didn't care.

She pulled away and held out a hand. "It's okay, dorogaya. If I had a chance at that kind of love, I'd take it, too."

I almost grunted. Innocuous words to wound, a jagged gash left in my chest, as if her hand had just reached in and casually torn through my heart.

She gave me a crooked smile, then, wearing it like a shield.

"But if you ever get tired of domestic bliss, you know where to find me."

A bitter laugh tried to claw its way up, but I gulped it down, nodding instead, swallowing against the shame and the ache. Still, I reached for her hand, letting her lead me further down the road, even though each step felt like a betrayal I couldn't escape.

CHAPTER EIGHTEEN

I wanted to get away from my roiling feelings, but I couldn't bring myself to release her hand. Instead, I gripped it a little tighter and ran a thumb over her knuckles. "Do you think it's an effect of the curse or a defense mechanism?"

Nastasia cocked an eyebrow, "What?"

"Our lack of compassion and empathy. I figure that it wouldn't do long-term to agonize over dead people when you have to feed on their blood to survive."

She looked at me, letting our hands swing with our steps. "Well, inevitably, some of them will die in the process, heart attacks, strokes, whatever. So, it's possible that it's a survival trait. Why do you ask?"

"No reason. Just curious what you thought," I lied.

"You're wondering why you're suddenly so different since you woke up," Nastasia said with an arch smile. "Is it the real you?"

I gave a half-amused snort. "Busted."

She nodded in affirmation. "Cait, you absorbed eighteen years of experience, and it is our memories that make us who we are. You are as much Skaja as you ever were Detective Reagan. And she was a disciplined soldier, or so you said."

"Yes."

"It follows that those memories would become a part of

you, adding to you're psychological makeup. What I find more interesting, though, is that Skaja was a hero to humanity, and yet you care even less for them."

I pursed my lips in disdain. "Are you fucking kidding? I watched them all clutch their fucking pearls behind the stockade that we built while we died for them. They never lifted a single finger in their own defense, and a few of them even tried to rape me at one point. They were cowards." I paused for a second, slowing our steps and lowering my voice. "Except Boudka. She died hopelessly defending four human serving girls."

"It might be confirmation bias on my part," Nastasia responded, tugging me into a faster gait. "But she was a woman, Cait."

"Not all men are cowards," I murmured solemnly. "I saw some truly heroic things done by men in Iraq, and the Bethadi knights were fearless, male or female." She nodded her agreement but said nothing else, instead pulling me along more quickly toward the east end of the city.

We crossed the Corrib River into the Latin Quarter and turned down Cross Street. Not that I wasn't already thoroughly sated, but if I'd expected a meal here, I would have been utterly disappointed. The streets were completely deserted, and all the clubs, restaurants, and venues closed. There weren't even any cops around. It was enough to give me a shiver—fucking eerie.

On instinct, I flicked out my tongue, tasting the air. My hand squeezed Nastasia's, and I pulled her to a stop. "Hold it." I smelled it again: burning autumn leaves and pressed apples, the same scent I'd caught at the coffee house. I looked around. There was no one, just the empty street. The scent wafted from a shallow alley to our left, maybe ten feet deep and vacant.

"I can't see you, but I know you're there," I called.

Nastasia frowned at me. "Cait, what are you—" she started but paused when soft footsteps sounded from the alley. Out walked the cute little barista from the coffee shop, literally materializing from the shadows. The way she had appeared jarred my memory. It was the girl from the coffee shop, yes, but I'd seen her before. Nastasia dropped back and hissed.

"Hi," the little vampire said, her brogue replaced by a British accent. Her lips curled into an impish smile. She really was short, maybe five feet tall, with the most strawberry blonde hair I'd ever seen. It fell very long, flowing wildly over her shoulders. She was pretty, in a girlish way, the kind of pretty that would send young teenage boys dropping at her feet. She wore a simple summer dress with a denim jacket. A pair of Wellies adorned her feet.

"Who are you?" I asked, placing a hand on Nastasia's shoulder and suddenly feeling relatively sober.

"I'm Rowan. And you are Cait Reagan and Nastasia Volkova."

Nastasia raised an eyebrow. "This is impossible. I know every vampire alive."

"Apparently not. But I know you," Rowan smiled, also in a slightly childish way, and kept her hands non-threateningly clasped in front of her.

For what seemed a long time, we just stared at each other. The same curiosity I felt lit brightly in her eyes. Her appraising looks and the way she tilted her head thoughtfully said she thought she recognized me but wasn't certain.

"You're her, aren't you?" I asked finally, breaking the rapidly thickening silence and referring to the little vampire I'd seen outside Nemhain's house. The one that had simply vanished right in front of my eyes.

"And you're her, aren't you?" She replied with a smirk.

"I am," I nodded casually, though I'd have been lying if I said I wasn't terrified. This girl was over two thousand years old.

Nastasia broke in. "Would one of you please tell me what the hell is happening?"

"What's happening? That's an odd question," the other vampire replied. "Well, we're standing on a wet street, talking. Unless this is another one of my weird moments. They do happen, so it is a possibility, but I don't think so. I don't see the badger anywhere."

"She's insane," Nastasia whispered.

I barked a laugh. "Without a doubt, but I bet she also knows where the soulstone is."

"You *are* her!" Rowan exclaimed with a broad, fang-laden smile as if she'd just found a long-lost toy. "I was right. I figured I was right. You look like her a little. Not the hair, of course, but you have your mother's eyes and nose, and you definitely have the bearing of an Óṣení-trained nutter. Do you still have it?"

"Cait?" Nastasia said, her tone now exasperated and on edge.

"Sorry, Nas, it's too long of a story. I've met Rowan before. As a matter of fact, I'm pretty sure she is the first vampire my mother ever made."

Nastasia looked skeptical. "Or, she's an insane vampire who's been hiding in the countryside for who knows how long and is just fucking with us."

I shook my head. "No, she's legit. She was at Maigh Tuireadh." I turned back to Rowan. "What's my name? My real name."

She smiled again, but this time, there was an odd amusement in it. "I'm rather surprised you don't know it already, to be quite honest."

"I do, but I want to hear you say it."

"Of course you do, but I doubt your human mother would approve."

I sighed and turned to leave. "Okay, I'm not going to play this game. Let's go Nastasia."

"No games," Rowan said quickly, almost desperately. "Weyna, or is it Skaja? Which do you prefer."

I cracked a crooked smile and turned back. "Cait is fine."

"But that's so boring. Weyna and Skaja have such deep meanings that span across time. Weyna, the great hero of the Valtárí. And Skaja, your Óṣení name that means, somewhat prophetically, I might add, shadow." She waved her hands about dramatically in a gesture meant to imply something spooky, but it just looked silly, and I almost laughed. "I've heard that the Valtárí brand is imprinted on the soul. Do you still have it?"

I nodded.

"I'd love to see it again, maybe just for a moment. I do miss it: all of the combat, the training, and," she smirked slightly, "the Óṣení women." She fanned herself with one hand. "Of course, not that I would ever, well, hardly ever. But you never know. I might like being crushed like a bug."

I slid aside my shirt, revealing the brand. Rowan laughed and clapped her hands, doing a bit of a hop step as she closed the distance between us. "This is so perfect. What a surprise it will be."

I rolled my eyes at the childish display. Nastasia was right. Rowan was absolutely bug nuts.

Nastasia walked over and leaned against the wall, crossing her arms, a petulant pout on her face. "Can I ask you a question?"

"Of course, it's a free country," Rowan answered, tracing my brand with a delicate little finger. "It's still raised."

"It's a brand, not a tattoo," I said, and she nodded.

"Were you at Oulu?"

Rowan froze. Then her head swiveled slowly toward Nastasia, an indecipherable expression scrawled across her features. She didn't answer at first, tapping her finger to her mouth. Then, in that little girl's voice, she said, "You want to know who set the fire?"

"Was it Marcella?"

I grimaced. I thought we'd been over this ground before. "Nas, really?"

"No, Cait, I want to know. I lost someone in that fire. We all did."

Rowan still stared at Nastasia. Finally, she turned fully toward her. "No. But you don't want anyone to know who did."

Nastasia's features fell, and she grew incredibly still as some unspoken thing passed between the two women. The color from Nastasia's earlier feeding that had blushed her cheeks drained away, and a look of horror slowly materialized. Her eyes glistened in the moonlight. "No." Her voice was small and quiet.

Rowan walked over and took Nastasia by the hand. "I'm sorry. Sometimes, they break."

As I watched the exchange, I thought to ask about it but decided against it. Whatever had just transpired, Nastasia would tell me if she wanted to. Rowan pulled the dazed younger vampire from the wall, tugging her down to her knees, and wrapped her arms around her. "Sometimes the truth is best left buried, little Anya."

I just waited in no small amount of shock as Nastasia Volkova, the evilest, most malevolent creature I'd ever met, bawled on the shoulder of the little blonde vampire, probably the oldest of us all. After a few minutes, I couldn't stand there anymore and watch. I dropped down and placed my hand on Nastasia's back, patting gently. "Anya?" I asked quietly. "What is it?"

She didn't answer, just kept repeating the same word as she clutched Rowan's jacket: "No."

I had no words, so I simply rubbed her back.

"It's okay," Rowan said. "It's not your fault—not really."

Nastasia lifted her head and looked into Rowan's soft gray eyes. Then she turned her face to me. "I'm sorry. I'm so sorry."

My forehead puckered with worry.

Shaking her head, Nastasia stood finally and collected herself.

I pulled a handkerchief from my pocket and handed it to her so she could dry her eyes. "What is it?" I repeated, but she just shook her head and pulled herself up. Eventually, Nastasia's tears slowed, and she returned my handkerchief.

"Thank you," she offered morosely but gave me no explanation, leaving me to wonder what had just happened.

"Come along," Rowan said when Nastasia was finally spent, tugging at both our hands.

"Where are we going?" I asked.

"You'll see."

"Cait," Nastasia said, turning toward me as we walked.

"Mmhmm."

"Please don't mention this to Liz or Marcella."

I glanced at her and spotted just the barest touch of tension at her jawline. She was really worried that I might. I squeezed her forearm. "I won't. I promise."

CHAPTER NINETEEN

Rowan, almost certainly not her birth name, took us to a tiny two-story attached home on Fairhill Road. The gray exterior made it look like something out of Soviet Russia. She pulled a large ring of keys, both modern and ancient, from her jacket pocket, sifting through them for what seemed like an eternity before she found the right one and opened the door, commenting, "I definitely have too many keys. But you never know when you might need one, so…"

Nastasia rolled her eyes. "Mad as a hatter," she mouthed at me. I shrugged. I couldn't argue.

Once inside, we were greeted by a woman in her late forties, clearly human and clearly a local. "Oh, Mary, honey. Where have you been? I've been so worried." She kissed Rowan on the cheek.

"Mama, these are my friends. Friends, this is Mama."

Mama? Okay.

Mama wrung her hands on a dishtowel. "Oh, it's so good to meet some of Mary's friends finally. I think I prepared enough for dinner."

"Mama, I'm not really hungry, and my friends already ate."

"Oh, Mary, but I worked so hard. Won't you just have a bite?"

Rowan sighed, held up a finger indicating we should wait,

and then went down a narrow hallway to another room. She came back a few minutes later. "Thanks, Mama. I'll finish the rest later."

Then she led us up a set of stairs to the second floor and into a room decorated with all of the latest teen idol posters, mostly K-Pop and J-Pop. Several gymnastics medals and trophies adorned a chest of drawers, and a tall mirror sat in one corner of the room. Everything in the room was pink: the wallpaper, the comforter on the bed, the pillowcases, even the makeup table. Pink, pink, pink. And not just pink, Pepto pink.

"Wow, this is—" I started but couldn't find a word.

"Atrocious," Nastasia said furiously, snapping out of her earlier malaise. "What have you done to that woman? Even I wouldn't do this, not without a good reason. It's abominable."

I raised my eyebrows in surprise. *Who would have thought Nastasia had limits?*

"Why?" Rowan asked innocently.

"Because you've stolen her will and made her think you're her daughter, whoever this Mary is."

She looked at Nastasia uncomprehending. "And that's bad?"

"Yes! Have you any idea the pain of losing a child?" Nastasia was becoming almost hysterical, and I put a hand on her shoulder.

"Slow down, Nas. Take a breath."

Rowan laughed at that. "What for? She doesn't breathe."

I rolled my eyes. The woman was obviously being intentionally obtuse, and I was getting a little irritated myself.

"No, Cait," Nastasia said, shrugging me off and reaching out to grab Rowan by the throat, hoisting her into the air. "This little shit has done something even I wouldn't do. It's hideous."

Rowan didn't flinch or make any show of struggling. But her face grew frightening as anger peeled away the childish front, and she glared at Nastasia. The scent of mixed magic blew through my nose and mouth, tasting of berries in soft summer breezes, ripe and ready for picking, coupled with harsh embers and smoke.

"Let me go." Rowan's voice was calm, but her eyes flashed dangerously. Nastasia's face went slack, and she lowered Rowan to the ground gently before shaking her head and backing away in terror.

Rowan's face cleared. "I came to her after her daughter drowned in the harbor. And before you assume the worst, because everyone always does, it was a sad accident, nothing more. I told her I could take away her pain, and she could have a daughter again. She asked if it would be Mary, and I said, 'If you want me to be.' And here we are."

Dear Goddess, I thought. *Who is this woman? She's fucking terrifying.*

I looked at Nastasia, taking her shoulders and turning her toward me. Her eyes were wide with shocked horror. "Are you okay?"

Nastasia stuttered in terror. "She...she glamoured me, Cait. That's supposed to be...no, that's impossible. A vampire can't glamour another vampire."

"Anything is possible," Rowan said softly. "It just takes the right magic."

"But vampires can't use magic," I said, looking back at her.

"Now, who told you that?" Rowan said, crossing her arms and raising an eyebrow.

I raised a challenging eyebrow in return, mostly because my mother had suggested it, but she'd never outright said it. Nastasia said nothing. She just moved further from Rowan, standing defensively by the door.

"Why did you bring us here?" I asked, tired of her games and thoroughly pissed off at the way she was fucking with Nastasia's mental state, something I had pretty much thought impossible.

"So we could talk." Her voice was very adult now and serious. "There are things you need to know. The Summer Queen has returned. The soulstone you seek is in Boudka's tomb. Tomorrow evening at dusk, I will meet you at the docks with transport to take us to Rathcroghan. Though it is possible that the Bethadi have already raided her tomb."

I shook my head. "Is Boudka alive?"

Rowan shrugged. "She was last I saw her, which was...let me think." She paused, counting on her fingers. Finally, shaking her head as if to clear it, she said, "A long time ago. Over a thousand years, for certain. Quite a bit more, I think. The brain gets full after a while, and you forget things. If only the badger were here, he'd know."

"Then how do you know the soulstone is in her tomb?" I asked, feeling my shoulders tense up even further in aggravation.

"Haven't you been listening? I was there when it was buried." She narrowed her eyes at me. "Are you being intentionally obtuse? If so, it won't help your current problem."

I raised an eyebrow, waiting for her to continue. I wasn't going to ask the obvious question. I wasn't. I sighed. "What, pray tell, is my current problem?"

"I believe that the Light Fae currently have your mother's mantle."

"So? The Light Fae can't use it. It'll consume any of them who try." The Dark Queen's mantle, also known as the Mantle of The Morrigan, was my mother's device of office, but it was more than that. It held a considerable amount of my mother's power. As I understood it, and I could have been wrong, it was the key to unlocking the full power of The Morrigan, though I didn't really understand what that meant.

"The Summer Queen seems to think that she can for some odd reason I can hardly fathom, though I always thought she was a bit mad, what with her insistence at eating olives on her toast."

You're one to talk about being mad, I thought, but I wisely kept that to myself.

"Besides," she continued. "They seem to believe that without you, it's only a piece of old cloth. Well, I mean, it's always been a piece of old cloth, but now it's really just old cloth. So, apparently, it's you they want now, Skaja."

"Nemhain probably bequeathed it to me," I explained. "That would be just like her, but I still don't understand how Áine thinks she can use it."

Rowan tapped her mouth with a finger, then she said, "There's something else going on here. Something I do not understand. Something strange. Something is terribly wrong with the Bethadi court."

I considered that. "So, I'm going to go out on a limb here and say that there's a reason you're telling us this."

"Just that you're a wanted woman here, little shadow," Rowan said solemnly. Then, her expression shifted back to an impish smile. "But look at the bright side. If you are captured, Bethadi law is very clear. You can challenge The Summer Queen, and if you defeat her, you take the throne. It's a win-win. Of course, you'll likely have to kill her. I don't think she'd just roll over and ask you to pet her belly."

I snorted. "That presupposes that Áine would accept a challenge from me. She wouldn't. Secondly, I'm no match for her."

"With magic? No. We'd need your sister for that, but," she paused, obviously for dramatic effect, "I don't think either of those things will matter."

"Uh-huh," I said, more curious than a cat peering into a mouse hole.

"Like I said, all is not as it seems with the court. Their magic has turned oddly dark in nature." Rowan grabbed a candle, lit it, and shut out the light in her room. Then she sat on the floor. "Come, sit. Let me tell you a spooky story."

Nastasia and I looked at each other, shrugged, and sat. It wasn't like it could hurt. Rowan, using her best ghost story voice, explained what she had seen so far. Periodically, she would do her best to make scary faces or make spooky noises. Of course, the little waif came across as either silly or cute, neither of which I found terribly comforting, but it did make me laugh from time to time. Even Nastasia was taken in by her charm for a bit, snickering at the expression of incongruous youthful exuberance.

The story also took much longer than it should have, and she spun off on various tangents as she spoke, but in the end, if she was to be believed, she was right. Something was seriously wrong in the heart of Roscommon, where Áine had apparently moved Luminara, the summer palace of the Fae. What was worse, though, was that it was going to be a long, hard slog to get to Rathcroghan, where Boudka was buried, and far more dangerous than I'd anticipated.

"So, why are you helping us?" I asked, finally when she was done, wanting to get to the beating heart of the matter, metaphorically speaking anyway.

Rowan looked at me, took my hand in hers, and said. "Because your mother asked me to guide you to Rathcroghan and parts beyond as needed. Mind you, she wasn't terribly specific about the time frame, so I've been milling about the west coast of Ireland for the last twenty years."

I looked into her gray eyes. I wasn't sure what I expected to see. Maybe I was looking for truth in her words or perhaps a lie, but her expressions and body language were so chaotic and weird that they gave nothing away. Finally, I nodded.

"Is my mother still alive?" I asked, feeling tears well in my eyes, knowing the answer. My life as Weyna had been her last gift to me, she had said, and the sad look that Rowan gave me was all the answer I needed. In the end, I just nodded and wiped my eyes. "So, when do we leave?"

"Tomorrow evening. I've already arranged transportation. Of course, I have no idea if it will suit you, but that's the fun of it all."

I shook my head and gave a mirthless, incredulous snort. We were well and truly fucked.

"We're back," I called as we walked back into Carrie's almost two hours after we left.

"So, what did you find?" Jess asked as she and Maggie lounged on the couch.

"Dinner and a movie," I said with a laugh. "Well, we had a bite, so that was good. And we made a friend."

Nastasia said nothing. She just brushed past us and stalked upstairs to the bedroom that Carrie had assigned to her and Jess.

"What's eating her?" Maggie asked, stuffing her face from a bag of store-brand popcorn.

I held up a finger to Maggie as Jess trailed after Nastasia. I heard them clearly as they whispered to each other. They knew that, of course, but neither seemed to care.

"I just want to go back to Boston," Nastasia murmured. "I don't want to be here anymore. Promise me, Jess. Promise me that you love me. Promise me."

I stood there in shock, motionless, Maggie watching me intently.

"Of course I do, Anya," I heard Jess whisper in the room above. "What on earth happened?"

"I—" Nastasia started, then she just broke down, quietly sobbing.

I still just stood there in the doorway to the common room. I felt tremendous pity for Nastasia right then, and I wasn't even sure what bothered her more. Had it been my rejection? Or was it something Rowan had said or something she'd done that had torn Nastasia's world apart? I suspected it was what the tiny vampire had said about Oulu. The sense of betrayal written across Nastasia's face had been heartbreaking.

Oh, Nastasia, I'm so sorry, I thought and stopped listening in.

"We should probably go to bed," I told Maggie, feeling absolutely numb. "You look exhausted."

"You don't look great yourself, chief," she replied. "Are you okay?"

"No, Maggie. No, I'm not. But some rest would likely do us both some good."

I turned and left the living room. Carrie was already asleep. I could hear her snoring from the other room. Nastasia and Jess were still talking, and I intentionally tuned them out. These were their private words, and I wouldn't intrude, but that look of shocked horror that I'd seen on Nastasia's face tore into a wound of my own.

It was the pain I'd felt when I learned what Marcella had done to me. That feeling of helpless rage returned and sapped the strength from my limbs worse than the midday sun. What had started as determination was rapidly turning into obligation. I wouldn't quit, but I was coming to realize that this was going to be so much harder than I'd thought.

I stripped and crawled into the small twin bed, pushing myself up against the wall. I let the tears come. At least they weren't for me this time. Who would have thought I'd cry for Nastasia Volkova, the woman I'd once thought was the most evil thing walking the planet? But then again, I'd since learned there were worse things out there—far worse, like me.

It wasn't long before Maggie stole into the room and crawled into the bed, curling up in the linens. "Cozy," she murmured.

I chuckled. "Yeah, welcome to our world, Maggie Sobrai. Welcome to our world."

"Is it always this dramatic?" Her voice was quiet, and her breath hot against my neck.

I gave a quiet snicker. "Yeah, pretty much."

Not once did she mention how warm I'd become as we lay there in the obscene stillness.

"How will we get home?" Maggie asked after the silence had become too thick. Her arm was draped across my midsection, and the way she had my shirt bunched in her fingers suggested that she believed I might vanish in the night.

"The Light Fae can create portals to other places. But even if they won't, we'll be sailing to Cardiff after we're done, assuming we can find a boat."

She scoffed. "Do you always do things with such a sketchy plan?"

I chuckled at that. "Pretty much. It's par for the course."

I felt her shake her head gently in disbelief. "Well, it sounds like you need someone looking out for you."

I smirked. "My wife looks out for me."

"Some wife, Nastasia's hot, but she's insane. She told me how you two met."

I laughed even louder, then lowered my voice. "Nastasia isn't my wife. She and I—" I stammered for a moment, unwilling to give voice to my feelings. "Anyway, my wife's name is—" I stopped. Nastasia would be able to hear us, and I didn't want to hurt her more than I already had.

"It's okay if you don't want to tell me, but where is she?"

"Back in Boston, looking out for our kids," I answered and waited.

"You have kids?"

There it is, I thought in amusement. "I did mention that on the plane, but you were preoccupied. They're adopted, of course. Vampires can't have babies. My youngest is a twelve-year-old human, and my oldest is a precocious sixteen-year-old vampire."

"Wait, you turn them that young?"

"No, not typically, but it was an emergency," I said, then I proceeded to give her the Reader's Digest version of my interactions with Schmidt, leaving quite a bit out. She didn't need to know about Liz or Nastasia working with him.

When I was done, she said, "Uh-huh. So it's all politicking and backstabbing."

"No," I said. "It used to be, but now we really are pretty much one big family."

We chatted back and forth until Maggie finally seemed to start nodding off, and I heard her soft breathing turn rhythmic. Truthfully, I was happy she was there. At least I wasn't alone, but Goddess, I missed Liz so fucking much right then. The problem was that I couldn't decide why. Was it because I just missed her? Or was it because when she was around, it was easier to stomp on my feelings for Nastasia?

I just didn't know.

CHAPTER TWENTY

"This is our transportation?" Maggie said as she stared at the collection of horses.

I smirked. "Yes. Yes, it is." I hadn't been horseback riding in two thousand years. Well, technically, I, Cait, had never been horseback riding. But Weyna was an expert, and, consequentially, so was I.

"But I can't ride," Jess worried as she spied the beasts.

"That's why there are three horses for five people," Rowan said as she suddenly appeared leaning against one of the animals.

Had she been there all along? It was a pretty big assumption that Maggie could ride. I turned to her. "Can you?"

She gave me an indignant stare and put her hands on her hips, and screwed up her face like it was the stupidest question she'd ever heard. "Of course not. I'm a city girl."

Oh, I thought. *Katie would just love you.*

"You're riding with me," Rowan said to Jess.

"No, she's riding with me," Nastasia replied darkly, glaring daggers at the older vampire.

Rowan stalked up to Nastasia, and the height difference would have made the resulting staring contest ridiculous if it had been anyone other than Rowan. But, finally, Nastasia just threw up her hands and said, "Fine. But only because you weigh nothing, and it won't tire out the horses."

I blinked. Nastasia had just folded like a cheap suit, and I wondered again what had passed between them.

Jess suddenly looked like a lost child, and she went over to Nastasia. "Are you okay?"

Nastasia looked at her, taking her by the shoulders. "No. But, Jess, I have to be honest. The only reason I would want you on the horse with me would be to protect you from her, but I won't lie. It would only be a matter of how fast she got to you, not whether I could stop her."

"You don't trust her."

"I don't trust anyone," Nastasia said automatically, but then quickly added with a soft smile, "usually." Then she kissed Jess, and it wasn't a chaste kiss either. It was a toe-curling, foot-popping, passionate smack on the lips. I gaped as I pushed down at the ugly feeling rising stubbornly in my chest.

"Close your mouth, child, or you'll catch flies," Rowan told me quietly as she pulled herself easily onto the horse. "Besides, that shade of green doesn't suit you." I cast an irritable glance at her but kept my peace. *It had just been a confession of feelings,* I told myself. *I had been blood-drunk. It didn't mean anything.*

"You should stay with Carrie," I told Maggie. "It won't be safe for you out there."

She shook her head vigorously. "And if you find one of those portal things you were talking about? Are you going to tromp all the way back here and get me? Or are you going to try to sail around the entire island to get to Cardiff when Dublin is right there? No way."

"We won't leave you," I said sincerely. "I promise." Of course, I had no idea what might happen that could change that. I didn't like lying to her, and I didn't really want to leave her behind. It made me anxious to think about it, but I didn't want to get her killed either.

Finally, Maggie looked at me pleadingly. "It's not just that. I need to be there. I'm not sure how, but I know it."

Of all the things she could have said, that was the most convincing. I didn't dismiss those kinds of feelings anymore, and as soon as I decided to give in, I felt a relief of my own. So, I said, "Okay, then get up here."

The rest of us mounted up. The others were all riding fairly large steeds while I was on a smaller mare, which was fine by me. She was well-muscled and looked to be quick and maybe a bit faster than the others. She was also a relaxed ride with a gentle nature, and I decided I liked her. If things were different, she'd be just the kind of horse I'd buy.

"She gotta name?" I called to Rowan as we started down the road.

"No clue. I stole them," she called back before we all kicked into a swift canter.

I just laughed. Of course, she had.

Downtown Galway had an eerie feeling to it. I hadn't been here in sixteen years, but the desolation of the streets, coupled with empty or broken store windows and the occasional bit of detritus blowing in the wind, seemed to dim the bright sunset. Behind us, far at sea, dark clouds threatened but appeared not to move, as if held at bay by some unseen force.

For all that, though, the city still felt alive. The emptiness wasn't complete. A tangible presence of human occupation remained. Any window boxes hanging from the floors above the street held beautiful blooming flowers. Chatter, noises of movement, and even the occasional bit of music lilted from the buildings. The front stoops of most of the residential buildings were still swept clean. The people were still here, watching us suspiciously from windows and, for the brave, the occasional doorway.

Several Garda officers pedaled through the city, their presence a thin illusion of security, though their good-natured greetings and waves belying the fear and worry etched in their eyes. Beyond that, though, most said little, and as a fellow officer, I understood the weight of their silence. The radios, their lifelines, were eerily quiet, a constant reminder of the now alien world that surrounded them.

For the few who spoke to us, I reminded them that the world was still out there and they hadn't been forgotten. Some of them knew my sister, which helped break the ice, and it didn't hurt that I could relate to their worries.

As for the rest, I didn't know what the interior held, but I did know that these people would starve if something didn't give. I'd heard that irregular supplies were arriving on the east coast, but here, in the west, there was nothing. A squadron of small rowboats, dinghies, and canoes had fled the harbor around four in the morning, seeking to stave off starvation with whatever meager fishing they could do. It wouldn't be near enough, and my rage against the humans faltered. Bereft of their electronics and mechanical devices, they were pathetic, floundering like beached herring. More importantly, they were our food source. If they died out, we would be locked in slumber until eons of moving earth crushed us to dust or the sun burned everything away.

Dead automobiles choked the N6 north of the city, so we took the horses down Old Dublin Road, the route we'd entered, being closer to the coast. Over an hour passed, and darkness had well and truly fallen before we caught the top end of the N67 past the outskirts, where things grew far more bleak. There were no sounds of civilization, and crows circled in several places.

At one point, we passed a man hanging from a tree, a simple faded note pinned to his shirt: "It's over." I insisted we stop to check his identification. Nastasia argued that it wasn't safe, but I fixed her with a glare, making it clear that it was non-negotiable. Besides, the sun had fully set, and we were in our element. Anything that came for us now would be in for a nasty shock.

"Someone would want to know what happened to him," I told her, finally. Unfortunately, there was no wallet, and even I didn't feel like checking the nearby homes or the smattering of abandoned cars on the road. We mounted up and pressed on after Jess made it patently clear she wasn't riding with Rowan anymore.

When I asked her why, she just pointed at the little vampire and said, "She's a fucking lunatic, and I'm sick of hearing about her imaginary badger."

A half-hour later, we cut back onto the N6 east of town, and Rowan called, "There," pointing straight ahead.

"Where," Maggie whispered to me, and I was reminded that she was blind out here.

"Ahead, maybe three hundred yards to the east, the road dwindles almost to nothing," I explained. "It enters dense forest." She nodded into my back, and her grip around my waist tightened slightly.

Darkness shrouded the interior of the tangled wood, just as we'd seen on the edge of Oranmore. The moment I laid eyes on it, I felt that abstract pull, the urge to kick my horse into a canter. *In here,* a disembodied voice whispered, *you will be free.* I shivered and worried at the reins as we drew closer.

The pall that had fallen over our band since the night before grew even deeper as we reached the edge of the wood. I looked around at the others and then scented the air. There was something off about it. The Light Fae in Weyna's time had always smelled of flowers and grasses and, occasionally, the loamy smell of fresh rain, somewhat like Morgan. That was all here, but there was also a sour-smelling, musty aroma. It was faint but definitely not expected.

"This route sucks," I grumped at Rowan, finally seizing on something to distract me from my worries and the strong desire to just lose myself in the forest.

"No, it does not," Rowan replied without taking her eyes off the line of cracked asphalt ahead. "It's the best and most direct way to Rathcroghan. Besides, little one, how would you know?"

"How would you?" I shot back. "You don't strike me as the Girl Scout type."

"Firstly," she retorted hotly. "I'm too old to be a Girl Scout. I was too old to be a Girl Scout when Juliette Gordon-Lowe was born. Secondly, this wood extends over almost the entire country, so there is no better way."

I opened my mouth to protest further, but Rowan snapped her head around. "Shush. It'll be fine. Besides, do you have a better one?"

I shut up and urged my horse into the woods behind her. Once we crossed into the forest, the trees weren't as tight as they had looked. Two cars could just pass each other on the remaining blacktop, which, for Ireland, was wider than most of the rural roads anyway.

"Cozy," Maggie whispered, tickling the hair on the back of my neck.

"That's one way to put it," I said wryly. "Do you smell it?"

"Yes," she said. "I thought faeries would smell like roses and daffodils. It smells like decaying flowers in here."

"Thanks for that," I said softly. "I was looking for a good description. And you're right. It should smell like flowers and trees and loamy things. Something is wrong."

As if to drive that point home, we pulled up short as a tiny little man waddled across the road in front of us. He wore a dark wool coat of brown and a pointed hat of the same material. He reminded me of a demented garden gnome, though much larger. Pausing in the center of the road, he turned his head toward us. A large bulbous nose filled the center of his face beneath two narrowly placed beady black eyes. Thick pointed ears sprouted from either side of his head, poking from beneath coarse, matted brown hair.

Jess hissed loudly from her perch behind Nastasia and moved to jump off the horse, but Nastasia grabbed her arm. "No," she whispered.

"Hello," Rowan said, but she did not smile. Her normally wild and childish demeanor was now deadly serious. "Can we help you?"

The man tilted his head. He brought his meaty left hand, far too large for his tiny frame, up to his mouth and bit a hunk out of a fat, wiggling rat. The rat gave a high-pitched scream and wiggled harder. He still didn't budge, though, watching us as he chewed greedily at the bloody flesh in his mouth, exposing ugly yellow razor-sharp teeth. "Fuck you," the little man said in accent-less English, and then he vanished quickly into the underbrush on the left side of the road.

"Well, that was rude," Nastasia said.

"Fuck you, too, buddy," Maggie called after him. "What a jerk."

"Shh," I hissed. "Let's try not to offend the Fae creatures while we're here."

"He started it," Maggie muttered.

"I know, but if you say the wrong thing to the wrong, well, thing, they won't care. They'll just eat you. Didn't you see his teeth." Maggie turned silent, and her arms gripped at my midsection.

"What was that?" I asked Rowan. "I've never seen anything like it."

Rowan shook her head. "I don't know, but nothing that looks like that can bode anything positive. We should keep our eyes open."

She urged the horse onward. I took a moment to move over to Jess and Nastasia.

"Jess, are you feeling okay?" Nastasia asked.

"Perfectly. He was a threat. I just wanted him to know we were, too," she said brightly as she reached into her pocket and pulled out a hairband.

"But you hissed at him," I argued.

"Yes. Don't ask me why; it was just a reaction," she said nonchalantly as she tied her hair into a ponytail. As I watched her, my eyes grew wide, and I noticed something odd.

"Jess, your ears!"

She frowned in confusion and reached up. Each ear was delicately tipped with a point that curved slightly, like an elf or faerie. Her frown deepened as she ran her hand along them. "Great. Just great. This is all I need." Then, with a sigh, she added, "Aoife said there'd be changes."

I nodded and gave her a smile I hoped might be comforting.

CHAPTER TWENTY-ONE

"How are you doing back there," I asked Maggie a few hours later.

"My legs hurt," Maggie said through a yawn. "And I'm tired. It's been a while since I've had to be up all night, not since AIT."

"Were you at Fort Sam?" I asked, referring to Fort Sam Houston which was where every medic got their training.

"It's Joint Base San Antonio now, but yeah. I hated that place."

"You don't like the army much, do you?"

Maggie shifted and sat up a little more, resting her chin on the back of my shoulder. "Nope. But I've only got another year before I go reserve. So it's almost over, and I'll have my GI bill. Assuming I get out of this mess."

"I'd say I'm sorry, but fate's a bitch. I was perfectly happy as a homicide detective with a mediocre boyfriend and a boring life. Then I got a new case, and poof, down the rabbit hole I went, Alice."

Maggie chuckled. "Yeah, I tried to make sense of life after Mama died, but I couldn't. I just figured that things are the way they are, and there's no sense or reason to it."

I patted her thigh. "Maybe, but look at the other side. Here you are, in Ireland, on a noble quest to save the life of a genuine hero. That's not too shabby if you ask me."

"I suppose," Maggie said, sounding none too convinced. "But it all seems pretty random to me. I was assigned to the patrol detail. You three wonderful people showed up," that bit was laced with sarcasm. "And now I'm just along for the ride."

"I suspect that you're here for a reason, Maggie Sobrai. Maybe it's just to be an observer, or maybe you'll do something amazing. But I'm going to do my best to protect you, I promise."

"I thought I was your hostage," she said, returning to her position, leaning against my back, arms tight around my waist.

"You are," I said with a wry smile. "Speaking of which, when we make camp, don't go wandering off. When the sun comes up, I won't be able to save you if you run into trouble. I'm not as old as Nastasia or Rowan. I can't stay up for days on end without needing to feed—a lot. And I don't think I need to remind you that you're the only human we've seen out here."

"What's it like?" Maggie asked tiredly, clearly struggling to stay awake.

"I'm serious, Maggie. You have to stay nearby."

"Yeah, yeah," she muttered. "I heard you."

"Now, what's what like?" I asked. "The bite?"

"Yeah," she murmured.

"Like sex in a can, honey. Like sex in a can."

The rest of the night passed relatively quietly, and near morning, we found a good space to camp. To our right, a small stream ran and fed a tiny pool of water that looked clean. The canopy had become even more enclosed overhead, blocking out most of the sky, but at least there hadn't been a hint of rain, and we were still clean.

Maggie and I dismounted. I laid out a sleeping bag on the road for Maggie so she could sleep while I set to standing up my tent.

"It's not going to rain," Rowan said. "It would be better to limit our need to pack our things in the event of a problem."

"Yes, but Maggie is human, and I don't want her eaten to misery by the midges, so I'm setting up a tent for us. Besides, it will be more comfortable for her." I didn't mention that, inside the tent, she'd be less likely to wander off without me knowing, at least, I hoped.

Rowan just shrugged and set about building a small fire.

I frowned at her. "What are you doing? We don't need a fire."

"I like poking sticks into them and watching the sparks. I find it relaxing."

"Let it go, Cait," Nastasia said. "We've already established that she's insane." Jess laughed and finished setting up their tent as well.

At Rowan's dark look, Jess struck a defiant stance, hands on her hips. "I don't like mosquitos, and I've already been bitten a hundred times. I'm with Cait here. We have quite enough bloodsuckers around."

"Hey!" I protested and heard Maggie's amused snort behind me as she crawled into the tent. "Screw you, Sobrai," I shot half-heartedly over my shoulder.

"You're not my type, Cait," Maggie said as she struggled back into her sleeping bag.

"I'm everyone's type," I shot back cheekily. "Some people just don't know it yet."

"Thinking a great deal of yourself these days, aren't you?" Nastasia chided as she sat down next to Rowan and started digging into the fire.

"You're not one to talk, dear," Jess told Nastasia with a laugh. "You couldn't wait to get your hands on her."

Rowan just kept digging at the fire and watching the sparks rise through a hole in the canopy above. Finally, she lay down on her sleeping bag, gazing away at the fading stars above.

I crawled into the tent and lay next to Maggie. "There's not a lot of room," I whispered, but she didn't answer. Finally deciding she was fast asleep, I curled up at her back and closed my eyes just as the dawn broke.

As the first rays of moonlight pierced through the darkness, my eyes flew open, and I tasted the crisp night air.

Immediately, I felt or smelled something wrong. Maggie's scent was extremely faint, and she wasn't in the tent. I also smelled smoke, too much smoke for our small fire.

"Where's Maggie?" I almost shouted, my voice carrying a strange echo among the canopy of trees. If there was a forest fire, we were in real trouble. I poked my head out of the tent.

Jess was at the still burning embers of the fire. She stood and glanced around. "She woke up in the middle of the day, and we chatted. She was here when I went back to bed."

"Fuck," I muttered. "I told her not to go running off."

"Do you hear that?" Nastasia said, looking off to our north into the woods. Even with our sight, we couldn't see very far. The curtain of tree trunks was too dense. I paused for a moment and listened. I noticed a faint whispering on the wind, like voices, and something else: music.

"Yeah," I answered and looked at Rowan, who shrugged.

"I'll cut the long way around," Jess said, taking off.

"Jessica! Wait!" Nastasia called, but Jess was already lost in the thick stand of trees.

"Fuck," I sighed, turning to Nastasia. "You need to keep her under control, Nas. We can't be chasing her, too."

She placed her hands on her hips. "She has her own mind, Cait. I can't control her any better than you can. Besides, despite what she said, she insisted on coming for you, not me."

I could see it rankled Nastasia. I patted her on the shoulder. "I'm not the competition, Nas. It's just a protective instinct."

"It's fucking inconvenient," Nastasia said hotly, then lowered her voice. "Well, let's go get them."

"Which way?"

Nastasia pointed at a shape in the ground. "That's Maggie's boot print. She went North, probably toward that insipid music."

We started inside, but I took a moment to glance back at Rowan. "You coming?"

"No," Rowan said bluntly. "I prefer to stay with the horses."

I glared at her angrily before following Nastasia into the thicket.

The gnarled trunks of the trees twisted and turned, guarding even darker secrets beyond, and they gave me the creeps. Though the trees were canopied in lush green leaves, the way the bark seemed washed of color and curled around the fat knots in the wood suggested something more out of a Washington Irving story rather than the beautiful, sweet greenery of my home. I had a bad feeling about this.

Worse still, I kept losing Nastasia, though she was only a few feet in front of me. It was more like bushwhacking in darkest Africa than a quick jaunt into a deciduous stand. The music rose in volume dramatically as we traveled further. Each step brought it closer than expected.

"I don't like this," Nastasia whispered almost imperceptibly.

"What's to like? We're moving through a thickly tangled, magical forest that looks very much like it doesn't appreciate intruders while trying to find our human hostage, whom I'm probably going to have to use for a drink box before this is over."

"Well, I hope Jess is having better luck because this is starting to get to me."

I shivered and slapped at my neck, confident I'd felt something there. "Fuck," I cursed. "Hold up. Is there something on my back?"

Nastasia turned, and I showed her my backside. "It's just your sword," she hissed. "Now come on."

"Did you even look?" I asked as I moved up next to her.

"Sure." Her tone was not at all reassuring.

We had traveled no more than a few hundred more yards, if that, when we caught a glimpse of light through the trees. *Well, that can't be good.* It was a soft glow of sickly yellow, reminding me of the weird ambient glow of the fog in Shaddan.

The music became much more distinct. A harp, a flute, and voices combined in a Locrian mode, mirroring the twisted nature of the landscape—horridly creepy yet alluring. I didn't know if we were chasing faeries or Metallica, and I seriously began to worry about what they might be doing to Maggie.

Nastasia picked up the pace, and we broke clumsily into a

clearing a few moments later. I tripped over a root and fell face down, dragging Nastasia with me.

"Shit," I swore as I looked up, face covered in dirt. In the center of the clearing grew a wide ring of oversized death cap mushrooms where danced a dozen twisted-looking Fae creatures around a large fire. Several of the brown-clad gnome-like creatures whirled about, their long coats flapping wildly, occasionally revealing their bulbous bodies. *Eww.*

Nude dryads with green-brown skin danced solicitously, but their forms were distorted. Rather than being fit and beautiful, these were overly sexualized, with huge breasts and widely curved hips. Among these primary dancers flitted emaciated sprites with almost skeletal forms. They were all Light Fae, to be sure, but they were deformed. Still, they moved with elegance and grace. Each step was so light as to almost miss the ground entirely. Through the press of Fae flesh, I finally spotted Maggie on the far side of the circle.

"Well, looks like she doesn't need rescuing," Nastasia said with a smirk. Maggie lay on her back, absolutely starkers, practically buried in the bodies of three of the voluptuous dryads.

I raised an eyebrow. "No," I whispered. "I suppose not. In fact, that looks like fun, don't you think?"

Nastasia turned toward me, her beautiful brown eyes shining in the firelight. Even in the sickly yellow that seemed to pervade the little hollow, her beauty was an expression of art. I took in a shuddering breath. "What was I saying?" I mumbled as Nastasia drew closer, her lips so very close to mine.

"You said it looked like fun," she whispered.

I glanced at the circle. Several Fae eyes turned toward us, hands reaching out and beckoning us to join them. Without thought, I stripped, leaving my clothes and weapons where they fell, before walking with halting steps toward the dance, the most beautiful woman I'd ever laid eyes on at my side.

No! the voice demanded in my head, but I squelched it.

Now, now—none of that. You'll spoil the fun. The voice struck something inside me, though, something nebulous and anxious. I had a moment of panic. Something was wrong. But then the arousing music flooded my senses, dousing my worries. These were my kinfolk, if not my people. They wouldn't hurt me, certainly.

Nastasia tugged at my arm, and I realized I'd halted at the circle's edge. I looked down at my feet, willing them to move in any direction, but they were fixed. Again, anxiety pulled at my stomach.

Stop! the voice protested once more.

With a jerk, Nastasia yanked me across the circle and into the frenzied dance of the fairies.

It was as if I'd stepped inside rapture. My whole body was filled with sexual need. Every nerve sang. Hands brushed my body at irregular intervals, occasionally eliciting excited noises. The more I danced with the faeries, the greater the urge became until I couldn't help myself. I jumped onto Nastasia, wrapping my legs around her waist, cupping her face, and hungrily driving my tongue into her mouth.

She moaned with the intrusion. My hands tore at her clothes as we kissed, ripping aside anything that stood in my way: top, trousers, underwear. The only thing I didn't get at was her shoes and socks as she kicked them off.

Nastasia shoved me onto the ground and spread herself over me, a knee finding my center and pressing hard. "Oh, Goddess," I gasped. "I missed you so much." Somewhere dimly, the anxiety boiled up again, but I pushed it aside, albeit with more effort.

The coppery spice of Nastasia's breath filled me, and I drew in her scent of pine and snow and mountain air. She gave me a devilish, fang-laden smile, and I returned it. The reckless abandon of the dance turned even wilder as Nastasia began running her tongue across my breasts. Several of the dryads dropped down with us, pinning my arms and legs. Nastasia bit at my wrist, sucking out pinprick wellings of blood that quickly subsided.

Her eyes were black, pupils blown euphorically wide as she nibbled at my abdomen and raked a hand down my side, digging furrows in my flesh. I arched as she shoved two rough fingers into me. My skin began to itch with hunger, but I ignored it as her mouth descended upon me, savaging my folds, my entrance, my clit, with the tip of her tongue, drawing me quickly toward what promised to be a powerful orgasm.

I tried to reach for her hair, dig in my fingers, and press her harder to me, but my arms were still held down in a powerful grip. I gazed upward to find beautiful, gold eyes staring down. Those eyes had gazed at me for eons of life, belying the curvy, youthful appearance of the woman who owned them.

"That's it," she whispered with a bright smile. "Just enjoy it."

No, that irritating voice in my head said again, more clearly this time. *No, sister. You must escape.*

I frowned. Where on earth was that coming from? I was sure now that it wasn't any internal monologue. It was an intrusion. The voice sounded like me, but it most certainly wasn't.

My back arched in sudden pleasure that crested across me. "Goddess, Anya," I breathed.

Without warning, hot blood sprayed across my face and into my mouth. I jerked in shock. The waves of pleasure and lust instantly died. The hunger flared across my body like fire, and the music ceased as the vast revel came to an abrupt halt.

I sat up and looked around in a daze. Fae creatures were running to and fro, trying to escape the long black claws of a red-haired demon. The dryad that had been above me only moments ago lay dead, her throat torn out.

"Don't run! Don't run!" The red-haired creature cackled with glee as it swept through, slashing at the Fae. The beast opened its mouth and bit into the neck of a dryad, coming away with half the flesh in its—no, her teeth. It was Jess. Her nails had grown long, extending into thick claws. Her fingers from the middle joint down were blacker than night. Worse still, her teeth were sharp, more like a wolf's or, well, I didn't know what. She chewed at the Fae flesh and swallowed. Her eyes narrowed as she walked over to the circle's edge and kicked at a death cap with one sneakered foot, dislodging it.

Whatever remaining hold the circle had on Nastasia and me

vanished, leaving me in shocked mortification. I scrambled to shield myself with my hands and let my hair fall over my face. "Oh, Goddess," I muttered. "What did we do?"

Nastasia, for her part, got up off her knees and began picking at her scalp. "Oh, good, just what I need, fucking faerie blood in my hair," she said and shook her head. Then she looked at me. "Not a word."

I didn't argue. I never wanted to talk about this—like ever.

Maggie wasn't so lucky. She lay on the ground at Jess's feet, unconscious and wheezing. Jess bent down, her hands flowing back to normal, though they were still covered in blood. She checked Maggie's pulse, examined her lips, then leaned in and listened to her breath. "I think she's dehydrated," Jess said finally. "We need to get her back to the campsite."

I stood. "Dehydrated? She was missing for eight hours at most."

Jess looked at me incredulously. "Cait, I've been wandering around this fucking forest trying to find you for two days!"

Nastasia's face contorted in rage, and she kicked the nearest corpse, another of those weird, twisted gnomes like we'd seen on the road. "Fucking faeries!"

"I thought you were immune to their glamour," I said, my voice low as I struggled against the sudden onset of the hunger. "You said—"

"I said," Nastasia snapped. "I was extremely resilient, and I know myself as well as anyone, but I'm not immune." She picked up Maggie and stalked back into the woods. I gathered my belongings, keeping them clear of my blood-covered skin, and staggered after, Jess close behind.

"How could you?" Jess whispered accusingly.

"It was glamour, Jess," I answered, but the words rang hollow, even to my own ears.

CHAPTER TWENTY-TWO

"We were glamoured," Nastasia told Jess for the third time. "It wasn't our fault."

"Don't lie, Nas. You wanted her," Jess shot back. "I've watched you two and your surreptitious glances when you think I'm not looking. You've been dying to fuck her ever since —"

"Jess!" I shouted far louder than I'd intended, and for the barest of moments, it was as if the universe flickered with darkness. "That's enough!"

Jess threw up her hands and stalked off toward a small stream we'd found just off the road and away from the circle, Nastasia close behind, still arguing her point. Rowan simply sat and watched us all, absently poking at the fire with a brand.

To say that Jess hadn't been thrilled at the way she'd found us, in flagrante delicto, as it were, would have been the understatement of the century. She was positively fuming. She ranted at Nastasia, who was taken aback by the outburst. They'd never had a closed relationship, and it was clear from the back-and-forth that Nastasia thought Jess was being unfair and a bit childish. I, for my part, felt guilty, and not just because of Jess. Liz's words echoed in my head yet again. *Not too close.*

"Fuck," I muttered, finishing the last of the blood we'd brought. I sat dejectedly on the broken asphalt next to Maggie, who was finally conscious and far too shocked by what had happened in the circle to say much of anything.

Now fully dressed and wrapped in a blanket, she watched the trees with wide eyes that darted with every twig snap or rustle of leaves. I saw the twisting emotions flicker through them as she sipped her water bottle. When her eyes welled up with angry, guilty tears, I finally loosed my glamour and quelled her misery. As bad as I felt, I wasn't a virgin to the preternatural like Maggie.

"Tell me," I whispered, trying my best to tune out Jess and Nastasia.

Maggie looked at me. "Did I want that?" she asked, her voice small and lost. "I said I did. I remember saying I did, but I just don't know. It was like I forgot about everything. I couldn't control myself."

"You feel icky," I said, raising an arm but not touching her. She slid into the offered shoulder, and I laid back, letting her rest her head on my chest before she nodded in confirmation. "But you liked it. While it was happening, I mean."

She nodded again, clutching at my shirt.

I gave her a gentle squeeze. "I have been right where you are. If you want to blame the Fae and their glamour for doing something you wouldn't normally do, you can. It's probably even appropriate, but you don't have to feel guilty for what you did. Sex isn't naughty, Maggie. It's fun. It feels good. And it keeps the human race alive. Do you have a girlfriend or boyfriend?"

She shook her head.

"Then you hurt no one. It wasn't your fault. Also, the Dryads were feeding on you, and it can leave you feeling spent and miserable."

She quieted and kept her head on my chest before wrapping an arm around me. "You're a good friend."

I said nothing. We weren't friends. It was just my glamour. But, for the moment, that was okay. She needed a friend. So, we watched, and I found myself bemused at how Jess vented all of her frustration on Nastasia, never once turning it my way.

Jess pushed away from Nastasia's offered hug as she stalked back to the camp, wet clothes in hand. "Get off me."

Nastasia grabbed Jess's arm. "Jess, I—" Her words failed as Jess slapped her across the face with her open hand, bloody furrows appearing in its wake. Jess's claws were out. To her credit, Nastasia didn't rend her limb from limb. She just backed away. "Jess?"

"Stop, Jess," I said, extricating myself from Maggie's grip. "We can't fight like this."

Jess spun on me, her face full of impotent rage, clawed fingers clenching and unclenching, blood dripping from her hands as her nails penetrated her palms. I stood and walked over, pulling her close and hugging her.

"Jess," I whispered and took her hands, showing her the claw marks. "You're hurting yourself."

She glanced at them and then back to me with pleading eyes. "Why, Cait? You could have resisted it. I did."

I might have, I supposed, but it had caught me off guard. Maybe I should have led with that, but there was something in her tone I didn't like—above her station as a lesser Fae. Hot anger colored my thoughts, and I lashed out.

"It's not for me to explain myself to you," I stated imperiously, my voice taking on an unearthly quality. Jess tried to shrink away, but I grabbed her shoulders and glared at her. "I am the Queen of Shaddan. You," I spat the word. "You are a lowborn pixie, no better than a common whore. How dare you question me?"

Jess flinched and averted her eyes. Nastasia rushed forward, hissing with rage, and snatched me away from Jess. She slammed me so hard into a nearby tree that it cracked the trunk, and the impact made me see stars. "Don't you dare call her that, you fucking bitch!"

Pain flared in my back and head. For a moment, I struggled, and I felt something hot and angry flare in my breast. "I'll—I'll —" I cut off the words abruptly and covered my mouth with one hand. *I'll kill you.* That's what I'd been about to say. *What am I doing?*

"Cait?" Jess prodded. The misery and betrayal that painted her face moments ago vanished. "What's going on? Why is this happening?"

"I…I don't know. I don't even know why I said that."

Nastasia let me go. "Are you calm now?"

I nodded. I was calm, but I wasn't okay. I was shaken, downright disturbed. I had sounded like Nemhain. *No*, I thought. *I sounded like The Morrigan, uncontrolled and enraged.*

Volatile, the intrusive voice unhelpfully added.

Rowan watched me impassively with those inscrutable, grey eyes as she poked her brand into the small fire. Something about the way she looked at me frightened me. It wasn't hostile, exactly. And it certainly wasn't judging. Her eyes were knowing. There was a truly vast depth of knowledge and experience there that belied her youthful appearance, and the alienness of those things combined unsettled me deeply. It was as if she knew me better than I would ever know myself. And that worried me even more for its implications when facing Áine. If this encounter with the fairy circle had been a test, I'd failed.

"It wasn't a test," Rowan said, her voice as clinical and impassive as ever.

"Stay out of my head," I muttered as I sat down between her and Maggie.

"Then perhaps keep your thoughts to yourself for a change?" she shot back, her tone clipped as she jabbed the brand deeper into the embers. "You're positively insufferable at the moment. It's not just that you're spiraling. You're practically shouting your every wayward impulse into the ether for all to hear."

"I'm what?"

She looked up from the fire, the light of the flames flickering in her eyes and giving her light strawberry-blonde locks the look of something ethereal. "Jessica isn't the only one undergoing a transformation, you know. All this rage, this simmering misery, the heavy cloak of dejection—it isn't floating in from nowhere. It's you. It's all coming from you."

A cold icepick sank into my stomach. "What do you mean?"

"Have you looked at yourself?"

I reached into my bag and fished out a compact, flipping it open, but Rowan shook her head with a sharp tut. "No, not that," she said, gesturing toward my chest with the glowing tip of the burning stick. "Inside."

"I can't. The curse—"

"First of all," Rowan interrupted with a tone that suggested infinite patience wearing thin, "it's not a curse, it's a gift. And second, you can do. It just requires a bit more," she paused, her brow furrowing as though rifling through her mental thesaurus before landing on the perfect word, "finesse."

"How?" I was lost and frustrated by her vague answer. I understood so little of magic except the weak emotional shit that Weyna had done.

"Here," Rowan said, her voice steady, and I felt a sudden, ice-cold tug deep within me. A startled squeak escaped my lips. Sparks crackled to life, dancing between the fingers of her left hand.

She didn't flinch, only carried on as if this were all perfectly routine. "You feel it all the time, Cait. You know you do. Stop fighting it. Just relax, take your time." Her gaze softened, though the command in her tone remained. "It'll come."

I stared at her a moment longer and closed my eyes, forcing all of my muscles to relax—easy to do when you're dead. I shifted my perception, but a thick black fog obscured everything. "I can't see the magic," I growled in frustration, "just the fog of the curse—or gift, rather."

"Push it aside. The fog is just a mental manifestation. It's not real."

I imagined the fog moving, letting my intent do the work. Nothing happened. Rowan's hand touched mine, and I looked up.

"Try again after you wake up. I'll keep watch today." She pulled a bit of twine out of her pack and tied Maggie's hand to mine. "This will keep her close. I'd rather move on, but dawn will be here soon, and you'll need your rest."

"Her is wide awake," Maggie murmured sleepily. "And I

have a name. Don't you think you should ask before you tie me to the sex-crazed vampire?"

Laughter erupted from the other side of the fire.

"Sounds like she's got your number, Cait," Nastasia said as she snuggled up to Jess. It appeared all was forgiven.

"Hey!" I protested, feeling my cheeks heat slightly, which was odd. I must have had some blood left in me after all.

"She's not wrong," Jess said, piling on. "You've slept with everyone in our little group except me."

"That's not true," I answered back. "Just—" I thought hard about it. Shit. She was right. I'd slept with Marcella, Nastasia, Liz, and Morgan, three of them in less than a one-month period. "Oh!" I exclaimed. "Shit. I'm a total ho-bag."

More laughter.

"Just so you know," Maggie said, stifling a yawn. "That was an observation, not an invitation." I laughed along with everyone. Even Rowan gave a tinkling snicker.

My tongue flicked out and tasted the air. "It's going to rain tomorrow, likely all day," I said and removed the bit of twine from my wrist so I could move the tent. I placed it as close to the trees as I dared, stringing up a tarp to fend off the rain. Once it was set up, I gently lifted Maggie and placed her sleeping form inside my sleeping bag, gathered up hers, and crawled inside to get some rest.

CHAPTER TWENTY-THREE

The storm clouds rolled over and broke with the dawn, dropping a torrent of rain. Jess and Nas's tent collapsed, and they argued about the right way to fix it. Once the amusement wore off, I called out and told Jess to can it and let Nastasia do what she does. I couldn't imagine the eight-hundred-year-old vampire didn't know how to put up a modern tent. Apparently, I'd been wrong, and the bitching continued until Nastasia finally gave up and let Jess take over.

"Are they always like this?" Maggie asked through a yawn as we lay next to each other.

"No clue," I answered. "This is the first time I've been around them since they hooked up."

Maggie chuckled. "They sound like an old married couple."

"Yes, they do," I said with a bit of a laugh. "They're a lot alike."

We did our best to tune out the bickering while I told Maggie the story of the Battle of Maigh Tuireadh and those I'd fought beside: Saya, Obín, and the rest. I tried to force back the thick emotions in my chest when I spoke of Zilly, but it was no use.

"There was one woman, Zilyana, she was an amazing fighter. She wasn't built like the rest. She had curves, you know?"

"You tell it like you were standing there," Maggie said.

I choked back a response. I wanted to tell her that I had, that Zilly had been real and wonderful, and that I had loved her. But I kept it to myself. I wasn't sure she was ready for that admission. She'd already had her world turned inside out. Instead, I asked, "What do you mean?"

She lifted up in the tiny tent and looked at me. "It's just the level of detail. You should write fantasy novels."

I laughed with unbridled mirth. "Maggie. Haven't you been paying attention? Fairies are real. Vampires are real. What makes you think it's just a fantasy story?"

Maggie shrank back a little. "You mean it's not?"

I shook my head. "You saw the attack on the Liberty Hotel, I'm sure."

"Oh! That was you!"

I nodded. "Yeah, that was me."

Maggie's eyebrows pushed together. "But then, why are they trying to kill you?"

"Politics," I stated matter of factly. "Senator Kim is using the attacks as an excuse to take over the country. We're a threat to that. But she doesn't want it to get out that she's known about us for years."

"Wait, what?" Maggie's eyes went wide. "I thought the interview with The Mermaid Twins was the first anyone had heard of them—you. You know what I mean."

I shook my head. "Senator Kim has known about us since she was the mayor of Boston, maybe even before."

"Jesus, they really did send us into a meat grinder." Clearly, she hadn't wanted to believe it, even then. "I don't want to be someone's martyr." Her voice was high-pitched and grief-stricken, and she looked up at me with wide eyes. "I can't go back. They'll think I cooperated or helped you."

"We'll make you forget it all," I said. "All you'll remember is being a hostage. You'll be fine."

Maggie shook her head. "Are you out of your mind?! That would be worse. If whoever set us up is as ruthless as you say, then I'll be killed or sent to a black site or Gitmo. I'll vanish without a trace, and I'll have no idea why. They won't want to take the chance I might remember something." Her voice rose more, turning panicky. "Besides, you said there's a risk of psychosis. I don't want to be psychotic. Would you want to be psychotic?"

I shushed her, and, thankfully, Maggie settled. "Let me see what we can do when we get back. I promise, though, we won't hand you over to anyone if I can help it."

"If you can help it?" Maggie asked tiredly. "Aren't you the leader?"

I laughed. "Hardly. I'm just a grunt. But it'll be okay. We won't let anyone hurt you."

With that, Maggie laid back down, though her body still trembled with fear. She sniffed, and a cold tear landed on my collarbone.

I tightened my grip and shushed her the best I could. I had an inkling of what she was feeling. She'd been sent to die by an uncaring apparatus that used the military for political goals. It was a betrayal. Unfortunately, it wasn't a new one.

We mounted up and continued our journey at dusk. I took a moment to count the days since we'd gotten here. Had it been three or four? A day in Galway, one day on the road, then we lost two in that fucking faerie ring and most of another recovering. Fuck, that was five, and this was day six. We'd been here six days, and we were barely out of Galway. This was taking too long. I gripped the reins tightly as the forest closed in, becoming darker and more ominous and forcing us to ride single file.

"So, are you really going to get married?" Nastasia asked out of the blue, probably just to make conversation.

"Yep," I said, smirking into the darkness.

"Wait, what?" Jess said, suddenly engaged. "You're getting married? To Liz?"

"Yep," I repeated.

"Wow," Jess breathed. "I never thought I'd see the day that Cait Reagan tied the knot."

"Happens to the best of us, Jess," I called back.

"Huh," Maggie grunted. "I didn't realize vampires had weddings. Is it all gothic and dark? Are there spiders and black candles?"

I barked a laugh. "Ha, I hope not. I have no idea what we'll wear. I'm not a huge dress person, but Liz is. Maybe I'll wear a tux. I'd like a banded collar, maybe." I daydreamed about that for a bit, occasionally offering additional details to no one in particular.

Nastasia finally snapped me out of my musings. "You two are mad, you know."

I chuckled quietly. "Yeah. We are, but we're enjoying the ride."

"I will tell you what, Cait. You come talk to me in a couple of hundred years after the bloom, as they say, is off the rose. I'll still be single."

"Hey!" Jess protested, and I heard the distinctive whap of a hand hitting a shoulder.

The rain hadn't let up since we'd broken camp. Despite our raincoats, we were all soaked to the bone. Both Maggie and Jess were shivering as the temperature dropped precipitously and the heavy rainfall turned to thick flakes of snow.

"Isn't it summer here?" Maggie asked through chattering teeth.

"Yeah," Jess said, her voice a little muffled as she clung to Nastasia's backside. "This is all wrong."

I said nothing. They weren't wrong, but no one needed the obvious confirmed again. I would have liked to have swapped places with Maggie and let her ride in front so I could shield her from the wind, but she was too big, and I wouldn't be able to manage the reins well. If something spooked the horses, I'd lose control. Abruptly, Rowan came to a halt ahead of us.

"We walk from here," she declared curtly. I peered around her. The forest had finally closed over the road, making passage by horse impossible.

"Fine by me," Jess mumbled. "My thighs are killing me anyway."

Nastasia said nothing, but we locked eyes as she

dismounted, and I saw the worry there. The two mortals were going to freeze if we didn't find some real shelter. We were all waterlogged and the now freezing temperatures were starting to stiffen up our clothes. I did my best to rub Maggie's body as she dismounted, trying to get more circulation going, but she was shivering, so it wasn't really doing much. We turned the horses around and let them loose.

"Should we just turn around?" I asked as I watched them walk away.

"No," Rowan said stiffly. "We continue on foot. We'll find shelter." I looked around skeptically, but I followed her.

We didn't find shelter, though. After almost an hour and a half of marching, the only thing we came across was a large clearing where the snow had begun to drift. It was almost a foot deep at the edge, and Maggie stumbled headlong into a bank. I hoisted her up as fast as I could to try to keep her from getting even more frozen, not that it mattered. We soldiered on for a few more feet, and Maggie fell again. I'd had enough.

"Rowan," I shouted. She stood at least a dozen paces ahead. "We have to turn back or find someplace to camp. We can't have them like this. Maggie is stumbling in the dark, and she and Jess are going to die if we don't get them warm soon."

Maggie picked that moment to sit down. "I'm really tired. Why don't ya'll find some shelter? Then come back for me."

I knelt. "No. That's just the hypothermia talking. I'm going to get you to safety and a warm fire." I looked over my shoulder. Rowan was staring at me impatiently. "What?" I demanded, my fury rising. This girl was pissing me off, and she might kick my ass, but I might just take my best shot if she didn't start showing at least some modicum of manners. I didn't expect compassion.

Rowan looked at me and finally said the one thing I most expected to hear. "It's best if we left them behind to find their way back on their own."

CHAPTER TWENTY-FOUR

"You look tired," a soft feminine voice came from my left, and I whirled, dagger in hand. Coal-black eyes that hid a thousand secrets and rested beneath a thick sable mane met my gaze. Cutting cheekbones and a narrow nose accented her full lips, painted in dark red. What little skin her heavy winter parka and ski pants exposed appeared tan, as if she'd just come off a few weeks in the Mediterranean. The aura about her was alluring—too alluring.

"Who are you?" I asked, sheathing my nisís and taking Maggie's hand. I wanted my hand on her if we needed to run.

"Oh, my, aren't you a specimen, all fit and combative," she chuckled. Her accent was American. "Well, I don't mean you any harm, or at least not much. But your compatriots look chilled to their bones and would do well with a fire."

"This is not good," Rowan hissed. "Anything this fortuitous has to be a trap."

I couldn't argue, but Maggie's hand was all but frozen, and she was almost delirious with cold, as was Jess. "We don't have much choice," I muttered through gritted teeth, irritated. "Jess and Maggie will die of hypothermia if we don't do something."

"Cait is right," Nastasia said, finally speaking for the first time since we'd released the horses. "We can't stay out here."

Rowan glanced at Nastasia and then back to me. "I'll say this once, child. We should look for other shelter, something less," she paused again, "occupied."

I lost my temper. "Look around you, Rowan! There's nothing here. We've been wandering for miles. I don't even know if we're going in the right direction."

Rowan's eyes smoldered with irritation. "We are. Our destination is only a day's walk that way." She jerked her thumb over her right shoulder toward what I assumed was the northeast. It was impossible for me to tell in this near blizzard.

"They won't last another day," I shot back hotly. "The mortals are going to die."

"Well, I didn't bring them. I wasn't expecting the human at all. What matters here, Skaja, is getting you to your destination," Rowan said coldly.

I blinked in astonishment, though I shouldn't have been surprised. "They're my friends." Then I shook my head and stared forlornly at the sky, watching the falling flakes. "You know what? I'm responsible for these people. I'm not letting them die." I turned to the woman. "Do you have a name?"

"You can call me Nellie," the woman replied and turned toward the trees. "Come with me," she encouraged as she tromped into the tree line. "I have a fire and sustenance for all of you."

I sheathed my blade, adjusted my pack for more comfort, and picked up Maggie before following Nellie into the trees. Nastasia carried Jess and followed close behind.

"Badb's ass feathers," Rowan cursed in Óṣenic.

"I heard that," I called back and kept walking.

Only a few minutes more of fighting through the underbrush brought us to a less than inviting cabin, one story tall with all of two windows and tiny, but a fire glowed within, and that was what I cared about.

"No," Maggie hissed, her voice barely audible. "Let go of me."

"Shh," I cooed. "We're almost inside. It'll be okay. I'll keep you safe."

"This place looks awful," Jess croaked tiredly.

"I have to agree," Nastasia affirmed.

"This is my home, girl," Nellie retorted. "Have some manners."

Nellie insisted we remove our boots before entering. I couldn't blame her; they were caked in mud. It took an agonizing few minutes to untie the frozen laces. Each second that ticked by heightened my anxiety, as if Maggie might just die in my arms. But we were inches from getting warm. After a few more minutes of fumbling, I managed to get Maggie's boots off. We all piled into the minuscule structure, and heat washed over us. Nellie muscled the door closed against the howling wind.

"Thank God," Maggie murmured as I carried her over and lay her in front of the roaring fireplace before taking in our surroundings.

"Cozy," I murmured wryly. The cabin stood no more than fifteen or twenty feet on a side. Jars of various herbs adorned the shelves and hung from the rafters, their fragrances mingling into a muddled mess in the air.

Two chairs and a small sofa, old but inviting, were arranged in front of the crackling fire next to Jess and Maggie, who were both a little revived and struggling out of their wet clothes. A small, two-seat wooden table, looking older than Rowan, stood in one corner. A thick center support ran from the floor to the pyramidal roof above. The most intriguing feature of the cabin was its walls, made of roughly hewn logs, many of them still bearing the remnants of their branches. I made a mental note not to lean against them lest I accidentally stake myself. Now I understood how a cat in a room full of rocking chairs actually felt.

"Hey," Nastasia said as she tended to the women, helping them undress. "Where's Rowan?"

I looked around. "Rowan?" I called, but there was no answer. I stepped to the door, but Nellie put a hand on it.

"You'll let the cold in. She stayed outside. I don't think she likes me."

Eyeing the woman warily, I moved to the fire and stripped, setting my clothes next to Maggie and Jess's. Nastasia didn't bother, just letting them melt on her body.

Nellie appeared next to us with a pot and two steaming cups of tea on a tray. "Here," she said. "This will help you warm."

I picked it up and let my tongue flick out, tasting the tea. All I got was spearmint and peppermint. If there was anything else in it, I couldn't detect it. Nastasia took a sip and nodded. "Seems fine," she said and handed the cups to Maggie and Jess, who sipped at them greedily.

"That is so much better," Jess commented as she downed the tea and poured a second cup.

"Yup," Maggie agreed and held her cup out for more.

I caught the scent of blood. I turned my head toward Nellie, who was dribbling a bit from her palm into a cup. She looked up. "This will take the edge off for you two," she said brightly. "I don't keep blood around."

I narrowed my eyes.

"Oh, don't look at me like that," she said, bringing the cup over. "I can smell your dark gifts like a dog scents a bone. I brought you into my home, didn't I?" She wrapped her palm in a clean cloth bandage and brought me the cup. "Here."

Nastasia reached out. "Me first," she said. I handed it to her. She took a drink and then handed it back. "Seems fine. Just blood."

Nellie looked at her as if to say, 'told ya,' and puttered back into the kitchen. I took the mug and drank. Immediately, the angry ants under my skin that I'd been fighting all day finally subsided.

"Just relax," Nellie said. "These storms are magical. It'll break soon enough. Then you can go on your way."

"Thank you," I said earnestly.

"No problem. I've been starved for weeks," she said with a sly grin.

I looked over at Nastasia, who had her eyes closed. Maggie and Jess were out cold. "Shit," I muttered and stood, stumbling forward, suddenly unable to focus. A few steps more, the world turned black. "Fuck," I mumbled before I knew no more.

CHAPTER TWENTY-FIVE

I'm sitting on the grass just over the fence at the Cliffs of Moher. A warm breeze slides over my skin. I watch the golden hues of the sunset turn the undersides of soft, cottony clouds to fiery hues of orange and pink. I remember thinking that Tir Nan Og, the land of the everliving and the Faerie, must be off in the distance somewhere, and I smile at the ignorance and flights of fancy in my youth. I wanted to be one of the Fae folk, flitting from tree to tree, playing my harp, away from humans. Even then, I didn't like people very much.

Of course, that was before I knew what the Light Fae were like: capricious bastards, treating people like chattel and driving them mad with glamour. "Mother, help me," I murmur.

"You're not alone today, sister," a voice whispers in my ear in Óṣenic. It echoes with familiarity and yet carries a seductive undertone. I turn, half-expecting to see Aoife, but it's not her. The woman before me is younger, perhaps eighteen or nineteen, yet she's the mirror image of us both at that age. Her hair is raven black, but my face from twelve years ago stares back at me. "Though," she continues. "I'm not sure that you should be judging anyone based on being capricious or driving them mad with glamour."

"It's been you reaching out to me," I whisper, and she responds with a smile. I brace myself for a smile like Nastasia's, laced with cruelty and seduction that matches her tone, but it's not. Her grin is innocent, much like the warm smiles Aoife and I used to share.

She says, "This is your dream, and Nellie can't harm you here. You're too powerful in your own head, but the others are in danger. Shall we off?" She holds out a beckoning hand.

I reach out to take it but pull back. "Who are you?"

"Call me Drusera," Her smile never wavers. "I am your sister. Perhaps you might think of me as your darker sister, but we all have darkness within that rises and falls more frequently than the tides, do we not?"

Taking a defiant stance, I scrutinize her expression, but she gives away nothing. "I'm not a fan of riddles," I say and finally take her offered hand.

Her grip is gentle, almost dainty. "Now, you must move us between dreams."

"I don't know who or what you are, but you've bet on the wrong horse. I don't know how to do that."

"Just reach out. They are near. Just think of them. Remember them. Think in as much detail as you can."

I think of Maggie, her scent, and the feel of her pressed against me that first night. She'd been scared and alone. In a way, she reminds me of Catherine when we found her, and Katie when I first met her. I shake my head, pushing aside an errant image of Katie lying on the floor of the cell. "Cozy," I whisper, echoing Maggie's words, and the image of Carrie's spare room comes to mind.

Moments later, we find ourselves at the checkpoint. The bodies of the dead soldiers lie around us. Before me, Maggie is leaning back against the tank, her fatigue top open. A woman with thick auburn hair is tucked into her neck. I hear the sounds of feeding. Maggie is groaning in ecstasy, clutching at her lover's shirt.

"Oh!" I whisper, aghast.

Drusera giggles next to me, and there's a bit of maniacal titter in it. "Seems she likes you, Cait."

"Not that she ever said," I answer, backing away. Maggie opens her eyes and gazes at me drunkenly. I can't help but smirk.

"She never told her love, but let concealment, like a worm i' the bud, feed on her damask cheek," Drusera quotes.

"Shakespeare," I mutter, recognizing the quote, though I can't remember the specific play. I have always hated Shakespeare.

"Twelfth Night, Act 2, Scene 4. Though I am more a lover of the

Tempest, myself."

"Yes, well, I'm not Orsino. I'm engaged to someone."

"Are you really?" she asks with a bit of a frown. "And how is that going to work? You're a vampire."

"So is she," I answer, though I frown at the question itself. If she were a concoction of my head, shouldn't she know that already?

Glancing around, Drusera announces. "Well, I see nothing amiss here. Shall we onward, dear sister?"

I snort in wry amusement. "Speak for yourself. This seems perfectly amiss in its own right."

Drusera giggles again. "What I mean to say is that I don't sense Nellie here. Come." She holds out her hand again, but I balk.

"Why are we looking for Nellie in Maggie's dream?" I ask.

She sighs as she might at a child who asks too many questions. "Nellie consumes the dreams of others. The psychological impacts can be quite disabling, permanently crippling, in fact. And time is of the essence."

"Who are you?" I ask as she grabs my hand. "I mean, who are you, really?"

"No time."

The world melts once more, reforming slowly into a clinical, cold room. A small girl, perhaps twelve years old, sits in the corner, crying in desperation. Despite her youth, I recognize Jess immediately. "I'm not here. I'm not here," she repeats over and over like some mantra of denial.

I try to go to her, but Drusera holds me fast by the wrist. "We're not here to interfere."

Jess looks up. "Can you help me? Can you get me out of here?" She sounds pitiful, eyes swollen from tears. Beneath that simmers a deep rage.

"How did you get here?" I ask.

"My parents sent me here for having sex," Jess mumbles irritably.

"At your age?" I was shocked. "You're what, ten? Twelve?"

"I'm almost thirteen. Sometimes a girl needs things," she says defiantly. "People will give them to you when you have sex with them."

"Dear Goddess," I whisper in horror.

"It doesn't matter," Drusera says. "Her dream is intact. Shall we

go?"

"But—"

Drusera's tone turns urgent and demanding. "Cait, we only have a few minutes. Nellie must be consuming Nastasia's dreams. We've lost too much time looking for her already."

I struggle against my urge to comfort Jess. Drusera is right. It's only a dream, and one I wish I'd never seen. Just the thought of being inside their minds, seeing their private subconscious wants and needs and fears, makes me feel disgusting. I take Drusera's hand.

Envisioning Nastasia is pitifully easy, and I shiver with the memory I choose, but it is the most powerful. The world changes faster than I blink. Apparently, the stronger the reminiscence, the faster the transition. Despite my misgivings, I wonder briefly how I might enter the dream of someone I don't know, but that's forced aside as the earth shakes, knocking Drusera and me to the ground.

"What the hell?" I cry out and glance around. Not far, perhaps only a dozen feet away, Nastasia stands fixed. Before her, an old lady has ahold of her head. Around us, the ground is familiar. I've been in this memory. It's different in many ways; strange lights sparkle in the sky, but the Mongol hoard charging toward the village is clear enough, though a great emptiness seems to be consuming them from behind.

"What do I do?" I say, picking myself up from the ground.

"It's a dream, Cait. Do what you wish. Dream it, and it will happen."

I imagine myself a massive dragon of glimmering ebony, shadows shrouding my body in wisps of smoky darkness.

"Not bad," Drusera says appreciatively, though her voice sounds far away, and I realize that I've become what I imagined. The power in my limbs and tail and wings is surprisingly real. I can feel each muscle twitch as I lower myself down to snap at Nellie, but she rolls away with surprising speed, her body shifting into that of Ryūjin, the dragon of the sea.

"That's my supper you're interrupting, child," she howls.

I flap my massive wings, buffeting her away, but she darts back in like lightning and strikes, digging her fangs deeply into my leg. I feel the poison coursing through me.

I become the tree of life, Crann Bethad, my body and limbs forming into its impossibly large trunk, splitting her mouth. The poison is pushed out with flowing sap as the wound closes.

Nellie shifts into a massive giant with an axe that will fell me in a single swipe. As she swings, I transform into a sparrow and dive at the giant's eye, spearing it with my beak. It breaks with a satisfying squish.

Nellie screams, clawing and trying to dislodge me. But I've already reformed again into the dark shape of a wevkrana with its metal-tipped legs, digging relentlessly at the back of the eye and kicking out at her digging finger, leaving bits of bone and gore in my wake.

It occurs to me that she probably can't shrink without blowing out her own skull, so I dig faster and deeper. With legs that can sunder concrete or steel, I pass through the bone quickly, and soft bits of gray matter give under my legs.

Goddess, I think. This is so gross. Ick. But it's only going to get worse as I transform once more into the form of a Balor, this time far too large for her skull to hold. It explodes into a shower of gore before the giant's body, and all its remnants fade away in poisonous green sparkles.

"Very imaginative," Drusera says as I return to myself next to her. "But you must wake. Nellie will kill you in your sleep if you do not."

"But, who are you?"

"Find the crystal within the crystal," she says cryptically before the world winks out, and I open my eyes.

"Shit," I murmured as I pulled myself up off the cabin floor and glared at Nellie. She had changed. Gone was the beautiful young woman with the raven hair who'd greeted us, replaced by the same old hag I'd seen in Nastasia's dream. Wiry gray hair twisted wildly about, barely contained by the ragged bit of leather keeping it hostage in a frayed bun. Slumped shoulders and a fat hump that stooped her scholiatic body supplanted the formerly beautiful figure.

Dark hooded eyes, milky and unseeing, turned my way and

widened with shock. "You meddler!" She half-barked, half-cackled at me in the raspy voice of an aged woman, all witchy and squealing. "How dare you interrupt my dinner!"

"You will release them," I demanded with a growl as I drew myself up.

"Oh, no," she said with a demonic smile full of sharp serrated teeth. "They're mine. You'll just have to fight for them."

The corner of my mouth rose as the prospect of violence flooded me with excitement. "I don't see a problem with that." I drew my bóllom.

"No, I don't think so," Nellie said, returning my smirk with one of her own. "I pick the weapons, child. I select cards. Thank you for accepting my challenge, though. That keeps us from having a bruising battle that wouldn't end well for your friends, no matter the victor."

"Huh," I grunted, stalking imperiously around the cabin, maintaining a measure of bravado that I didn't feel. In truth, I was terrified. She seemed small and feeble, but I knew better. Looks, in the land of the Fae, were never to be believed.

I picked up a silver teacup and made a show of polishing it with the hem of my shirt, looking at my reflection. Even setting aside the distortion of the curved demitasse, I looked a little frightening. Green fire sparked in my eyes, and there was a furor in those eyes that reflected the rage riding just under my skin, ready to leap at any moment. Rowan had been right; I was changing.

I set aside the anxiety of my musings. It was a distraction, and Nellie had already maneuvered me to a disadvantage, taking away my obvious superiority of strength. "The game will be fair, then?"

"Of course," Nellie said, though her cunning smile did nothing to inspire confidence in that statement.

Moments later, we were sitting on either side of her tiny table, and Nellie dealt out seven cards each from a deck of simple playing cards. The suits and styles were minor tarot arcana: swords, cups, pentacles, and rods. "My stakes are the release of my friends," I said. "And no tricks, hag. If I have the slightest inkling—"

"No tricks," she said with a sly smile. "And if you lose, you leave them to me."

I closed my eyes and steeled myself. "Agreed. What is the game?"

She grinned. "Gin. One hand."

"Fuck," I swore to myself. "I really wish Aoife were here." When we were kids, Gin was one of the few card games we knew, and we often played it in the evening hours during holidays. My Aunt Mary was the queen of the game, but Aoife was a strong second. I sucked at it. We were all fucked.

CHAPTER TWENTY-SIX

Of all of the more fortunate moments in my life, I suspected I'd count that evening at Nellie Nettle's as one of the most. It might have even rated higher than when Saya had decided to just charge Weyna and bowl her over in overconfidence rather than fighting smart.

Nellie shuffled the cards like a Vegas dealer. It wasn't faster than I could follow, but damn, she was deft with a deck. The already niggling anxiety and doubt bloomed into icy fear. I was going to lose this game for sure. I lifted my hand. It was a shitty split of just about every suit with three fours, two threes, a five, a knave, two queens, and a seven. *Yup,* I thought. *I'm fucked.*

Nellie snatched up the ten of cups sitting face up and replaced it with the three of swords. I kept my face carefully neutral, but that didn't help. My eyes drifted back to the silver teacup. Nellie's cards showed in the reflection, and I almost tilted my head in curiosity as I glanced at it. Nellie's cards looked blank. I blinked slowly and glanced back to Nellie and the vicious smile on her lips. I drew a card from the deck, the king of swords matching one of my queens and the knave. I discarded the queen of cups. I didn't need it.

Nellie snatched it up with a smirk. In the mirror image of the teacup, the card turned blank. It was all I could do not to frown at the image, and I flicked my eyes back to my cards. I couldn't decide if it was a trick of the light or if she was cheating. If I stopped the game and accused her, I'd forfeit the contest, and she'd win. But if I waited too long and she still won by nefarious means, there would be no opportunity to contest the results. Such were the fucked up rules of a Fae challenge.

I pressed my lips into a thin line, switched my cards to my left hand, and re-arranged their order as I considered what to do. Nellie wouldn't give up her supper in a game of chance without an edge, would she? Of course not. I didn't think she was Fae, but she sure had a bead on using their tactics. Deception had been her whole bag from the start, so the odds were better than even that she'd cheat to win—far better.

As she set the four of rods in the discard pile, my hand shot out, snatching her other wrist and twisting her cards to face me. She squeaked in protest. "Let go of me." But it was too late, I'd seen. The cards had been blank, the faces only appearing as they were turned—a simple glamour.

Something dark and malign twisted in my chest, and I completely lost control of myself and my temper. With a single swift motion, I sent the table flying across the small cabin to splinter into pieces against the central pillar, bits of wood narrowly missing Nastasia.

"You bitch!" I roared as I snatched the woman from her seat by the neck and barreled her to the back wall, impaling her shoulder on one of the sharper stubs. She yowled in pain.

Thick black nails grew from my fingers. I ignored the agony and blood as they pushed forth. My hand grew larger, neatly wrapping around Nellie's throat as my vision tunneled in on her. A sharp blast of cold wind snuffed out the candles and lamps. The fire in the hearth flickered and died.

"You cheat!" I screamed in outrage, my voice dropping an octave and taking on a resonance full of magic and menace. "Do you know who I am?"

The hag shook with terror, her clawed fingers scrabbling at my wrist, trying to tear it loose. Her nails dug deep, but she might as well have been a baby for all the good it did. The wounds closed instantly. Finally, she gave up and just held on for dear life, shaking her head.

"I am the Crown Princess of Shaddan," I shouted, drops of saliva hitting her face. "You have forfeited the challenge. Release my friends, or I will rend you to pieces." I leaned in closer, my voice a guttural growl. "I will rip your heart from your breast and eat it while you watch."

She squeaked out something harsh, and I loosened my grip. "What?"

"Yes, Your Highness," she croaked out.

I jerked her from the wall and threw her to the floor with a crash. A knock sounded at the door.

"Fix it! Now!" I commanded. Nellie didn't move, still gaping in surprise and terror.

The knock at the door became more insistent. I stomped over. "What?!" I demanded as I opened it.

Rowan stood there looking irritated, icicles hanging from her hair, but her aloof expression crumbled, and a note of fear widened her eyes slightly. She seemed somehow shorter than I remembered—for that matter, so did the doorway.

"What?!" I snapped again as a puff of snow blew in.

"I'd like to come in," she whispered, almost inaudible, even to me, under the howling wind. "The temperature has dropped a bit further, and I'm finding it less comfortable than I'd like. Also, lightning seems to be falling rather close by. Electrocution is uncomfortable, to say the least."

I grabbed her by the arm and pulled her in, slamming the door shut and sending a dangerous shudder through the entire place.

Rowan glanced at the bleeding hag cradling her arm, the shattered remains of the table, and our companions slumbering on the floor.

"Oh, looks like you have things well in hand, then." Her air of quiet confidence returned as she moved to the counter, picked over it, and snatched up an apple. For a moment, I thought she'd actually take a bite, but she just polished it on her shirt and watched me with penetrating eyes.

"Get up!" I shouted at the hag, jerking her to her feet. "Go make an antidote or whatever you need to bring them back." Hastily, I added, "with their dreams intact."

"Y—Yes, Your…Your Highness," Nellie stammered breathlessly and set to work. She scrambled about the tiny kitchen, pulling herbs down from the ceiling and the jars on the shelves, grinding them in her mortar and pestle.

Slowly, painfully, my body returned to normal. Blood coated my fingertips, staining them red as the claws retracted and normal, healthy nails regrew in their place. The room seemed to grow around me as well.

"Nellie Nettle. Why am I not surprised?" Rowan said, her arms crossed as she leaned against the tiny counter before glancing my way. "I told you not to trust her."

"Fuck you," I muttered angrily. "You could have been more specific."

Rowan looked at me, anger flashing in her gray eyes for the first time. "I would have thought, 'Don't go with her,' was quite specific enough, my child."

I pursed my lips in irritation. "Maggie and Jess were all but frozen," I argued. "What the fuck was I supposed to do?"

"Kill her first," Rowan offered.

I scowled at her. "I don't kill for no reason."

Rowan raised a skeptical eyebrow, then looked around pointedly.

"Let me rephrase," I said, leaning against the wall near the fireplace. "I thought three vampires and a Dark Fae could handle her just fine." I turned back to the hustling hag. "You done yet?"

"Almost," Nellie said, regaining a bit of her composure. Her hands flew across the table, gathering ingredients and crushing them in the mortar and pestle before dropping them into a teapot. "It won't be long now."

"No tricks, hag," I spat at her. "I haven't decided to let you live yet."

Rowan placed a hand on my arm and switched to Óṣenic, whispering, "Threatening her further isn't going to help, girl. Now get control of yourself."

"Don't touch me," I barked, jerking my arm from her grasp.

Rowan slammed me to the wall. My head impacted right next to one of the stakes. She opened her mouth as if to say something, thought better of it, and let me go. But I could see that she was seething. We were both on the edge of a serious disaster.

I nodded quickly and bit the inside of my cheek, tasting the coppery tang of blood. It steadied me, keeping me from starting a fight with Rowan that would likely get me killed and certainly level the cabin. Rowan released me, and I cast my gaze back at Nellie, who stood before the teapot on the little iron stove. "Well?"

Nellie wrung her hands and glanced at me from the corner of her eye. "Tea only steeps so quickly. It will need to cool before we administer it."

I tried to force myself to relax, taking stock of Rowan's comment. She was right, of course. But as much as I tried to ease back on the throttle, my body stayed taught, and the firm desire to murder Nellie for her betrayal stuck in my head. I couldn't calm down, and fear niggled softly in the back of my mind.

"Control," I murmured to myself. "I need to control this." It wasn't the curse. I knew what that felt like. This was something else, something darker and meaner and more—unpredictable. My thoughts stumbled as Drusera's voice returned. *Don't you mean—capricious?*

"Cait?" Rowan prodded, and I realized she'd said something.

"Huh?"

"We're ready. I will take the first dose to ensure it's safe." She still spoke in Óşenic. I assumed to keep our host from understanding.

"No," I stated firmly. "This is my risk. If she's going to poison them—"

"Then I should be the guinea pig," Rowan finished in a whisper. She leaned in close, lowering her voice further, "I can't take Nellie Nettle alone, but she's afraid of you."

I nodded my assent. Truthfully, who was I to argue with her? She was over two thousand years old—well over, I suspected.

Nellie walked toward the others balancing a small tray holding three tiny steaming cups of her concoction with one hand. Her right shoulder looked to be healing rapidly, but the arm stayed at her side.

"You know," she commented idly, gingerly shrugging her injured shoulder with a wince. "I shouldn't have made my house from ash, but it's quite effective against faerie and undead alike. See that you remember that, Your Highness."

I raised an eyebrow and, reaching over, snapped one of the sharp stubs from the wall. I picked at the bark with a sharp, black fingernail, speaking in a dark, somewhat menacing tone. "I will."

Rowan stopped Nellie, taking one of the cups. "This isn't all of it, I'm sure," she said, not waiting for an answer before downing the cup.

"Rowan!" I hissed, but nothing happened.

Moments later, she vomited up the mixture. "Well, that was rather like drinking rat piss."

"You sound experienced," I said in a cheeky tone.

Rowan gave me a wry look.

Nellie rolled her eyes. "I'm not going to poison them. I will do as I promised. I like my head right where it is."

"Nice try, hag," Rowan said. "We both know it's the heart we'd need."

I made a mental note of that. If I never met another hag, Maki would still be fascinated by all this.

Nellie gave Rowan a scornful look before returning to the pot to refill the cup. "Spoilsport."

Rowan's features coalesced into a bored expression, and she waved her hand dismissively but said nothing.

Nellie returned to Nastasia, Jess, and Maggie and dribbled bits of the concoction into each of their mouths. Like, well, magic, one, two, three, they all sat up wide awake and puked on the floor.

Nastasia looked confused. "What happened?"

I glanced at the refuse on the floor. In each little puddle of sick sat a tiny piece of brown root. I bent down and picked one up with two fingers. "Is this Mandragora?" I asked, narrowing my eyes.

"It can bring one to a dreamlike state," Nellie said dispassionately. "Though, too much will kill. It takes a touch of magic, of course, to create that potion. Weeks of work, wasted. I'll have to start again. Thank you for making sure I starve."

"A touch of asceticism might do you some good, my dear," Rowan said and helped Jess off the floor. Maggie was next.

"Don't be impertinent, girl," Nellie shot back. Rowan only gave her a smirk.

Nastasia stood on her own. "I'll kill you, you crusty bitch," she snarled and reached out for Nellie.

"No!" I commanded. "I need information." Nastasia narrowed her eyes and glowered at me. I held her gaze. "Seriously, Nas."

"Fine," she bitched and grabbed a doily off the end table to clean bits of blood off of herself.

"Not my doilies," Nellie said with a groan.

"You're lucky it's not your head," I shot back.

"Heart," Rowan corrected with a smirk.

"I had the strangest dream," Maggie said. "It was—" She paused and looked at me. "You were there."

I waggled my eyebrows. "Do tell. You know, I always thought I looked good in green."

Maggie's eyes went wide with surprise, and she turned away with a blush.

I glanced at Jess. Her hands were shaking. "We need to talk later," I told her, and she nodded.

"Now," I said to Nellie, fixing her with a pointed glare. "Tell me what's going on around here. Why is the magic so chaotic?"

Nellie put her hands defiantly on her hips. "I roused your friends, but I'm not in the habit of giving out free information."

"What do you want?" I asked.

"Please tell me that you're not going to make a deal with Baba Yaga here," Nastasia said incredulously.

"Shh—" Nellie hissed, a warning in her tone. "She'll hear

you."

Nastasia gave Nellie a skeptical look. "Who?"

Nellie widened her eyes and stared at Nastasia like she was stupid.

"Baba Yaga? She's a fairy tale," Nastasia said, and then her face shifted as it dawned on her what she had just said. "Nevermind."

"Kostyanaya Mat is my sister," Nellie said. "And she's a nasty one."

"The Bone Mistress," Nastasia translated for us. "It's what some call her in Russia."

"Anyway, she's up and about," Nellie commented as she began straightening up the kitchen area. "You don't want to meet her, Your Highness, I assure you."

"The missing Ukrainian girls?" I asked, thinking back to a news story I'd read after I'd awoken. "Everyone thought it was a Russian-backed separatist group."

"Sure, that's a logical assumption given the war, but it was my sister, no doubt," Nellie responded, waving her hands around. A brush of magic, earthy and sour, wafted through me as the bits of the table I'd smashed flew through the air and cobbled themselves back together. With another wave, all of our clothes turned instantly dry.

"Much better," she said with a creepy smile. "The storm is breaking outside, and the sun is rising. You all need to shoo. And stop using my sister's name if you know what's good for you, missy."

"You're not of Shaddan or Bethad, are you?" Jess asked out of nowhere.

Nellie smiled mysteriously but ignored the question. Instead, she opened the door. A warm wind blew into the house, carrying with it a wafting of melting snow. "Now, get out. And, you," she pointed at me rudely, "don't come back."

I gave her a crooked smile, bringing up the rear as we all filed out. "Don't give me a reason to," I said as I stepped across the threshold. She slammed the door with a muttering curse.

CHAPTER TWENTY-SEVEN

"It's this way," Rowan said as we made our way back toward the clearing. Strangely, the walk back seemed much longer than the trip to the cabin, probably the effect that Nellie wanted. The snow melted far more rapidly than I would have expected, turning the ground into a marshy mess, bog-like and hard to navigate, and raising a thick fog. Several times, Nastasia and I had to help Maggie pull herself from the mud, having sunk in several inches. Jess, strangely, walked on top of it as if it were solid earth, leaving almost no print.

We cleared the trees and were no more than three or four steps into the clearing when Rowan held up a hand. We all froze. A quick glance at the trees and the air revealed nothing. I scanned the ground, trying to gauge where Rowan was looking. Then I saw it, a low bulge in the ground about halfway across the clearing.

"That wasn't there before, was it?" Maggie asked.

"Shh," I hissed, but it was too late. The bulge in the mud sped right toward her. "Fuck," I swore as I timed a strike to drive down into whatever it was. That, as it turned out, was a mistake, as a black and brown tentacle lifted out of the ground. My bóllom, jammed deep into the appendage, went right along with it, carrying me into the air with a painful jerk at my shoulder that nearly dislocated it.

"Help!" I squeaked, and Nastasia drew her ninjato and began squishing her way slowly toward the center of the clearing.

It took me a moment to realize that it wasn't a tentacle at all; it was a sinewy arm, maybe twenty feet long and disgustingly rubbery, bending in weird places and capped by a five-fingered clawed hand. It shook wildly, trying to dislodge me.

"Is that a grindylow?" Maggie blurted, and I really wished she'd shut up and stop making herself a target because another arm protruded from the ground, snatched her by the leg, and pulled her into the mud.

Jess ran forward and jumped onto the arm that had Maggie, her teeth sinking into the thick flesh as she bit it. A massive, bulbous head, misshapen and ugly, with two yellow eyes, skeletal nostrils, and a wide mouth, emerged from the center of the clearing and howled in rage. The arm thrashed, sending Maggie flying through the air to land in a heap, but it failed to dislodge Jess, who bit it again. Finally, the hand curved around impossibly and yanked Jess loose, tossing her off into the gnarled treetops, where she disappeared.

Nastasia was at the center by then and stabbed into its eye just as I finally pulled my bóllom free and slid off the slimy arm. The fall to the ground was about twenty feet, and I landed hard on my right leg. It snapped, and I screamed in pain. It would heal, but, fuck.

Clearly, the creature wasn't terribly smart. As soon as I yelled, it forgot about Nastasia and started reaching for me. Jess darted out of the trees, looking none the worse for wear, grabbed the other arm this time, and bit it again. *Goddess*, I thought. *The woman is fucking tenacious.* Finally, the nasty thing stopped snatching at us and gave up, slithering back below the ground and burrowing away toward the tree line.

"Thanks for the help, Rowan," I muttered, my voice dripping with sarcasm as I drew myself up.

"I don't recall naming myself your royal guard," Rowan retorted. "Besides, you had the grindylow in hand."

"Pluh-pluh. I thought they were tiny and lived in water," Jess said, spitting dirt and slime out of her mouth.

"Less movies, more study," I said. "Go hang with Maki for a bit. Maybe she'll rub off on you."

Jess nodded and continued spitting. "Pluh. Ick. It tastes like shit."

I slogged my way over to Maggie, who was still unconscious. "Maggie? Hey! You okay?" I prodded and checked her airway and breathing. Both were fine, and her pulse was steady. She didn't have any obvious injuries, so I did the only thing I could. I bit her and gave her changed blood. As soon as it went down her throat, she woke in a panic.

"What the fuck are you doing?" Maggie demanded, scrambling away.

"Keeping you alive" was all the explanation she was going to get. I marched over toward the northeastern tree line where Rowan stood. "You know, for the oldest vampire on the planet, I'd hoped for a little more solidarity, or at least a bit of esprit de corp. We could have used your help."

Rowan gave me an infuriatingly pleasant smile as she said, "I fail to see how. I am carrying no weapons. And while my strength and speed are probably considerable next to yours, it's only by degree. You are Valtárí, Skaja. I saw you take down a koṣant all by yourself the night Boudka was murdered. I'm not, as you Americans would say, 'the heavy' in this group."

That pulled me up short. *Why am I bitching?* After a moment's thought, I finally reasoned that it was because Maggie got hurt. And whose fault was that? Mine. I was putting my shit on Rowan, and she didn't deserve it. But still, my chest squeezed with runaway anger. I stomped on it. I had brought Maggie along, and it was my responsibility to protect her. Jess and Nastasia were different. They had volunteered and were holding their own.

"You're right," I said with a sigh and stomped my way back over to Maggie, every step making a sucking splorch sound in the muck.

Maggie eyed me with suspicion.

"You hit the ground hard," I explained, deciding she deserved better. "I wanted to make sure that you didn't have any lasting injuries. When we feed, the blood gets changed. It takes on a bit of magic that can heal wounds. I gave some of that back to you. I was afraid you had a closed head injury or worse."

Maggie looked at me then, her nasty frown curving up into a crooked smirk as she raised a hand. "I must be growing on you. That sounds suspiciously like compassion."

"Oh, shut up," I murmured half-heartedly, pulling her from the mud and turning back to Rowan. "We need a place to rest for the day."

"There's a cave just a few hours walk from here," she replied. "You're likely familiar with it, I suspect. But then again, it only gained fame long after you died—the first time, I mean."

"Oweynagat." The name alone was innocuous enough, often mistranslated as 'The Cave of Cats.' But it was the one place in all of Ireland most closely tied to The Morrigan and, supposedly, the site of all manner of unnatural activity that frightened locals for generations.

It was said Nemhain had lived there for quite some time. I seriously doubted that. My mother, an almost religiously clean individual, would never take that as a home. The cave was, as Agent Schaeffer would say, all damp and oozy throughout most of the year.

The one time Aoife and I visited Oweynagat with my great aunt Mary, it was just a dark cave with a few tourists. Even then, those weren't common, just people interested in Irish folklore or the occasional remnants of my mother's worshippers.

"Do you think it will be dry?" I asked Rowan.

"How would I know, child? Do you always ask so many questions? Perhaps you should let fate take you where you belong for once."

I snapped my mouth shut with a frown and followed Rowan into the trees, bushwhacking for another hour. Finally, when we'd reached the Carnakit road, the tree line broke on vast pasture. The sun shone down on the grasses, and a cool breeze blew in from the southeast. There wasn't even a hint of rain or snow to be seen anywhere. Apparently, the tangled forest hadn't yet covered the entire country. Still though, we encountered not a soul.

A hundred or so yards down the road to the west stood a small two-bedroom ranch-style home, but the roof had collapsed, giving its once inviting quaintness an eerie haunted look. Moss and ivy covered the remaining walls, making it seem as if it had been abandoned for several years, but the Sinn Fein flag flying in the yard told otherwise, looking nearly brand new.

"Where is everyone?" Jess asked again as we wandered across the pasture.

Nastasia stared at the house, then looked across the pasturelands. "For that matter, where are the cattle? And the sheep?"

I realized we hadn't seen a single domesticated farm animal on the entire trip. The countryside should be full of them, just wandering around and munching on the low grass, but there was nothing. A feeling of intense foreboding, far worse than when we entered the forest, crept upon me.

Rowan gave us an exasperated look over her shoulder. "As I explained previously, had you been paying attention, something is amiss in Luminara. The Light Fae have taken the country and everything in it. Not long after the power failed, humans from every corner of the country began walking toward the palace. None of them have been seen since, except at the coasts. Even Dublin is mostly empty now."

"I don't understand," I said, stepping carefully over a cow patty. "The Fae came to save humanity, and now they enslave them?"

"Well, technically, I think it was to defeat the Kaushkar. Saving humans was kind of a necessary byproduct, but I take your point. I don't think this is about slavery, though. There are more and more Fae making their way across the country, replacing the humans: redcaps, brownies, and the like. Also, more dryads are appearing than I would expect."

My eyes widened suddenly, and my steps slowed for a second as I considered the implications. "How many Fae?" I asked in almost a whisper, terrified of the answer.

Rowan looked up and waved her hands as if doing some mental math. "Hmm. . .multiply as a percentage of landmass. . .carry the one." Then she bobbed her head as if deciding she was close enough. "Probably tens of thousands, perhaps more."

I halted in my tracks. "Fuck me!" I breathed.

"What?" Nastasia asked, dodging her own set of livestock-made hazards.

"They're transforming them," I whispered. "They're turning them into Fae. My mother said it could be done, but that kind of transformation takes almost unfathomable magic just to change one person. On this scale, I thought it was impossible."

"The kind of magic that one might find right next to the gate?" Nastasia asked sardonically.

"Mother of Waters," I swore softly. "This is insane."

Rowan giggled as if I'd said something very funny. "You expected something different, Skaja?"

"Great," Jess said behind us. "Just what we need, more of those assholes."

Rowan laughed even harder. "I think I like you," she said to Jess. "You remind me of a friend of mine."

"You won't let them turn me into one of those things, will you?" Maggie asked, her voice a little shaky.

"Hey!" Jess interjected. "I'm one of those things, you know. And you'd be dead without me. So go easy on our kinfolk, yeah?"

"Can all of you just give me a fucking break," Maggie screeched, scratching at her leg and slapping at a mosquito on her neck. "I'm just scared. I don't want to be some oversexed chick stuck in a tree. And I sure as hell don't want to be a short, squat man with bad manners and fat fingers, okay? I only learned that faeries were real the day before yesterday!"

Jess stepped in front of Maggie, jabbing a finger into her chest. "How do you know you're not already one of them? I didn't know until it happened."

Maggie stopped and just sat down in the grass. "You know what? Fuck all of you. I didn't want to be here."

I stomped over and pushed Jess aside, kneeling in front of

Maggie. "It will be okay."

"No, it won't," she said, tugging at her pant leg. "It's already started."

I frowned in confusion. "What are you talking about?"

She undid her belt and pulled her pants down. On her left thigh, just above the knee, the skin held a large patch of black goo that covered most of her quadricep. "This," she said shakily. "What is this?"

"Shit," I cursed under my breath and covered my mouth in shock. "When did that start?"

"After the Faerie ring. I felt fine when I went to sleep, and then it started to itch when I woke up. It was just there, maybe the size of a quarter."

"Why didn't you say something?" I asked, my tone mild and kind. Not that I could have done anything when it started, anyway. Hell, I had no idea what to do now, and I couldn't figure out how she'd gotten infected with the stuff. As far as I knew, it was something localized to Boston.

"I hoped it would go away by itself," Maggie replied as tears flowed down her cheeks. "Am I going to die?"

I shook my head. "Not if I can help it. Pull up your pants and stand. It's not going to get fixed here."

She did as I asked, and I helped her up.

"It's Dark Fae magic," I told her as we got underway. "It shouldn't even be here. I know someone who can help you, though." In truth, I had no idea if anyone could. I thought maybe Carol could. From what Bian said, she worked in earth magic. Of course, I didn't know where to find her, and she was an ocean away besides. But I couldn't let Maggie lose hope. That certainly wouldn't help anyone.

CHAPTER TWENTY-EIGHT

"Nope," Maggie said flatly, staring into the triangular maw that constituted the entrance to Oweynagat. "Nope. No way."

I laughed. "Yeah, it's not terribly inviting. At least it looks mostly dry. You should see it after it rains. It's one long slick of mud all the way down. I almost busted my ass in there the last time I was here. You know, though, it might be our best bet." I pointed around at the surrounding landscape, all blissfully clear of the spooky woods that had cropped up all over the island. "Maybe the Bethadi are afraid of it."

At that moment, a flock of copper-colored birds swarmed out of the cave. Their loud squeaks were followed by a sickening feeling that made both Nastasia and I turn away in disgust. Maggie and Jess doubled over and puked, even as the grass at their feet curled up and died.

"Then again, not," Nastasia said sardonically. "I don't think this is a good spot to camp."

"Nonsense, child," Rowan said and started down into the cave without looking back. A moment later, she poked her head out of the entrance. "Besides, I wouldn't encourage us to be out here during the day. Luminara is no more than a two-hour walk to our northeast, and honestly, I feel it's best we avoid the patrols."

"What patrols?" I asked. "We haven't seen hide nor hair of

the Bethadi Knights so far."

"That them?" Maggie asked. She stood near the top of the low rise next to the cave entrance, peeking over the road toward the southwest.

I hiked back up the slope and looked. In the distance, a group of men on horseback in shining armor rode across the field.

"Well, shit," I cursed and grabbed Maggie. "Into the hole, we go." I pushed her into the cave in front of me, and we both made our way down into the dark.

The tiny entrance to Oweynagat was a little treacherous. The slope was relatively shallow, but the stones were slick with bits of mud. I held her up as best I could. She'd be blind down there. For that matter, I suspected it might be hard even for us. A vampire could see at night or in near-dark conditions, but the lack of light in the cave was so extreme that it would be, at best, dim to our eyes and, likely, completely black at night. Interestingly, Jess seemed to be managing just fine. Fortunately, Rowan lit up a small kerosene lantern.

We reached the cave floor about two dozen feet down the incline, and a strange feeling of comfort fell over me, calming my thoughts and steadying my emotions. It even helped a bit with the antsiness of the hunger, which still hadn't faded completely. Of course, I hadn't consumed much in the last two days.

"Good Christ," Maggie said once she reached the bottom, her voice echoing loudly in the cave. "It's fucking dark in here."

I shushed her, hissing, "We need to be quiet right now. The Bethadi may not come down here, but they will investigate the entrance, I'm sure." I turned to Rowan, who just shrugged. *Great*, I thought. *Some help you are.*

When I realized that Rowan was likely the first vampire, I'd been a little startled by the revelation. Then, I'd been disappointed. Maybe I'd read too many books as a kid, but I'd expected the first vampire to be more like Marcella, maybe, or perhaps like the Queen of the Damned, but not a snot-nosed brat with a tendency towards creepy Stephen King vibes. I had finally had enough.

"Rowan?" I said quietly as I tugged my tent from its bag, letting the supports and stakes clatter to the cave floor. I was setting it up to give Maggie and me a place to sleep where she wouldn't feel so exposed. Even in this cave—no, especially in this cave—it was easy to get antsy and feel like things were crawling on you. The tent would help with that. Besides, I thought it might be a little chill down here for Maggie.

"Yes, my child?" She answered, sounding paradoxically like a teenage mother superior. I half expected a ruler in her hand. I also silently thanked my lucky stars that Ma hadn't sent us to Catholic school like Mike had wanted.

"Whom do you serve?"

She glanced at me, the cold eyes in her startling cherubic face revealing nothing. "I'm quite certain I don't understand the question."

I continued assembling our tent. Nas glanced over at me from behind Rowan's back, mouthing, "What are you doing?"

I ignored her. "It's a simple question, dear heart. Whom do you serve? Do you serve my mother, for example? Or perhaps, Áine? Or someone else?"

Rowan shifted, looking a bit taken aback and uncomfortable. "One does not simply serve a person. One should serve a purpose," she said after a long moment. "Perhaps, little one, you should ask a better question."

I smirked. "Do you serve the House of the Morrigan? Because, if so, I would expect that, as the Princess Regent and eldest scion, you would be more helpful."

"Ah," Rowan said. "And in what way would you have me help more than I already have?"

"You can start by giving me a straight answer to a few questions," I said, now threading one of the fiberglass tentpoles. I paused for a second and looked up at her. The imperiousness returning to her gaze, but I held it firmly. I wasn't going to back down this time. "We deserve to know what we're walking into."

Rowan sighed and looked away. "It would be better to say that I show favor on your house, Skaja, not that I serve them.

However, if you must know, I was asked to wait for you in Galway at the proper time—when the black gate was opened. I must confess, though, I had expected it far closer than Boston." *Point for me,* I thought.

"You had expected it to be Aoife," I said casually. "Instead, you got me, correct?"

"I was expecting Skaja," she answered, not quite so casually. Clearly, she didn't like me prying, but I also noted how she had abruptly disposed of her usually long-winded prevarications in favor of straight answers. I'd invoked the privilege of my station, something I wasn't altogether comfortable with, but apparently, it had its uses besides being an absolute albatross around my neck.

"What are the Light Fae up to?" I asked, glancing back up and watching her expression.

"In all honestly," she said as she set up a small lantern. "I haven't the foggiest, except invasion, or so it would seem. I believe, based on all that I've seen, that they intend to set up a permanent presence here. As to why their magic is corrupted or why they would want to be here at all, I'm honestly flummoxed. It's simply not like them."

No, I thought. *It wasn't like them at all.* They were rude and unpredictable, yes, but they generally only fucked over the foolhardy. That wasn't just how they were in myths; it was the reality of their culture. I didn't understand them, not really, but to my knowledge, wholesale transformation of an entire population wasn't something they had ever done before, and I wouldn't have expected it of them. I turned silent as I thought about that and went back to assembling the tent.

"You know, Skaja," Rowan offered a few seconds later. "I do have a life outside of what you and your mother and your aunts would have me do. Your mother bid me help you, and I'm endeavoring to assist, but I would wish to return to my own affairs soon. So, I do have an incentive to help you get what you need as quickly as possible."

"Mmhmm," I hummed in acknowledgment, then turned to Maggie after the tent was assembled. "Come on, Maggie, let's get a little rest."

Maggie stood in the tall cavern and shambled over. She looked miserable. Her eyes were downcast, and her face drawn. Honestly, I didn't blame her. I'd dragged her into a situation so far beyond her experience that she was struggling just to cope.

"I'm sorry," I whispered once we were settled. "You were right. I should have found another way."

Maggie grasped my arm as it wrapped around her midsection. "Was there one?"

I sighed. "I just don't know. I didn't think so at the time."

"I just can't understand why this is happening to me. All I ever wanted to do was help people."

She sounded small and frightened and desperately alone. I needed to end that. She wasn't alone. And with that thought, I realized that the kid was growing on me. I knew I shouldn't get close to her; she'd be in danger, and when I inevitably failed to protect her or save her from that creeping blackness on her skin, I'd be heartbroken. But I couldn't help it. *Can anyone?* I wondered. And that was the real question. I was happy with Liz, and all I wanted was to live in peace with my family, but that didn't seem to be possible. I would have to navigate the road that had been laid for me, like anyone, and so would Maggie. But she didn't have to do it alone.

I know you're scared," I continued. "It will be okay. I'll find a way to keep you from getting sick or turning into something else." *If I can,* I finished silently and hugged her close.

She turned toward me then, locking eyes with me in the dim glow of the lantern outside. "I'm not cut out for this," she whispered. "The army, I mean."

I frowned. "What makes you say that?"

"I haven't been in serious danger, not really. Yes, the grindylow was terrifying, and I was afraid those pilots were going to shoot us down, but I came through it okay. You haven't been mean to me. In fact, you've been downright civil for the most part. At first, I was sure you'd kill me."

I shook my head. "Why would I do that? You never raised a finger to us."

"Well, Nastasia—" she started, but I cut her off.

"Nastasia's thoroughly practical and a bit sociopathic, but she doesn't dislike you. But why do you say you're not cut out for the army? What does the army have to do with what's going on here?"

Maggie took a deep breath as if she were about to plumb the savage depths, and her hand squeezed my arm. "I'm in an uncomfortable situation. It's foreign and weird, but it's not the end of the world. And still, I've completely come apart like the frayed end of an old bullwhip. If I can't handle this little bit of the unknown, even given the circumstances, how could I handle war? I'm afraid to die. The men I was with were dying all around me, and I just sat there and wet myself. I did nothing."

Understanding dawned. All she had endured so far had only compounded survivor's guilt. She also probably felt bad for clinging to me, her captor, so hard. A soldier's duty was to plot escape, and all she'd done was go along for the ride.

"It's okay," I said, laying down, letting her rest her head on my arm and tuck her face into my chest. "It's not your fault." I stroked her head. "You should be scared. If you weren't, I'd say you were insane. But, Corporal Sobrai…Maggie, I watched a hardened Scout Sniper, a war veteran, completely implode when I threatened him. Nastasia has had kings at her feet begging for mercy. We're a scary bunch. But that in no way reflects on you. And I can tell you without a doubt there was nothing you could do. You would have been throwing your life away, and I wouldn't have met such a wonderful person. I'm going to protect you. I promise that."

Maggie shuffled, rolling over and clutching at my arm like a kid.

"So, let me tell you a story," I whispered.

"A story?"

"Yes. A story about a girl who went off to war, and it destroyed her. About a woman who has the blood of Goddesses in her veins and still doesn't know who she is. About a woman who survived some of the worst things that can happen and is still alive, despite how fucking terrified she is of what's coming. And she knows what's coming."

Maggie stayed still, but I felt her tears soaking into my shirt. I hushed her for a minute, then told her my tale. While I spoke, I knew that Nastasia and Jess and Rowan could hear me, but I didn't care. Maggie needed to know there was something on the other side of this. It wouldn't haunt her forever. So, other than the sordid details of my personal liaisons, I left nothing out, finally ending with my proposal to Liz and her acceptance.

When it was over, Maggie settled quietly and inexorably drifted off into what I hoped would be a peaceful sleep, still clutching my arm.

CHAPTER TWENTY-NINE

"Good evening," I whispered softly as Maggie stirred against me gently.

"Thank you," she said. "I needed a good rest."

"Nightmares?" I asked quietly, my voice filled with genuine concern.

"No," she admitted. "I don't remember dreaming anything." She turned over and looked at me.

"Then I have a favor to ask," I said cautiously, my voice tinged with a hint of trepidation. This was going to be a doozy.

"You're hungry," she murmured.

"How did you know?"

"Unless it was sex, which I doubted, given that you're recently engaged, what else could it be? I don't have anything else to give."

Smart kid, I thought. "True," I nodded. "But I won't without permission. I can go a little longer."

"It won't change me, will it?"

I gave a quiet laugh. "No, that's not how it works. That part is like the movies. I would have to drink you almost to death, then give you my blood. There's also a bit of intention required as well."

"Will it hurt?" she asked, her eyes reflecting a deep and genuine curiosity rather than fear.

I shook my head. "Not really. There's a pinch, like getting a shot, then it's all bliss and roses. But I'll warn you, it'll be a little on the erotic side."

She looked at me, her eyes searching my face. I heard her heart race and her breathing turn a little shorter. She wanted to say yes, but she was scared.

"You literally have nothing to fear from this," I said and swiped a hand through her hair.

"It's not that," she breathed. "I'm afraid of how I'll feel after."

"How do you want to feel?"

"I don't want to be insane if you're talking about that hypnosis thing you do."

I smiled. "That won't happen. It's when you screw with someone's memories or make them believe something that they just can't accept that they can break."

Maggie seemed to think about that for a moment. Finally, she said, "I just don't want to feel dirty, like I've done something wrong. How does it work?"

I could still feel the jackhammering of her heart. "You're still afraid. Do you want me to take that away?"

She shook her head. "No."

"Okay," I said and lowered my fangs. She gasped a little, and her whole body trembled with a mix of fear and anticipation. Her sudden desire for my bite was intoxicating. It was like my first feeding all over again, like young Pauline. I felt my glamour slip free and reach in, heightening her desire while doing nothing to suppress her fear.

"Please, do it," she almost moaned.

I pushed her on her back, straddled her hips, and pressed her hands to the mat. She turned her head to the side, and I lowered myself to her neck, biting in.

She whimpered a little, then breathed a soft "Oh" as I released her hands and pushed my arms underneath her, drawing her upward, holding her upper body suspended just above the floor.

Maggie's arms clamped around me as she bunched my shirt in her fingers, clawing at my back. With the first pull, she let out a shaky breath and squirmed underneath me.

I felt powerful and suddenly full of life. The heat of her soul flowed into me, and I pulled again as it suffused every part of me. Her head lolled backward as she trembled in sexual ecstasy, grinding herself into me. I gave a third and final pull. I wanted more, but I could do without, and I didn't want to take too much.

Still holding her up, I stroked her face and cupped her chin. Her eyes were fixed on mine, dilated. Her nostrils flared as she breathed in full, lustful lungfuls of air. Her lips split in a soft smile as I finally pressed my lips to hers. Her tongue shot out, sweeping my mouth. I pushed a bit of changed blood between her lips.

"Swallow," I mumbled, and she did as I asked. Her neck mended itself.

Finally, I laid her back on the floor. "Did you find it unpleasant?"

"No," She chuckled dreamily and turned extremely bashful. "I liked it."

I gave her a crooked smile. "I thought you might."

I wiped down her neck and face with the last of my alcohol pads as a blush slowly filled her face, and she buried it into my chest.

"Are you alright?" I asked.

Maggie nodded vigorously with a muffled squeak of "I'm fine" as she tucked herself in closer to me. "You smell good," she hummed. "Like Christmas."

I laughed. "Yeah, I've heard that. It's something about vampires. No one really knows why, but we all have a distinctive smell. Nas smells like pine forests on a crisp winter day just before the snows fall."

Maggie pulled her head from my chest and gazed at me. "And how would you know how Nastasia smells?"

Giving her another laugh, I changed the subject. "You look like you want to ask something."

Drawing herself fully onto her back, she propped a knee and clasped her hands together. "You seem to have everything under control, and I— wait, what did I say?"

I had started to laugh. "Nope. I am marching to the drums of fate. I have literally nothing under control, Maggie. There's no such thing." At her puzzled expression, I continued. "We don't even control ourselves, Maggie. A—" I paused, trying to find the right word for Marcella. "A friend once told me that we have no control over others and little enough control over ourselves, if any. The decisions we make and their consequences are the conclusion of millions of years of actions and reactions. I crawled into a tunnel in a fit of anger and was infected by nine different little parasites, each one trying to claim my body for its own and reshape it. I died from it. After a little CPR, I was turned."

"I don't understand," Maggie said.

She had her head on one arm, resting the other on my belly and flexing her fingers in an almost intimate way. For a moment, I wondered if she was coming on to me. I dismissed the idea and continued speaking, placing my hand over hers as I laid back and stared at the roof of the tent. "If I hadn't been in Iraq, I wouldn't have spent time searching underground. If I hadn't been in that cellar and I weren't so impulsive, I wouldn't have gone into that tunnel after a person I had no business chasing. But I was full of myself and full of anger, and I decided I could take a vampire on my own. Of course, the vampire wasn't actually down there. It was someone else entirely. And I got trapped in the tunnel with a beast from my worst nightmares. How much of that was actually under my control?"

Maggie shrugged. "You went into the tunnel. That was a choice."

I snorted a laugh. "Was it? I'm impulsive. I didn't make myself impulsive; I'm just wired that way. So I ask again, how much of that was my actual choice?"

Maggie raised an eyebrow. "I see what you mean." She unzipped the tent flap. "It's getting stuffy in here," she said absently. "You know what's really weird. When you showed up, I…I couldn't keep my eyes off of you."

Someone outside barked a laugh, Jess, probably. I ignored it. "Like you needed to be with us?"

"Yeah," she whispered. "I don't understand it. When we were on the plane, I wanted to get away, but I couldn't bring myself to even think it, let alone try anything. I'm not gung-ho or anything, but I'm not usually this passive. Is this you?"

"No," I stated truthfully. "I can't answer the question you have. I don't know why you feel that way. I will tell you that I couldn't bring myself to harm you either."

Maggie laid her head on my chest again and squeezed close.

"Comfortable?" I asked wryly.

"Oh! Oh, God, I'm sorry. See, that's what I'm talking about. It's like being close to a long-lost sister or something."

"No, it's okay," I said quickly. "I don't mind physical contact. I appreciate it." I didn't have any answers for her, so I let my glamour slip and spoke to her in quiet, hypnotic tones. "You look a little tired. Another hour of sleep wouldn't hurt you."

She yawned. "Yeah, I am tired." Her eyes turned glassy, and a moment later, they drooped shut, and she was asleep. I smiled as she gave a soft snore.

Gently, I lifted Maggie off of me, finished unzipping the tent, and crawled outside to three smirking expressions. "What?" I hissed. "I was practically starving."

Jess rolled her eyes and shook her head. "You've been waiting to do that for days."

I blushed. She wasn't wrong. I had kind of been thinking about it for a while. Being a vampire had its perks. Liz and I wouldn't sleep with anyone else, but feeding was pretty much the next best thing. Nastasia said nothing, but her arch grin gave away her thoughts pretty clearly.

"You're a big eater and so untidy," Rowan said. "I truly prefer to just take little bits here and there."

"You're also like two thousand years older than me. I can't imagine you have to feed too terribly often."

She shrugged. "Truly, it depends on my mood and what I've been doing, but I find small bites here and there to be less messy."

I pursed my lips and rolled my eyes. Rowan was just a little bitch, I decided, as I fished in my pack for an alcohol wipe to get the blood off my face. Of course, then I remembered that I'd used the last one on Maggie, so instead, I snagged a bit of water from Maggie's pack and wiped down my neck with my t-shirt. A few seconds later, my stomach gurgled, and something cold and nasty-tasting made its way into my mouth. I spit, and black goo splattered on the rocks. I worked my tongue and spat a few more times, finally using the water bottle to wash it out.

"Ew, yuck," Jess said. "What's with that?"

I looked at it. "It's in her bloodstream," I commented. I thought I should feel anxiety over it, but I didn't. I was fascinated. The goo wasn't moving. It had lost its viscosity and turned watery, lying in drops on the ground. "Huh. It's dead."

Rowan nodded and examined it. "Yes. The magic that was in it is gone. There should be remnants, but there's nothing at all. It's completely drained." She looked up at me, then back to the rocks, and set her finger tapping on her lips for a minute. "That's terribly interesting."

"Did the curse kill it?" I asked. *Goddess,* I thought. *There is so much about magic that I don't know.*

Rowan cast me an annoyed glance. "It's a gift, child, and it saved your life, but no, I don't think so. The dark gift shouldn't have any effect on it other than to stall out its growth, replacing cells affected by it."

I pursed my lips in aggravation. "If I could just see the magic, I might understand better. You said that vampires could use magic. But every time I've tried shifting my perception, all I see is a hazy blackness."

Rowan smiled, and for the first time, it seemed heartfelt, not arrogant or condescending. "Come with me, Skaja."

CHAPTER THIRTY

I followed Rowan out of the cave. We took a bit of time to walk the perimeter, threading our way around the copse of trees to the north and east. A home sat abandoned to the east of the cave, but it was untouched by the ravages of whatever had destroyed the house we'd seen earlier. This one was locked. To my shock, outside sat a small Yorkshire terrier, no bigger than my forearm, watching us from the porch next to a huge bowl of food. His liquid eyes followed us as we passed through the yard, looking forlorn.

My heart ached at the sight of the dog. "Come here, kid," I coaxed, my voice gentle and sweet. But the dog remained rooted, whining quietly with an echo of loneliness. He rested his head on his paws, his liquid eyes stirring in me a harsh feeling of absence. "Yeah," I said, my voice barely a whisper. "Me too, buddy."

Rowan, seemingly oblivious to the dog's presence, continued to share her wisdom. "To perceive magic as a vampire, you must understand that it's not your eyes that see. The perspective may appear to come from the eyes, but the true sight emanates from the soul." She paused, her hand gently touching my chest, directly over my heart. "Right about here." I felt an intrusion stirring through my emotions.

I tried to jerk back with a whimpered, "Please, don't," but

she snatched my arm, holding me close.

"I realize that it is rather unpleasant, but you must see." Her magic pushed even deeper. As it had been with Bian when I'd been sick, a thousand emotions flickered through me: bright joy, deep longing, powerful grief, even a touch of ecstatic love. It roiled and twisted, sending me to my knees and wrenching tears from my eyes to roll hot down my cheeks.

"Now, concentrate and shift your perception," Rowan said gently.

It took long moments, but I was finally able to fight through the tumult of emotions.

The blasting of tarzhi from the Bethadi gate filled my view as if I were stepping from a dark cavern into the noonday sun. Strands as vibrant as honey-laden sunshine and finely polished silver hummed with a pulsing visual rhythm. They whirled about, mixing with the fabulous greens and turquoises of the land itself. Threads from the Shaddani gate floated amid them, adding even more color. They sang in my heart despite the churning hurt that Rowan's touch had stirred.

"What did you do?" I murmured, awestruck.

"I opened your perception beyond the Dark Gift," she replied. "The gift appears black, but there is no 'black' magic, not precisely. What you see is like the light produced by flame. Harmless in its own right, but powerful when coupled with the heat."

She withdrew her hand, and I crumpled down. The vacancy of her passing yawned inside me, and I broke into sobs, suddenly wanting her back.

Rowan crooked a finger under my chin and pulled my gaze upward into her vast grey eyes. "Try to remember how this feels, not the petty human emotions that are overwhelming you, but the magic, the way your soul is perceiving the world around you. Hold onto that while your feelings settle."

I struggled to find the sensation, elusive and lost, as my chest squeezed with guilt and sorrow and my heart burst with euphoric joy. It seemed impossible amid the violent emotions. I swam in a sea of contradictions, seeing Liz's smiling face, feeling the fear that Katie had engendered when she'd had her last regression so long ago, and the depths of loss and grief when I'd been pulled away from Zilyana at the height of our triumph up north. And love, painful love, for Nastasia. Still, though, the visibility of the tarzhi persisted everywhere around me. I held it like that for a moment, hearing the song of the magic pure and bright. Abruptly, it flickered out as my gift snapped back to black, clouding my sight.

"You had it," Rowan said, helping me off my knees. "Just for a moment. Let's finish our sweep and return to the cave. You can try again."

"Why are you really here?" I asked meekly as we journeyed around the copse of trees.

She ignored the question and pointed northward, "Look!"

We stood on the far side of the trees that surrounded the house we'd found, maybe a hundred yards northeast of the cave entrance. I followed her line of sight and almost gasped. A soft light glowed in the distance with an ethereal quality, as if it were living silver hanging just at the horizon. "What is that?"

"That, Skaja, is the light of Luminara. Despite the strange dark nature of the forest and the Fae folk it has produced, the citadel itself is untouched. It leads me to believe that whatever this," she waved her hands around comically, turning in almost a complete circle, "is, it can be repaired.

"Come," she said, guiding me back to the cave entrance. "Sit here and practice. Find your gift from within and look past it; focus and see. It'll be obvious when you succeed."

I sat and concentrated, trying to discern the shroud that was my curse. *Gift*, I admonished myself. *It's the Dark Gift, Skaja.* The blackness seemed impenetrable. I couldn't push it aside; its dark tentacles rushed back in to fill any space I tried to make.

When I found the key to seeing, it turned out to be pitifully easy and so obvious that I'd completely overlooked it. "Glamour," I uttered in sudden realization. When I glamoured someone, the magic became translucent, allowing me to see the mind of my victim.

"Ah," Rowan answered, and I could hear the arrogant and

irritating smile in her voice. "Now you understand. Your Gift is yours. It will obey your commands if you know how to ask."

I drew on my experiences, limited as they were, with glamour, reaching out for a mind that wasn't there. As it turned out, my lack of experience with either glamour or magic didn't matter. As soon as I sought a presence, the shroud vanished, and the tarzhi popped into view, overlaying my vision. A light tear flowed down my cheek.

"I can see again," I whispered, my voice laced with the absolute awe and joy I felt. Cait had never seen it, but I had. And in that moment, I realized that I really was Skaja. My perception followed a thread of silver winding away from my center. It pulsed and moved. Other threads of tarzhi swam around it in every direction as my perception projected faster and faster down the thread until I found my soul once more, its pulse slightly different. I recognized the resonance of it. It was definitely my soul, but absent the changes that my life, Cait's life, had wrought.

"Skaja," I breathed, realizing that this was my past life.

"Careful," Rowan warned. "Look, but don't touch."

Cait's life before Nemhain's revelation seemed like a shell, a glove that had been wrapped around my true self, a shroud of pain and hardship. My hand drifted up between my buttons, feeling the raised brand over my breast. I had thought of my life as Skaja as being something separate and distinct, someone else's life. But it wasn't. It was all part of the whole.

"Oh!" I gasped as a flood of memories erupted in my head, years of life. My love for Zilly had endured. We had lived a long and happy life after the battle. I'd trained warriors and heroes. I'd had children, a daughter and a son. Zilly and I had raised them with love to be strong. I died on the Isle of Skye, and I was to be buried there.

"I see so much," I said, my voice barely a breath on the wind.

"And you will see more, I promise. Now, let go of the past and reach for the present!" Rowan hissed encouragingly in my ear, her voice demanding. "Touch the magic. Hear its music."

The tinkling of the magic sounded in my head. All around

me, the music sang in harmony but for one dissonant melody that seemed to scrape across my mind like the screech of a harpy or nails on the proverbial blackboard. It raised the hackles on my neck. "What is that?" I asked in exasperation, looking up at Rowan.

"That, my child, is what is amiss in Luminara."

CHAPTER THIRTY-ONE

In a daze, I practically stumbled down the tunnel into the cave. The depths of a peace I'd never known had settled over me. In the dim light of the small lantern now burning low, I gazed at my friends with new eyes. Nastasia was shrouded by her gift, but her soul burned white hot beneath, peeking through periodically, reflecting her passion.

By contrast, Jess was breathtaking. Shaddani magic spiraled and wove about her. The hues, ranging from serene blue to deep violet, culminated in a brilliant blood red. This crimson aura unfurled behind her, blooming like massive wings. "You are a vision," I whispered, and her cheeks flushed scarlet.

"Cait," Nastasia said, a look of concern on her face. "Are you feeling okay?"

I gave her a broad grin. "I've never felt better, not in two thousand years."

Nastasia's eyebrow arched in suspicion, her gaze shifting to Rowan. "What have you done to her?" she accused, her voice hot with anger.

Rowan put her hands on her hips. "Why do you assume, child, that whenever something happens you don't like, that I'm either derelict in my attendance or have had some hand in it? I showed Skaja how to see magic again, that's all. I haven't a clue what's in her addled brain at the moment."

I ignored them, turning my attention to Maggie, who sat by the lantern in her skivvies, brushing her fingers over the moving substance on her leg with a deep frown. Her body flowed with the white of her soul and the green of Earth, and yet a sliver of Shaddani magic pulsed within her.

She's Dark Fae, I realized with a start, not like Jess, something else, something different. That pulse of deep purple Shaddani magic seemed to hold an almost sinister nature, not exactly threatening, but powerful, as if it were waiting for something.

I didn't know why, but part of me knew, somehow, that there was a terrible potential for violence trapped within Maggie, and, with my sight re-opened, the call of it to my blood was like a clarion. Her Fae line, whatever it was, had a purpose.

Unfortunately, the goo on her leg seemed to swallow everything around it, black and twisted with a few frayed strands of midnight-blue tarzhi bent at angry right angles. The jagged infection rose and crossed her body. Bits of latex-like skin spidered over three fingers of her right hand. I narrowed my eyes and stalked to her. "Hold still," I said, gently brushing her hands aside.

I placed a thumb on the mess of angry blackness, and it parted like oil hit with dish soap. I lifted my thumb, revealing that the skin beneath was all but gone, showing bits of fat, muscle, and blood. Maggie howled in agony and jerked violently, then settled as the goo flowed back into place.

"Ow, Jesus! What the fuck did you do that for?" She shouted. "That fucking hurt."

"I'm sorry," I said, giving her a sympathetic look. "I didn't know it was so bad underneath, but I needed to understand what we're dealing with and how far it's gone." I cupped her cheek and thumbed away a tear. "But this means that we can fix this. We have time. I just can't do it here. I need to take you back to—" Before I finished, pain flashed through my chest like a hot knife, burning through to my back.

"Oh, Goddess," I groaned and fell over. Outside, thunder rumbled, and lightning crashed close by, shaking the dust from the ceiling. My vision stuttered like a bad film as I watched Úmbra and Aoife huddling close, Déra's home shaking itself apart. Then, as quickly as it had come, the pain diminished. "Shit," I breathed. "We're almost out of time."

Nastasia came and took my shoulders, helping me out of the dirt. "Cait. Are you okay?"

I shook my head, quelling my rising panic. I swallowed hard. "It's Aoife," I said breathlessly. "She doesn't have much time left, and I think I might have been wrong. I think she's going to die with Úmbra."

Nastasia wrapped her arms around me. "No, dorogaya, she's not. We won't let that happen."

Jess scooted our way and joined in the hug. "Don't worry, Cait. We're here with you."

All I could think at that moment was that I must be doing something right if these two sociopaths were comforting me in my hour of need. Of course, then, Rowan had to ruin it.

"Well, we best pack up and be off," she said cheerily. "We—wait, what are we doing?"

"Boudka's grave?" I reminded her flatly.

"Oh, right, I'm sorry, I was watching the badger."

Maggie looked around. "What badger?"

"Let it go, Maggie," Nastasia answered as Jess got to packing their things. "She's insane."

"Yeah," I agreed.

"And yet, child, you are following me as if I'm not," Rowan retorted with a devilish smirk.

"That's Your Highness Child to you," Jess said and giggled.

"Maybe I don't like you after all," Rowan pouted.

"Did you ever think we don't like you much, either?" Maggie muttered as she helped break down the tent. "Pretentious little bitch."

My eyes went wide. "Oh, you're definitely coming to stay with us after the army," I said with a grin.

Maggie actually smiled at that. "I have another year, Cait. A lot can happen in that time, but I appreciate the offer. Of course, that depends on how long I end up in the stockade when all this is over."

"You're a hostage, Maggie," I said with a sardonic grin.

"You didn't have a choice."

She shook her head and grinned back. "But am I? I mean, really?"

I snapped closed the tent bag, strapping it to my backpack before hoisting it on my back. "Let's go."

"You want me to carry it for a while?" Maggie offered after we'd gotten outside, indicating the pack.

I laughed. "Maggie, this thing might as well weigh nothing. I can pick up the engine block of a semi without breaking a sweat."

"You don't sweat," Jess pointed out as we started down the nearby road.

I rolled my eyes. At least everyone was feeling a little better, though that might have been just me. I was certainly feeling a lot better.

We chose to finish our journey to Rathcroghan by the road. We followed the gravel wheel ruts west until we reached the paved stretch that led north to the N5. Low rock walls, so common across the country, flanked either side of the narrow avenue. We passed two cars sitting in random spots. The glow of Luminara, some twenty miles north, steadily grew as we followed the pavement.

We cut off the road once we reached Rath Beag, a group of rising concentric rings that had been a small ring fort, even during Weyna's time. We stooped low and crawled our way to the top of the rise, where Nastasia extracted a set of field glasses. "That's unfortunate," she said, handing them to me.

Even at this distance, I could see there were moving figures to the north of the central mound of Rath Croghan. Through the field glasses, it was clear that there was an excavation going on already. A dozen or so people, Fae by their breeches and tunics that looked fresh from the Renaissance Festival or a Lord of the Rings cosplay, were digging around an old toppled megalith. "No," I whispered. "This is perfect."

Nastasia looked at me like I'd lost my mind. "How, in any

way, is this situation fortuitous?"

I smirked and whispered, "There's only about a dozen guards. And we don't have to go to Luminara to solve our problem. I was dreading that, given the state of things here. Goddess only knows what's got the Light Fae all fucked up."

"Weren't they supposed to give us a ride home?" Jess asked. "I'm not looking forward to dodging British warships in a dinghy on the Irish Sea."

It was a fair point and one I'd forgotten about. I didn't like our chances if we had to try to get to Cardiff, and I certainly didn't like thinking about how long that would take. I kept my mouth closed, though—no need to snap at Jess for pointing out the flaw in my plan.

I turned back to Rowan. "Are you joining us for this?"

"And spoil your fun? You're Valtárí, a true Mage, a vampire, and the daughter of a Goddess, Skaja. Why would you need my help?" Rowan quipped as she finally crawled up to look at the assembled host.

I gave her an incredulous glance. While I couldn't argue three of those, I hadn't consciously used any magic in over two thousand years, and I still didn't know how to influence the tarzhi. That being said, there wasn't a single Fae knight among the people we watched, so it would probably be a fairly swift victory. I handed the field glasses back to Nastasia. "Can you make that distance without being spotted?" I asked her.

Nastasia nodded. "Of course."

"Okay, I'll come in from the road to the north of their position. You come in from this side."

Nastasia grinned. "Finally, something real to do."

"And what should we do?" Jess asked, her eyes alight with something truly disturbing, and I wondered if Light Fae were somehow natural enemies to her kind, whatever it was.

"Sit tight," I answered. "We'll call if we need you. This will be over almost before it starts."

CHAPTER THIRTY-TWO

Me and my big fat mouth, I thought as Nastasia, and I fought back to back, struggling to fend off the small group excavating the grave. In our favor was the fact that Boudka's grave was fully uncovered, even if her sarcophagus was still half buried. We wouldn't have to dig. Of course, I'd discovered that fact when I'd gotten knocked into the grave, landing hard on the shadowsteel cover.

It wasn't that the Fae were faster than I'd expected, but Nastasia and I were moving much slower. Somehow, they had dampened our Dark Gift. On top of that, the entire contingent turned out to be Bethadi knights. They were just out of their armor, which, against us, made them more, not less dangerous. So, in the end, six to one turned out to be about an even fight.

"You know," Nastasia said with a grunt as she parried another blow and barely avoided tripping over the dead knight at her feet. "I'm actually glad this is a stand-up fight. I need the practice."

I dodged low, deflecting an incoming blade away from Nastasia's back and rolling around, catching one of the knights in the leg with my nisís. "Speak for yourself. I thought I was done with all this sword and sorcery shit." I kicked out with one leg, sweeping a knight off his feet and plunging my bóllom into his chest. Smoothly, I came back up to a ready position, feeling my butt pressing into the curve of her back. "Sorry about your ninjato; it looked really nice."

"It was made of high carbon steel," Nastasia bitched. "I didn't expect it to break on the first parry."

"That's Fae-steel for you," I said, barely deflecting an arrow from one of the guys in the back. "Yo! Rowan, we could use some help!" I shouted, then more quietly to Nastasia. "This really sucks. I hate the idea of asking that brat for help."

"You and me both," Nastasia grunted, driving a stolen Fae blade into the heart of another attacker. I had to hand it to Nastasia; as soon as her ninjato had broken, she'd managed to snatch away a sword from one of the knights like stripping candy from a baby.

"Four down, eight to go," I said during a momentary breather while the Fae knights re-arranged themselves into a wider group, giving more room for the archers to shoot. Not that anything but a heart shot would do them any good. I'd already taken four arrows and tossed them aside. They just hurt.

The archer whose arrow I'd deflected disappeared almost comically, flying backward off his feet into the darkness. Moments later, we heard horrible screaming that cut off abruptly. Another archer vanished into the night a second later, though she didn't scream; she was just gone.

"Make that six down, six to go," I huffed.

Then, the most remarkable thing happened. Maggie Sobrai, the terrified medic, scared of her own shadow and afraid she wasn't cut out for warfare, jumped out of the darkness with a scream, landed on the back of one of the knights, and stabbed him in the throat with a long knife. As soon as he dropped, the drain on our gift vanished.

Nastasia gave a hoot of victory and glanced back. "Is that the medic?"

"Sure is," I said, grinning wildly despite my shock. I charged forward and went on offense, executing a Valtárí pattern against two of the remaining knights. Nastasia scooped up a second-long sword and took on two of her own. The other two had vanished from view, which I found disconcerting until I realized they were just gone.

Goddess, I thought. *I missed this.* This was the thrill of battle, heart-stopping moments of pure terror filled with the delight of matching blades with an opponent. And, for all her comments about me being the better fighter, Nastasia was fucking amazing. She kept up with my every step. She wasn't trained in the Valtárí way, but she was fast and agile, and we worked together like a well-oiled machine of death.

One of my opponents tried to dance away, but she tripped over Maggie, who had run in and rolled into her legs. I stabbed that one and blocked the blow her compatriot aimed at Maggie. A Fae dagger sailed in from my left and dropped him a split second later. I looked over. Nastasia was pulling one of her borrowed blades from the dirt.

"You looked like you needed a break," she said and shrugged her left shoulder where a wound was closing rapidly. Fortunately, Light Fae weapons, while made of stronger stuff than steel, didn't suppress magic like shadowsteel.

"You okay?" I asked, reaching down and helping Maggie haul herself up off the ground. She just stood there, trembling like a leaf, thunderstruck. I wiped my weapons on one of the dead soldier's cloaks and then pulled Maggie back down to sit on the ground. "It's going to be okay."

"I've never killed anyone before. I don't even know why I did it. I saw you guys fighting. Then I noticed you and Nastasia weren't moving as fast as you should. I knew something was wrong, and I just took off running." She put her head in her hands, accidentally smearing blood across one cheek. "Fuck. I just want to go home."

I pulled her close, resting my chin on the back of her bowed head. "You did the right thing," I murmured quietly. "We needed the help."

Rowan appeared next to us, and I looked up. "Thanks," I said softly, but she just tugged me away from Maggie. "Just a second," I muttered as I followed her. "What? Maggie's struggling."

"That is what I pulled you aside to discuss," Rowan said,

her voice low. "That girl is a detriment to your mission. You should have left her in Galway."

My temper spiked again; this time, there wasn't the consideration of destroying the cabin over everyone's heads to quell it. The area around us grew almost pitch black, and thunder rumbled in the distance. My arm snapped out and wrapped around Rowan's neck, lifting her off the ground. "I have had enough of your callousness. She wanted to come, and I didn't want her to miss her chance to go home should we convince Áine to create a portal. But I will not have you suggest one more time that we should leave her or Jessica. Is that clear?" I lifted her to my face, nose to nose.

Rowan stared at me for a long moment. Her eyes were no longer the soft gray of childhood but had once again taken on that hard, steely color. "Let me down," she growled, about as well as she could with my hand squeezing her windpipe.

"And if I don't?" I spat.

"Cait, let her go," Nastasia said, tugging at my arm. "This isn't helping." She turned to Rowan, who hung in my grip like a rag doll. "What's happening to her?"

Rowan's attention turned to Nastasia momentarily. Then her eyes flicked back to me. "She is her mother's daughter, but there is quite a bit of Badb in her as well. The closer she gets to Luminara, the more that it shows. This will pass, but—"

"The hell it will," I hissed at her, but even as I said it, the rage fueling my actions seemed to be fading. I lowered Rowan to the ground and released her. I squeezed my eyes shut, dropping to my knees as regret and worry replaced the anger.

"But what?" Nastasia prodded Rowan.

"The Morrigan is coming. She cannot stop it. It's what she was made to be."

Made to be, I repeated in my head and sighed. "I don't want this. I never did."

It's what you are, sister, Drusera sang in my thoughts, oozing with malicious delight.

Rowan knelt down and pulled my chin up to her eyes, her words flat and precise, almost clinical in tone. "Nevertheless, little shadow, she is upon you, so you must take care to keep a tight rein on your temper."

I screwed up my face in irritation. "Let me guess, it's my destiny."

She just shrugged. "When someone falls ill with a fatal and incurable disease, is that their destiny? If someone is hit by a car in the middle of the street, is that their destiny?"

Shrugging, I just said, "I have no idea."

"Do you think it matters to them?" Rowan asked pointedly.

I understood immediately what she was driving at. This is what I was facing, and if I wanted to survive it, I had to deal with it, whether I liked it or not. "Okay," I muttered in resignation and pulled myself off the grass.

Maggie was still rooted where she sat, looking at her hands as Jess cleaned the blood off them with a wet rag. I sighed and pursed my lips. This wasn't at all how all of this was supposed to go. No one was supposed to die or, in Maggie's case, get infected with that morphic gel crap, as the government called it. And Jess, I didn't even know what to make of her changes. She was turning feral, and I didn't know how to stop it or even if it should be stopped. I was pretty sure she shouldn't be eating people.

"I don't know if I can do this, Nastasia," I said as she joined me next to Maggie. "I just want my life to be stable and normal."

"One must still have chaos in oneself to be able to give birth to a dancing star," Nastasia quoted.

"Leave it to you to quote Nietzsche," I commented distractedly as I watched Jess care for Maggie. I followed each slow movement of the rag as she wiped away the blood and whispered encouragement with such tenderness.

"It's one of the truths I live by," Nastasia continued, placing a hand on my shoulder and tugging me around to look her in the face. Goddess, her beauty wouldn't be repressed, even now, under the dirt and grime and blood. "I embrace the chaos that is my life and wrestle it into whatever form it will take. For me, I make it into whatever amuses me. But if you need more, then make it more. If your own amusement isn't enough, Cait, then turn your chaos into justice or destruction.

It's yours to command."

"And destiny?" I asked. "What about that?"

Nastasia's expression shifted, showing more kindness and compassion than I'd ever seen from her, and she ran a thumb along the line of my jaw. "Cait, your goal is to save Aoife. So, save her. If you want to save Maggie, too, then save her." Then she leaned in conspiratorially with a goofy grin. "Whatever happens after that, these fools will call it destiny."

Rowan raised her eyebrows and crossed her arms. "I'm quite certain you are aware that I can hear you, you Russian trollop."

Nastasia raised a serious eyebrow but couldn't hold it as she burst out into gales of laughter.

I stared down into the open hole. The image on the shadowsteel sarcophagus was eerie to look at. There, staring back at me from the lid, captured in relief and surrounded by an opulent Óşenic knot-work pattern, was the picture-perfect likeness of Boudka. The bas-relief looked almost as if it had been molded directly from her face. I could imagine her hauntingly beautiful eyes and blonde hair. I recalled her sweet smile, spun a bit off kilter after she'd been turned. Even then, she'd been one of the most beautiful things I'd seen, perhaps more so as the undead.

"That looks nothing like her," Rowan said with no small amount of cheek. "She did make a fabulous queen, though. She really came into her own after you died, Skaja. So, are you going to open it?"

I stood frozen, memories of passionate nights flooding my thoughts and overwhelming my emotions. A pang of sorrow and rage, like the crack of lightning, struck me as I remembered how she'd died, worse still, how she'd glamoured away my love like so much smoke, sending me onward to Zilly. The memory broke my heart, and light tears fell over my lashes, leaving rivulets in the dirt smeared on my cheeks.

"What is it?" Maggie asked, touching my shoulder. The tendrils of black goo beginning to cover her fingertips quivered as if attempting to escape.

"I was in love with her," I said through thin tears. "For a while, she was everything I aspired to be. Then she died."

"Cait," Nastasia said. "You weren't her. Those memories were someone else's."

"Perhaps," I responded, my voice slightly choked with emotion. "But it feels real. Everyone I love leaves me." Even as I said it, it sounded more like maudlin whining than truth. Liz hadn't left me, though she might if she knew what had happened here. Even that, though, I doubted. She knew I had a thing for Nastasia, and she certainly wouldn't blame me for what happened in the faerie ring, even if I did.

Without another word, I hopped off the dirt ledge and dropped down into the grave. The sarcophagus gonged with the impact of my hiking boots, echoing around me with weird reverberations. It reminded me a bit of the Xarpras. If we got out of this, if we succeeded and saved her, I would make Úmbra a new one. I wanted to hear her play in person, I decided, and there was enough black steel here for a hundred blades or a thousand such instruments.

I slid off the lid and stood in the cramped, thin valley of earth between the coffin and the dirt wall. Again, I paused. Would she recognize me somehow? And what might she think of what I've become? Did I know what I'd become—was becoming? A million questions swirled in my head. I looked back up at my friends. We'd been through so much already just to get this far. My eyes landed on Nastasia, and I gave a wan smile. How could I have let myself fall for her? I still loved Liz, but this gravity between Nastasia and me seemed inescapable. What would I do when we returned home?

Nastasia nodded encouragingly. "I'm here, whatever happens," she said, only adding further to my conflict.

I brushed that aside for the moment, though; I had a job to do. I examined the latches on the left side of the casket. They had no hinges or keys or any visible way to open them. I gave a brief tug with my fingers, putting a fair amount of strength into it, but they didn't budge. "What did I expect," I said to myself. "It's shadowsteel."

"Maybe it opens from the inside," Maggie offered helpfully. The others chuckled, and I smiled, happy the tension had been broken.

"Where was the Mantle?" I asked, realizing that the sarcophagus seemed unopened.

"In a separate box," Rowan said. "I told you. I was here when it was buried."

Of course you were, I thought. I rapped on the lid. Gong. Gong. Gong. "Boudka? Are you in there?" I spoke in Óșenic, knowing for sure she would understand. A minute ticked by, and I rapped again, but there was nothing.

"There must be some kind of catch or something buried on the side," I said a few minutes later. "We need to bring it up."

"No," Jess said, climbing down into the pit with me. "Look. The knot-work here and here is different."

I examined the twisting ribbons of decoration imprinted on the lid. She was right. On either side of Boudka's face were several twists in the knot-work around five round indentations. I examined each one in turn. They were ridged with fingerprints. "Wow," I said. "That's interesting."

Jess leaned forward and checked the fingerprints. Before her work in general forensics and computer crime, she'd spent over a year doing almost nothing but print analysis. She could tell you everything about them. After a moment, though, she recoiled and nearly toppled over trying to escape the grave.

"Out!" She all but screamed. "Get me out. Get me out of here." Her face was flush and wide-eyed with panic, and dirt fell in as she tried desperately to scramble out of the grave. "Help," she cried in a hyperventilating wheeze.

Nastasia leaned down, caught Jess's scrabbling fingers, and pulled her up. Then I felt as much as saw Nastasia's glamour land on her like a hammer.

"What is it," Nastasia asked. "What's wrong?"

"They're mine! It's impossible. But they're mine." Jess's voice was shrill. Nastasia's glamour wasn't working on her like it used to.

I looked up at her horror-filled expression. "How do you know?"

"I spent years looking at prints." She said, still clearly frightened. "I've looked at my prints a zillion times for spot checks, equipment calibration, elimination prints, you know? I know every finger and both palms. I had to. It was part of my job. Those are my prints, Cait. How are my prints on there?"

"Now that's fucking Vegas magic right there," Maggie said with a laugh. "Like serious Criss Angel shit, but real."

"Criss Angel is a douchebag," Rowan said with a slightly maniacal titter. "Give me Doug Henning any day."

I stared at the lid in wonder. I'd always known my mother was powerful, but this—this was— well, I didn't know what to call it. Next level shit, maybe? "The Goddess of Magic," I whispered in absolute awe. Clearly, I hadn't understood what that meant. All I'd ever seen her do was conjure storms and cast magical lightning—and the occasional prophetic vision. Shit, I'd done all of that. But this, this simple detail, was beyond my wildest imaginings. I looked back up at Jess. "I need you to open it, honey."

"No, Cait," Jess said defiantly. "I'm not touching that thing again."

"Come on, Jess," Maggie said. "We've come this far. We gotta see what's inside; it's bugging me like a three-inch mosquito on a hot day."

Rowan snickered again. "I like you," she said to Maggie. "If I didn't have other plans, we could have fun together."

Maggie grinned, and I shook my head. She was such a far cry from the little girl who'd peed her pants at the checkpoint. Rowan patted Maggie on the arm, gave her a wink, and then walked over and shoved Jess back into the grave. "Open it," she commanded in that creepy, childlike voice, and the rush of magic from her glamour was palpable.

Nastasia grabbed Rowan, but Rowan was quicker, twisting Nas's arm and taking her to the ground almost faster than I could see. Jess obediently got back on her hands and knees and pressed her fingers into the depressions on either side of Boudka's visage. A ping sounded as the latches popped loose.

"Turn me loose," Nastasia demanded.

"Then behave," Rowan said. "We're out of time."

"Let her go, Rowan!" I called up, and surprisingly, Rowan turned Nastasia loose without another word.

"I'm going to—"

"Stop, Nas! Save it for later," I said, then helped Jess off the top of the coffin.

We lifted the lid. It opened like your standard coffin, revealing a three-foot-deep space. I stared, then sighed in relief. It was empty, save three objects: a bóllom, a nisís, and a fat crystal the length of my forearm and roughly half that in width. It was a soulstone. I took the crystal, gingerly lifting it from the bottom. I twisted it around in the moonlight and held it up. "I got it!"

"Can I look at it?" Jess asked, and I handed her the crystal. It wasn't like she could hurt it. She had Nastasia help her out of the hole and then started examining it.

I retrieved the weapons, still in their Óṣení sheaths. I froze as I noted the pattern of knotwork. With trembling hands, I removed the bollóm. "Skaja ni Nemhain," the Óṣenic inscription read. I looked at the nisís. It held the same inscription. These were my blades.

Boudka wasn't here, but this proved three things. She was 'The Queen' that Marcella had been looking for. She was Queen Maeve of Irish legend, and Queen Maeve had been a real person despite the naysayers. She'd known I would come. She'd left these things for me.

"Cait," Jess called down. "I think we have a problem here."

I leaped out of the grave and landed next to Jess. Nastasia stood next to her, scowling at Rowan, who wore that creepy passive face she always had, as if she could slaughter us all in seconds, and it wouldn't matter one bit.

Jess turned the crystal over several times and stopped, examining one side. Then she turned it over again slowly, studying it more closely. "There's a defect. Is that going to matter?"

I scowled. "Where?" I reached out, and she handed it to me, pointing.

"Here." I followed her finger and saw what she did. Right in the middle of the stone was a molecule-thick crack that ran halfway through it.

"Fuck!" I shouted. "It's fucking broken. I can't use this." Tears welled in my eyes, and I dropped to the dirt, my shoulders shaking from the sobs.

"Cait," Maggie said, dropping next to me.

Gently, I peeled her hand away and stood, stifling my tears. "I'd like to be alone for a minute." Then I walked away toward one of the old overturned stone megaliths and sat down to bawl. This had been my only hope.

Rowan sat down next to me. She didn't touch me. She just picked a flower and twisted it in her fingers.

"Did you know?" I asked miserably.

She shook her head. "No."

I nodded. "The stone is useless." I sighed, defeated. "What am I going to do?"

"I might be able to answer that if I knew why you wanted it in the first place."

"My sister and a Kylr named Úmbra are inhabiting the same body," I said.

Rowan raised an eyebrow at that. "That sounds like a bit of a bind." She smiled at me as if one might smile at a disappointed kid. "But, Skaja, I know where you can find a better option."

I wiped my nose and eyes and looked at her. "Where? What?"

"Your mother's mantle," she grinned.

"Is my mother really dead?" I asked solemnly. I still didn't want to believe it.

Rowan nodded. "I believe so." She looked genuinely sad. She didn't even call me a child or little one or anything else condescending. "I'm sorry, Skaja. She began to fade only a few years ago. I think she used the last of her power to connect you to the past, to give you the skills you would need to survive."

"I wish she'd just come to see me instead," I muttered. "That would have been a better gift."

"Perhaps," Rowan said and squeezed my hand. "Perhaps."

CHAPTER THIRTY-THREE

"That's a problem, isn't it," Jess said as she and Maggie stood.

I followed her gaze. "Shit," I cursed as I spied what she'd spotted. South of us, a wide swath of Bethadi Knights in full armor rode on horseback toward us. They weren't charging, but they were moving at a solid canter.

"Run," I said, and we took off. I stowed my weapons and scooped up Maggie, running toward the woods to the north. Once inside, we'd be able to lose the mounted men. Their horses couldn't traverse the dense thicket like we could. Unfortunately, two dozen archers exited the woods with bows drawn as soon as we closed on the tree line. Several loosed arrows, knocking Nas and me to the ground with well-placed shots to the leg. Maggie spilled across the grass but hopped up, holding one of the Fae daggers.

"Come on!" she shouted, clearly as sick as I was at all of this stupidity.

I yanked the arrow from my leg with a grunt and stood.

"Well, fuck," Jess said, hands on her hips. "We're going to faerie jail, aren't we?"

I turned toward Rowan, hoping she could do something, but she was just gone, vanished into the aether like a wisp of smoke. "Yeah, Jess," I muttered quietly. "We probably are." I blew out an exasperated breath. "Fuck."

"Skaja ni Nemhain?" One of the archers said in Bethadi, lowering his weapon and stowing it. "You are to come with us to Luminara. The Queen wishes to speak with you."

Interesting, I thought. *Just 'The Queen,' not 'The Summer Queen.'* "My friends are not to be harmed," I called. "As the current reigning queen of Shaddan, I demand parley." I had no idea if it would work, but it was, I thought, actually a good bluff.

"We do not recognize your ascendancy," he said. "However, as a Princess of the House of the Morrigan, you will be welcomed as a guest. Your friends will be given accommodations."

"That's not a promise of safe passage," I challenged.

"I have none to give," the man answered just as the clopping of hooves stopped behind us.

I turned to glance back at the Knights, seeing one that I recognized. "Lugh? It's me, Skaja."

He nodded. "I know who you are, Skaja. The Queen has demanded we take you and your party into custody." I frowned and narrowed my eyes, but the pain on his face was evident. He didn't actually want to do this.

Several of the Knights dismounted and approached. Nastasia drew weapons, but I shook my head.

"Nas, Don't," I told her. "It'll be alright."

She looked at me, but then her eyes rolled back in her head, and she dropped to the grass, as did Maggie. A group of knights tackled Jess and swiftly trussed her up. I made to move, but the world spun and turned black around me.

CHAPTER THIRTY-FOUR

The blackness resolved itself into a room with bright fluorescent lights that glared down from overhead. I was strapped to a bed with thick but padded leather restraints. I tugged at them and found that they held me fast, but then, I'd expected that. This wasn't real. None of it was real, not the bed or padded walls, not even the door which stood just in view to my left, closed tight. It sported a small window of thick glass, just like in the movies. I snorted in mild amusement. *So,* I thought. *This is the game. I'm in an insane asylum, vampires aren't real, and I'm suffering from delusions.* It was sadly unimaginative for the Bethadi.

The door creaked open, and Nastasia strolled in. "Feeling any better? You had us all worried," she chirped, her kind smile a stark contrast to her sinister countenance. She might have been glamoured out of her gourd, but she was more likely just a construct of the glamour itself—a figment of my thoughts brought to life by Fae illusion.

"Sure," I said with a cold smirk and narrowed eyes. "You know, this isn't original—the whole insanity thing. It's been done in the movies and on TV a million times." I chuckled. "Even Joss Whedon used it for Buffy the Vampire Slayer. I mean, come on."

Nastasia sighed and wrote something on her pad. As I

watched her, I had to admit they'd done an excellent job. Gone was Nastasia's porcelain skin, replaced by a healthy, if still pale, human glow. Otherwise, the likeness was perfect, right down to those fabulous legs.

"Are you going to be a little less combative?" she asked dispassionately, her expression turning a little less welcoming and a little more grim. "I don't like having you restrained, or," she waved absently at the room with her pen, "in here. You've already put two orderlies in the hospital. And, while I know that you are restless and have been trained to fight, I'd prefer you kept that to a minimum."

I rolled my eyes. "Áine, or Wisteria, or whoever you are, this isn't going to work. You can't play on my guilt, and you won't send me around the twist. So, let's get on with the shock therapy or whatever other petty torture of the mind you have planned. I've already seen this plot. I'm going to promise to be good. You'll let me out of these restraints. Out there, I'll meet all the people who are in my life playing roles within what is supposed to be the real world, people my psyche has supposedly co-opted as villains or heroes in my delusion."

"Do you remember who I am?" Nastasia asked, and I rolled my eyes.

"Sure, you're Doctor Popov," I responded automatically. "No, wait. That's not right. You're—" I stared blankly for a second, digging into my thoughts. It took a moment to remember. "You're Nastasia Volkova, a—well, friend probably isn't the right word. But we were intimate, so I guess you could say we're allies."

She scribbled on her pad. "I see. Can I ask you something?"

"Sure, Doc," I said, still distracted by what I'd called her. It wasn't exactly a memory, but I'd had a moment of deja vu, for lack of a better term. I had been in this room before. I was sure of it, but I couldn't remember when. Something tickled at my right wrist, and I went to scratch at it, only to find I was still secured to the bed.

"Ms. Reagan?" The doctor said, getting my attention. "Did you hear the question?"

Had she asked me something? I must have lost my train of

thought. "No. I'm sorry. What did you say?"

"Which do you think is more likely? That you are a vampire struggling against some unknowable, nameless force of evil and the predations of humanity, or that you are struggling with your own guilt?"

I looked at her and was reminded once again that, Goddess, she was beautiful: her liquid brown eyes, that shoulder-length, silky black hair, her long legs crossed at the knee slipping into the darkness beneath her pencil skirt. It was all the same. The high heel of her left foot was trying to wiggle loose to dangle from her toes. But I supposed that was to be expected. This was glamour, after all. Interesting that she was the shrink. But then again, I never met one that didn't need one, so I went with it.

"Did I lose you again?" She asked.

"No," I said, keeping my tone neutral. I wasn't going to figure this out from the bed, so I needed to at least be cooperative. "Yes, all things being equal, if vampires aren't real, then it is more likely that I have deluded myself into believing I'm one because of trauma. But what trauma?"

The doctor raised a cool eyebrow. "That is a conversation for the psychologist. I'm going to give you something that should help you think more clearly. Hopefully, we can avoid any further full-blown episodes."

"What's wrong with me?" I asked, already knowing the answer.

The doctor stood and looked down at me with a fake smile that fit her face perfectly. "In medical terms, you are suffering from a severe depersonalization and derealization disorder complicated by complex post-traumatic stress. In simpler terms, you're imagining a better world because you are so traumatized as to believe it is easier to deal with than coping with this one."

I smirked. "Like I said, not original. Whoever cooked this up needs to stay away from screenplays."

The doctor nodded sadly. "Perhaps, but since you seem lucid, I think we can release you from your restraints. Please stop tonguing your medication, though, Ms. Reagan. It really is for your own good."

I sighed and felt a disconcerting lessening of my stress. Breathing wasn't supposed to affect me that way.

A nurse stepped in with a tiny dixie cup and a medicine dispensation cup. "Open up," she said.

"You're the boss, but it'll come up in an hour."

She smiled. "Let's hope not," she said. "You're my hero, Ms. Reagan. Remember?"

I frowned at that but did as she asked, taking the medication and the swallow of water that accompanied it. I opened my mouth and moved my tongue around to show I'd taken it. I'd seen the movies. I knew how this worked. And this was just like them, to a tee.

About ten minutes later, an orderly, a black man in his forties, came in to let me out of my restraints. He looked familiar, but I couldn't place him. Once I was up, I thanked him and followed him out of the padded cell and into a hallway. A little further down, he pressed a button, and a pair of double doors opened, letting us in. Beyond was a short hallway with two small meeting rooms, one on either side. A side passage on my right led to a veranda where a few folks were smoking cigarettes. I had the urge to go bum one but suppressed it. At the end of the hallway on the left corner was an observation room with thick glass, and a common room sat beyond.

It was what I'd expected: some tables, a few blandly colored chairs, two mid-sized couches from Cold War East Germany, and a small flat-screen television hanging from the wall playing an old John Wayne western. Again, it was the same cliché setting as everything else. The far wall had a long series of thick windows with bars that looked out over a small garden area surrounded by dense trees. I had to admit, the view was peaceful, even if the bars made it seem a bit confining.

Who was I kidding? It was very confining. This was a minimum security state forensic unit—a hospital for people who had committed crimes but were deemed incompetent to stand trial. I'd never seen the inside of one before, so clearly, not everything had been pulled from my own memories.

I sat down at one of the tables and tried to shift my perspective. Nothing happened. I frowned. If this were glamour, I should at least be able to see it. Something of this complexity should show itself in the tarzhi, but there was nothing. I tried again. Again, there was nothing, and the edge of panic began to creep under my skin.

I stomped on my fear as best I could and looked at the clock. It was twelve-thirty. I did a quick mental calculation. I figured I had about forty-five minutes before the pills came back up, assuming they were even real. I had to admit, this was the most realistic glamour I'd ever heard of. Even the crappy burlap-like upholstery on the furniture felt real.

With nothing else to do, I dropped into a plastic chair and watched 'Hondo.' It was a good movie. I wasn't a big fan of John Wayne like— I stumbled, losing the thought. I'd been thinking someone's name, but it slipped away. Had it been my da, maybe? I couldn't remember.

The specter of doubt began to creep in despite my best intentions. Could this be the real world? Maybe I had lost it. I remembered my nightmares of Mosul vividly, but my memories of Marcella and the Caldwell case seemed more fuzzy. What was worse, something about this place seemed terribly familiar, and I didn't know why.

I tried to ignore it and focus on the movie, but it just wouldn't go away, and it scared me more than I wanted to admit.

CHAPTER THIRTY-FIVE

When I sat down, the movie was about over, so I only saw the last fifteen minutes. Afterward, I found a set of colored pencils and some paper, so I decided to draw. At first, I wasn't sure what I was drawing. It was a narrow face with high cheekbones and soft, full lips. Over the course of a few minutes, it began to take shape. It was good, actually. Better than I expected. The face, the emerald green eyes, and the blonde hair made me feel a pang of loss.

"Hey, stranger," someone said to me. She had a bit of an East London accent.

I looked up, and a mixture of both joy and a hint of something painful swirled inside me. It was Liz, or at least, an excellent facsimile of her. Like me, she wore basic, ugly brown scrubs. However, underneath her top, she had on a long-sleeved undershirt, and lace-up sneakers adorned her feet rather than slip-ons. But in every sense, including her dragon's blood scent, she looked and sounded and smelled like Liz.

"Hi," I said, then lowered my voice. "You know who I am?"

Liz raised an eyebrow and smiled. "Of course I do, Cait. We've been cooped up here together for six months now."

A mild itch started in my right wrist, and I scratched at it absently. "Six months," I repeated quietly. "Has it really been that long?" A vague memory twisted around in my head like a slippery thing. I was in chains and an orange jumpsuit, being dragged through large hospital doors. I pushed it aside.

I had been in Ireland, headed toward somewhere. It didn't matter. I remembered the plane, the fighters, the horses. That was the truth. But a small niggling part of me had begun to question it. My meeting with Nastasia or Doctor Popov had seriously fucked with me. *No*, I thought. *No. These are memories planted by the Light Fae.* But my feelings, when I saw Liz. Those were real. And the way she smiled at me like she always did was filled with love.

"Katie is still having lunch, but she'll join us for cards," Liz said, and then she frowned. "Hey, are you alright?"

I shook my head, feeling lost. "Katie?"

"Our adopted daughter, remember?" Liz said, and I breathed a sigh of relief.

"Wait, what are you doing here?" I asked, now thoroughly confused. "I don't understand?"

Liz laid a hand on my forearm. "Bad day?" Her voice was gentle, but her eyes were full of pain, glistening, almost wet.

"Liz?"

She sniffed and used her free hand to paw away tears. "Sorry. I thought we agreed not to talk about it, you know? How I got here. I don't want to think about it." She blinked away the tears and then muscled her lips back into a smile. "Besides, you look like you could use a happy face." Her voice was still a little choked.

I shook my head, not sure what to say. "I love you," I said and put a hand on hers.

She nodded. "I know you do."

"Hey, mama," Katie said, walking up to us. I was thankful, feeling awkward and unsure of what to say. This couldn't be Liz and Katie, I knew. But after Doctor Popov, I needed them close, and it was easy to give in to the temptation to lean into the glamour. *Just a little bit*, I told myself.

"Hi, Katie," I said. "How was school?"

"Oh, you know. The usual, on-line classes. But Auntie Liz has been helping me with my math assignments."

Emotions swam in my chest. This seemed so right, and yet,

everything was wrong. I was stuck in Fae glamour, that was certain. I didn't know how they'd stripped me of my magic or why I suddenly felt the need to breathe and eat, but it had to be part of the same thing.

"Mama?" Katie prodded. "Are you okay?"

"No, Katie," I said, my voice small and afraid. "I'm not."

"I know," Katie said brightly. "Maybe you'll feel better if you tell us a story about who we are in the real world."

I screwed up my face. "Huh?"

"Another story. I really liked the Christmas story. That was really sweet. Or maybe you could tell us again about how we all met. I really like that one, especially the part where I couldn't remember anything. I'd give anything for that right now."

An icepick of fear drilled into my chest. No. That wasn't right. I felt abject terror. I quickly pulled away from Liz and slid my chair back, then stood and backed away.

"You're not real," I said in a panic. "You're not real." They couldn't be real. Were they escaping in my delusion? Had I actually lost it? *You lost it a long time ago,* a voice said in my head. It sounded familiar, but I wasn't sure. There was something weird about it. I'd heard it before, but I couldn't remember when. *Just go back. Be with them. They're your family now.*

"Mother?" I whimpered. It sounded like my mother, my real mother, the one with jet-black hair and green eyes—the tall one who liked to fight. Wait, no. She wasn't my mother, was she? I had her eyes, but… "Goddess, why am I so confused?" I clenched my fists and squeezed my eyes shut, trying to remember my mothers, both of them. But the only face that came to mind was a woman with my eyes and beautiful black hair, strong and powerful. My thoughts twisted. It wasn't her.

But I am, the voice said, and the tone was achingly sweet. I never wanted it to go.

Seeing my distress, Katie turned to Liz. "Bad day?" She asked, and Liz nodded.

"Doctor Popov," Liz commented. "Cait, honey, try to relax. It's okay. I know you're having a bad day. Try to remember

Christmas. That was sweet."

I blinked and looked around, confused. "Christmas," I said to myself. "Right." Katie, Liz, and I had been in Marcella's sitting room. I was sick with the flu. I gave Liz the earrings. Liz gave me—something—my thoughts stumbled. I couldn't remember. It was in a bag. Or was it a box? Or both, maybe. I couldn't remember. *Why can't I remember?*

Because it wasn't real, the voice said. *It's okay, let it go.*

"No. It was real. I was there," I muttered and pushed my chair back so hard that I fell over onto the floor.

Two orderlies rushed out of the observation room and helped me up.

"You okay, darlin'?"

"Carlos?" I said, looking up at him. "But—"

He cocked his head forward, waiting for me to say more, but I snapped my mouth shut. It was him. It was Carlos, in a white uniform. An embroidered rainbow patch was stitched into his collar. I looked at the other orderly. I didn't recognize him. He was a tall, broad-shouldered white man, maybe in his forties, but his hair had already gone gray, making him look much older.

"Yeah," I said finally. "I'm okay."

"Reagan," someone called from the unit entrance. "Therapy."

Carlos looked at me with concern, stroking his beard. "Are you going to be okay? Do you want to skip therapy today?"

I shook my head. If anyone was going to shed some light on this madness, it would probably be the therapist. I just needed to keep my wits about me. "No," I said, my throat feeling a little thick. "No. I'm fine."

Carlos led me to the double doors and pulled up a set of keys on a short wire, rifling through them. "You're not gonna give me any trouble now, are you?"

"No," I said, shaking my head. "No trouble."

There was no point. I'd already figured out that the only way out of this was through. I needed to figure out what the game was. There was always a game. The Light Fae toyed with people, seeing how far they could push them before they broke. But I wouldn't break. I couldn't. Aoife was counting on me. "I need to help my sister," I said. "It doesn't do to make my situation worse. It'll just take longer."

"Uh, huh," Carlos said skeptically and unlocked the doors.

I looked back. Katie and Liz were talking and watching me. Katie looked a little heartbroken and for a moment, I thought I saw a tear fall across Liz's cheek. *They're not real,* I told myself. *None of this is real. You can't get sucked in.*

Who are you trying to convince? The voice in my head replied. *You can't escape your own guilt.*

Carlos escorted me from the room, and the doors closed behind me with an ominous thunk. For a moment, I felt like Jack Nicholson being taken to shock therapy in 'One Flew Over the Cuckoo's Nest.' But that was just a movie and not at all what mental treatment facilities were like. No one did lobotomies or shock therapy for psychosis anymore. In most cases, they were reasonable and humane.

After a quick right and another left, we arrived at an office. Carlos opened the door, and I walked in. I snorted and shook my head. "Of course, it would be you," I said.

CHAPTER THIRTY-SIX

"I'm glad you decided to come this week," Jennifer said as I walked in. "Grab a seat."

Jennifer was in her usual jeans and Bryn Mawr sweatshirt. The office looked in many ways like her office in real life. *No,* I thought. *It looks exactly like this.*

Behind her was her bookshelf, loaded with psychology books and a few older bits of literature, mainly philosophy. On the credenza beneath the window sat her happy little fern, its fronds waving gently from the air conditioning. I sat down on the long couch adorning the right-hand wall, and Jennifer, as usual, came around and sat in the soft, gray, cushioned chair opposite. She even had her shoes off, like she always did when I came to see her.

I pushed down the sense of panic that was gnawing at me. "So," I said with forced glibness. "This is a new concept, faeries putting the vampire on the couch. You know, in real life, you're my therapist, too." I scratched absently at my wrist again. It still itched.

"Why do you think that is?" Jennifer asked.

I shrugged. "What does it matter? They can't keep me in here forever."

Jennifer nodded and then gave me that disarming smile she had when she was humoring me. "That may be so, but for now, you're here. So, why not make the most of it?"

"Okay," I said, drawing out the word in exasperation. "Fine. What would you like to talk about?"

Jennifer chuckled. "I think that's my line."

"You want to talk about the war?" Reclining to get comfortable, I leaned back, kicked off the slip-on sneakers, and put my feet up on the couch. "Oh," I said, forestalling Jennifer's reply. "You don't mind, do you?"

"Do you?" She asked, and it occurred to me that they must have dug fairly deeply into my psyche at some point to get all of these details right. Whenever Jennifer wanted to challenge me on something, she would tilt her head slightly, just as she did now.

"Not at all," I answered with a smirk. "I think it's very comfortable."

"No, Cait," she said dryly. "Do you want to talk about the war?"

I raised a hand nonchalantly in a 'whatever' gesture.

"How are you coping with your memories of the war? More importantly, though, I'd like to know specifically how you're handling your incident with Sgt. Holley."

"Why are Liz and Katie here?" I asked, avoiding the obvious trap. I didn't feel like digging into Holley at the moment, anyway. That was too raw. It was too soon.

"We've talked about this, Cait. You already know why she's here. She told you."

Then I remembered. "She killed her children. Is that why she's here?"

Jennifer nodded in confirmation. "Are you having trouble remembering that?"

I shook my head, but that was a lie. I was having problems remembering everything. It was as if the life I was sure was my own was a dream, and it was slipping away, being replaced by this worse, far more awful existence. "Katie killed her parents, didn't she?" I asked, my voice starting to tremble slightly.

"You know that, too. But I want to know why you are avoiding the question about Sgt. Holley and your assault."

I frowned. Jennifer would never push me to talk about something unless I wanted to. If I deflected on something, she generally left it alone until I came back around to it. This wasn't like her. But I had this awful feeling that maybe, just maybe, it was. Maybe Popov had been right. Maybe I was running from something. No. That couldn't be. I remembered other things in perfect detail. My memory of— Aoife. It took a second to remember her name.

"Cait?" Jennifer probed. "Where are you?"

I shook my head. "I'm right here. What is the question?"

"No, I want to know what you were thinking about."

"I was thinking about Aoife, my sister."

Jennifer gave me a puzzled look. "You mean Drusera," she said.

I shook my head. "Right. Umm—Drusera, sorry. I—" My head felt fuzzy, and my thoughts were slow. It might have been whatever they made me swallow. "What was I saying?"

"How are you handling your trauma?" She asked. "What are your thoughts around Sgt. Holley?"

"Oh. He's dead," I answered, almost automatically, as if it didn't matter.

"Is he now?" Jennifer asked, scribbling something on her legal pad. "And how did he die?"

"Heart attack," I said blandly. "Real shame." My right wrist itched again, and I rubbed it. *What is up with that?!*

"I see. So you had nothing to do with his death?"

I shook my head. "Of course not. I'm not a murderer."

Liar, the voice whispered. *You're a cold-blooded killer. You shot him.*

She scribbled something on her legal pad. "Are you sure that he died of a heart attack?"

I looked at her then. Why would she ask that? It was a dead giveaway as to the nature of the delusion. I frowned. "Of course." I shook my head again as an image of Holley intruded on my thoughts. He was kneeling in front of me, begging for his life as I held a gun to his head. *No,* I told myself. *That's not right. That's not what happened. I glamoured him. He…*

"Cait?" Jennifer prodded, tearing me from the violent images.

I focused on her once more. "Yes, Doc?"

"How did you come to be here?"

"I told you. I… I…" My thoughts stuttered to a halt. An arrest. I'd been arrested. Blood covered my hands. "No," I said, getting agitated now. "This is all Fae glamour."

"Perhaps, but what do you remember?" Jennifer said. Her tone had turned gentle and coaxing. It was meant to be encouraging, I was sure, but it was getting on my nerves, especially because what I remembered seemed broken.

I remembered two different scenarios at the same time, and I couldn't keep them straight. I remembered watching Holley die of a heart attack, but there was another image that kept popping into my head. Holley was on the ground, a bullet in his head. I was beating his dead body with the butt of his own .45. That wasn't right. That couldn't be right. But it felt right. Certainly more right than the other memory. "No, no, no," I said, my voice rising in pitch. "That's not right. I didn't. I didn't do that."

Jennifer set her pen and pad down on the desk and then turned back to me. "Talk to me, Cait. What is it?"

I looked up at her, first in horror, then rage. "You can't do this to me," I shouted. "It's not what happened! I'm a vampire. I—"

"Cait," Jennifer said, a warning in her tone. "I'm going to need you to take a breath."

"A breath?" I laughed maniacally. "A breath? I don't fucking need to breathe!" But I did. I tried to stop breathing, but it only took a few seconds before the need forced me to take in air.

"No," I whispered. "It's not possible. Curses can't be undone. They can't." The room began to spin, and my head buzzed. Lights and spots clouded my vision. I couldn't get air.

Somewhere, dimly, I knew that I was hyperventilating. I crumpled to the floor, desperate for oxygen. "No," I tried to say through my wheezing gasps, but all that came out was a strangled noise.

"I have a medical emergency in my office," Jennifer said to

someone. Was she on the phone? Then she was next to me, whispering in my ear. "It's okay, Caitlin. Try to take a breath."

My right wrist burned, but I couldn't move. "No," I finally breathed. My voice sounded tiny and distressed. "No. I can't go through that again." Another memory of kicking in the door of Holley's shitty apartment. I tried to push it aside, trying to remember what had really happened. I was with someone, someone who needed my protection.

Liar, my head screamed at me. *You were exacting your own revenge. You shot him!*

"No." But my denial sounded hollow. *Did I? Had I shot him? If I did, then what? Am I delusional? Like—like Gabe.* Another memory. Something different. Gabe in my doorway. He was drunk. I was screaming at him, beating him with my fists. I scratched at my wrist again, trying to alleviate the accursed itching. *God, it won't stop.* Where was that bloody voice now? Where was Drusera? Where was she when I needed her most to tell me what was real and what wasn't? *Where are you, sister?*

Something bit into my upper arm, and moments later, my panicked thoughts turned foggy, syrupy, and sluggish. My breathing slowed as a drowsy bliss took hold, stealing away the fear.

"Take her back to her room," Jennifer said. Her voice sounded worried, but it was so very far away. "No restraints. She just had a panic attack. Let her sleep it off."

Strong arms hoisted me up and dragged me away. I didn't remember getting to my room, but I found myself in my bed sometime later. I tried to keep my eyes open, but the lids wouldn't stay up.

Sleep, the voice in my head said. It sounded close. It was Drusera's voice.

"Nice of you to finally show up," I murmured drowsily.

I'm here, she said seductively. *It'll be okay.*

I couldn't resist the tug of sleep, and my eyes fell shut. The sounds in the hall outside filled with cottony, muffling goose down, and then they vanished.

CHAPTER THIRTY-SEVEN

I awoke later to a darkened room. The door was open, but the hallway lights were dimmed. A small bowl of red jello with a plastic spoon sat on the nightstand next to my bed, along with a neatly written note: "So you don't starve. With love, Elizabeth."

"Liz," I murmured, seeing her in my thoughts, beautiful and pale, not that facsimile I'd seen in the lounge. *I have to get back to her,* I thought. *She's not really here. This isn't real.* Just then, my stomach rumbled. That felt real, as did the brief pang of hunger that followed. I picked up the bowl of gelatin and took a bite. At least it was cherry and not lime-flavored. I really hated the lime crap. They always served it here on Tuesdays. I'd started calling it Limey Tuesdays, mostly to dig at Liz playfully.

My eyes narrowed at that. *Limey Tuesdays?* I thought. *No. This is wrong. It's powerful glamour, more powerful than I'd ever heard of, but it's just glamour. Isn't it?*

Rage instantly flooded my chest, squeezing at my lungs and licking my ribs. I tried to throw the foam bowl across the room, but it flew about three feet before tilting and dropping the jello to the floor in a clumpy mess. *Leah would have a fit if she saw that. Red's her favorite.*

"Leah," I whispered to myself. "Hold onto that thought." I

could see her face, her gray eyes watching me brightly as she, Katie, and I played cards. Katie had a bag of A-negative. I remembered thinking that she should be drinking the AB-positive, just in case I had some kind of relapse, but I never said anything. Leah was laughing. I didn't make her up. How could I have? And Katie? And Marcella? And Mother Lamia? *No way. I'm not that fucking imaginative.* I scratched my wrist.

"What *is* that?" I bitched quietly as my nails scraped at the underside of my arm. My wrist itched to absolute distraction. As I scratched, for just a split second, I felt something hard and metallic brush my fingertips. That jarred loose a memory, warm and loving—*Liz and Cait, best of friends.* A grim smile crossed my face, and I relaxed. I knew what it was.

"Remember Christmas," Liz had said.

Someone had once told me, "Love, my daughter, is one of the most powerful magics in all worlds. It binds others to us and us to them."

Liz and Katie were actually here. Their presence was drawn into the glamour because I loved them, and they loved me. They might not even be aware of it, or perhaps it was a dream for them.

I closed my eyes and focused on my wrist—the feeling of it —the itch. It wasn't an itch at all—it was cold metal.

Another memory came to me. I had been in the bath with— with that woman who said the thing—the thing about love and magic. She had said, "Boudka has magic in her, for sure, but I've yet to figure out how to unlock it. And given all the interest you've shown in developing your own skills, you'd be at the mercy of those flippant dimwits, too."

Yes, Drusera exclaimed in my head, exuding a triumphant glee. *It's a lie. You know it's a lie.*

My grim smile turned to quiet satisfaction as I began to unravel what was happening. This wasn't the Light Fae at all. This was Shaddani magic, amplifying my gift. That's why I hadn't been able to see it.

I concentrated on the sight once more, willing myself to see. I reached out with that familiar sense, that feeling inside I got when I glamoured someone. An ache set itself up behind my eyes, but the world flickered. Whoever held me fought back, snapping this fake world back into focus. But this was my body and my mind, and I now knew these memories to be false, this world to be nothing but glamour.

Instead of continuing to look outward, I closed my eyes and looked inward toward my own soul. My mind's eye exploded with light, shadow, and silver as I saw my soul shrouded in the Dark Gift. My Dark Gift. It was mine, it answered to me. I still couldn't see anything around me, not yet, but it was final confirmation of what I suspected.

Now, I focused outward. I lashed out at the blackness, seeking a mind, any mind, to invade with my glamour. I found seven. My Gift faded from sight, revealing a massive spherical construct, an egg of sorts, fully enclosing my body. I felt a moment of disorientation as the glamour faded and gravity seemed to twist violently. I was kneeling on a stone floor, marble by the feel of it.

I only caught a glimpse of the cocooning magic before my gift slammed shut once more, but it was enough. *Oh, but this is a brilliant magical construct,* I thought with admiration as it all made sense. It was two spells. One, Shaddani, tremendously powerful, shielded my perception and bolstered the power of my gift to keep me in the dark. The other hovered a hairsbreadth beyond in the brilliant silvers and golds of Bethadi glamour, wrapped incredibly closely around the first, fed from six different directions. That was the one I needed to disrupt.

"Caitlin?" A voice called from somewhere, the door, I thought. "Oh, God, Caitlin."

Arms grabbed me. I was running out of time. Whoever controlled the glamour was trying to slam it shut and distract me. I tugged at the arm, and the darkness grew thicker. That was the wrong move. I needed to ignore them.

"Medical Emergency!" someone yelled. I dismissed it.

I couldn't possibly unravel something so massive without being able to see it. Maybe Aoife could, but I just didn't have her raw talent. What I did have was brute force. I pushed at the shroud of my gift from within, using the energy of my soul. The curse didn't want to let any slip away, and it drank greedily at it, but I pushed harder anyway, reaching out for those minds again.

My head hammered, and my nerves sang with prickling pain. The rifling bees of the hunger traveled across my skin like ripples over and over, each increasing tenfold in intensity. The light of my soul flickered beneath the shadows, dying out like a sputtering flame. Still, I pushed and reached out, grabbing the minds I found. I couldn't get them all, but I was able to see six. They were staticky and strange, muffled somehow, but I had a hold of them. I dragged at their memories, trying desperately to hold on.

Finally, I broke through like a flashlight piercing a thinning fog. Blue, purple, and vermillion magic swirled around me in a lattice, binding me. Beyond lay the magic of the glamour. I eased the pressure slightly and tugged at the strands of Light Fae magic. Shockingly, they responded, deforming close to the egg of Dark Fae magic before slapping back into place with an almost audible THWACK. I tugged harder, feeling my skin start to burn and flake.

I focused on just a few of them and yanked. They deformed again, and for just a split-second, the real world shone through, filled with gold, white, and silver tarzhi. I was definitely kneeling on a marble floor. It flickered into view, and then it was gone again as something yanked back hard.

"Oh, no," I growled defiantly. "You will not keep me here."

I yanked with all that I had. Cold, syrupy blood ran down my cheeks from my eyes. I was killing myself with the effort, but I would have to free myself from this prison. If Nastasia or Jess had been able to do it, they would have already. I was on my own.

A scream of rage and power sang from my throat. Blood seemed to be pouring from under my lids, trickling from my mouth, and falling in thick drops from my ears. I tore at the tarzhi, looping the threads of Bethadi magic, forcing them to touch the Shaddani construct. When they did finally touch, there wasn't some big explosion, which I'd expected, just a soft pop.

The entire structure unraveled like so much yarn and spun

away. The fog in my thoughts, the false memories, they all snapped away, almost as if they'd never been there. The world around me materialized in gorgeous, glowing focus, full of life and color. The tarzhi of Earth, Bethad, and Shaddan swirled in a dissipating maelstrom. As a last hateful act, I tore violently at the six minds I'd found, clawing chunks of whatever I could find within.

I lay half sprawled, half kneeling on a blood-splattered white marble floor. Encircling me, six magi in the mustard and brown master's robes of the Bethadi Magical Academy lay stunned on the floor, several of them bleeding from their ears and attended by men and women in robes of white. I didn't think they were dead, but they didn't look fabulous. Not far behind one of them, I spotted a face I knew: Wisteria. Her hair was colored a pretty fuchsia, but it was her.

I knelt on hands and knees in a long hall with grand white columns stretching to a vaulted ceiling high above. Beautiful frescoes that would have taken Michaelangelo to tears adorned the ceiling.

The artwork appeared to be historical depictions, but I only recognized one. It depicted a single knight on horseback casting a glowing spear at a great six-legged beast with one huge red eye.

The interpretation is a little loose, I thought. I'd been there. My mother, who had saved Lugh from certain incineration, was nowhere to be found in the painting. I wasn't shocked.

"Your raw power is impressive," a voice called from ahead of me. "It took six of our best magi to hold you in glamour. And now look at them."

Trying to rise, I found my hands shackled in gleaming gold bonds that held me to the ground, sapping my strength. I looked up at the throne and swallowed hard. The source of the Shaddani magic that had encased me sat quietly on the throne of The Summer Queen: Badb.

"Hello, Auntie," I wheezed out raggedly with a bloody grimace. "Long time no see."

Badb stood, green eyes intense and alight with curiosity. "I had my doubts, but it really is you, Skaja. Though, it seems that something is missing."

"Maybe you could let me out of these cuffs and treat me like family."

She gave a bark of laughter. "But, Skaja, this is how we treat family, don't you know that? Keeping a child locked away, unable to move." She strode in long, languorous steps toward me and drew out a wicked-looking dagger that glowed a luminous white. Placing it under my chin, she tugged my gaze further up by the point to meet her eyes. "I think perhaps I don't need you after all." She drew back with a cruel smile as if to drive the knife into my chest.

"Get away from her!" Nastasia cried from somewhere behind me. There was a scuffle, and a whoosh of air ruffled my hair as Nas's booted feet shot past me. Surprisingly, she made it, sinking a blade into my aunt's chest. "Die, you faerie bitch!"

Badb simply snatched Nastasia by the neck and stood, dangling her above the floor. With her other hand, she plucked the blade from her chest.

"Oh, child," Badb said menacingly. "You shouldn't have."

"No!" I protested through a bloody cough, but there was nothing I could do. Badb plunged the glowing dagger into Nastasia's heart.

I gasped in horror. Jess screamed. Badb dropped Nastasia to the floor, and Nas turned back, looking not at Jess but at me. She gave me a sad smile, one hand on the dagger hilt. "I love you," she whispered, and then her body just disintegrated, the magic of her Dark Gift unraveling like the frayed edge of a badly woven rug. There was a moment of stunned silence as we all watched Nastasia's body crumble to ash.

Jess went berserk, tearing the throat from the knight that had hold of her and charging across the floor toward Badb. But as soon as she got within reach, she stopped cold and fell to her knees. She screamed in helpless rage, unable to move any further, no matter how she struggled. It took six knights to restrain her and drag her back, forcing her to kneel next to me. This time, they locked manacles around her wrists and ankles, clearly not wanting to make the same mistake twice.

"And I think that will just about cover the heroics for

today," my aunt said, her cold, pretentious smile returning.

My eyes burned with tears as my vision tunneled in on Badb. The entire room dimmed, and thunder rolled outside, rattling the stained glass windows. My fangs lowered, and I growled at her. "I'll kill you for that. I will tear your heart from your chest and eat it in front of you."

Badb took a half step back, a startled look in her eyes.

"What, auntie?" I spat. "Scared?"

She composed her features quickly and gave an imperious wave. "Take them away. Lock the feral pixie in a cage, but keep her close. I want a word with her. Take the infected human and my—" She paused for a moment, her face showing a sudden conflict of emotions. "Take the infected human Veria for treatment and take my niece to the dungeon."

Maggie clenched her fists and started to struggle as they began to manhandle her, but I shook my head at her questioning gaze. "Don't," I mouthed at her, and we were both dragged from the room.

CHAPTER THIRTY-EIGHT

I ended the night stuffed into a tiny oubliette-like cell about three feet square, the only exit an iron grate twenty feet above me. I could have easily climbed to the grate, but the sun had risen, and there was no opening it for now.

The trip down here had been long, especially given my limited movement. I had snorted in a sort of enraged amusement as I shuffled along, realizing that I now knew how all of those poor bastards I'd put away must have felt as they were shipped off to jail, in many cases for life.

Every step was a short scuff of my feet, and each and every stair had to be traversed one step at a time. If I stumbled, there was no real way to catch myself, as my wrist shackles were attached to the ankle chain by a long, inflexible pole. It was slow and certainly gave me ample time to consider every dark feeling pooling in the pit of my stomach and crushing my chest.

Somewhere, probably halfway down, Veria, Aine's Magi Advisor, took Maggie away. At least he promised to try to help her. I took little comfort in that, though I did believe him. He'd certainly tried to help Boudka. Perhaps it would be different this time, but I doubted it. Maggie's body was suffused with the darkest of Shaddani magic, the kind that fed on everything you threw at it.

Finally, we reached a door, and I shuffled into a long hallway stinking of damp, mildew, and dust. Green algae and moss bloomed on the walls, probably a result of sinking the palace into the high water table so close to Lough Key.

Along one side was a series of Fae-steel grates covering a long row of oubliettes like the one in which I currently stood. Along the other was a series of cells with thick metal doors, reminiscent of the cells the council had constructed near the gate chamber.

At least the shackles had been removed when I'd been dropped in here, vanishing from my wrists and ankles when I hit bottom and reappearing in the guard's hands. They hadn't even bothered to lower a rope, just shoving me into the deep stone hole and letting me crack my elbows and head on the way down. *Assholes.*

Fatigue dragged at my limbs as I leaned against the wall. Goddess, I was tired. My chest felt as if it would collapse in on itself; it hurt so badly. I remembered Morgan telling me at one point that when Aoife had been shot, she'd been shocked at how much physical agony a vampire could feel with such painful emotions. I had just nodded. I knew all too well.

I'd failed. It was that simple. Nastasia was gone. I'd never faced a loss like this. I'd come close with Liz and Katie, but this, never. I'd loved Nastasia more than I ever realized. Maybe I had no business marrying Liz. It seemed like I was born under an angry star, and she certainly deserved a better life after all she'd been through, she and Katie and Leah. I'd let myself be just a little bit selfish, believing I could have that happiness and of course, a minute later, here I was.

"Fuck," I muttered morosely and let my tears of desolation fall; there was no point in hiding them. *It never stops,* I thought. "What did I do to deserve this?"

"Those sound like tears of grief," a voice called from a tiny vent near the top of the oubliette. It had a slight sickly rasp to it, but underneath was a mellifluous cadence that spoke of an aristocratic upbringing. It was almost familiar.

"Who's there?" I called shakily, trying and failing to hide my misery.

"Why are you crying, child?" The voice asked, ignoring the question.

I thought perhaps it was just one of Badb's tricks, but I had nothing to hide. I wasn't a spy, and I didn't have any helpful intel. It wouldn't hurt to be honest at this point. "Because I fucked up. I trusted the wrong person, and she led me into a trap."

"Ahh." I couldn't identify the speaker, though I'd definitely heard her before. "Are you sure you were led into a trap or just stumbled into one?"

"Well, my guide just fucked off when the bad guys showed up," I answered angrily. "Same result. All I know for certain is that we found Boudka's tomb—she was a former lover of mine —and now here we are. I'm trapped down here, and my friends are captives elsewhere. Both of them are very sick. One seems to be losing her mind, and the other is infected with this black goop that shouldn't even be in Ireland." I dropped back to the floor and let my hands fall into my lap as the tears flowed again. "And a woman—a friend—someone that I loved dearly, she's dead. Badb killed her, and it's my fault."

"I'm sorry," the voice said as gently as its ragged nature would allow. "But it's not the first time you've dealt with the death of someone you loved, is it?"

"No," I said dejectedly. "But not like this."

"Are you quite sure?" The voice asked, and I could almost hear the raised eyebrow.

"Who are you?" I demanded, scowling at the vent now.

"Do you not remember me?" There was an edge of melancholy to the voice, but beneath that, something almost manic. "Perhaps not. We spent so little time together, and yet a part of me lives on in you."

I blinked and furrowed my brow, puzzled. "What are you talking about?"

Humorless laughter filtered through the tiny hole. "They used to call me The Summer Queen, though that title has little meaning now."

Shock ran through me. "Áine, I thought you were dead."

"No, not yet, but soon, Skaja." I could hear a slight smile in her words. "Skaja is okay, yes?"

"Sure. What difference does it make?" And indeed, that's how I felt. It made no difference who I was, Skaja, Cait, Weyna —three names, same fate.

"We all fail. The greater the risks we take, the greater the consequences. It is the nature of living, I'm afraid. I failed my daughter. Badb took refuge in Bethad after she attacked me, biding her time until she found the perfect moment. She knew she could never take me in a stand-up fight, so she took Wisteria hostage and demanded the throne. But Dark Fae were never meant to rule the light."

"The corruption," I said, slowly beginning to untangle the web in which I sat.

"Yes. Her rule manifests itself not as darkness but as a twisting of our people toward malevolence—well, more malevolence, anyway. Now, she has command of our world, our magic, and my people. She cannot wield our magic directly, though, not yet. But in time—"

"In time, the magic will become so twisted that it will bend to her will," I finished for her.

"You understand. I see you've become quite the quick study." She gave a horrid rasping cough, wet and thick. "I'm sorry. I'm not long for this life, it would seem, which is a shame. I would very much like to talk to my daughter before I am gone."

"I just saw her in the throne room," I countered. "I don't understand."

Her voice took on a deep, despairing tone. "Badb has commanded her neither to hear my words nor speak with me. My isolation has been almost complete for thirty of our years now. But now, you are here, and despite your rather dire circumstances, I am grateful."

"At least I know why my mother never found Badb for all her searching," I said.

"Indeed," Áine responded quietly, her tenor almost thoughtful. "I understand that you are grieving for your lover, but I have to ask. How much of you is Skaja, and how much of you is…"

"Cait. They call me Cait now." I swallowed hard. "I don't know, to be honest. I don't think I can tell the difference anymore."

"Pardon me for being forward, but it seems you need a kick in the proverbial arse. You didn't curl up into a ball when Boudka died."

"Not helping," I shot back angrily. "Especially given that you could have saved her."

"Yes," Áine sighed. "Possibly not my finest moment, but if I had saved her, who knows what would have become of you? And you were instrumental in closing the gate. That, however, is neither here nor there. I seem to recall you setting off a veritable riot in the camp when Boudka died. So, it's hard to imagine you just giving up."

"But it's my fault," I argued, still not seeing her point.

"Is it? Let's say that's true. What does it matter?"

"You're not listening—" I started, but she cut me off.

"I most certainly am. You have friends that are still alive, yes?"

"Yes," I replied, seeing where she was going, but I had nothing to rebut her following words that wouldn't sound like a whining child.

"I think you know the rest, then," she continued. "I will ask how this lover of yours died."

"She died trying to save me from Badb. Goddess, if she'd just stayed put, we'd have had time to figure this out."

I could almost hear Aine's eyebrow raising as she said what I was already thinking. "Don't you dare besmirch her sacrifice," Áine snapped. "She made a choice to try to protect you. It may have been the wrong one, that is yet to be seen, but it was her choice. Now, the only thing you can do is forge onward. I'm stuck here for the moment, but you are not."

"I feel very stuck. How can I get myself and my friends out of this in one piece?"

"Perhaps," Áine said, her voice becoming much more clear and gentle. "Perhaps I can help you."

I snorted. "I'm not sure there's much you can do."

"Well, suppose I could do anything you require. What

might it be?"

"Duh. I need to get out of here, rescue my friends, and leave."

"That I cannot do. But you will have your chance. Badb wants the mantle badly, and she has always been short on patience. She'll pull you out of there soon enough. Tell me, what brought you here in the first place? What were you looking for?"

"I came to Ireland to collect a soulstone. My sister is alive, but her body is also occupied by a Kyliri lehos."

"A soulstone would not help you with that problem. Unless you've suddenly exceeded all my expectations of your training since we last met, the problem is beyond your expertise to untangle neatly. But, not to worry, your sister's soul will likely consume the intruder, and she'll be fine."

"No," I spat hotly. "I can't let that happen. The Kyliri is a friend, or, well, the friend of a friend. I can't let her die. I wouldn't be here otherwise."

"Well, that certainly burns the euphoris flower, I suppose. What you need is power, dear. In this instance, skill isn't required, brute force will do. You need to detach the Kyliri soul from the body and stuff it back in the lehos."

"I'm still the same shitty mage I always was. I don't have dyscalculia anymore, but I haven't learned much."

"Yes, but you can see a soul, grasp it, and pull, can't you?"

She made it sound so simple. "Sure, but souls don't just pop loose because we pull on them, or every mage would use that trick for who knows what."

"A moment, the guards are coming through," she whispered, and I heard the door to the cell block open with the jangle of keys.

I sat quietly and listened to their footsteps. I even forced out a few tears and some loud sobs as they passed. *Yup, this is me,* I thought. *Just sitting in this hole and being miserable. Nothing to see here.*

A few minutes later, the hallway door opened and closed.

She gave a raspy chuckle. "Indeed, as I said, it requires power. What you need is your mother's mantle. If you claim it, you'll have all the power you need."

"What will it do to my sister? I know she won't die, but…"

"The Kylr are incredibly robust. Do you remember Daneen?"

I shrugged, even though she couldn't see me. "Sure. The short, cute Kylr night watch who wore the one thick braid. She was the only one who would talk to me at any length. Though most of what she said was deeply philosophical and thoroughly boring."

Áine laughed. "Yes. That's her. Well, during the final push to send the Kaushkari home, she was wounded, shot through the eye, and her lehos destroyed. And, wouldn't you know it, it grew back."

"Wow," I murmured. I couldn't think of anything else to say. Aoife was almost impossible to kill.

"Okay, so riddle me this, Batman; how do I tell the difference between them? Souls don't exactly have name tags."

"I can't help you with that, Skaja. You'll have to figure that one out on your own. You said she's your sister, we're you close?"

"Not really. We were separated sixteen years ago. Since then, we've grown apart."

"That's a shame. If you knew her well or had a strong connection with her, perhaps you could use a more precise technique."

I scowled. "We're twins," I commented. "I'm not sure how much more connected I could get. She feels my pain sometimes."

There was another ugly cough, then a wheeze, then silence, and I thought perhaps she'd just died on me. "Áine?" I called.

No answer.

"Áine?" I hollered once more. "Are you still alive?"

"Shush, child, I'm thinking," she scolded. "Keep your mouth closed for a moment."

I raised my eyebrows. "Okay," I muttered. "No need to snap."

A few minutes later, Áine spoke. "I think I know how to help you. Listen closely."

I did. She explained to me what she thought might be the best way to do everything. It sounded pitifully simple, but the devil was in the details, and I would most likely die in the process.

"That's a shit plan," I muttered.

"Yes, but it's all you have," she retorted. "And I have faith enough for both of us."

CHAPTER THIRTY-NINE

I was dragged across the marble floor of the throne room and dropped unceremoniously at the foot of the large dais, once again chained. The High Fae court of the Summer Queen stood scattered to either side of the long throne room. Sitting on the throne of white marble shot through with veins of gold sat Badb, and laying over one arm of the throne was a cloak of darkest black that seemed to suck up all of the light, the Mantle of the Morrigan. Áine had been right. She was impatient. She wanted it badly—badly enough to put it in easy reach.

"Enough nonsense," Badb said and waved her hand.

The court's glamour shifted and faded, replaced by something far more sinister. The beautiful white columns flowed into tall black cylinders of black basalt stone, twisting with carved eels, crows, and wolves. The white marble floor was whisked over with a black sheen shot with red reflected the burning moonlight from above, casting dark reflections. The beautiful golden lights that hovered quietly in the corner began to move, twisting and darting this way and that and taking on dark cobalt, vermillion, and violet shades.

The surrounding spectators all looked the same, but the brilliance of their presence was dimmed a bit. The barely controlled anger and terror that had colored their expressions was laid bare with sunken eyes and the look of a battered people.

I shook my head, looking at the spectacle of misery. "Why?"

She squinted at me, her eyes smoldering with hatred. "Because of you. And because of this." She stroked the Mantle once more. "Áine and Nemhain plotted to murder my child. I couldn't let that happen."

"Your child? I don't understand." I couldn't imagine my mother doing such a thing. Badb had gone insane. I closed my eyes for a moment, feeling a twinge of deep sorrow for the woman I once knew. "And Áine? What of her?"

Badb stood, and the chains shackling my arms took on tremendous weight, pulling me to the floor with the slap of my hands to the marble. I didn't bother to look up. She didn't deserve obeisance or to see the helplessness in my eyes.

"Your mother, Macha, and I were the closest that sisters could be. We shared in all things. Then, Nemhain stole our world from us. She stole my daughter from me. And then, to add to the insult and pain, she stole *you*! You were supposed to rescue my daughter, not replace her, not destroy her!" Badb was almost screeching now.

I glanced, eyes wide. The truth had emerged, and it was far more horrid than I could have imagined. The dreams had been her memories. "Mother Darkness," I whispered. "Hel. She was your child."

"Drusera," Badb nodded, her voice turning somber. "That is her birth name. And somewhere beneath the thousands of years of loneliness and insanity, she still lives, I know it. I sequestered the essence of her psyche away, keeping it dormant and saving it from the thousands of years of loneliness. My little girl is preserved, and there's still a chance for her."

My shock was palpable as I tried to square what Badb said with the creature I'd seen in my dream at Nellie's. "She's awake now," I mumbled to myself. Maybe I could save Drusera, but who would she be in the end? The child? Or the beast? Or worse, both? *Oh, Mother,* I thought. *What have you done?*

Badb reached into the small box next to the throne. From it, she produced a deep red liquid in a crystal bottle and swirled it before her. The liquid moved and flowed, coating the container's interior. "Do you know what this is?

"It looks like blood, but I suspect not."

"We call it the Blood of Shaddan, actually. But you are correct. It is not blood. It is a distillation of the sacred Spley Flower, which grew on a hillock near The Vermillion Palace. There are none left alive who know how to make it. But, for Goddesses, those destined to lead, defend, or hold domain over the magic of our land, it will expand their minds, giving them sight and unlocking all that they are. It was a simple rite of passage for those of the bloodline. A sip, some pretty fireworks in the head, and done. For all others, it is deadly." She walked forward, holding the bottle before her. "You will drink, and we will see, Skaja, if you are human or Shaddani. Are you one of us or one of them? And you will know my daughter's pain." She stepped down to the floor level, glaring imperiously at me. "You will know your true purpose, not that nonsense Nemhain promised."

"Don't," Wisteria hissed. "It is poison."

"Silence," Badb roared, and Wisteria shrank back.

I shook my head. "No. Not unless you release my friends."

She knelt down to one knee, her cheek to mine, and whispered in my ear. "I promise. You will drink it. Drink or another of your friends dies." She drew her dagger as Jess and Maggie were dragged into the room and forced to kneel behind her. Jess was manacled, but Maggie was in no fit state to offer any resistance. Her face was pale, and her clothing sweat-soaked. The glassy state of her eyes suggested that either she'd been glamoured into obedience or that the goo on her leg had taken hold of her thoughts, like Reynolds.

I lifted my head, glaring at Badb with hatred and defiance and trying not to hear Jess's mixed whimpers of sorrow and growls of rage. I opened my mouth, and Badb grabbed my face roughly by the jaw. She upended the contents of the bottle into my mouth and forced it shut, whispering sharply in my ear, "Now you will know my pain."

The liquid was sweet and reminded me a bit of port, perhaps, traveling down my throat with the lightest burn. But when it reached my stomach, fire lanced through me. My fingers curled as the agony reached my head, making it feel as if it were bursting from the inside. My entire body screamed with pain, and I fell to the floor. The marble felt ice cold against my cheek, but it brought no relief. Tears of blood streamed from my eyes, and a cold, wet trickle slid from my ears. It was like the hunger, yet amplified a thousandfold. In desperation, I screamed.

I will kill her, I thought through the haze. *I will kill her.*

The world winked out of existence.

CHAPTER FORTY

I floated in a sea of darkness, with no light and no feeling, and yet there was, every so often, a sound. It was the latent thump of my cold heart.

A pinprick of light appeared, illuminating my body in a faint red glow. My limbs appeared hazy, and their edges seemed to flow like water as they moved, leaving behind fading soft streaks that painted the blackness in glowing blues, purples, and reds.

The pinprick of light grew. I wasn't sure if I was moving toward it, it toward me, or if it was simply getting larger. The cold rush of Shaddani magic blew through me like a fierce wind, and I gasped with the power that filled me. My chest felt crushed with it. My head felt stuffy and full of pressure as if it were crammed with some cottony mass. A thousand emotions, a tumultuous mix of fear, hope, and longing, moved through me, bringing tears and pain and joy and other feelings with no real name.

The beacon of light resolved itself into a figure. It was Leah.

"Hello, Mama," Leah said with a smile that melted my heart and reminded me how much I loved her. She wore a blood-red cossack robe adorned at the breast with the triple moon emblem of the Shaddani court.

"Leah?" I whispered.

"Yes, Mama?" She answered, holding out her hand.

"You can't be here. It's impossible."

"Of course not, Mama. I'm not your daughter. I am all that came before you. I am the memory of our world. I am Shaddan —all that it has ever been and will ever be."

"Are you The Morrigan?" I asked, not understanding.

"No, but she is of me. She was born of my existence almost as soon as I came into being in the swirling primordial dust of our world millions of years ago."

"You're the embodiment of our world—of Shaddan," I said, more answer than question.

She gave me that cute, timid smile that Leah always did. "Yes. Think of me as an avatar of Shaddan itself."

"Then why do you appear this way?" I asked, confused.

The blackness ebbed away and was replaced by an island in the middle of a massive lake—the lake north of the Heroes Field. I recognized it from my dream, Lindon Danu. Leah still stood in front of me, and my body grew less vaporous and more real. The fragrances of the land assaulted my nose. Some were familiar, like grasses and the muddy smell of fresh rain. Others were strange, filled with the scent of sweet flowers or the musky aroma of animals that I didn't recognize.

"Are you not the protector? Are you not the next in your line?" Leah said in answer to my question, pulling my attention back to her. The juxtaposition of her words with the image of my young, innocent child twisted at my heart, but I understood. That was the point. She appeared as the one person that I most needed to protect. And I knew instinctively that it wasn't a manipulation. It was my mind providing the form.

"You are partly my creation, then? You exist. I give you form."

"Clearly, you understand," she whispered, looking up at me with eyes both young and far beyond old or ancient. Her stare seemed almost primordial in its depths and yet so full of need, hurt, and want. In it lay the gaze of a battered child—my child when I'd first seen her so long ago.

I knelt to one knee, eye to eye with her. "I do. I will keep you safe. I will restore what's been lost."

She nodded and held out her hand. "Come with me, and I will show you what you must see."

Reaching to take it, I asked absently, "Am I really dead?"

She paused and pulled back her arm, wringing her hands with a pensive expression. "Well, you did die, but I plucked you from the Ma, the space between worlds. So, now, you are between life and death. How you will move on is difficult to say. For each who drinks, the outcome is a little different, and Mama," she giggled slightly, just like my baby, "you are definitely different from all who have come before you." She reached out again. "Take my hand."

As my fingers closed around hers, the world flashed around me, blurring by in splashes of chaotic color and light. The transition passed quickly, and I found myself in a beautiful room with a tile floor. I stared out a vast picture window across a stunning nighttime vista of flowing hills and forests. Amid the forest were large modern buildings, each standing hundreds of feet high like fingers of steel and glass reaching into the night. Dotted about the landscape were smaller structures, like unfinished-looking skeletal pyramids of shining girders and beams. A single moon, more like a world unto itself with water and green spaces, hovered huge in the sky.

Great airships, massive and bulbous, rode beams of light toward the distant world.

Behind me, a woman screamed. I turned. Aunt Badb lay upon a small hospital bed, not all that different from any bed in any hospital on earth, though strange symbols adorned the control panel. Badb's belly lay swollen as she cried with the pains of labor.

I looked down at Leah, who still held my hand. "Is this Drusera's birth?"

"It is," she said dispassionately. "This is Kaushkar, fourteen thousand Earth years before your battle at the Giant's Causeway."

"That's almost a half-million Shaddani years," I said, doing some quick mental calculations.

"No," she said flatly. "The time difference between Shaddan and Earth is not always stable, but that is unimportant. Look."

I watched as Badb struggled and pushed. Several women in black smocks swarmed around her. They all looked human enough, though I had the sense that they were different somehow. I wasn't sure what I'd expected of the Kaushkar. I'd never seen one. It was then, though, that my eyes were drawn to Badb's wrists. They were shackled by loose chains to the bed. "Is she a prisoner?"

"Yes," Leah said. "She is the Queen of Shaddan. She came as an envoy to the palace of the Kaushkari King, Dyeuspater. Though, here he is simply Dommus. There is no magic here that she can work with, nor is there a direct gate to Shaddan. He refused to let her leave."

A woman, a doctor or midwife, I assumed by the patch on the shoulder of her smock, said, "You're doing great. Just one more push."

Badb screamed through gritted teeth. From my vantage point, I couldn't see the birth, but moments later, I heard the cry of a baby. Tears flowed from Badb's eyes as she gazed at her daughter. She, too, looked so human, and I wondered just how close all of these people were to us genetically. *We can't be that different*, I thought.

The woman swaddled the baby in purple cloth and laid her in Badb's arms. "Drusera," she whispered. "You shall be Drusera, the guiding light."

I began to cry softly. I couldn't help it. The love in my Aunt's eyes hurt to see, knowing how it would all turn out. Now, my vision made perfect sense. "Cousin," I whispered just as the door opened and a man strode in.

"Sister," Leah corrected, but I was too engrossed in the procession of images to comprehend what she said.

The man was tall with a thick dark beard and cold, penetrating eyes. In some ways, he reminded me of the photograph I'd seen of the Maltese, though in truth, other than the cruel eyes, he looked nothing like the old vampire. First of all, he was olive-skinned, not black. Broad shoulders rested on a thick, muscular body, and his style of dress wasn't all that different from what modern men wore on Earth in my time. His black shirt looked for all the world like a golf shirt, absent the buttons and collar. Light brown trousers covered his legs and sported an elastic waist. A pair of brown lace-up business shoes adorned his feet. I almost laughed at the mundane nature of his appearance. This was the great Dyeuspater. *Dommus*, I corrected mentally. He looked like a corporate CEO on holiday.

Marching over, he gazed down at the baby in my Aunt's arms, ignoring Badb's hateful gaze. From the way Badb held her daughter, trying desperately to shield her away from him, I knew what would come next. Dommus reached down. When my aunt resisted, he backhanded her without a word, snatched my cousin from her mother, and whisked her away. Badb said not a word. She only gazed balefully at his retreating backside as he exited the door.

My hand flew to my mouth. "She's his child," I whispered in horror. Strangely, the expected vision of my own trauma didn't make an appearance. But then again, I had closed that chapter with absolute finality.

"Yes," Leah said, and this time, she wasn't dispassionate. Her words held a grim undertone of anger and sorrow that chilled me to the marrow. It was a stern reminder that this wasn't my child next to me. It was the living embodiment of my home.

I walked to the bed.

"No, you must not," Leah hissed, and I stopped, glancing back at her in confusion.

"I don't understand. I just wanted to get a better look at her."

"Look, Mama, but don't touch or interact with her. This isn't a dream or a vision. Until someone perceives you, you remain in flux, a passive observer without existence."

I blinked at her as comprehension dawned. "We're really here. In the past. But that's impossible."

Leah gave me a knowing smile that looked so out of place on her innocent face. "Is it? How did you defeat Saya?"

"I sidestepped, and—" I broke off. It had been my past life, that much I had known but had struggled to accept. The truth was far more twisted, and the part that really baked my noodle was the moves I'd used. As Weyna, at that particular moment, I'd had no active memory of being Cait. I'd had no training in combat, but still, I had used my knowledge—Cait's knowledge. My future self had been connected to my past self in a way I hadn't fully understood.

"You see now," Leah said, more statement than a question.

"Yes," I confirmed, then gestured back to Badb. "What happened to them?"

Badb looked so young. If she'd been human, I'd have guessed she was no more than eighteen or nineteen, just a few years older than Katie. Such a young age to wear such sorrow and responsibility. It hurt so much to watch.

"I wish I could do something," I murmured, my voice choked.

Leah took my hand once more. "There will be a time for you to help her, but not now."

CHAPTER FORTY-ONE

"Where are we now?" I asked, glancing around at the massive throne room, for that's what it was, despite the modernity of it. We stood in a great hall with more massive picture windows running the length on either side of the rectangular room that gave a spectacular view of the world to the northeast and southwest; at least, I assumed that was the case given the rising sun. From our vantage point on a narrow ledge in front of the windows, we gazed down across dozens of Kaushkari citizens.

"The Kaushkari Royal Court," Leah whispered and gave a slight giggle. "More of a boardroom, honestly."

Dommus stood on a slightly elevated dais in front of a large throne at one end of a long table. To his right sat an empty, slightly smaller throne, Hera's—or Eria's seat, rather, I assumed. But my eyes momentarily drifted to a large portrait of a beautiful woman with dark skin and long black hair resting on the wall behind him. Badb kneeled, shackled in the center of the room.

"You will never speak of how she was conceived," he said to her. His voice held no venom, and yet, the rage that filled my aunt overwhelmed me. I wanted to dash across the throne room and tear out his throat.

"You would never reach him, even with your speed," Leah

said. "Be patient and watch."

I turned back to the proceedings, again noting his wife's absence from her throne. I wondered what machinations he must have used to secure his place next to her. Something about this entire arrangement struck me as off.

"You will tell your child that she was a child of love and never reveal the truth. You will never take her from this world," Dommus said. "Otherwise, I will kill you both."

"I understand," Badb ground out. "Though, Sky Father," she spat the name like poison, "tell me, is this how you treat all your invited guests?"

He ignored the question. "It is an agreement, then?"

Tears slid down my cheeks as I watched my aunt, the mighty Goddess of Battle, humiliated at his feet. He was arrogant, too. That agreement had a million loopholes. *Another Holley,* I thought. *He is just a man. Powerful, perhaps, but still just a man—arrogant and fallible, a beast in human form.*

"Agreed," my aunt growled through clenched teeth. I altered my perception and noted the brief pulse in Badb's magic, binding her and Dommus to the agreement. As I glanced around and out the window, I was shocked to see so little ambient magic, though. My aunt glowed brightly with the tarzhi of our home. The rest of Kaushkar was bereft, except for massive glowing points around the steel pyramid-like structures below. Powerful lines of magic connected them to Dommus, funneling into a pair of bracelets on his wrists. Beyond my view, a few other lines splayed out to other parts of the world, likely connected to others. Still others disappeared altogether, only a short distance from the pyramids.

"Dear Goddess," I muttered in horror. "They've harvested the magic of their world. No wonder they're so powerful. It's an abomination."

"Yes," Leah confirmed once more. "It is a remarkable technology, though, don't you think?" Her voice held a bit of annoyance.

"Technology?"

"Hush, mama," she said.

Dommus waved his hand, and the shackles around Badb's wrists vanished. "You may see your daughter. But be aware, Badb, Queen of Shaddan, that this is a mercy. Do not tempt me to dispose of you."

"Does he ever stop?" I hissed.

"No," Leah replied. "Not even for the queen he married. He has become more powerful than she. After thousands of years of this, Eria's heart has become twisted by rage and jealousy. She cannot strike against him directly, so she strikes against his paramours and their children."

"Eria cursed Lamia and murdered her children," I whispered, mostly to myself.

"Eventually, she will. But that has not happened yet. Not for a long time. Come."

The world swirled again. Chaotic lights and shadows blasted across my vision until, almost sick with dizziness, it stopped like we'd slammed into a wall.

I found myself in a dark garden. The moon, covered in its alien landscape, filled the western sky. Flowers bloomed all about us, moving and stretching, straining toward the moon above. In the center, surrounded by a ring of glowing runes, Badb sat with a small girl in front of some kind of strange game board that reminded me a bit of the chess game from Star Wars. The girl appeared no more than ten or eleven.

"Is that her?" I asked, noting that the girl looked so much like her mother. She had our family's brown-flecked green eyes and a smallish nose. There was no doubt that we were somehow related. Her face was a bit wider, though, accounted for by her father's influence.

"It's been ten years since her birth and eleven since Badb arrived," the avatar said. And though she had Katie's voice, the cadence was the same, carrying that sense of vast power and knowledge. I didn't bother to look at her, knowing what I would see.

"Is it time?" I asked. The previous scene in the throne room had stoked the fire of hot rage in my chest, and it demanded action, some response to my Aunt's horrible humiliation.

"Listen," Katie said, ignoring the question.

"Oh, I wish you could see Shaddan, my daughter," Badb whispered. "But I cannot take you there."

"Father says I must not go there. That your sisters will use me against him."

Badb shrugged. "Perhaps. Such things as I cannot choose are hard to see. Such things as must be resolved in far-flung years are even more difficult."

I turned to the avatar. As expected, she now wore Katie's body and face. "Did she know that I would come? That I would be here now?"

Katie showed me her trademark smirk but said nothing.

I snorted mirthlessly and turned back to the scene before us. "Wait and see, then," I muttered. "Fine."

"Will you have another baby?" Drusera asked, moving a small fairy forward on the game board. There were no squares, and for a moment, I wondered how they knew how far to move the game pieces.

"No," Badb said, a little too sharply, causing the child to stir uncomfortably.

"I would like a sister," Drusera continued as Badb slid a large black dragon next to the fairy. As I watched, the dragon reached down and devoured the small fairy rather violently. There was no blood, but it tore the small creature's limbs off before crunching down the head and torso. There were even sound effects. It was horrifying.

"You will have, one day, after a fashion," Badb whispered conspiratorially. "But I will not give birth to her."

My lips parted slightly as I drew in a surprised breath. "Is she talking about me?"

Katie didn't answer the question, instead saying, "Hush and watch, Mama."

"You don't like father much at all. I don't blame you. He's always angry."

Badb gave a soft laugh. "Your father wants what he cannot have. He begs for adoration, and yet, no matter how much anyone gives him, it is never enough. He believes that the women of his life reflect poorly upon him."

"Even me?"

"I don't think he believes that you are living up to your potential," Badb replied diplomatically, moving a black-winged succubus across the playing board. "Check," she said.

Drusera rolled her eyes. "All parents think that of their children at some point."

Badb chuckled, and the sound was light and happy. I realized that despite her circumstances, this time with her daughter filled her with joy. No wonder it had all driven her mad.

"Even Eria?" Drusera continued, dragging a huge six-legged behemoth between Badb's succubus and what I thought might be her queen or king; I wasn't sure.

"Even Eria," Badb said and reached for another piece.

At Badb's mention of Eria's name, though, a cold wind blew through the garden. In several places, lilies sprung from the soil, blooming instantly. They did not seek the moon, however. Instead, they simply drooped in place as twinkling magic flowed from them into the other flowers until they withered and died.

"She's coming," I hissed and looked around. There were no other outward signs, but I could feel it like an immense power hovering nearby, waiting to strike. I shifted my perception to see perhaps if she was hidden somewhere and noted something odd. Only a few feet away from Badb flowed a pinprick of Shaddani magic seemingly from nowhere. It was a rift. I was sure of it. A natural schism in the fabric of this world that led to our home.

"Now?" I asked, but Katie said nothing. She didn't respond at all, as if she hadn't heard me.

The immense magical pressure I felt grew almost unbearable, and I darted forward. *Consequences be damned*, I thought. *The child won't die here. My aunt can take care of herself.* Though, I wasn't sure if that was true. But she must, I thought. I need to keep Drusera safe.

"Stop, Mama!" Katie called, but I sprinted the distance anyway. As I reached the ring of runes, I was hurled away to land in a heap on the ground in a flash of heat and light. My chest was burned horribly, but the wound began to close almost immediately, and I pulled myself up.

"Mother of Waters," Badb swore as she turned her eyes toward me. Her eyes grew wide with surprised recognition. "Daughter?"

I paused, suddenly stuck on a distant memory of Badb's voice, something said almost as an afterthought: "I told you, a warrior."

"This is the moment," Katie whispered in my ear, so close I could feel her breath. "This is where you live or die. You must choose rightly."

The recognition of the truth hit hard, causing me to lose my concentration. I turned away from her. "Is it possible?" Of course, it was possible. Even the Shaddani die, Nemhain had said. Two thousand years was such a long time. But in Bethad, barely fifty had passed. Nemhain was Weyna's mother, yes. But who was Cait's? I kept grasping at those memories.

"I always knew you were more warrior than witch," Badb had said. "Something seems—missing," she said, as if I were no longer whole. I whirled, looking at Katie, looking for confirmation. My life depended on it. Was this what I was supposed to do? Was it already too late?

A resonant, feminine voice boomed from the far side of the garden, maybe a hundred feet behind me. "Now I know why he sent me away! You harlot!"

Bad stood, her chair rocketing back. She grabbed Drosera and dragged her back. They were so close to the rift. Badb was almost touching it.

I spun. A woman gazed at us with black eyes, her long dark-brown hair cascading over a simple but elegant dress that Liz might have worn to the office. She even wore heels. It would have struck me as funny if the circumstances had been less dire. As it happened, though, I found her presence absolutely terrifying. Even my aunt, the Goddess of Battle, looked quailed by her.

"Fear isn't something that stops you," Nastasia had told me. The memory sent a pang of loss into my gut, but I batted it aside. I had already failed the test of the Blood of Shaddan, of that I was sure. The path of destiny could not be changed. And there were no mentions of Cait or Weyna or Skaja in any history I'd ever heard or seen. I had never battled Eria, or if I had, I certainly hadn't won. I would die here and now, not even a footnote in history. Badb certainly would have mentioned it if she remembered me at all, wouldn't she? It didn't matter. I was committed.

"I won't let you harm them," I said in perfect Shaddani. "They are my family, and family is all that matters."

Eria laughed. "Move aside, woman. I am not here for you, but I will destroy you if you get in my way."

An insane idea came to mind as I stared defiantly across the intervening space. It would certainly mean my death, but it was the only way. I cocked a hip and gave her my most arrogant smile. "Perhaps, but I have a better idea. What if I could give you the thing that you most want?"

Eria's eyes narrowed. "What could you possibly have that I could want?"

"Vengeance," I said flatly. "And freedom."

Disbelief colored Eria's expression, but she was also intrigued. "How could you offer me that? I can tell that you couldn't stand against me for terribly long, let alone my husband."

I thought again about Nastasia and what she had said. "I really wish I were different," I muttered to the empty air as it occurred to me that these were likely my last few minutes and that I would never see Katie, Leah, and Liz again.

The threads of Shaddani magic still fluttered about, but they were even less cohesive than moments before. The rift would close soon. I was about to die, but no one deserved what my aunt was going through, and Dommus certainly wasn't a fit father for Drusera. It did occur to me that I was about to set off a paradoxically looping series of events, but I buried that thought. It made my head hurt.

I spun and gave Badb a powerful kick. She flew backward into the rift and was gone.

"Mother!" Drusera screamed, charging through the rift after her. Then it just faded away in a wisp of magic, leaving only Eria and me in the garden.

I turned back to Eria. "So," I said cordially. "Let's chat."

Surprisingly, Eria only smirked at me. "Clever," she said. "Clever enough that you now have my undivided attention." I cringed inwardly at that, but I'd made my bed. Now I'd have to lie in it.

Fortunately, the chat was brief, the plans were laid, and when it was done, I had no idea if I'd chosen the correct path, but I thought so. Of course, the world just winked out as if it had never existed.

Fuck, I thought.

CHAPTER FORTY-TWO

She is an agent of chaos, a beacon voice overwhelming my entire being with the fire of magic, the rage of battle, and all the presence and command of an entire world. She is the Queen of Shaddan.

A vast and wondrous land unfolds, reminiscent of Earth yet distinctly different. Two moons hang suspended in the sky, full and bright. The magic of this realm surges from all directions like a tempest, whirling in a maelstrom and funneling to a single point below. It's captivating in its raw power.

Badb stands, bathed in the ethereal glow of both moons, their brilliance casting shifting shadows on her face. She stands on a small island covered almost entirely with vegetation within a vast inland sea. We are at the center, a clearing set with a circle of megaliths sculpted into twisted shapes. In the far distance to the east climb tall peaks.

She speaks. "Mother of Waters! I command the magic that flows within this world on a night of holy creation." The very stars seem to flicker above as beautiful tarzhi of orange and autumn yellow spiral into a jewel sitting on a raised stone table at the very center of the circle. The grass around curls and dies, withering from both the rising power and the loss of magic.

"Holy Goddess," I whisper in awe from the dark. "She's channeling the magic of a planet." She cannot hear me. This is a memory, the memory of my birth, etched into my very soul in this

single moment. My vision is both narrowly focused on this place and all-encompassing. Creatures of both land and sea scream in agony as the magic is ripped from this place. I can feel their suffering from every corner of this world, and yet, I can do nothing.

"Can I stop her?" I whisper through the pain.

"No," the avatar responds, now wearing Liz's face. "This is just a memory. One that I think you should see."

"Grant me the power of creation and transformation that I might cure the injustice dealt to me and mine. That this soul, this daughter of mine, may one day break my banishment and bring me home!" The magic waivers, almost dying out. Mother Danu has delivered her denial.

Badb remains fixed in her purpose, unholy as it may be. "Fine then," she mutters. "If that is your answer, Mother, I'll do it myself." With tremendous effort fueled by her rage, she pulls harder on the magic. The stream is renewed, the magic moving faster now. Across the entire world, creatures are suffering, vast numbers dying amid the cataclysm she wreaks.

"A siphon of the soul of my sister Nemhain to steer magic and command the dead," she says, her words almost lost in the roar of the magic. She holds forth a small gem, glowing in deepest blue. The blue light empties from the gem, streaming into the soulstone.

"A bit of Macha to command it." She holds forth another stone, this one alight with bloodied vermillion. Again, the soul-stuff within streams into the soulstone. There is a brief burst of light and a concussive thump as it fights to enter the stone.

"The offering of the Summer Queen, that she may be more than a creature of death." She presents a third stone, this one shining bright in gold and silver. The magic flows effortlessly into the stone, this time with a blast of blinding light so powerful that Badb has to shield her eyes.

"And all that I can give to my child that she may become the hero we need," she says, this time both more solemnly and with more determination. Deep purple tendrils of magic snake to the stone, take hold, and draw taught, pulling directly from Badb's soul.

"And thus is the true vessel of the Morrigan born of the three made one," Badb intones; then her hands rise, and the power of the world is forced into the stone in a single colossal act of creation.

Around the entire world on which we stand, all that remains are bits of translucent tarzhi filtering up from below, the remnants of the once-rich magic of this place. At least the suffering has stopped, but the world seems dimmer somehow, less alive.

With a final blast of light and the clap of an explosion, the last of the stolen magic flows into the crystal. For a moment, there is nothing, and I think maybe she's failed. But then the crystal flickers to life. A soul is born.

Badb walks to the soulstone and lifts it carefully. "I created you, child, to right the scales. When the moment is right, you will become flesh and take me home."

The stone is silent as the vision fades.

CHAPTER FORTY-THREE

I opened my eyes and stared at the floor of the throne room, where I knelt, still stunned by the tragedy and wonder of it all. In a horrible, dark epiphany, I understood. Mother Darkness was one of us, a daughter of Shaddan, a child of Badb, a cousin, a sister after a fashion. She was family. My mother had promised to protect her, but when the Kaushkar threatened to invade, she forced Badb to leave her in the field of heroes in an effort to save our home. And yet that betrayal had brought the cataclysm that ended our world, giving rise to the blasted wasteland and twisting Drusera into the monster she had become. And in her grief and anguish and reckless desire to redeem her child and return to Shaddan, from which she was barred, Badb nearly murdered a world to create a single soul: mine.

"I didn't ask to be created," I whispered, my voice trembling with rage. "I'm not some chosen one." I looked up as Badb stopped mid-stride—she had been pacing.

Her eyes turned to me, confusion twisting and furrowing her brow. "What?"

"Your holocaust is almost complete," I said. "Our world is in ruins. Thanks to Macha, Mother Darkness has control of its magic. And you! You nearly murdered an entire world, leaving it all but bereft of its birthright. I will not bear the guilt of this.

I didn't ask to be created."

"I would have expected gratitude," Badb said.

"Oh, I'm grateful for living and for the love that I have found. But that wasn't your doing, was it?" I demanded, my voice rising. "My mother, Nemhain, gave me a life—twice. Even though she knew what I was, what I was likely destined to be, she wanted me to live. She believed in me. More importantly, she left me with the choice. That is a greater gift than anything you've done and certainly better than you planned."

"Nemhain didn't give you life. I did!" Badb roared. "She gave you a body, that's all!"

I yanked at the shackles, but they held firm. "I will not take you home," I growled. "You're mad with grief and can do nothing but harm."

"A few years here might change your mind," Badb said firmly. "It is your destiny. You cannot run from it, daughter."

"I'm not your daughter, but if I were, then that would make Aoife your daughter, too, wouldn't it? She'll die if you keep me here."

That seemed to pull her up short, but she recovered and stepped over to me, kneeling down. "When Weyna died, Nemhain returned your soul to the soulstone I used to create you. But you were too powerful, and the stone was already worn. The stone cracked. Aoife was an accident."

It took me a moment to understand. "Then so was I. Neither of us alone is the soul you created. We are each part of the whole. If I deserve life, then so does she."

Badb lowered her head then and sighed. "Skaja—Cait, don't you understand? I'm tired. I want to go home. I want to rescue my child. Is there anything you wouldn't do for your own child?"

I shook my head in disappointment. "I know you suffered at his hands. I've been through that myself. I know it was all wrong. And yes, I would do anything for my family. I've done things I never thought I would, but you need to stop. This has gone too far. Look at everyone you've hurt or killed. Just let me have the mantle. Give Áine the throne. Let it go. Haven't you done enough damage?" That last was spoken in the barest whisper.

"I can't. I needed you to see the truth, and now I know that I cannot trust you—not yet." Her words were so sad, so full of disappointment and despair, and yet so damning. "Guards, take her back to the dungeon."

"You accepted my challenge," I said with a defeated air. "I choose the mantle, your magic, and our freedom, all of our freedom."

"What?" Badb asked, clearly at a loss.

"Skaja challenged you. Don't you remember? On the day of my induction into the Valtárí. I said, 'Care to go a few more rounds?' And you said—"

"Anytime, anywhere, young one," she finished for me. "That was just banter."

"No," I responded. "It was a challenge, and you accepted. By our custom and laws, I choose here and now. I have named my stakes. I'm sorry, Aunt Badb, but I have no choice. I have my own family to save."

"You may not refuse," Wisteria called from the assembled group. "You may only forfeit once the challenge has been accepted. This is Bethadi law as well. And you are the Queen of Bethad now, are you not? You were oath-bound when you took the throne from my mother."

Badb glared at Wisteria.

"Sorry, Badb," Wisteria continued. "It comes with the chair, I'm afraid."

Momentarily at a loss for words, Badb turned to me and then back to Wisteria. Finally, she stalked with her imperious grace to a side table and snatched up a pair of blades. "Fine, then. You cannot win, daughter. What do I get if I win? My magic is all that sustains me now. What could you offer that would be worth that?"

"My obedience," I said.

"No, Cait, you can't," Jess shouted. "She killed Nas!"

We ignored her.

"Prepare yourself, my daughter," Badb said, waving her hand. "I choose no limits."

"No limits," I affirmed.

The shackles fell away, and the feeling of fatigue left me. I stood. There was a shuffling among the Bethadi as they all moved away.

"And I'm not your daughter," I spat. "I'm your monster."

CHAPTER FORTY-FOUR

Fuck, Áine, I thought. *I really hope you know what you're doing.*

Badb stared at me with those black and blue crow-like eyes. They were the eyes she wore in battle. I'd once envied them for their sight and perceptiveness and their unblinking, intimidating stare. But I pushed that feeling away, stuffing it down. There was no room here for sentiment. I was about to lay on with the Goddess of Battle. This would be the fight of my life.

Looking around, I found Wisteria. Stepping over to her, I whispered in her ear. "I need a bit of a favor if I'm to win this. I need some of your blood."

"What are you doing?" Badb demanded, eyeing me intently.

"I'm preparing to meet my maker," I barked. "You wouldn't begrudge me a moment's preparation, given how lopsided the odds are."

"You're insane," Wisteria whispered back to me, but she tilted her head back anyway, and I wasted no time. Her knees buckled as the pleasure of my glamour washed through her, and she gave a soft sigh of contentment. Her blood was like liquid sex itself, flushing my entire body with power.

I tried to ignore the rush. It could easily become addictive. The Bethadi power that flowed through her veins blossomed my dark gift from a ribbon that wound lightly around my soul into a vast curtain, and strength flooded every muscle. My own legs almost gave out in the wash of pleasure that filled me. It was like drinking fire, and I wanted as much as I could take. Fortunately, I grew sated after only a moment. She recovered quickly, fingering the blood off her neck with a lascivious grin.

"And a devil, too." She giggled wickedly, but beneath the playful tone, a deep-seated need flickered in her expression. A split second later, it was gone as she shook her head and then took the golden cuff from her wrist, placing it on mine. "A token of my favor, as in days past. Fight well, Skaja of the Valtárí."

I leaned in and kissed her on the cheek. "Thank you—sister."

She winked. "Remember, no limits."

"If you're done snacking," Badb snarked before she turned to one of the Fae next to her, a man dressed in the sunset orange and black of the Summer Queen's Battle-master. "Thorn! You will oversee the match. Shaddani combat, no rules, no limits. Victor is the last one standing by death or capitulation." She then turned toward me with a cruel smile and added, "Or decapitation."

"Yes, Your Majesty." He practically spit out the title. Thorn had been one of Lugh's retainers when I'd known him. Now, he was the keeper of the palace guard and, normally, the Summer Queen's champion. Given the stakes, though, there was no way Badb would let him stand in for her. I'd crush him in seconds. She knew that.

A young Fae, a page girl, appearing perhaps of twenty years by human standards, with dazzlingly beautiful brown hair and an exaggerated swish to her walk, sauntered over and handed me my bóllom and nisís. She winked at me. "My rations are on you staying alive for at least three minutes."

My jaw dropped. "Rowan?" I hissed. "Where the fuck have you been?"

She angled her back to Badb, placed a finger to her lips, and then pushed a strand of hair from in front of my eyes. "Events must unfold as they were foreseen," she said cryptically, then added, "The strength of the Pack is the Wolf, and the strength of the Wolf is the Pack."

I frowned in confusion. "Are you quoting The fucking Jungle Book?"

She kissed me on the cheek and moved away with a wink and that impish smile.

"Are we finally ready?" Badb griped once more. "This is growing tedious."

I moved back to the center of the floor and gave my bóllom a few swift practice swings. "Yup!"

She didn't wait, launching straight at me like a fresh recruit. I dodged low, sliding between her legs and putting a slice into her left calf, damn near taking off the leg, then I came up on one knee, facing her. I got a bolt of lightning to my chest that spasmed my muscles and sent me skidding backward across the floor. If I'd been human, that would have killed me. As it was, it just pissed me off, and I was back up instantly, feeling Wisteria's blood burning in my veins.

To my disappointment, Badb's leg healed almost as quickly. *Goddess, you dope!* I thought bitterly.

"You know, Badb. You can surrender now. You're clearly outmatched," I taunted as I circled right.

"You were always an insolent child. Even Nemhain couldn't stand you."

"Oh, auntie, how hurtful," I said with mock hurt, then grinned. "Of course, the truth is, I just reminded her too much of your sorry ass."

She swung a wing from my left; it might have taken my head off if I were still human, but I was far faster than she remembered. It whisked harmlessly by as I ducked under. Unfortunately, it provided cover for her left hand, which snapped out and raked across my chest, leaving three long gashes and cutting a long furrow across my breast.

The cuts healed quickly, but it still hurt like a bitch. "Ow! I just had those done!" I quipped. Faster than I could see, her blade was back in her hand, and I realized she was toying with me. *It looks like I don't have to goad her into a mistake,* I thought.

Badb snapped her weapons back to their sheathes and

jumped forward, snatching both of my arms quick as lightning and breaking my hold on my blades. Then, she began pushing me down to the ground. Even with all of my vampiric strength and Wisteria's blood, my left leg buckled, sending me to one knee.

"I thought you were better than this," I snarled in her face.

"Oh, but I am, child," she shot back with hot menace and a gleam in her eye. A hot wind blew through the middle of me, and I felt as if my very soul was being crushed. My curse grew into a pulsing smoky black mass as purple stria of Shaddani magic coursed into it. Badb quickly turned the Dark Gift back on me, trying to snuff out my essence.

Two could play at that game, I thought. *And I have a surprise.*

I hadn't spent the entire time in the oubliette chatting with Áine. Some of it had passed while I practiced a few tidbits of magic that Áine had taught me. Bloody sweat beaded on my brow as I drew hard, not on Shaddani magic, but on the silver and gold tarzhi flowing from the gate, beating back Badb's power and transforming myself. "That is my Dark Gift," I grunted, my voice turning deep and distorted. "You can't control it."

My clothes exploded as great black bat-like wings tore from my back, and a new form erupted from the old in a rush of blood and gore. I stood, pushing back on Badb, every bit the succubus of old: horns, cloven hoofs, and all.

I jerked my left arm free and punched her in the face repeatedly. "I. Have. Had. Enough. Of. You." My tail swung around, the spearlike tip gashing her chin before stabbing into her arm with the thick barb at the end.

She let go and staggered back.

I slashed at her throat with clawed fingers, catching her wing, though, as she brought it around to defend herself. The following swift kick knocked her back across the floor, where she skidded to a halt on her backside, her savaged wing hanging perilously torn.

I shifted back and picked up my weapons. Fatigue dragged at me. The transformation had burned a lot of blood, but it had bought me time. I pulled once more on the tarzhi, flooding my curse with strength and keeping it from consuming Wisteria's blood. The hunger within me roared, and I felt my control slipping. It was perilous, trying to maintain the focus to draw on the magic, fend off the raging hunger, and fight her simultaneously, but I didn't have a choice. She had infinite reserves. By comparison, I had almost none.

Badb shifted back to her humanoid form and stood, looking for all the world as if I hadn't touched her. I couldn't beat her, not like this.

She smirked. "New tricks are always fun to watch, but this is over." She drew her hands together. I hurled my dagger, catching her in the shoulder, but it only delayed her momentarily. Charging forward, I snatched the dagger back and struck out at her, but she pushed me backward with the terrifying power of her scream.

Shockingly, I didn't fall. I didn't cower. My courage didn't fail. Wisteria's golden bracelet flared hot and white. *No limits*, I thought, realizing that I wasn't alone in this fight.

Badb's eyes shifted ever so slightly, focusing for a split second over my shoulder—at Wisteria, no doubt.

The bracelet may have saved me from losing my nerve, but the power of Badb's scream was also a physical thing, and I skidded backward, barely keeping my feet, unable to fight the vicious headwind. She followed with a blast of raw magic aimed at my chest, even as her scream continued. I crossed my blades in front of me, and the maneuver gave me a bit of shielding, but the skin bubbled and peeled from my arms and chest, and my blades began to fume a sickly, foul-smelling black smoke.

From nowhere, a black dagger spun through the air and hit Badb in the neck, straight through her windpipe. Her voice faltered and failed. The magic died, and she dropped to her knees, hands clutching at the dagger. I blood-stepped behind her, placed my smoking bóllom to her neck, and plucked the dagger from her throat.

Badb froze.

"No limits. And you have no allies here," I whispered in her ear. "You shouldn't have toyed with me, Auntie. You should have finished it, first shot." I pressed the blade into her skin, drawing more blood from her slowly healing wound. "Yield or die."

"I yield," she choked out in a hoarse, gravelly whisper.

I looked up, expecting to see Rowan smirking or Wisteria giving me a haughty look like I owed her. Instead, They were all staring gape-mouthed at the back of the throne room. Maggie stood there next to the small weapons table with her arm still outstretched like a statue, taking deep, ragged breaths.

"Rowan told me to do it," Maggie said defensively as if she were a child caught mid-naughty.

Badb's head remained bowed. I couldn't tell if she was expecting me to do something rash, like beheading her or something, but she just knelt there in silence. Finally, I crooked a finger beneath her chin, lifting her eyes to meet mine. "All you had to do was ask."

The pain in her face tore at my heart, and for the first time in all the time I had known her, and perhaps as long as she'd been alive, a single tear slid down her cheek. "Please promise me that you'll save her."

"I'll try," I said, biting my lip to keep from crying at the tragedy of it all.

"What does it matter?" Wisteria interjected hotly. "She has all but murdered my mother! And she's kept me from her for thirty years! Kill her!"

I held up a hand, but I kept my eyes on my aunt.

Badb slowly stood, her hands raised in surrender. "You'll get your justice, Wist. As soon as Skaja names a successor, I will fade."

I shook my head and stared at the ground, then turned to Wisteria. "Please, Wist, give me some time. A few hours at least."

Wisteria stared hard at Badb. "Two hours, then you must name a successor. And before you do, there is something you must see." She turned and dismissed the rest of the Bethadi host. Several attendants, who had been all but invisible to that point, brought in a long table and chairs. "Come, let us sit. It will be more comfortable, at least."

Badb stood and walked to the table with a slight limp before dropping heavily into a chair. Her perpetually youthful appearance already shone with deep lines as she sagged in her seat. She was dying already. I could see it.

A Fae servant brought me fresh clothing, and Maggie and Jess joined us as we sat down. I had a million questions and not much time. *Maybe no time*, I thought as Badb leaned heavily on her elbows and coughed loudly. A few drops of blood appeared on her lips.

Wisteria conjured water in a glass and set it before Badb. Despite her anger and hatred, she was close to getting what she wanted, and the grace befitting her station seemed to take precedence.

"How did you escape Kaushkar?" I asked, trying to understand how, after what I'd experienced, how I had saved her and Drusera, all of this could happen.

Badb snorted mirthlessly. "It was thousands of years ago, and even we can't remember everything. Eria came for us, and a woman, maybe a servant—I'm not sure—stepped in between us and pushed me through a rift that appeared in the garden. Drusera followed me. That's all I remember."

I nodded but said nothing. To tell her the truth would only cause her more pain. The deep welling of anger and hatred I'd felt when she'd killed Nastasia was nowhere to be found, only a profound sense of sorrow.

Badb coughed again, and her face took on a disturbing pallor. "You have to save her," she pleaded once more.

"Save who?" Jess asked.

"My daughter," Badb replied. "What you call Mother Darkness."

"Save her?" Jess said incredulously. "She'll destroy everything! She's insane!"

Badb turned on Jess, speaking in an angry rasp. "You don't know that. No one does. No one has been able to even speak to her in over sixteen thousand Shaddani years."

"Someone has to go to her," I whispered. "It's my responsibility to set things right."

Jess shook her head, turning angry. "Why is it always your responsibility? Why do you always have to be the one, Cait? When are the sacrifices enough? Who else do we have to lose?"

Ouch, that hurt. I looked at Jess sympathetically, but I didn't have a good answer for her. "Jess, you just said it. She's going to destroy everything we care about. If I don't do it, everyone we know will die eventually, and we don't even know why."

Jess bared her fangs and hissed before turning away, likely to hide her misery.

Wisteria reached out a hand, placing it on Jessica's. "It won't be long now."

"You know what's happening to her?" I asked, briefly shifting away from the topic at hand.

"She's in mid-maturation," Badb interjected. "You need to get her home and back to the garden from which she sprang. She has time but not much, or she'll regress and grow feral, and all she could be would be lost. If your mother were here, she could induce the change, but…" She trailed off.

"I will."

Badb stood, stumbled, and then slipped to the floor. "It looks like I might have been a bit optimistic as to how much time I have left."

I rushed down to her. "Please, Badb, you can't go. This isn't what I wanted. You taught me so much. I can't lose you now. I just found you again."

Badb's hand caressed my cheek. "Our relationship was always fraught, Skaja. This was our destiny. You are my successor. I will always be with you. Please save her."

Tears fell over my cheeks. I couldn't help it. Despite all that had happened between us and what she'd done to Nastasia, I leaned forward and pulled her to me, holding her close, willing her to stay with me, but the tarzhi didn't respond, and her breathing became more shallow. Finally, I whispered in her ear. "I will try."

"It's time," Badb said.

"I name Wisteria," I breathed and felt her nod into my shoulder.

Slowly, Badb's body turned completely gray, then to ash,

coming apart in my arms, as she collapsed into a disintegrated pile on the floor. I scrabbled up handfuls of the ash and squeezed them, smearing it across my chest and face, wracked with unassailable and incomprehensible grief.

My gut hurt, as it had when I'd thought Marcella had died, when Semi had brought me Boudka's body, when I'd watched Nastasia breathe a last 'I love you.'

I felt twisted and wrong, and I screamed out every ounce of rage and sorrow. The throne room shook with the sound and fury of it. My aunt, the battle crow, one of my greatest heroes, was dead. Once more, I dug my hands into the pile of ash that had been my aunt, my mother's sister, the last of the Morrigna.

Bright motes of vermillion sparkled from the ash and flowed into me. I gasped as an electric, powerful magic flowed through me. It was like nothing I'd ever felt, warm and alive and shining with the dark music of a home I'd never known. More motes, purple and blue-black, floated around me, forming into Badb's armor and whisking away the blood and grime from my body. And then, it all settled. All that Badb had been, the remains of her magic were mine now. I had become the battle crow, the queen of swords, the reaper across the fields of the dead. I was the Goddess of Battle.

It occurred to me that I had no idea what it even meant to be a goddess, and it wasn't over yet. There was still the mantle, the remains of my mother's power. I had a horrible moment of pause. *What will it take for me to have my life back? When all is said and done, and Drusera is rescued or dead, Dommus is packed off to Kaushkar or dead, how will I go back to being just Cait Reagan, homicide detective?* I simply had no idea.

CHAPTER FORTY-FIVE

"Will you be okay?" I asked Maggie, who looked horrible but at least conscious and aware of her surroundings. "I promise we'll be going home soon."

She gave me a weak thumbs up. "I'm okay for now. But tomorrow or the next day? I don't know. Doctor Veria was very kind, though. He said that the key is Earth magic. He said to tell you that you just have to reset my lines, whatever that means."

I shrugged. "I don't know, but we will figure it out."

I moved to Jess, who gave me a dark look. "What is it?" I asked.

"She loved you, not me," Jess mumbled miserably.

I pursed my lips in aggravation as my temper began to slip, but I tried to keep my tone gentle. "First, she loved us both, and if you couldn't see that, then you're a fool. Second, it's not okay for you to make her death about you."

Jess turned away and stared toward where Nastasia had died just the day before. She turned back to me, anger flashing briefly in her eyes, but then her expression cracked, and tears welled. "I want to blame you. I want to throw things at you, but I know it's not your fault. It just sucks."

I pulled Jess to me, wrapping my arms around her. Strangely, she settled then, nestling into me. I said, "I'm sorry. I know she loved you. When you were sick, she was devastated. And I know you loved her, too. I wish I could do something."

She didn't answer. She just clutched closer and began to wail. Her whole body shook.

"Shh," I murmured gently. "I know, Jess. I know. I'm going to miss her, too."

"I loved her, Cait," Jess moaned. "I want her back. I want her back."

Maggie shifted in her seat uncomfortably, watching us. I sniffed back my own tears and glanced up at her. "I'm sorry," I said.

She shook her head. "You don't need to be sorry, not for this. I've lost people, too, you know. I know how it feels." Then she did something surprising. She stood, limped over to us, favoring her infected left leg, and wrapped her arms around us. "Nastasia seemed like she wasn't easy to make friends with, but you two managed to worm your way into her heart. I'd say that's quite an accomplishment. I'm jealous, really."

Jess barked a laugh despite herself. "Yeah, she's hard to love. I won't lie."

"Sometimes," I agreed.

When Jess and I had cried as much as we were going to, at least here and now, we stood. "I think it's time to go home."

"Thank you, Skaja," Wisteria whispered. "I owe you a debt I can never repay."

I shook my head. "Absolutely not. I only did what I had to do to save my people. Now, I just need to get them home."

Wisteria gave a wan smile. "A moment longer, please. I have something for you, and there's something I wish to show you."

I nodded and turned back to Maggie and Jess. "Will you two be okay without me for a few minutes?"

"Some food would be good," Maggie said. "I'm starving."

Wisteria snapped her fingers, and several people in the court sprung into action. A few minutes later, fruits and cold meats arrived, and Wisteria assured us that hot meals, showers, and clothes would be provided.

"What about your mother?" I asked as she led me away from the burgeoning banquet.

"She's already been released. While you were talking with Badb, I helped her back to her rooms." Wisteria turned very quiet. "It's a bittersweet moment for us all, I'm afraid. She won't last much longer, a few days, maybe a week, I suspect. It's hard to say. I offered to return her to the throne, which would give her more time, but she refused. In truth, Skaja, this isn't a responsibility I've ever sought, nor will I savor it."

I paused, tugging her to a stop. "I know you don't think much of me, but someone once told me that the best leaders are often the people who want it least. "

"Good advice, cousin," she said with an arch smile. "Perhaps you should take it yourself."

I shifted uncomfortably from foot to foot. "I guess. I don't know the first thing about leading, and I certainly don't know anything about my own kind."

Wisteria gave me an appraising look and then cupped my cheek. "That first part is a lie. You've led an army, if only briefly. As for the second, I'll give you your first lesson. Your friend, Jessica, is that her name?"

I nodded.

"You need to take her back to the garden where her transformation began. If she'd been born on Shaddan before the fall, she would have been taken to such a place at birth. Her exposure at this age is already a risk, but the process has started. She needs to finish it as soon as possible."

"I don't even know what she is?" I said as we continued down the switchback stairs leading to the ground level and the rear garden. "My head says some kind of pixie."

"She's a night pixie," Wisteria said casually, pushing wide a set of double doors just off the bottom of the vast staircase, which opened onto a veranda overlooking a vast garden of beautiful flowers, some familiar, some truly alien. "The truth is, it's a bit of a misnomer. Night pixies aren't really pixies at all. They look like pixies—if a pixie were over five feet rather than three inches tall. When she completes her transformation, her wild swings of behavior will settle, but her powers will come into full bloom. Like all Fae, she has the power of glamour, and like pixies, she will have insectile wings, butterfly in her case, but that will be where the resemblance stops. Night pixies are predators. They will stalk almost anything except Shaddani royalty."

I raised an eyebrow. "Jess is a police officer. This doesn't sound conducive to that life."

Wisteria chuckled. "It will depend on how in control of her instincts she is. Her senses and abilities will likely serve her well enforcing the laws of your world. Give her time and try to coach her. It might help you as well."

I frowned. "How so?"

"Skaja, Shaddan was a paradise, a world of beauty, yes, but it was also a dark place of chaos and nightmares. Creatures of smoke and fire lived in vast deserts. Great serpents and women who sang songs that could charm the soul lived in the seas. Dragons full of darkness once ruled the skies. Your ancestors rode them for millennia if the stories I was told as a child are to be believed. Unfortunately, that was before my time. Look, though, and see the true state of things in Bethad."

She took my hand and guided me forward to the edge of the veranda. I followed her gaze across the garden, spilling out in all directions to the massive sphere that comprised the gate to Bethad, and I gasped in horror.

"Oh, Goddess," I breathed. The gate opened on a high clifftop overlooking a vast landscape beyond, and it was a mottled mess. Some areas were green and glowing with life; others were dark and twisted, and still more were positively barren, looking desertified. I didn't know that much about Bethad. I'd never been there, but I did know it shouldn't look like that. The entire world should be green and verdant.

I turned back to Wisteria. As I watched her, Wisteria's hair lost its luster, turning long and stringy, pale white as its thick fuschia curls simply fell away, vanishing in glittering light. The long, flowing gossamer gown she wore faded into a threadbare shift that barely covered her, and the silver threads of magical lights weaved into her clothing vanished.

I reached out again and placed my hand on her shoulder, turning her toward me.

Her face was pale and gaunt, as if she hadn't eaten in weeks.

"Oh, Wist, I'm so sorry. What happened?"

Wisteria hugged herself. "It's almost gone, Skaja. There weren't many of us left after the last battle. The lesser Fae that Badb didn't kill just faded away shortly after her magic took hold. We're all that's left. Coming here to bolster our numbers was a last effort to save ourselves."

"Like Shaddan," Wisteria continued through her tears. "Bethad depends on us to keep it alive and beautiful. The magic persists and flows, but to truly make it what it is, we all participate, guided by the Summer Queen. And now—"

"What happened to Mother Danu?"

She gave a mirthless laugh. "No one really knows. Most of us believe she rejoined in the magical harmony that is the source of all, but honestly, none of us can be sure. It's clear, given what we have learned here, that our work was never completed. Mother Darkness lives, and this world is still under threat, and now, so is ours. And there are even less of us than there were before.."

"Badb caused this?" I asked, still staring at the patchwork quilt of living and dead landscape.

Wisteria nodded. "Yes. Now that she is gone and I have taken her place, the land will heal, but it will take time. We cannot return until it rights itself, so we're stuck here in your world. Ireland was the only place we truly knew well, so it was the only logical choice. Also, the humans are defenseless against us. We couldn't afford a protracted fight."

"And the people who live here still?" I prodded, mostly curious what her long-term plans were.

"The ones on the coast, we'll leave for now," Wisteria said, her eyes turning hard, almost daring me to object.

"They'll starve soon. You should either take them or at least turn the power back on and let the other humans help them. Don't make them suffer needlessly."

Wisteria laughed a cold, brittle laugh. "I won't let them starve, Skaja, not to worry, but Jess said that you hated them."

"Big mouth," I muttered. "I do, some of them, most of them, even. But Maggie is my friend, and there are others. How many others might I count as friends if I only knew them better?"

"You are far wiser in your youth than you give yourself credit for. I can promise this. I will make sure the remaining humans are fed and clothed. I'll do my best to keep them from being tormented, but this land is ours now, and we won't be giving it up anytime soon."

I nodded, then I gave her a quick hug. "Would a thousand or so Fae creatures and a few hundred Bethadi help matters?"

She looked at me, puzzlement etched on her features. "Of course, it could be no worse than it is now. And the presence of more of our magic here would certainly help keep us protected."

"A Fae bargain, then," I said firmly. "You have to promise me to come to my aid when I call, not in a hundred years either, the moment I ask."

Wisteria scowled in disappointment. "My mother made such a bargain with yours, and look where it got us. I know what you wish, Skaja, but I can't promise what you ask. Mother Darkness has already taken so much from us."

I sighed in resignation. "I understand. And you can call me Cait."

"You will always be our Skaja," she said with a crooked smile. "It suits you better. Or perhaps Weyna, it means—"

"—hero." I finished with a humorless snort. "I was never that. No one sings songs of Weyna."

Wisteria laughed. "No, perhaps not. But it makes you no less a hero to me, and we will sing your praises as long as we live, which is quite some time. Now, there is something else I need to show you."

I took her hand, and we walked back into the castle. The building itself was still beautiful and timeless, but the decorations were tattered and threadbare. The furniture was old and worn. Everything looked less than it had been for certain. In the throne room, the floor and walls were once again white, but they had lost some of their luster.

The rest of the court still waited, and Jess had a grim expression. Her eyes screwed up in sympathy as she spoke to one of the Bethadi men whose beautiful silver and gold gilded armor had turned tarnished and worn. Maggie likewise looked on in quiet sadness even as they all ate the lovely dinner the cooks had prepared.

Rowan stood at the back, watching the whole affair with her typical vampiric detachment, while the rest of the Bethadi court held their heads in what I could only describe as a horrid expression of group shame.

Beauty and glamour were their expressions of self, their whole identity. It sometimes seemed vapid and shallow, but it wasn't. It was artistic and beautiful, and it was how the Light Fae expressed their joys and sorrows in ways that made human hearts soar and fall. Yes, they were fickle and toyed with humans often, but that was simply who they were. My aunt had stripped everything from these people, and many had perished as a result.

Wisteria stepped to the throne and gingerly lifted the mantle. As I watched, her fingertips turned black as night where they touched the cloth. She held it out to me. "Take this, Skaja. It's yours."

Rowan appeared out of nowhere as soon as I took it. "I suggest that you put it on in a safe place here rather than wait until you return home."

I took the garment and gave her a puzzled look. "Why?"

"Must you always question every bit of sound advice I give you? By the blood, you're just like—" She broke off. "Never mind. Just do as I say for once, child. It's for the best."

That didn't sound good, but I didn't argue, and I needed it to save Aoife; otherwise, what was it all for?

CHAPTER FORTY-SIX

"Are you ready for this?" Jess asked as I unfolded The Morrigan's mantle, and Maggie helped me spread it out. It didn't look special, just a black cloak with the symbol of the House of the Morrigan embroidered on it: three circling crows —but I could feel its call. It wanted me. My fingers buzzed with it. My head rang with the need to throw it over my shoulders. The desire to have it swallow me tugged at every part of my being. It was all I could do just to hold it there as it spilled down to the floor.

"Honestly," I answered. "I'm fucking terrified, which is why I want to do it here, where there are people to stop me if it goes wrong."

We stood in the palace's laboratory because, well, gotta have a magical laboratory in a faerie castle, right? Wisteria and the six mages of the court that I'd seen earlier moved into a circle around me as Maggie and Jess moved behind them.

"The floor beneath you is inscribed with our most powerful runes of protection. They should contain you." Wisteria commented, rather blithely, I thought.

"Should?" I asked, feeling even more uneasy.

"They will," she nodded. "This is the most well-reinforced room in the building and is designed to handle a significant blast, so…" She trailed off and took a step back as the Magi raised their hands, and the runes inscribed on the floor lit up one by one. Each shimmered with golden light as the magic moved around the circle like some massive clock hand. As the last rune lit, my ears popped gently, and the room turned eerily silent.

Wisteria said something to me, but I couldn't hear her. No sound penetrated the magical dome created by the runes. I reached out and found the air between myself and my companions solid. Jessica wore a fascinated expression, but Maggie looked worried.

"I'll be okay," I encouraged silently, giving Maggie a thumbs-up. She returned the thumbs-up and nodded.

"Okay," I muttered to myself and waved to Wisteria. She answered with an Óṣení three-fingered 'fuck off' gesture and a wink. I gave her a wry look with pursed lips, but they slipped into a grin. She grinned back and waved, mouthing, 'Goodbye.'

This is it, I thought. Either I could handle the powers of The Morrigan, or it would kill me. I slung the cloak over my shoulders with a flourish. Wisteria's expression shifted, turning pensive.

For a second or two, nothing happened, and I shrugged at her. Wisteria frowned back at me. Then her eyes went wide. Dark Fae tarzhi swirled around me. I dropped to my hands and knees as agony flooded my chest and limbs.

Fuck, I wondered dryly. *Why does everything I do have to be so fucking painful?* It wasn't as bad as my Valtárí brand had been, and certainly nothing like being infected by the white worm, but it wasn't pleasant. And at least it wasn't my head this time. That was blissfully clear. The pain passed quickly, but I found I couldn't really move much. I was stuck on my hands and knees as my arms and legs jerked spasmodically. Electricity danced within the circle between me and the ground.

With effort, I pulled my gaze up. Wisteria gesticulated wildly, pointing behind me and screaming something. It was then that I realized the entire room had gone completely dark except for the glow of the runes.

"Oh, shit," I murmured as the electrical discharges ceased,

and I heard two soft footsteps behind me. Finally, able to move again, I stood and turned.

I wished I hadn't.

I had expected to see a person, my mother perhaps, or Badb's spirit, but this apparition drove ice water into my veins. Tall and shrouded in ragged clothing, it looked more like the Grim Reaper than anything else. A pale white hand extended and pointed at me.

"Do you accept?" Its terribly hissing words echoed within the circle. The runes were flickering now, and I was worried they would fail before this was completed.

"Are you The Morrigan?" I asked shakily, feeling a shiver down my spine as something akin to tiny clawed feet seemed to scramble up my body.

Without warning, the creature launched forward, slamming me into the shield that surrounded the circle. "Do you accept?" It hissed again as its pale hand wrapped around my neck.

A memory, dark and twisted, floated into my thoughts. I had been in this position before. No, not me. Úmbra!

This was a test, I realized. But what was the right answer? The memory was incomplete. Úmbra had pulled on the powers of Mother Darkness to banish this creature, but I didn't know what had happened after that. What had she been seeking? It wasn't The Morrigan. It couldn't have been. She had been trailing Avra, hadn't she? The memory had no context, and I had no idea what I should do.

"Fuck," I ground out. "Get the hell off of me!" When it didn't let go, I hissed, "I'm the Queen of Shaddan, and you will obey!"

The creature instantly stilled, and its hand relaxed. With a slow nod, it crumbled to dust. Around my shoulders, the mantle fell to rags, and the smell of burning embers and soft summer fragrances filled my nose and mouth. A thousand images flooded my mind as I slid down the shield to the floor, enraptured by the vision.

"Mother," I whispered in awe, a tear running down my cheek, my voice childlike. "I see it."

Shaddan spilled out as I flew above it. Not the Shaddan of

today, but our world at the height of its civilization. I flowed over the land gracefully, catching the sights, sounds, and smells of the landscape. A vast ocean came and went, bringing with it the scents of saltwater and brine. The field of heroes passed beneath me. The great branch of Crann Bethad stuck out from the island where Drusera would be left thousands of years hence.

I still sat in the circle. I was aware of the stone beneath me and the shield pressing at my back with a light warble, but the images continued until, finally, I found myself within the vast city of Nochtanmore, the capital of Shaddan.

People of all kinds moved to and fro, going about daily tasks so mundane and simple: trade and commerce, parties and occasional conflicts, even acts of kindness and love. Many of them were obviously Óṣení. Some were High Shaddani. And some floated on colored wings, Night Faeries like Jess. Still others moved about, creatures of every shape and size. It was beyond breathtaking, but that wasn't the end.

Ahead, the Vermillion Palace stood, glowing like a beacon of magic, its blood-red crystal towers seeming to touch the sky above. And the sky—it was unbelievably beautiful. In one portion, a massive nebula of greens and browns puffed like clouds and hovered beautifully, alight with the birthing of stars. A vast spiral galaxy, its arms twisted around a bright center, floated far away, distinct but no bigger from my perspective than a thumbnail. The moons floated in the sky stuck in their perpetual phases, one full, one waxing, one waning. Thousands of years of knowledge drifted within my head, all at my proverbial fingertips.

"Not too shabby, is it, Weyna?" A voice said to my left.

I knew that voice, and tears immediately sprung to my eyes. "Ma!" I cried, jumping up and launching myself at her, wrapping her in a firm hug. Suddenly, I was Weyna at eighteen again, memories taking me back to her cabin, my arms wrapped around her as we forgave each other and found our peace at last. "Oh, Ma, I missed you so much."

"And I missed you, dear daughter," she said as she hugged me back, holding me tightly, her tears dripping onto my cheek.

"Are you—alive?" I asked, swallowing hard, wanting it to be true but knowing that this was just an afterimage, a bit of her left in the mantle.

She smiled down at me sadly. "No, child. This is all that remains of me. When I gave Róisín a child, I placed within her almost all that I was. My body died shortly after, and what little magic I had left of my own, I used to show you what you needed to know, but my soul lives on in you and your sister." She ran gentle, warm fingers down the side of my face and tugged at the high collar of my leathers. "I see that you have inherited the power of the Battle Crow. And now, for a time, you will have my power, too. But, remember, three there must be to rule Shaddan. You have a choice to make."

I pulled her back to me. "I don't want you to go."

"Child," she whispered softly. "I am always with you in your heart and soul. We will be forever a part of each other."

"And the power of The Morrigan?" I asked cautiously.

"Such is our burden. She is always with us as she has always been a part of you." She backed away, her body losing its cohesion at the edges, like smoke or fog. "Try to remember who you are and what you have come to be. That is all that will save you from tilting over the very edge of chaos. Be wary, my daughter. She is upon you fully."

My mother reached out her hand, and I took it one last time before she disappeared in a sprinkle of tarzhi that flowed into me. The breath of her scent blew into my lungs, filling me for just a moment, and I squeezed my eyes shut.

"No," I whispered, the cold hand of grief squeezing at my heart once more. "It's too much," I whimpered. "I can't do this. Please, Mother of Waters, make it stop. I can't take any more."

An abrupt chill stole over me, and I turned back to the center of the room. The images that had floated there were gone, replaced by a nebulous blackness, deep and dark. If my heart could beat, it would have been a jackhammer in my chest. As it was, despite myself, I breathed in a shuddering breath, feeling the anxiety and fear.

I forced myself to relax and accept my fate. "I'm as ready as I'll ever be," I whispered into the darkness.

The black mass shot forward, tunneling into my nose and mouth like smoke, making me gag and lurch as it seemed to be choking the life from me. The sensation ended abruptly, though, replaced by rage and a tittering madness that drew a malign smile to my lips.

The Morrigan, the entity that stirred in all of us of the royal line, had taken her hold.

And the mystery of our trinity became clear. One soul, split and bound, becoming three and yet still one: Aoife, Drusera, and me. As it was before with Nemhain, Macha, and Badb, so it was with us. It was destined.

In that moment, I became so much more than even Nastasia had ever suspected I could be. I was a Goddess, and yet, still more than the whole of my ancestors. The floor floated away as I rose, and vast raven's wings unfurled behind me. The magic of Shaddan, Bethad, and Earth all whorled around me like a slow-motion maelstrom. It moved and danced to my whims. I looked at the circle of runes designed to keep me pinned to this place. I laughed almost maniacally.

"No." With a grim smile, I tugged gently at the magic of the runes. It just unraveled and floated away, and they went dark.

"Cait?" Jess asked.

"Yes, my child?" I replied, feeling the vast well of strength within me like some devilish high. It felt so good, euphoric, and powerful. I could take this world apart with my bare hands if I wished.

"Are you still in there? Is it still you?"

I paused at that, turning toward her. "I am the Goddess of Magic. I am the Goddess of Battle. I am the conductress who guides the dead. I am the seer. I am the mother and the crone." The lab dimmed to almost total darkness as the magical lanterns flickered and died, one by one, until only a single sconce burned nearby.

"Oh, God," Maggie breathed, dropping to the ground in terror and hiding her face. She felt it—I knew—the desire in her chest. It was like a physical thing, calling her to me.

I whipped my head around at the sound of her voice. "Hmm," I murmured gleefully. "What should I do with you?"

Wisteria backed away, whispering to the Magi and shooing them out. She locked the lab door, leaving only the four of us inside. I ignored her. Maggie was much more interesting.

"I can save you," I whispered, lowering to the ground in front of her as my magic wormed in and stilled her tremors. I could feel her terror, her desire to run that fused with a deep-seated need to embrace me, and it sang in my blood. It felt so good that I wanted to take some time and revel in it, but I set that aside. Through the tarzhi, she was a shining star, and yet, in places, I saw a touch of purple here, a bit of blue there, and there, deep within her soul, sat a mote of red that pulsed with the life of a world long gone.

"I don't want you to save me," Maggie whispered, sounding small and terrified. "I just want to go home. I want someone to take this stuff off of me and let me go. I don't need to be saved."

"But you do," I said with a dark smile. My ruby red lips parted, showing my fangs as I ran a cruelly clawed black nail down her cheek, tugging at the soft flesh. "You can't just go home, Maggie, not to that dingy apartment and incessant loneliness, always wondering if the companion of the night even likes you, always waiting for the other shoe to drop until they leave. It never matters, man or woman. It never seems to be right. And there's a reason you never fit in, never feel whole."

Maggie's eyes ran with tears as I cracked wide her soul and exposed the raw pain within to the open air. The power of it was heady, but I wasn't done. Without an ounce of glamour or manipulation, I had crushed her resolve with a few words, but not to leave her that way. "You are special," I continued. "You need a real life, the life you were supposed to have. The life that there was no one left to give you. And so, you will be the first of my true children."

Maggie sobbed, but I pressed on mercilessly, probing into her deepest, darkest pain. "You are one of us. Didn't you feel it? When you took the life of that Bethadi knight, perhaps? Or, maybe, when you threw the blade perfectly and struck down Badb?

"Our connection guided my hand to save you when we first met. I wasn't sure at the time if it was real, but such things like this have their own rhythms, their own rhyme and meter. They are like a song unsung and hiding amid the myriad chords and notes of possibility, but I hear it now, in all its glorious detail. I know what you are." I let that last sentence hang in the air over Maggie's head like the sword of Damocles.

Maggie stopped struggling against my glamour, surrendering to my words. The tears still stung her eyes no matter how desperately she tried to blink them away. But they were hopeful rather than terror-filled. "What—what am I?" she asked, her voice tremulous and small.

I gave her a soft smile full of love and cruelty, dark and pungent with my intent and her need. "Beneath the moons of Shaddan, which forever glow, fixed in place, one full, one waxing, one waning. Below their light, forever sliding across the world, is the penumbra, the edge where shadow and light combine. And the center of that place is what you truly are, a shadow born of light and darkness."

I pulled hard on the Bethadi magic, drawing in a vast pool of energy. My human heritage and that little bit of Aine's soul gave me the power to do in seconds what would have taken my aunt years. I spun Bethadi tarzhi, twisting and changing it into the Shaddani magic I needed. It was pitifully easy. The power built, rising toward a crescendo. Both Jess and Wisteria backed away from us, crying out in pain. I drank that in as well. It was delicious.

"Are you prepared to live as you never have?" I asked, giving a kind, darkly angelic smile.

"Please help me," she begged, tears streaking her face. "Make me whole and new. Take it away."

Her eyes went wide as she finally felt it inside her.

"Do not be afraid, my daughter," I whispered, now kneeling with her, my arms wrapped around her shoulders, my mouth to her ear. I was already changing her, had been before she'd even asked. She stared down at herself, eyes flashing in terror.

So much the better, I thought, still drinking it in. Her body spun apart from the ground up, first her legs, then her torso and arms, and finally, she disappeared entirely into a floating pool of inky darkness. Rapidly, though, she reformed. The corruption spun by my demented sister washed away in the transformation as Maggie became something else, something not human, a creature of the darkest of human nightmares and the most malignly prurient of their dreams, more frightening even than me, and yet so beautiful.

"You are a Night Maiden," I said. "You are my herald and my daughter. I have remade you and now name you for the Nerin, the sacred twisting shadow of the moons."

The creature I'd wrought solidified prostrate before me. She still looked much like Maggie, if she had been formed of smoke and moonlight rather than flesh and blood. Her eyes glowed with a savage, silver light that wafted with power. Her body still held its feminine shape, but the skin was light gray beneath her wild black locks. Bits of random magic floated from her like wisps.

"Rise, Nerina," I said, and she stood, resting so lightly on the ground as to almost be floating. The tears were gone, as was her fear. The horror she'd just experienced became a forgotten, distant memory as I consumed it.

"Why?" She asked, her head tilted in curiosity.

"As a child, you always wanted to whisk yourself away under doors or through cracks in the wall, disappearing into the night," I said. "Now you can go where you like, see what you wish. You will never die. You will never grow old. And no one will hurt you."

She stared at me, dumbstruck and confused, not by her transformation but by her feelings. I could see it in her face. I'd drunk in her fear and used it to fuel her transformation. I'd also entered her mind, giving her purpose and need. I'd taken a meaningless life full of hardship and graced her with power beyond her imagining. I'd remade her, and impossibly, she felt beautiful and complete, not like a horror at all—at least, not yet.

"Not to worry, little Nerina," I said, running a hand through her hair, disturbing the magical vapor that wafted around her. "There is so much more that I need from you, but for a time, you will be free to do as you please, and when I call, you will return to me."

"Yes, Mistress," Nerina said.

I leaned in and whispered instructions to her. She drifted away, vanishing into a dark corner, and was gone. I turned to Wisteria, advancing on her. She pressed harder to the wall as if she could simply fade into it. I felt her fear and drank in the richness of it, so like the taste of her blood. I reached out and touched her face, watching her flinch away. "Mother Morrigan," she whispered. "Please, don't."

I cupped her cheek. "One good turn deserves another. You helped me, fed me from your very blood. Call this repayment." I left my mark upon her cheek, a spiral of black, not unlike the brand that still lay burned upon my breast.

She touched it gingerly. "What have you done?"

"We are family," I said lovingly. "I have only marked you as such. Look." I turned my cheek, showing the gold spiral that had appeared there. "Today we are sisters, you and I. Where you were alone, you are now one of four." Turning away, I gazed at Jess, who stared at me eyes like saucers, her mouth agape. "If you have need of me," I said absently to Wisteria, "I will know. But when I have need of you, you will come."

Wist stared up at me; her eyes were wide, and her nostrils flared. "You can't. We can't."

"You took my home, Wist," I said, placing a firm hand on her shoulder. "You can keep it, but there is a price. I need your magic."

"Cait, stop," Jess said, a tremble in her voice.

"Don't look at me like that, Jess," I said. "I only gave Maggie what she most wanted, to be free of the confines of her life and her pain. I gave her purpose. I've made a solemn vow to Wisteria. And though it comes with strings, she will be stronger for it."

"Cait," Jess said through trembling lips. "This isn't you. You don't do things like this. You don't just make people what you want or change them how you see fit."

"It's not? I don't?" I asked with a wicked smile. "Are you sure?"

Jess took a step back. "Cait, stop, please." In her voice flowed the icy breath of fear.

"Jess," I murmured to her. "You don't have to be afraid. Wist needed to know she wasn't alone. Now she can see she has allies, and she and I need allies. You need my help, too. You're out of time."

"Wisteria," Jess said, running over and shaking the Bethadi Queen by the shoulders. "Help her. Stop her."

Wisteria looked at Jess, eyes pleading. "I—can't. I couldn't even if I wanted to. You don't understand the gift she just gave me. But you... You need to let her do what she must. You don't want to go feral, do you? You'll become nothing more than a savage eating machine."

Jess shook her again, but Wisteria didn't blink or budge. I had her, for the moment, at least. Jess backed against the wall. "What are you doing?"

I stepped forward and reached out my hand, calling forth the transformational magic once more. *No,* my sister said in my head. *She is right, Caitlin. This is not you. You must take control.*

"Oh, shut up, Drusera. You and my aunt conspired to steal the magic of our home," I answered aloud and blocked her out. I was sick of her meddling. I was chosen. I was— I paused. Something nagged at me, a touch of anger—no, rage —a feeling of being used.

"N-No," I ground out involuntarily, my teeth chattering on the word as I fought to maintain control. "I'm not done." I quelled the flailing attempts to push me down as my hand snapped out, grabbing Jess by the arm and pulling her close to me. The slender ribbons of Shaddani magic twisted around her.

"Stop, please," Jess whimpered, but it was too late. She didn't understand now, but she would. I was saving her. She was on the edge. The feral nature of the Dark Faerie within her was trying to take her. I wouldn't let it.

"See, Jess," I whispered as the magic began to change her.

Jess's eyes turned vacant as she saw the future that awaited her, absent intervention. A creature, not even a woman anymore, pounced on anything that moved, tearing it to pieces and consuming as much as it could. That demon-like monster terrified her, more so because it *was* her. She saw herself killing the innocent and taking bits of them.

She knew it to be true. She'd already been there, seen it, done it. And it horrified her because I'd twisted her psyche, stealing in like a thief in the night and unlocking a deeper sense of empathy. Every horrible thing she'd done, every horrible feeling she'd engendered in others, crashed back into her mind. In the end, she begged.

"Help me," she breathed in terror, her voice small, like a child's.

"I will," I said as she sank to the floor, curling up fetal.

Soft moss, the color of grape soda, grew in an almost perfect circle beneath her, spreading out from her body. Without another word, Jess closed her eyes. Thin gossamer threads spun straight from her pores, covering her entire body in a rapidly thickening translucent carapace, not altogether unlike a butterfly cocoon. Fascinated, I enjoyed my front-row seat to one of the most precious life cycles of our world.

It was only a few minutes before a deep, blood-red glow erupted from the cocoon. The beautiful light sparkled like the sun through wine, shimmering as Jess moved within. I put a hand on the carapace-like covering, finding it hot to the touch.

Strange muffled popping and cracking noises sounded from the chrysalis. An occasional, if faint, pained squeak or agonized cry erupted from within.

Somewhere, that anger peeled at my thoughts again. I wanted to tear at the cocoon and free her, but I held the urge at bay. "No…" I grimaced. "Not yet. You'll kill her or leave her deformed."

I lay myself across the chrysalis protectively, feeling every movement, every stroke of the creature inside. My child, my dark, beautiful child. The touch soothed the raging human within me, if only for a moment—just long enough.

The cocoon jerked several times in rapid succession. Part of it began to press upward on the flat of my palm. I drew back, watching in a weird mixture of abject horror and wild fascination as a bulb protruded outward like some weird pseudopod. As it grew up and away from the main body, the skin of the cocoon thinned, and the appendage within slowly resolved itself into the stretching fingers of a hand.

Blood-red nails, so sharp that they looked as if they could rend stone, broke through with a wet sucking sound. Another hand erupted behind the first, pushing apart the cocoon. The sticky material slid over the arms with faint elastic creaks and pops. Very slowly, Jessica emerged, head first, eyes still closed. She licked her lips in an almost sensual way and took a soft breath before flopping over onto her side. The shell still stuck to her lower half in places.

"Jessica?" I whispered when she didn't move for what seemed too long a time.

"Give me a minute," she replied, voice quiet and drunken, before pulling herself up and rubbing her face. Her skin was baby-smooth, and there wasn't a freckle on her anywhere.

I didn't dare touch her. Somehow, I knew that even this late stage needed to take its normal course.

Her hair, an unnaturally deep shade of red, cascaded long and gorgeous like a bloody wave down her back. Ethereally pale skin covered her entire body, scattered with bits of twinkling red, flawless and mesmerizing in the dim light of the chamber.

A few minutes later, she pulled up and extracted herself from the sticky mass of now rapidly dissolving husk. As expected, when her nude torso finally appeared, I could see gorgeous, vermillion moth-like wings protruding from her back and slowly unfolding. They were enormous, and her fabulous, deep emerald green eyes were much larger than they used to be, but not freakishly so. She blinked them several times and languidly focused. "Mother Morrigan," she murmured and bowed her head.

I slipped to the stones, spent and tired, unable to move. The laboratory sconces sprang to life, and the pulsing purity of chaos diminished until I could think clearly again, but still, she was there. I could feel her intensity, her power, her voracious desires. It seethed deep inside me, a siren call I so longed to answer again.

"Mother Danu," I murmured in prayer. "How did my mother keep this power in check?" Just as it was for my mother and her sisters, so it was for me. I was now The Morrigan's vessel, and she was mine, and the implications were terrifying.

"Cait?" Jess prodded, kneeling and cradling me, stroking my hair. She was uncomfortably close, but the feel of her skin on my cheek was so pleasant and soothing that it lifted some of the fog.

Slowly, with trembling fingers, I reached up and found her face. Just running my fingertips on her cheek gave me such a sensation of belonging, but I couldn't hold it there. Fatigue wracked my limbs. I was so tired. "Yeah, just—just give me a second." My hands still shook with a lingering anxiousness. "I'll be alright. I just need to recover."

Jess held me like that for a long time. "What's wrong with her?" she asked Wisteria.

"Transformation magic is taxing," Wisteria said. "And though it is far less so for her than for us, it still takes a toll."

I waited there, cradled in Jess's arms, feeling an almost euphoric love for her. Finally, the bout of fatigue waned, and I could finally pull my head up and look into her eyes. "I'm sorry."

She just laughed and smiled. "You're always sorry," she said lightly, and while I thought she might lose her temper and rail against me or slap me with those sharp nails, all she said was, "Okay, so am I still me? Or am I a bug-eyed monster?"

I snorted a wry laugh and whispered. "You're good people, Jess."

She helped me up, and when she was sure I wouldn't drop, she stepped away and spread her arms. Her wings spread to their fullest. I gasped. "You look—oh, Goddess, Jess—" I paused, and her eyes went wide with worry. "Jess, you're beautiful. Its—" Tears burned in my eyes at the sight of her. "I have no words."

She seemed happy with that appraisal as she inspected herself. Looking over her shoulder, she cocked a hip. "Now, how the fuck am I supposed to get a uniform over these?" she bitched, and I couldn't help myself; I laughed.

"It's not funny," she groused. "This is fucking inconvenient. I can't run around nude. And I certainly don't want to be on Kim's pickup list, you know?"

"Jess," I said in a way that suggested I was making a solemn vow. "I would never let anyone hurt you. You are a precious thing."

"Woman," she corrected softly through pursed lips.

"Huh?"

"I am a precious woman," she repeated more forcefully. "I'm not a thing."

"I'm sorry, I couldn't control her," I muttered, ashamed and closing my eyes against the memory of what I—no, what The Morrigan had done through me.

Jess put her palm to the side of my face. "This is what I am," Jess murmured. "I just never knew it before. You freed me. You made me complete."

I wasn't convinced. I couldn't tell if this was Jess talking or what The Morrigan had done to her.

"How do you feel?" I asked, pushing aside my guilt as best I could. What was done was done.

She barked a laugh. "Fucking amazing. I feel like I slept for days and I'm ready for a night on the town. Do these seem too small to fly to you?" She gingerly tested her wings, letting them fan out to an almost ten-foot total wingspan and flutter for a second.

"I guess there's only one way to find out," I replied sheepishly.

Jess threw her arms around me, eyes tearing up. "I was afraid I'd lost you, too. Now, can we please go home?"

"Yes, Jess," I said, holding on to her for dear life. "We can go home."

Wisteria stared at me darkly. "That's an excellent idea. You have overstayed your welcome."

I looked at her, my brow furrowed and my eyes pleading. "I'm sorry, Wist. I couldn't—"

"Enough, Sister," she snapped. "It's done." Then she turned

to Jess, her expression softening. "I'll get you some clothes."

CHAPTER FORTY-SEVEN

We didn't stay much longer, but Wisteria gave us long enough for showers and fresh clothing. The momentary break gave me a little time to explore my own body. I was different. I was still a vampire. That hadn't changed, for which I was eternally grateful, but I found myself able to change my shape in ways I hadn't expected. Beyond the wings, everything was mutable. With a thought, I could change all or part of me into almost anything I could imagine. I provided the image, and my magic provided the form.

When Jess came back, I had to admit, she looked incredible. The high-collared jet-black jacket hugged her figure perfectly, paired with a crisp white shirt and matching pants that somehow managed to look both professional and effortlessly stylish. The jacket and shirt had openings in the back, and apparently, some of Wisteria's Light Fae pixies had shown Jess how to roll up her wings and guide them through. I hadn't been there for that part—I couldn't even begin to imagine how it worked—but Jess seemed satisfied, which was what mattered. She was also holding a large parcel, which contained another six work-ready suits Wisteria had commissioned for her.

I crossed my arms, eyeing Wisteria. "Do you have Rumplestiltskin working back there or something?"

Wisteria arched a perfect brow, the picture of unbothered elegance. "I like Jess," she said pointedly, making it very clear who wasn't on her nice list. Then, without missing a beat, she added, "But no, I gave Rumplestiltskin the day off."

I blinked at her, caught off guard. "…Wait, was that a joke?"

Her expression stayed as cool and serene as ever, but there was the faintest flicker of amusement at the corner of her lips. She handed me a small book of spells. "To get you started," then with a soft smile, she added, "sister."

I placed my hand over hers. "I'm sorry. I couldn't—"

She gave me a smirk. "I know. I'm not really angry at you. Now, page twelve."

"Now remember," Áine, who had joined us, said after I'd been studying the portal spell for a bit. "it only works for places you know intimately or can see directly. Trying to go places you've never been or, worse yet, off-planet will just get you killed."

She punctuated the warning with a spluttering cough as I recited the incantation for what felt like the hundredth time. Though she still looked pale and drawn, there was a hint of color in her cheeks now. She seemed to be improving, which was a relief. She deserved better than what my aunt had done to her. Everyone seemed resigned to her impending death, but something inside me suspected that the old bitty had a lot more years ahead of her.

Wisteria, who had been watching with an air of mild irritation, finally spoke, her tone clipped but not unkind. "If she doesn't get it now, Áine, she's never going to."

I glanced at Wisteria, half-expecting her to take the book back and tell me I wasn't worth the trouble, but she only raised an eyebrow as if daring me to argue.

Áine waved a hand dismissively at Wisteria and nodded toward me. "One more time, Cait. You've almost got it."

I took a deep breath and recited again.

"I think you're ready to return home," she said at last, satisfied I had the words right. All that remained was to see if I had the control.

"But," I said, suddenly feeling rather small and unprepared

for the responsibility that had been heaped on me. "I don't know the first thing about any of this. People pray to my mother, you know? I mean, she wasn't an actual goddess, but still."

"Yes, she was," Áine rasped. "And you will hear those truly dedicated if you pay attention, but that ability only comes with time."

"Wait, I have to answer prayers?" I asked, not liking the direction this was taking.

"I really don't recommend it," Áine replied. "Honestly, it will only lead to heartache. But there are responsibilities that come with power, and you will likely feel unable to resist the urge to help others at times.

"Do yourself a favor and be discerning. Ask questions. Look before you leap, as they say. Some prayers should not be answered, and some, ultimately, deserve a flat no."

I snorted in amusement despite myself at that last. "I think I can certainly discern a flat no. Also, what can I actually do to answer prayers anyway?"

Áine raised an eyebrow at that. "You would be surprised at just how little it takes to move things along. A spot of an inspired feeling here, some dissuasion there. Again, though, it's terribly busy work and not worth the hassle."

I had no idea what she was talking about, but I suspected I'd get a feel for it. In any event, there was something else that I was hoping she could answer for me. "I also have this odd feeling, like there's more to me than there was—a weird splitting of my consciousness. If I concentrate on them, I see things far away and in distant places. I don't know how to describe it."

"You're the Goddess of Death," Wisteria said as if I were being obtuse. At my bemused expression, she put her hands on her hips and spoke to me like a child. "Part of you is sifting the dead and sending them on. When you have time, explore that feeling, and you'll understand. No one can really help you with that, unfortunately."

I shook my head and blinked, letting my eyes drift around the room. "I don't know if I can do this," I said finally. "I had no idea that my mother was doing all these things behind the scenes."

"It's interesting when we find ourselves in the shoes of our parents. If they're worthy of the term 'Mother,' we truly come to appreciate all that they have done for us and others," she said with an arch grin. "It's not so easy, is it?"

Surprisingly, it was Jess who broke in and offered me encouragement. "You can, Cait. Nas believed in you—more than you know—and so do I." Hearing that from her helped soothe me immensely. Jess knew me. She knew what I was capable of. At least she thought I could handle what I'd been blessed—or cursed—with.

Wisteria came and embraced me tightly. "Thank you, Skaja. Maybe it won't be all doom and gloom. Here." She handed me a satchel.

I hefted it; it was relatively heavy for its size, and whatever was inside sounded like stones sliding together.

"Tablets. The last two remaining Earth tablets. You might need them."

"Is this all that's left?" I asked. "My mother had six pairs."

Wist gave me a cryptic smile, then patted me on the shoulder. "Just take those. Remember, if you can get to Shaddan, you can always make new ones."

I realized that she might have just given me the only bargaining chip we'd had so far in this subversive war against Mother Darkness. *Drusera, Cait, your sister,* I corrected silently. "Thanks, Wist. I won't say I owe you for this, but I appreciate it."

She smirked and waggled her eyebrows. "What? You don't want to owe me a favor?"

I chuckled. "Absolutely not, but—" I placed a hand on her face, thumbing the spiral mark. "I'm sorry for this. I don't know why I did it. It was as if—"

She reached up and pulled my hand away, glancing down at our joined fingers. "I know. She is hard to control."

"What is she?" I asked. "I don't understand."

Wisteria gave a wry chuckle. "None of us do, really."

"I'm so confused."

"She is an entity of pure chaos. She is alive and is part of you. She thrives on battle. She relishes changing things, sometimes just to change them—and she's possessive. That's all I know. Perhaps there are better answers in the Vermillion Palace, if it still stands."

Nodding, I hoisted the pack onto my back and kissed Wisteria on the cheek. "Thank you, sister."

Wisteria grinned up at me. "I never understood why you never tried to get me in your bed all those years ago."

I snorted a laugh. "Skaja couldn't have handled you then."

"And now?"

"And now, she's engaged to be married and has sworn off all others," I replied with an embarrassed smile. "Besides, we're sisters. That would be icky."

She gave me a childish pout, then took my hands and looked into my eyes, lowering her voice. "Well, you'll never know what you missed, and now it's time for you to go home. Such a shame. Maybe next time." She gave me a wink.

I looked at the floor. "Uh. . .Wisteria, I—"

"Oh, Skaja, you are just too easy," she tittered. "Now, make us proud and do it like we showed you. Oh, wait. I believed you would want this." She took a small urn from one of the Fae serving girls and held it out to me.

I stared at it, not wanting to take it, feeling emptiness and loss suddenly clench my heart. I took it from her anyway, though, and fought back the burning in my eyes.

"I'm sorry for your loss," Wisteria said and placed a hand over mine. "She was incredibly brave."

"You don't know the half of it." I looked at the jar of ashes. "I just don't understand why she had to be so fucking heroic right then." Nastasia's words echoed in my head. *Everyone loves a good redemption story.*

"You are redeemed and then some," I whispered and looked up into Wisteria's eyes. "I'm ready."

She smiled compassionately and moved away with her mother to the dais. Very carefully handing off the satchel and urn to Jess, I lifted my arms and called on the magic from the Shaddani gate so very far away, following the steps that

Wisteria had given me. They weren't hard, but the forces in play were powerful. The portal spell fucked around with spacetime and gravity. I couldn't hurt the planet in any significant way, but I could do a lot of damage locally if I wasn't careful. I kept Marcella's house firmly in my mind and said the incantation.

There was a spark of blue. The tarzhi snapped into a circle in front of me, maybe ten feet across. A fat, fuzzy image appeared within rapidly solidifying into a view of Marcella's foyer with an almost comical pop. Liz walked in from the kitchen and stopped mid-stride, staring right at us.

"Cait?" Then her eyes bugged. "Jessica?"

With a last look at the Fae around us, Jess and I stepped through, and the portal snapped shut behind us with a mild whump.

"Hi honey," I said through bittersweet tears. "I'm home."

"Oh, thank heavens," Liz said, throwing her arms around me and pulling me into a firm kiss. My foot may have lifted off the ground a little. I was such a sucker for the sappy stuff.

Jess walked slowly past us and into the kitchen, tears welling in her eyes. Liz glanced around. "Where's Nas?"

My eyes fell on the jar, and I shook my head. "She didn't make it." My voice was thick with unspent emotion.

Liz stared at me in pronounced shock. "What? What happened?"

"Badb," I said as I let go and stepped into the kitchen, dropping the satchel on the floor with mine and Déra's weapons before I placed the urn gently on the table. I dug a bag of blood from the refrigerator the suppress the bees under my skin. "Badb fucking happened." I dropped into a chair, scooting closer to Jess and sucking on the blood.

Jess grabbed a banana from the fruit bowl and started picking at it. "Nas did something incredibly brave and incredibly stupid."

"What? Will one of you tell me what happened?" Liz repeated, more forcefully this time.

"Badb took over Luminara, the Fae palace. It's a long story, but my aunt captured us, threatened me, and Nas went nuts.

She shot across the throne room and stabbed Badb."

Liz blinked, obviously confused. "She stabbed the Celtic Goddess of Battle?"

"Yes." I shook my head. "My aunt killed her on the spot for it. Stabbed her through the heart. I saw it, Liz. I watched her curse unravel like so much fucking silk thread right in front of my eyes. Then she just turned to ash. It was fucking terrifying. And there was nothing any of us could do. Jess tried, but all it got us was thrown into the dungeons."

"So, how did you get away?" Liz asked, sliding heavily into the next seat around the table.

Marcella walked in then. "Liz, have you seen Catherine? I need—" She stopped cold. "You're back."

"Yes. And Nas is dead," I said coldly. "She's gone. I got her killed."

"Quit saying that, Cait," Jess argued. "Not everything is your fucking fault. Just like you said, we volunteered to come. We knew the risks."

"Mama! You're home!" Katie cried as the elevator door opened and ran into the room, Leah hot on her heels. She wrapped her arms around my neck and squeezed me tight.

"Okay, honey. Yeah, I'm home," I said somberly, then I raised my voice. "Can everyone just give us a minute? We're not mad at anyone here, but we're worn out, and frankly, I don't know what I can handle right now."

"Did you find the soulstone, Mama?" Leah asked from the doorway. "Was the dark lady there?"

I looked at her, blinked slowly, and then said, "Yes, the dark lady was there, and we found something to help Auntie Aoife, but Mama's pretty tired right now."

Leah walked over, wrapped her arms around me, and whispered, "I'm just glad you're home. I was afraid."

"Wow, Jess! You have wings," Katie exclaimed and reached out tenderly. "Can I touch them?"

Jess gave a half-hearted wave, and Katie began feeling them. "They're not like butterfly wings at all. They feel like silk."

"I know, honey," I answered Leah and pulled Katie away from Jess for a group hug. "I missed you all, and I never want to be that far away from you again."

Jess stood as if to leave, but I grabbed her arm. "No, Jess. You don't need to be alone right now." She gave me a brief, forlorn look before sitting again and returning to her grief.

Leah took her hand. "It's okay, Jess; I'm going to miss Auntie Nas, too. But she'll watch over you." Jess bawled harder, turning completely inconsolable.

I leaned over to Katie, whispering, "Did you tell Leah that Nas was dead?" I thought maybe Katie had overheard us when they were coming down.

Katie shook her head and pursed her lips with worry, whispering back to me. "No. I didn't know. Nastasia's dead?" Liz and I shared a worried look, but we said nothing. Leah couldn't possibly have overheard us from the third floor.

It took a few minutes to quell the sudden chaos that had ensued upon our arrival. There were a million questions, but eventually, we shooed everyone away. It was all just too much in our battered state. Jess and I were cooked. Eventually, Katie and Leah took the hint, hugged each of us, and disappeared elsewhere. Jess vanished upstairs, for which I was grateful. I felt horrible for her and, despite what she'd said, terribly guilt-ridden. It was survivor's guilt, I knew, but still.

"Come on, love," Liz said after the kitchen emptied out. "Let's go up to our room and get the road grime off you."

I nodded and followed her to the elevator in a daze, just happy to be alive and to have come home in one piece. I decided right then that I had too much at stake to keep risking my life. Katie and Leah would be adults before I knew it, and this family Liz and I had accidentally cobbled together would be different. I wanted to savor it while we had it, even if I'd never be rid of The Morrigan; maybe I could pass the whole Goddess thing to someone else. Aoife and Morgan, maybe. I certainly didn't want it.

CHAPTER FORTY-EIGHT

"Where's Jess?" I asked later when Liz finished getting Katie and Leah settled in front of a movie.

"She's sound asleep down the hall in Catherine's room," Liz said as I stripped awkwardly out of my aunt's armor and got into the shower. For a while, I stood in the spray, just happy for the creature comforts.

"Can I join you?" Liz called from the door a few minutes later.

I leaned back so I could see her poking her head into the bathroom, a ridiculous smile on her face. "I'd really like that," I said, my voice low and hoarse with sorrow. "I could use some quiet time together."

"I'll wash your back," Liz said playfully, and I watched as Liz stripped, carefully folding her shorts and t-shirt on the toilet lid, followed by her panties and bra.

"Like what you see?" she asked, glancing back at me with a quirky grin, catching me staring.

"Yeah," I said. "I do. I missed you. And I was afraid for a minute that it was all over. Badb had me in this twenty-foot-deep oubliette covered with a Fae-steel grate."

"Sounds like she was a horrible person, to be honest, Cait," Liz said, washing my back with a soapy scrubby. I leaned forward, dousing my head in the spray and letting it rain

318

down through my hair and around my face. The hot water felt good.

"You saved me," I murmured.

"Hmm?" Liz asked as she turned me around and started washing my arms and chest.

"I can reach that part," I whispered.

"I know, but you look like you could use it. So, just let me do. Now, what were you saying?"

"Can I ask you something?"

"Sure, love, anything, you know that."

I tilted my head and giggled slightly as she washed under my left armpit. "I said, you saved me. Did you have any dreams while I was gone? Maybe of a psych ward?"

Liz's strokes slowed to a crawl, and she looked up at me, her eyes wide and searching. "How do you know that?"

"The Bethadi, they glamoured me. They did the whole your life is a delusion bit, psych ward and all. It was all really cliché, but they pushed false memories into my head that made it harder to tell reality from glamour. Anyway, you and Katie were patients in the unit, and the doctors, in the illusion, tried to tell me that we'd created this delusional family. "

Liz hummed thoughtfully, turning me back around and working on my legs. Then she said, "Remember—"

"Christmas," I finished for her fingering the bracelet. "This —it kept itching, and eventually, it helped me break the glamour."

Liz raised an eyebrow. "You broke Fae glamour? You're not putting me on, are you?"

"It took six mages and my aunt to hold me under, and I still broke it." Even as I said it, though, it sounded impossible, and I started to worry.

She started washing me again. "Well, I should say that I'm surprised, but I'm not. Truthfully, I'm just glad that you're home."

"Am I?" I asked honestly, feeling that same sense of dread from the worst moments of the glamour. "Am I home? I keep expecting to wake up, you know? I keep thinking that maybe the last few days have all been an illusion." My voice rose in pitch as panic flooded me. "Or worse, a delusion. Tell me it's not, Liz. Tell me I'm home. That it's over."

Liz cupped my face. "Cait, you're home. I promise. Now, let's get out of this water and curl up in bed. It's early yet, but you look like you could use time to unwind."

"Liz?" I whimpered. "How did Holley die?" Tears were running down my cheeks.

Taking my shoulders firmly, she said as gently as I'd ever heard her. "His heart failed him when you confronted him. I wasn't in there, but it sounded like you scared him literally to death."

I nodded, finally feeling my chest relax a little. "I need to take care of Aoife," I said softly, trying desperately to unload the obsessive thoughts.

Liz frowned and grew stern and demanding. "Now you listen to me, Cait Reagan. It's almost dawn. You just got back, and the entire journey clearly unnerved you. You need rest. So, no, you're not going anywhere until you sleep. Aoife's still stable. If Bian calls for any reason, I'll wake you."

I gave up and didn't argue. She was right. I was mentally exhausted. I tried changing the subject again, but I felt raw, and the grief over Nastasia returned with a vengeance. "So," I said, my voice breaking with a slight stammer. "What—what's the word on Senator Kim?"

"The vice president is addressing the state assembly to show support from the White House on rebuilding efforts. That's due to happen on Friday. Kim will be there."

I opened my mouth and then closed it again. I couldn't speak. My throat was constricted, and I blinked furiously against the pressure in my eyes.

"Want to talk about it?" She asked.

"It turns out," I began, my voice trembling, "that I cared for Nastasia way more than I thought I did. It was awful, Liz. So awful." I paused, swallowing hard against the lump rising in my throat. "There was this moment—just a split second—but I'll never forget it. I saw it in her eyes... she knew. Nas knew she was going to die. And she looked right at me."

The words burned as they left my mouth, dredging up the

memory I desperately wanted to bury. "She didn't beg for help. She didn't scream. There wasn't fear, not even anger. Just…" My voice cracked, and I clenched my fists, shaking my head violently as if to rid myself of the image. "…resignation. Like she'd already accepted it. Like she thought it was okay."

Liz's hand pressed against my back, steady and grounding, but it wasn't enough to stop the spiral. I buried my face into her shoulder, sobbing in broken gasps. "And her last words… God, Liz, her last words were to me."

I stopped. My chest heaved as I tried to pull myself together, but it was no use. The memory of Nastasia's face, her voice, hit me like a knife to the gut. "She said…" I choked on the words, unable to say them aloud, but they scorched my thoughts. *I love you.*

The silence stretched between us, heavy with the weight of what I couldn't bring myself to share. But in my mind, it was deafening—*I love you.* Her voice was still so clear, so heartbreakingly certain. She'd given me that, even knowing she wouldn't survive to see what I'd do with it.

"Why?" I wailed, clutching Liz's arms as though she were the only thing keeping me tethered to this world. "Why did she do that? Why would she…" My voice cracked again, splintering like glass under too much pressure. "Why would she leave me with that?"

Liz held me tighter, murmuring soft words I barely heard over the sound of my own ragged sobs. "Shh… It's okay."

"But—"

She placed a finger on my lips. "No, Cait," she said gently. "Let it go. It's okay to grieve for her. Just let it out. I knew you still loved her. I'm not a fool. It's okay."

I broke at those words, curling up on the bed like a child. Liz spooned up behind me, stroking my hair while I wailed. I hadn't wanted to. I had wanted to spare Leah and Katie from hearing it. But I just couldn't hold it in anymore. Nastasia was gone. And despite every stupid thing she'd done, I'd loved her. Seeing her that first night in this very room, the way she'd shared our pain. She'd unlocked the darkness inside of me and taught me it wasn't something shameful; it was beautiful and powerful, and she'd given me permission to know it. And now she was gone, and it hurt so much. And when I just didn't have any more tears, I pulled Liz under the covers and held tight to her. "Please don't leave me," I whispered like a broken little girl.

"I'm not going anywhere, love," Liz replied, stroking my head.

CHAPTER FORTY-NINE

I woke early that evening and made my way downstairs. Now, I was starving. My skin and extremities literally hurt. The bagged stuff from the Traulsen was running low, given that we had five vampires in the house at the moment. Even though it wasn't helping much, I grabbed some anyway. The specter of Aoife's possible demise pressed hard. Áine had given me a theoretical understanding of what I needed to do, but that was a far cry from executing it in practice, and my lack of any significant magical experience scared me. Souls were powerful, and what nature seemed to build effortlessly had taken my aunt the magic of an entire world to duplicate. *And it had almost killed her,* I thought irritably.

It was probably a testament to my hungry state that I was easily distracted by maudlin thoughts as I ruminated over my own predicament. My soul had been a lab experiment and an abhorrent use of magic. Badb had murdered thousands of species in pursuit of her goal, the perfect soul constructed for a single purpose. Yes, what she did was wrong, but that purpose was one I could easily understand, "Save my little girl."

I'd kill the world for my children—or Liz. Despite that, though, I chafed at the idea of being a construct—something artificial.

"You look deep in thought," Liz said, wandering tiredly into the kitchen.

"Mother Darkness is my sister," I muttered tiredly, taking another sip of the goopy blood. "I want to save her."

Liz's brow wrinkled, and she sat down, placing a hand on mine. "How is that possible? You said she's thousands of years old—tens of thousands."

"I'm a science project," I told her with a wry and rueful smile. "My aunt Frankensteined my soul together from bits of my mother, her sisters, Áine, and, I think, some of Mother Darkness, too." That got me an arched eyebrow and a curious look.

"Tell me more," Liz said.

"My aunt put me through a right of passage for the Shaddani royal family called The Blood of Shaddan—"

"No," Liz said gently, sounding like a therapist as she rubbed the back of my hand softly with her thumb. "Not that I don't care about the details, but I want to know how you feel about that.."

I blinked, suddenly unsure what to say. "I—I don't really know." I gave a nervous laugh. "How do you feel about it?"

Liz chuckled. "Love, I have no opinion on that whatsoever. It's irrelevant. I love you, and I just want to make sure you're alright. You've been a wreck since you got home."

"Have I?" I asked a little distractedly as I absorbed her words.

"Mmhmm."

I raised the bag of blood. "Must be hungry, I guess."

"No," Liz responded. "It's more than that. It's deeper."

I sighed and lowered my eyes. "It's The Morrigan. She's a part of me now," I whispered, feeling a cloying anxiety. "And I'm afraid of her."

"What does that mean?" Liz asked.

"She is a Goddess, Liz. And not like the Kaushkar or my Aunt. She is an entity of unfathomable reach and power. She was born from the primordial magic of Shaddan not long after it was formed, that much I know. But she's not an entity in her own right. She is attached to my bloodline. Without us, she would evaporate back into the magic of our world, I think.

She's been part of me since I woke up. I can feel her, like a rage-filled demon hiding behind my eyes, a being of chaos that the Goddess Queens of Shaddan channeled to rule and protect our world. But I don't know how to do that, so I just keep her locked away."

"Is that wise?" Liz asked, her tone level, but curiosity sparkled in her eyes. She was intrigued, and I couldn't blame her. How often does your lover, your wife-to-be, become a true Goddess?

"I don't know. But when I first allowed her any leash at all, she took over. I transformed Maggie, the girl we'd taken hostage after the fight to leave town, into a Night Maiden, one of Shaddan's secret guard—they're assassins. She was just a kid, Liz, and I changed her fundamentally. She's not her anymore. I remade her into a creature destined to do the bidding of my sister and me."

Liz pursed her lips in thought. "Can it be undone?"

I shook my head and spoke in dark tones as the reality of what I'd done truly landed on me. "No. Shaddani magic remakes things or takes from them. The Dark Gift is Shaddani magic, but it's just a curse, a transformation of energy into the benefits we have. What I did to her was much more basic. The Morrigan provided the knowledge and the power, but I was the conduit. I simply snapped my fingers and rewrote her DNA from the bottom up. I twisted her mind, reshaping it like clay." I paused, licked my lips, and swallowed hard. Then I whispered, "And I loved doing it. It was thrilling, like nothing I've ever felt before, except maybe when I'd glamoured Pauline. Or, maybe…" I trailed off.

"When you killed Holley," Liz finished for me.

I nodded. "If I let The Morrigan loose, I could do amazing things, almost anything, but Goddess, Liz, the damage I could do."

"How can I help?"

"Just be there to keep me sane. Don't let me turn into the monster."

Liz patted my hand and cupped my face, pressing her lips to mine. "I won't," she said, her eyes gazing into mine. "I promise."

I nodded. "I'm stronger than all of my aunts put together. No one should have this kind of power."

"I can't think of anyone I'd rather have it, but use it wisely, love." She wrapped her arms around me, and I melted into them.

Marcella stormed into the kitchen. "Cait, Liz, go get dressed and take care of Aoife. I have to go. We have a crisis. The fucking National Guard just invaded Camp Eight. It's a fucking nightmare."

We both looked up. "What?" Liz asked.

"I don't know the full extent, but seventeen redcaps and brownies are dead; there may be more. The details aren't clear, but it looks like two National Guardsmen disobeyed orders and entered the camp."

"Oh Goddess," I whispered, and hot burning rage sang through my chest. The room immediately darkened, almost to pitch. I fought to control my instincts, but I wanted to go there, to kill every last human and be done with it. I wanted to burn away this human infestation, leaving only enough for breeding stock and food. I gripped the table and stared at the grain of the wood, fighting for stability, my eyes following the long crack in the surface.

Liz's gentle, cool hand landed on the back of my neck. "Easy," she whispered. "Easy, love." I looked up into her eyes, kind but firm, and the urge vanished, instantly washed away by her coaxing voice. "Easy, love. It's okay."

"Bloody hell," Marcella breathed as the lights brightened. "What was that?"

Liz's reply was calm and professional showing not a hint of fear. "That, Marcella, was The Morrigan."

I glanced up at Marcella. "I'm still working out some things from the trip," I said wryly, then turned to Liz. "I can't do this anymore. I'm going to save Aoife and find a way to give her this albatross. You can't marry me while I'm like this. I'm not even safe to be around."

Liz frowned, the hurt flashing in her eyes, but she took my hand. "Hey," she whispered. "I'm with you no matter what you decide, and it's my risk to take."

A loud whump sounded from somewhere in the city and shook the entire house, rattling the chandelier in the foyer and the dishes in the cabinets.

"Fuck. What now?" Liz swore.

CHAPTER FIFTY

"How did that thing get through the gate?" Liz shouted over the boom of the F-35s, screaming down the Charles River toward the Balor and dodging shots from its great red eye. Fortunately, it was either too slow or too dumb to hit the fighters, but they didn't seem to be doing any damage to it, either. The thing was like a living tank, just sluffing off the 25mm shells they shot at it.

"I have no idea," I yelled back, jerking the wheel of the Jeep to dodge bits of debris lying across Memorial Drive. Jess abruptly stood in the back, and her vast red wings swung forward, covering the open top of the Jeep just as the Balor fired another blast, plowing through the Mass Avenue bridge behind us.

Fortunately, it was deserted. A few abandoned cars fell into the Charles, along with the steel and concrete debris. But every shot had so much energy that the very concrete exploded, sending pebbles and bits of blasted material raining down. Evaporated water billowed across the river, hiding the far side from view. I had to swerve several times around wevkrana, scurrying across the road as I stood on the gas, desperate to get to the Lamia compound and Aoife.

Glancing ahead, I spotted the F-35s turning for another pass. As they leveled out, I noticed the open bomb bays.

"Shit," I shouted. "We need to get off the street. They're unloading heavy ordinance." I peeled off into the parking lot of a tech store just a hundred yards from the Lamia tunnel.

As I watched, waiting for Jess and Liz to climb out, the Balor crept further up the Charles, breaking through the BU bridge a half-mile downriver. The beast had been upgraded somehow. Huge red runes glowed on its plated hide. It was a protection spell, for sure. I could unravel it if I could get close enough, but that meant letting Aoife wait even longer, and I couldn't do that. The military would just have to handle it until I was done.

"It's on the move," Liz said as she exited the Jeep. "But I don't know how they'll stop something like that."

The hair on the back of my neck stood up, and I swung around, pulling my bóllom and slicing through the emisai that had been creeping up on us, felling it, and, of course, coating myself in ichor.

"Fuck," I bitched, trying to shake the foul-smelling stuff off my arms. "We can't stay out here. The city is crawling with emisai and wevkrana."

I took off toward the water tunnel entrance at a dead run, carrying Jess, Liz hot on my heels. Yeah, Jess could fly, but not fast enough to be anything but a target.

The two fighters roared past, fifty feet off the deck, each dropping a pair of bombs on the Balor.

"Get down," I shouted, and we dove for the deck. The ensuing explosions were massive, blowing out glass all across the riverfront.

"What was that?" Jess asked as we dusted ourselves off and ran on.

"That was four one-half ton guided heavy explosives," I answered, pausing briefly to look back, praying they'd killed it. Through the fog, I saw that the Balor was smoking but still just trundling along, clearly unharmed. "And it did fuck-all. Damnit."

We reached the tunnel entrance at the edge of the Charles, and Liz tore the gate open, motioning us inside. "Go, go!"

Liz and I dove in to swim for it. Jess, with no other real

options, fluttered her wings, jumped, and flew straight in as if she'd been born to it.

Minutes later, we were through the main hatch to the compound. Inside, the massive stone blocks supporting the wall and ceilings over the stairs had shifted dangerously. We didn't waste time gawking and ran on.

The swiveling doors into the Hall of Memory were propped wide with iron rods. Humans milled about, pressing body to body in a panic. It looked like a trainload of commuters from the T that they'd brought in through the Harvard Station entrance. Four lamia guards tried to keep them orderly and moving, but it was pandemonium.

"Order!" I commanded. The lights dimmed, and everyone stopped. They stopped talking, screaming, or moving. I grew to a height of twelve feet, my head just brushing the ceiling. The humans all stared up at me, terrified.

"Good," I said with a pleasant smile. "I have your attention. Two abreast, women and children first. Is that understood?"

No one spoke. They were all obviously too frightened, but a few nodded. I pushed my way to the front. Jess and Liz followed. It wasn't much effort; the crowd parted like the Red Sea as they tried to form themselves into two orderly lines.

"Excellent," I said and spun smartly, ducking through the massive door and calling, "Carry on," over my shoulder.

Jess and Liz followed me as I returned to my human form—well, human-ish, anyway. The hunger spiked again. "Goddess," I muttered. "I'm starving." Of course, my preferred food source was happily making its way inside. I'd get one alone later. Just that realization seemed to quell some of the itchiness.

When we reached the temple, another loud boom sounded, and the entire room vibrated with the intensity. "Sounds like the Air Force just dropped the hammer," I commented as we moved a little quicker, finding our way to the infirmary.

Inside, the chaos continued; easily twenty or so people lay around on gurneys and the floor and sat in chairs as Bian and a couple of Lamia struggled to treat them all. Most had minor injuries resulting from being trampled, pushed against something, or being hit by falling debris. Aoife still lay in repose, now pushed to the far corner to make room for others.

The emisai that had been Matt Reynolds still hunkered in the corner, watching everything with predatory eyes. I tried to ignore him, but his eyes tracked me as I approached the table.

"Cait," Bian said. "Finally. Please tell me you know what to do."

"I do," I said firmly. "But I can't do it here. There's too much noise. Is there an open room?"

"Déra's busy arranging defensive plans with the other Lamia, so you can use hers." Bian gave us directions, and I picked up Aoife, taking her to Déra's room, where I kicked closed the door to drown out as much of the ambient noise as possible. I needed to concentrate.

I set Aoife on the bed, and she shifted, saying something in Óşenic. Whatever it was, it was garbled, and I couldn't understand.

"I'm here, sis. I've got you," I whispered, then knelt on the floor.

Her tarzhi were a mess, tangled and warped around the two bright souls orbiting frighteningly close together. I pursed my lips. Úmbra needed her lehos, but so did Aoife.

Another explosion somewhere above rattled the room. More dust and bits of stone rained down on my head, breaking my concentration.

I put everything out of my head and closed my eyes, diving back down into Aoife's body. Aoife's soul was like a massive star, drawing energy away from Úmbra's as they spiraled together. Already, Úmbra's soul was dimming, losing cohesion. The normally beautiful silver ball of light was fuzzy at the edges, the magic of her soul fraying in places.

I yanked at my own soul, tethering her to me by a silvery cord, allowing it to draw from me. The agony of diving through my curse like that was hellish, and the hunger drove to eleven, but there was nothing I could do.

It was one thing, drawing together tarzhi outside my body or examining my own soul, but linking through the curse was torture. My chest heaved with pain as if I'd been shot or perhaps were having a heart attack. My skull burned from the inside. It hurt so much that I whimpered with it. But I kept going, tying myself to Úmbra's fate. If she died, so would I. It was dangerous, but it didn't matter. Some things were worth it. Katie would understand.

"If I don't survive this," I ground out painfully. "Tell Katie and Leah that I love them."

Someone said something in reply, but I couldn't make it out through the raging whine in my ears. It might have been Liz or Jess. I wasn't sure. Once the thread took hold, the pain vanished, but the drain felt like every ounce of strength was fading. Exhaustion pulled at my muscles. My body felt heavy. My thoughts started to turn sluggish. My soul was draining away from two different directions: the transfusion to Úmbra and my Dark Gift.

I steeled my thoughts and followed the twisting tarzhi away from Úmbra's soul until I found it: her lehos. It was magnificent, spun with all manner of magic that vibrated and twisted like spun glass in motion. I focused deeper, finding its core, an empty place where Úmbra's soul had once sat.

Now what, I thought. I struggled to remember what Áine had said. *Most magic, dear cousin, doesn't require some massive calculation. Be simple in application. Use what you know.*

I watched it again. Each cell of the tarzhi had a trillion tightly packed strands of tarzhi, all in motion, pulsing to a rhythm. Deeper still, the center of a cell—I assumed because it just looked like a collection of highly organized threads—pulsed as well. As I watched, more tiny clumps of tarzhi spun toward it, shifted the rhythm, and then floated away, spent.

Holy shit, they're memories. *The lehos holds every memory of every lifetime. All that Aoife and Úmbra are experiencing are being added to the whole.* And then I had it. I knew exactly what to do.

The tarzhi delivered the memories. If I could simply replicate the process in another cell, a new lehos would grow. It was just a bunch of neurons—and an incredibly sophisticated DNA chain, but my intention should be enough. The magic of the lehos should do what it was designed to do.

I drew out until the entire beautiful little parasite that had almost killed me was in full view. I snatched a single thread from a cell in the roughly brain-shaped mass that held Aoife's consciousness. Only one thread of trillions from one cell, not even an entire neuron, I suspected. It tried to snap back into place, but I didn't let go. I attached it to the lehos and then drew my perception back to watch.

At first, it seemed to work. But then it stopped as if something was missing.

An explosion rocked the entire camp. Dust blew under the door from the hallway outside. I pushed it aside. There was nothing I could do now. I was committed. But I rocked slightly, my head beginning to feel light, the hunger rippling under my skin like insects.

"Why isn't it working?" I murmured.

"Why isn't what working?" A voice said—my mother's voice.

"Mama?" I murmured. When had she entered the room? How long had she been standing there? I looked, but there was no one.

Still, though, I explained with increasingly slurred speech what I was trying to do, and she stated simply, "The lehos move, dear."

"Drink," Jess said, and she pressed her wrist to my mouth. I bit in and sucked at it greedily. The sudden influx of pleasure almost threw my concentration, but it helped, and it drove away the hunger for the moment. Jess pulled away at some point, and the hunger returned with a vengeance. I was being consumed.

I tied the nerve cell with a nearby muscle cell, and the process started again. This time, it didn't stop. It accelerated.

"It's working," I whispered in awe. "I can see it. It's like watching music become thought." My head turned fuzzy and everything seemed to take on a silvery quality.

"Cait? Cait?" Liz shrieked far away. Then, it was quiet, and I was floating in warm, tranquil waters of beautiful turquoise blue. The warm sun beat down upon my nude body as I floated on my back. I was in the shallow waters of a half-moon beach. Small fish schooled nearby.

"Oh," I whispered. "This is nice." I was dead—again. I wondered absently if I'd saved Aoife and Úmbra or if they'd died.

Light splashing caught my attention, and I sat up. Not far away, at the shore, two women stared at me, hands on their hips. Their forms were blurry. "Well, come on," one of them said. "Get out of the water, ya eejit. Gods, how thick can you get?"

I didn't want to get out of the water, but the current began pushing me toward the two women. Finally, realizing that I'd get no rest here, I stroked for shore.

As I approached, the female figures resolved into Úmbra and Aoife. "Oh! Did you die, too?" I asked. I thought maybe I should feel bad about it, but our troubles were over, and I couldn't bring myself to care too much.

Úmbra gave me a stern look. "No, stupid, we're saving you. Now get up!" Her voice resonated in my ears as if she'd shouted.

My sister joined in. "Come on, Cait! Wake Up!"

The beautiful waters vanished, and my eyes flew open. I was lying on a gurney. Liz and Aoife stood over me to one side. Úmbra perched on the other, a hand on my forehead.

"Is this another hallucination?" I asked.

"No," Úmbra said in perfect English and stuck a bag of blood in my face. "You're awake. Now get up. We have problems."

"But how?" I asked, gratefully taking the bag of blood.

"Caileigh," Morgan said from next to the door. She was leaning against the wall, arms crossed. "It was urgent, and her dead body wasn't helping anyone."

Úmbra laid a hand on my arm and kissed my forehead. "Thank you," she murmured.

"How long was I down this time?" I asked, giving Aoife a nervous glance.

"Just over an hour," Liz said, walking around the gurney into view—tears of relief on her face. "The Balor is still tearing up the city. The VP is trapped at the Capitol. The National Guard and the SWAT team are fending off a bunch of wevkrana, but it won't be long before—"

"Mother Darkness sends emisai," I finished for her.

She nodded. "Their bullets will be useless. And, Cait," her eyes turned hard, "Kim's there with him."

"Fuck," I swore, pulling myself off the gurney. "She picks now of all times to attack the city."

I froze, my gaze locking on the Matt-emisai thing. Its unblinking, eerie blue eyes seemed to pierce right through me, and suddenly, everything clicked: Senator Kim, Avra, Drusera —Mother Darkness. The ogumo.

"Shit," I whispered, the realization hitting like a freight train. "Drusera and Mother Darkness aren't one person. They're two."

Úmbra frowned. "What are you talking about?"

"They were whole once, maybe," I said, pacing. "But they were split—intentionally. Drusera is alive, sane, and in stasis somewhere. Badb hid her body and consciousness within the crystal. But Mother Darkness? She's all the rage, chaos, and hatred left behind. Festering. Alone. She has no real body—just the twisted, monstrous soulstone—and no actual eyes."

"Eyes?" Úmbra asked, still not following.

I nodded. "That's the key. She's blind. She can't see the way we do. But Avra—" I paused, a darker realization taking hold. "Months ago, before I entered Shaddan for the first time, Carol told me she'd had a vision. She described a woman's eyes, pleading, begging for help. It was Avra."

Úmbra held her hands out, exasperated. "And?"

"The attack on Óṣen," I continued, voice tightening with anger, "it wasn't about conquest. It was a feint. A trap. It was designed to lure Avra to Shaddan—and it worked. She's trapped there now, at the pinnacle of the soulstone, forever staring into a giant black mirror, maybe even karanite. And through that mirror, Mother Darkness sees. She's invaded Avra's mind and uses her to watch us. The emisai, the ogumo —anything she's created. They're her eyes."

I turned toward Matt, whose unblinking stare hadn't wavered. "And Kim—"

Aoife interrupted, her voice sharp with urgency. "The night

Kim accepted her senate appointment, she wore a black pendant. She's been wearing it ever since."

"Fuck," I muttered, my stomach dropping. "She's either in league with Mother Darkness or under her control."

The infirmary rattled violently as another shockwave rolled through the compound, shaking dust and bits of stone loose from the ceiling. A few people screamed. Aoife turned toward the trembling walls, her lips pressed into a grim line.

"That thing is going to bring this place down," she said, her voice low and tight.

I nodded, my mind racing. "If we don't deal with it, the Air Force is liable to nuke it."

Umbra's hand landed on my arm, her grip firm. "You just died—"

"I know," I interrupted, meeting her worried gaze. "But if we don't stop the Balor now, it won't matter. The compound, these people, maybe even the city…"

Aoife stepped closer, her expression hard. "We can't let that happen. I'll go with you."

I hesitated, glancing at her. "Are you sure? You've barely recovered yourself."

"I'm fine," Aoife cut in sharply, squaring her shoulders. "Besides, why else did you save me?"

The ground shook again, more dust raining down, underscoring the urgency.

"Fine," I said, relenting. "But we do this smart. No charging in without a plan."

I turned to Aoife. "If we can strip its protection, it might actually go down."

Aoife nodded. "And if the military drops another payload while we're close?"

"Let's just hope they're empty of heavy ordinance." I grinned faintly, and she rolled her eyes.

Aoife and I moved toward the exit, each step pulling me further into a haze of adrenaline and resolve. As we reached the door, the compound shuddered again, the distant sound of the Balor's roars mingling with the dull hum of jet engines above.

"Ready?" I asked, glancing at Aoife.

She nodded and gave me a crooked smirk. "Are you?"

Before we could step out, Liz grabbed my arms and gave me a fierce kiss. Then she dusted off my shoulders with deliberate care, her hand lingering as she cupped my cheek. "Go get 'em."

CHAPTER FIFTY-ONE

A few minutes later, I was feeling much better. I'd found a random guy to feed from. Dragging him into a private room had been pitifully easy: a spot of glamour, a snack, and a spot of glamour. It wasn't at all satisfying in an emotional sense, but it got the job done. I also realized why Katie had always acted like a starved leopard when she'd fed on men. *Blech.* The beard alone was enough to put me off, all scratchy and irritating. How did I ever think that was cool? As it was, I left the poor guy in a sorry state, but he was young and muscular. He'd recover. I hoped.

Once we'd made it back outside to Harvard Square, I pulled Aoife aside. "Do you know how to do this?"

She nodded, but her expression was less than confidence-inspiring. "I think so, but I don't understand how it works."

"Leave the formulas and mathematics for real spells. This is a shift. It's all about will and imagination." At her still skeptical expression, I added, "Trust me, sis. I won't let you fall. Now, let's see some wings, okay."

Aoife closed her eyes, and I felt the brush of magic run through me—far more powerfully than I expected, too. She shifted instantly, the massive wings unfurling behind her. Unlike mine, the feathers were a gorgeous silver. The tarzhi spun into her, swirling around in the visible spectrum as it added the necessary mass to increase her size.

I clapped. "Damn, you look good," I said encouragingly. "Okay, now, just follow my lead." I launched high into the sky, my wings unfurling and flapping, pulling me up further. Looking back, I watched as Aoife tentatively jumped, flapped, and then, with a bit of effort and not a small amount of wobbling, managed to get herself moving. I chuckled to myself. At least I was better than her in something. And to think, I used to be the big nerd in the family, and she was the jock.

A few minutes later, she reminded me just how athletic she was as she pulled up next to me. "This is— Holy shit, Cait! We're flying!"

Despite how serious things were, I couldn't help but laugh. "Just so you know, it's my first time, too. I just wish we had more time to play around." We made our way over to the Charles, where I dropped down to the deck, just a few feet off the water. Aoife followed.

"This is a little low, isn't it?" Aoife said, narrowly missing the mast of a sailboat floating loose in the river.

"We need to stay low—" I never got a chance to finish that sentence as an F-35 blasted by above us and nearly sent us tumbling into the water. "That's why we stay low. I don't fancy being a bug on anyone's windshield."

Aoife nodded vigorously, eyes wide. As she barely recovered from the jet wash, her wingtips brought up a heavy spray. "Gods, that was close."

I slowed and shook my head. "No. That was easily fifty feet from us, probably more. You sure you're ready for this?"

Aoife smirked. "Come on, Cait. Put some magic into it." She shot off ahead of me far faster than her wings could have carried her, and I realized she was surfing the tarzhi, using it to propel her. I followed suit and nearly bought it on one of the BU bridge supports that was still standing. This was all going to take some getting used to, but I did manage to pull up next to Aoife.

The Balor finally came into sight, stomping toward Science Center. "Distract it," I shouted as I drew my bollóm and rocketed forward. "And watch the helicopter!"

"How?" Aoife shouted.

"Hit it with some magic," I called back. "And watch out for the chopper!" I pointed off toward the buildings on the south side of the river, where a news chopper from Channel 8 hovered among the rooftops.

A lance of hot fire threaded in gold and purple blasted inches from me, and I had to dive sideways to avoid getting cooked. "Fuck, Aoife, really?" I muttered as the shot impacted the Balor, and it began to ponderously turn to see what had struck it. The rune on its flank where the shot had hit sputtered for a second, then flared back to life. *So,* I thought. *It's not invincible.*

The F-35 we'd seen before rolled in from the east and shot its flank, but now that I was closer, I could see that the bullets were pancaking on a magical shield. As the plane passed overhead, it pulled up and went ballistic. The great red eye of the Balor loosed a bolt and caught the F-35 on the wing. There was an explosion, the plane spiraled away, and a parachute opened maybe four hundred feet above us. Another shot just missed the tiny pilot but vaporized the parachute.

I yanked on the tarzhi, feeling it blast around me in a bubble as I took off. A half-second later, mist and pressure gathered around my head and shoulders, but it dissipated as I reached the pilot and used my wings to draw to an almost standstill, catching her in my arms. "Gotcha," I grunted as I dove for the deck, narrowly avoiding another shot from the Balor. I couldn't see her eyes through her visor, but the grimace of terror on her face was clear enough.

A ball of light flashed past us and into the Balor. Aoife had fired off another shot. I glanced back and caught lightning flashing over the Balor's body, lighting up the night. What I should have been doing was watching where I was going as I clipped that same fucking sailboat mast Aoife had just missed earlier. We tumbled into the water, skipping across to a painful and ungraceful landing before we both sank into the river.

Shit. She's gonna drown. I went to dive for her and discovered, much to my embarrassment, that we were on the shallow bar near the shore. The water was only three feet deep. The pilot had already pulled herself up and stood, peeling off her helmet. My eyes went wide. It wasn't the time, but damn, she was fucking gorgeous. Her tightly bunned brown hair just fell out around her shoulders. Hard green eyes, not all that different from my own, stared at me as I sat on my butt.

"Thank you," she said, holding out a hand.

I didn't take it. I had to weigh almost five hundred pounds in this form. "Sorry for the rough landing. I got distracted."

She smirked, and then her eyes narrowed. "Do I know you? Your voice sounds familiar."

Now that she mentioned it, hers did, too, and I glanced at her nametape. It read Captain Elise Frost. My heart fell into my stomach as I read the callsign embroidered below. "Frost Queen." Shit.

"No, I don't think we've ever seen each other before," I said, trying badly to add a little husk to my voice.

She raised an eyebrow, her voice taking on that icy cold tone she'd had when she'd intercepted us on the way out of town. "Are you sure? I'd swear you sound really familiar."

I nodded and pulled myself from the water, glancing down at her before turning my back. "Nope, never seen you before in my life."

"Cait," Aoife's voice said from somewhere nearby, though it was really faint.

I cleared my throat. "Look, sorry about your aircraft, I—uh —I need to get back to it."

I took off, suddenly ruing my luck and, maybe, just a little, my engagement. Goddess, she was hot, and there was no ring on her finger. I sighed and took off back toward the Balor. A few seconds later, I caught up with Aoife, who was hovering just over the river.

"It must be nearsighted or somethin'," she joked. "It's a terrible shot."

I shrugged. "It's just a siege engine; it's not intelligent, really. They seem to be designed to wreak havoc on the battlefield and not much else. I just can't figure out what it's— uh oh."

The Balor's eye glowed. I pulled the tarzhi into a tight shield in front of us as it fired. Aoife and I were blown backward and sent skipping across the water again. I managed to pull out. Aoife skidded and sank before popping back up.

"You were saying?" I asked as she shot back up into the air next to me.

"Fair play to ya," she replied. "So now what?"

"You hit it again, and I stab it in the eye and hope that the explosion doesn't kill me," I said flatly.

"That's a shite plan," Aoife said as she took off. "Absolute bollocks."

She wasn't wrong. It *was* a shit plan, but it was the best one I had. The only shadowsteel I had was my sword, and then I paused, looking at my hip. Badb's dagger hung there, the bright white glow. The memory of Nastasia flashed in my mind, and a dark, chaotic rage pulsed in my chest, squeezing it hard. "No," I ground out, but it kept pushing at me. "I don't have time for this."

Aoife loosed another shot at the Balor, drawing it further down the river toward me. I narrowed my eyes and shot off toward the beast faster than I thought I could. Vapor condensed in a funnel around my feet as Badb's armor coalesced across my body. I drew the dagger. A ragged sort of joy filled me, drawing a malicious smile to my lips.

Lightning flashed down across the water as the power of The Morrigan rained down, pelting the river, the trees, the Balor, and anything it could find to ground it. I didn't care. This is what I lived for.

I screamed. The beast turned toward me, firing another shot. The shield I conjured this time was stronger—much stronger. The beam simply stopped and petered out as I dove for its great red eye. I couldn't believe I'd finally channeled her. I still had control. I would stop the thing and then ease back, quelling the chaos that swirled within me. I hurled the dagger and watched it spin through the air.

It never made it. The dagger smacked into the shield, flared brightly, and then simply fell into the river below somewhere near the lumbering hulk's massive foot. Rage flared inside my chest at the denial of my victory. I screamed with the fury of Badb, and the beast recoiled, but only for a moment. Then, the flash of its eye caught me again as the tight beam of red magic lanced into me, hurling me across the sky. I had been unshielded, but I'd survived.

I slammed through a heavy glass window, tumbling into an office full of gawkers in the John Hancock tower, some three hundred feet above the street. A bit of blood leaked down my face, dripping to my lips. I licked it away with a smile. The wind whipped into the office like a gale and sent my hair flying. With a grin of satisfaction, I hurled myself into the night.

I had been going about this all wrong, I decided.

"Come to me, Mother, bringer of Chaos, the beautiful siren of battle," I cried, and the chaos filled me. I caught sight of my reflection. My eyes burned bright in fiery blue. My form began to change as the tarzhi flooded me. My wings took on a leathery appearance, my neck stretching as my head and body swelled, my hands and feet twisting into massive claws. Moments later, the image of a great black dragon, like those of Nemhain's stories, met my eyes. My mouth split wide in a toothy grin. The Morrigan had me, and I didn't care.

I twisted around in the air, flying for the great beast in the river. Drawing in a breath, I felt the heat in my belly burn brightly, and I exhaled a gout of liquid flame that doused the creature with a bright blue fire, bits splashing away onto the remains of the Science Center, setting it ablaze.

A lance of magic fired past me into the beast. The runes flared again. *Oh, Aoife, if you could only know this power,* I thought as I plummeted down to land on the massive Balor, tearing into its flank with my claws. Finally, after plundering the city without a sound, it roared in pain. A black-clawed nail tore through its thick hide, rending one of the runes, which flared and flickered out.

The creature bucked harder than I had thought it could, hurling me upward and off as it turned and blasted me again, sending me sprawling into the northern shore, leaving a long furrow in the grass.

Another lance of light, this time far to my left, fired into the Balor's flank, and it roared.

"No!" I screamed. "It's mine!"

I pulled myself up, but Aoife fired again, taking a chunk out of the Balor. More runes flared and died.

"No!" I screamed. "Mine!"

I sought out my sister and spotted her, flying around the great monster like an insect. I breathed a gout of flame at her, but she dodged aside. She fired again, finally digging deep into the wound for the third time. The Balor roared, faltered, and collapsed into the river, its bulk sending water crashing across the shores and into the streets on either side. Some of it sluiced across me, and I shook my head to clear it.

"You bitch!" I screamed and launched myself upward, dropping a stream of fire on Aoife's position.

She emerged, her body aflame, but it didn't last long as her body exploded with light. At first, I thought she'd died, but that wasn't it at all. A great dragon covered in opalescent scales, long and serpentine, like something from Chinese myth, burst from the light and charged me.

CHAPTER FIFTY-TWO

"That was mine," I said as we faced off. "You can't leave anything for me, can you?"

"Cait," Aoife said. "This isn't you. It's The Morrigan. She's controlling you."

"No," I roared. "This is me. For all of my life, I walked in your shadow, never good enough, never strong enough. Always fighting to be like you. And then you were taken away, protected, and loved while I was left to rot and scour a shitty life from what was left. No more!"

I lunged forward, jaws snapping on empty air like a thunderclap, but she twisted away, her sinuous body undulating with lethal grace. My teeth clicked on nothing a second time as her coils whipped around me, crushing and unrelenting. I wrenched free, my scales scraping against her, just as her head darted close.

Her maw opened wide, revealing dagger-like fangs dripping venom that hissed where it struck the air. A shimmering mist burst from her throat, and agony erupted across my midsection as my scales blistered and burned away. I roared and fell, spiraling toward the Charles below.

Pain seared through my abdomen, but instinct drove me. With a beat of my wings, I rocketed upward, narrowly avoiding the dark waters. Aoife followed, snapping at my tail.

Desperate, I banked hard and twisted mid-air, sending a gout of flame in her direction.

I missed. Instead, the fire licked over the shoreline, igniting a row of houses. My roar of frustration drowned out the screams below. *Fuck. She's too nimble.*

She closed in. I soared higher, the cold air burning my lungs, but I knew height wasn't enough. I needed more than speed— I needed her off guard. As Aoife's shadow swept beneath me, I spun sharply, tucking my wings tight. The sudden plummet left her no time to react.

I hit her like a comet, and we collided with a force that sent shockwaves rippling through the clouds. Her claws raked my sides, drawing blood, and I felt her coils tighten, crushing the air from my lungs. My wings, trapped against my body, fought uselessly. Her fangs drove toward my neck, and I twisted, sinking my teeth into her instead. The metallic taste of her blood hit my tongue as her dripping venom began seeping into my wounds.

We plummeted together, a tangled mass of teeth, claws, and fury. The city below raced toward us, growing larger by the second. She writhed, trying to overpower me, but my sheer weight dragged her down. The rooftops loomed. Panic clawed at the edges of my mind, but adrenaline drowned it out.

With a violent jerk, I broke free of her hold and shoved her aside. My wings snapped open, catching the air just in time to veer up, a whisper away from crashing into the earth. Aoife hit the ground with a deafening crash, scattering debris, crushing cars, and sending shockwaves through the streets.

But she wasn't finished.

Storm clouds churned in the sky, summoned by her wrath. Lightning streaked dangerously close as I shot upward, aiming for cover in the roiling tempest. The air grew heavy with electricity, and the first droplets of rain stung like needles against my raw skin.

I need a plan, I thought, every beat of my wings sending agony flaring through me. I can't beat her like this. Not in the open.

Above the city, cloaked in the storm, I hovered. My breath

came in labored gasps, every moment stretching taut with anticipation. Below, the chaos continued: fires burned, people screamed, and Aoife's shadow moved, relentless, hunting. My time was running out.

Why would you want to beat her? Drusera's voice broke in. *Let it go, Skaja.*

"Shut up!" I roared and blocked her out. It had been a mistake. In my maddened state, I wasn't thinking clearly. Like an arrow fired from one of Déra's bows, Aoife shot from the misty clouds and latched onto my neck, her jaws crushing down on my windpipe. As a vampire, it wouldn't matter, but the dragon needed to breathe. I raked down her body with my claws, finally finding purchase and leaving bloody furrows behind and shaking her teeth loose with a sickening tearing sound.

"Cait, stop," she pleaded. "Get ahold of yourself. This isn't us. We don't fight. We've never fought. I love you. Liz loves you."

"Shut up," I growled as we broke through the clouds into the night sky high above. "Just shut up! You bitch. They loved you the most! Every holiday, every year after you were gone, Ma went to you, leaving me behind like dead weight."

"Cait. That's not my fault, nor is it yours. Can't you see what this power is doing?"

My eyes narrowed. "It's made me strong! Stronger than you. I'll kill you."

Pain echoed in Aoife's slitted eyes as she wrapped her coils around me one more time, compressing my wings painfully to my side. "Then we die together."

The air thundered past us. Lightning flashed as I called on everything I could to dislodge her, but she hung on, even as the heat of the flashing electricity scorched us both. Finally, I looked at her and opened my mouth, loosing a great stream of liquid blue fire right into her face.

"We go together," she grunted, eyes burned away, mouth savaged by my fire. "It'll be alright. I'm not letting go."

The clouds fell away as we plummeted into the city. I struggled and screamed, but I couldn't get free. The world went black as we impacted like a meteor from the heavens, a burning star pulled from the sky to crush whatever might be below.

I woke with a start. I lay in Boston Common. Fires burned all around; bodies of people littered the ground, crushed as we'd hit. To my left, only a few feet away, Aoife lay, her silver hair splayed around her head.

I scowled. "I am the Queen of Shaddan," I whispered. "And this is what comes of challenging me." I leaned down, though, and put a finger to her neck. Her pulse was strong. She was alive.

Somewhere inside, buried deep amid the rage and chaos that suffocated my psyche, relief tickled at me. Slowly, I surveyed the destruction we'd wrought.

No, I thought. *This is my fault. I did this.* The chaos tried to rise again, and hot rage burned in my chest, but it guttered as I spotted a body, a human, a cop.

"Cardozo," I whispered in horror. "Mother of Waters, what have I done." Tears stung my eyes as I realized what I'd become.

Ever so carefully and gently, I lifted Aoife from the ground, cradling her to me. "Mother Nemhain, help me," I cried in pain as I took off into the sky. From the air, I could see the destruction. Half the city was on fire.

Boston, my home, was a battered landscape. The seaport was devastated by the flood brought by the Akkorokamui, and now this. *How many,* I wondered. *How many had died at my hand tonight? I am the monster.*

I landed at the tunnel entrance to the Lamia compound and carried my sister inside, walking across the water until I reached the dock. A line of people stood outside the water door, looking shocked and beaten. Inside, the line expanded, still running two by two into the compound. Desolate faces covered in soot and grime greeted me with grim expressions. A woman held an unconscious child. She was alive, but whether she had been caught on the edge of the destruction or was simply sleeping, I wasn't sure. Her mother watched me pass with hollow eyes.

Inside the Hall of Memory, Lamia moved around, handing out supplies and helping the injured. I couldn't look at them. There were no accusing gazes. They didn't know who I was. They couldn't reconcile the dragon they'd seen with the creature that now passed among them. I was just another bearer of the injured to them. But their furtive glances at my attire and the strangeness of my sister's body burned like damnation.

"Cait?" Liz called when I entered the temple proper. She was standing at a table, writing down names of missing loved ones and promising to help find them. "What happened?"

I blinked slowly as her words filtered in. "I did," I answered in a daze. "I happened." My voice was empty, devoid of emotion. I couldn't let myself feel anything. I'd break. So I kept walking, finally delivering my sister to a gurney in Bian's lab. Liz followed, plaintively begging me to talk to her, but I just couldn't.

Morgan rushed over. She'd been treating minor injuries with what minimal medical training she had. "Aoife, baby! Aoife?" She turned toward me. "What happened?" The lack of accusation in her eyes, her ignorance of my part in Aoife's state, felt like a dagger in my chest. I didn't answer. Instead, I turned and walked away, leaving the room, Liz still close behind. Finally, as I reached the secret exit in the back of the compound, far north of the main water door, Liz grabbed my arm.

"Cait," she said. "Talk to me."

"I—I can't," I whimpered almost inaudibly. "It's my fault. It's all my fault."

I stepped through the door and into the dark tunnel beyond. Liz followed. "Cait, what are you doing? Where are you going?"

I spun on her. "Liz, you can't be near me. No one can be near me. I'm too dangerous. Don't you understand? I just destroyed half of the city and nearly killed Aoife. I have to go someplace where I can't hurt anyone."

"No!" she snapped. "You aren't leaving me. You're not leaving us. Katie and Leah need you."

I snorted mirthlessly. "That," I said, raising my arms and calling a portal, "is the last thing they need." I turned and looked at her one last time, tears running down my face. "Goodbye, Liz."

Liz sniffled. "No, Cait, you're not going without me, without us."

I turned and stepped through the portal, snapping it shut behind me.

The wevkrana parted in front of me as I approached the black gate, scurrying aside at just the threat of my existence. The last time I'd been here, I hadn't understood. I'd thought the land beyond was hell—and in most respects, I'd been right.

Now, it is home. I stepped through.

EPILOGUE

Elizabeth

I stared at the television, watching troops, tanks, and other miscellaneous military equipment take up positions around the city. These images were mixed with bits of footage from two weeks ago, both amateur and professional, replaying the battle on the Charles River. Katie and Leah sat on the couch huddled with me, and Marcella stood behind us as we saw Aoife and Cait fall over and over, interspersed with footage of Aoife and Cait taking on what people were calling 'The Boston Kaiju.'

"When is Mama coming home?" Leah asked softly as we watched the two dragons plow into the chaos on Boston Common. Fortunately, they'd opted not to keep replaying images of the dead and battered on the field.

"We're going to go find her," I replied.

"Mama?" Katie said, giving me a hopeful look.

"She's hurting, Katie, and she thinks she's too dangerous to be around us. We're going to help her."

"Yes," Katie said. "Finally. When do we leave?"

"Tonight," I said, then added, "Now be quiet. We need to hear this. Leah, I need you to go to the other room for a minute."

Leah didn't argue. She knew what was coming and what

was happening. She trotted away into the tiny side bedroom of the little apartment where it had all started. Cait's apartment.

The decor was better, but it was still a tiny dungeon. Even so, I felt strangely at home in this place, as if Cait had left part of herself behind. I even thought that I caught the smell of cinnamon and burnt embers from time to time, though that was certainly my imagination.

Finally, an image of the East Room of the White House, hovering as a split in one corner of the screen, grew and replaced the constant violent replays. President James stalked from the wings, striding purposefully to the podium. Despite his kind blue eyes and a salt-and-pepper beard, he had the look of a man on a mission. *A mission*, I mused, *that would be rudely interrupted.*

"My fellow Americans, I come to you this evening with a heavy heart. I have ordered that all federal facilities fly their flags at half-staff as we mourn Vice President Calvin Elridge and all the valiant men and women of both the Massachusetts National Guard and the Boston Police Department who laid down their lives in a valiant attempt to defend the Massachusetts Capitol. But there are bright spots. The Senate has confirmed Mina Kim, the Junior Senator from Massachusetts and my nominee for Vice President Elridge's successor. As such, she will fill a vital role—"

The screen abruptly blanked before returning with an image of a nondescript figure with their face hidden in a dark hoodie. Behind them, barely glowing with a menacing red light, great butterfly wings shifted slowly.

"Ooh, spooky," Marcella joked.

I didn't laugh. I was too angry. "I thought it was a good touch. Jess, with her bubbly personality, makes a great psycho bad guy in the shadows. It's right out of a good anime."

"I'm sorry, ladies and gentlemen," Jess said from the depths of the hood. Somehow, she still sounded bouncy. "I know you were expecting a Presidential announcement about the recent events in Boston. However, there are some things you should know."

"This is the part you wrote, right, Mama?" Katie asked,

looking about to jump out of her seat.

"Yes, now hush," I hissed. Katie tossed me an irritated look, but she snapped her jaws shut at my returning glare. I wasn't in the mood.

Jess continued, "You have been led to believe that the preternatural creatures living in squalid poverty beneath Boston are somehow to blame for the series of events that have befallen the city. We assure you that nothing could be further from the truth. They had nothing to do with the Liberty Hotel, the rogue tsunami, or the recent attack on the city by a group of monsters." The screen flipped over to a black-and-white video. "But our leaders have decided that such is true without judge or jury, only executioners."

We watched through cameras that had been mounted at all of the camp entrances as tactical teams ran inside, looking for the preternatural creatures that had lived there until just a week ago.

In Camp Two, we observed them gaping in awe at the massive entrance warehouse. When they arrived in the next chamber, they found it all but abandoned. The brownies and redcaps were all in Ireland now, their very existence providing a supporting bulwark to the magic Wisteria needed to restore her home and people.

We all watched as the dryads, whom we had been unable to move, trapped as they were within their trees, all appeared. They all raised their hands in surrender and knelt down. But it didn't matter. The tactical officers began shooting them down. It only took a few seconds before all fourteen of the dryads in the camp were dead. It was horrific.

Further still, inside the camp, the men searched, finding the empty home of the mermaids, who were back in the ocean, thanks to the serum cooked up by Marcella, Mother Lamia, and Bian. There was little left but the bungalows, an empty pool of water, and sand. A solitary mermaid sat, her red hair flowing around her soft, tan shoulders, half transformed on a rock by the pool, singing a lovely song. There was no glamour in it, though. She was no threat.

When the men walked to the pool, she stopped singing and

looked at them, her sea-foam eyes searching and afraid. A tear flowed down one cheek.

I closed my eyes. I couldn't watch it again as the leader of the team, an Army captain by his rank insignia, shot her in cold blood.

Marina had been her name. The serum had failed on her for some unknown reason, and we hadn't had time to sort it out before we'd had to evacuate. Marcella had begged her to go with the others. But in Ireland, though the Light Fae could likely keep the air and water clean, she would have only large lakes and ponds, and Marina had said she couldn't abide being cut off from the sea any longer. In the end, she'd chosen to stay behind, partly in solidarity with the dryads but mostly because, as she had said, she wanted her death to make a statement. And it would. Billions would see this.

Another monitor displayed Bian's lab, where men in lab coats looked around for anything but found only a few wiped computers and the ashes of burned files.

Camp Eight, where the Bethadi had lived, was empty. After what would become known as the Battle on Boston Common, they had simply left, returning home, but not before making a valiant effort to save the VP. Unfortunately, it took only one koşant to infiltrate the capital and kill almost everyone—except for Senator Kim, of course. Somehow, in the chaos, she'd slipped away.

All of the other Camps were likewise empty, their occupants having either fled to the countryside where they could or having journeyed through Light Fae portals to stay in Ireland.

When she returned, Jess spoke again, her voice choked with emotion. "There is your government. These are the people who lead you, murdering innocent girls in the dead of night. Now look to your children, your spouse, yourself even. Anyone could have the blood of the Fae running through their veins. Until now, they have been living peacefully among us for thousands of years. Eventually, the government will round them up, too. Is this the world in which you want to live?"

The screen went blank and then flipped back to the East Room, where President James stood transfixed. In a rare moment for the man, he seemed at a loss for words. He looked to his left, seemed to get some offscreen queue, and spoke. "This country will not be intimidated by thugs, hackers, or—or —" He stopped speaking and was hustled away from the podium by a cadre of secret service. The screen switched to the presidential seal before the CNN anchor returned with the talking heads all sputtering to figure out what just happened.

I flipped it off. "So," Marcella said, "do you still think it was a bad idea?"

I shook my head. When M. had suggested this entire plan, I'd been skeptical, but I couldn't deny the power of the images we'd seen. "You ready for the next step? It's about time." I gave her a cruel smile. Sometimes, you just had to let the devil out of the box.

Marcella donned her headset and opened her laptop. Unlike the previous videos, this image was in full color with sound— and it was live.

As we gazed on, Senator Kim clacked her way across the marble floor of Marcella's home, now abandoned and completely devoid of furniture. I glanced at the massive Traulsen against the wall to my left and smirked, remembering how much effort it had taken to get it in here, hoisting it over the balcony.

Marcella's ensuing, ice-covered smile drew a shiver from me. It held no real emotion other than malign glee as she reached out and pressed the button on the desk-bound transmitter in front of her. "Hello, Madame Senator, or should I say, Madame Vice-President." Her tone could have frozen fire in place.

"Where are you?" Senator Kim replied, looking around.

"No, Madame Vice-President, that's not how this works. You're under the misperception that you are the predator, and we are the prey. I assure you, it's quite the opposite."

Kim glanced over to the Secret Service man behind her. He had his hand to his ear, but he shook his head silently at the Vice-President.

"Don't bother, Miss Kim. We've been quite thorough. I know with whom, or should I say what, you have made a deal, and you should know that such deals are easy to undermine when you have something that the other party wants more." Marcella glanced down at the two tablets sitting to her right, the Earth tablets.

The Vice-President blanched in Ultra Hi-Def, and Marcella smirked. I wasn't entirely comfortable with what came next, but I wasn't given a vote. I understood the threat this woman and her political aspirations posed to all of us, but still, it was a risk.

"What do you want?" The Vice-President asked. She tried to show courage and bravado, but I could hear the tremble in her voice.

"From you? Nothing. Not anymore. There was a time, perhaps, when we could have come to an arrangement, but you had to go full Nazi on us. And that was—" Marcella paused as if searching for the right word. But I knew better. She'd probably rehearsed this little speech several times. "—unwise," she continued.

"There's a reason that everyone believed that we were a myth for all this time. We were very good at covering our collective asses. You, however, are a public figure with a very short lifespan. Very short. Understand that we are not interested in negotiation. We have no demands. We have no worries, either. But I will tell you this. Your lovely little relocation bill will not pass through the Senate despite the way you orchestrated the death of the previous Vice-President. Congratulations, by the way, on your appointment, though I did watch your confirmation hearing. It was brutal, to say the least. The Democrats really have it out for you and your agenda, don't they? If I were you, I'd watch your back."

Vice-President Kim finally spotted the camera mounted on the wall next to the staircase and turned fully to face it. "You can't threaten me."

Marcella half-laughed sarcastically: "I'm not threatening you at all, Madame Vice-President. That would be a crime, after all. I have been alive for over a millennia, and I know how to play a very, very long game with absolutely ruthless efficiency."

"Ma'am, we should leave," her secret service detail said, looking around.

"Oh, not to worry, Madame Vice-President. We have no plans to harm you." The implied 'yet' hung in the air for a moment. "But suffice it to say that we are out of your reach. That being said, I do have a question for you."

The newly minted VP was visibly shaking now. "What is it, Miss Carson?"

"How does a woman, elected as Mayor on a platform of equality and justice, decide one day just to become an ambitious fascist? More importantly, how smart do you think it was for the Vestry to side with you given that when your use for them is over, they'll be your next target, hmm?"

The surprise on the VPs face was certainly worth the price of admission. She was, as Morgan, or maybe Carlos, would say, 'about as spooked as a chicken in the fox den.'

The chill in Marcella's voice was terrifying, as was the look of absolute pleasure in her eyes. "It was good talking with you, Madame Vice-President. We'll be seeing you around."

She clicked off the microphone.

Kim glowered at the camera for a few moments, then turned and stalked out of the building.

Marcella laughed and grinned. "Goddess, I love my job sometimes."

I rolled my eyes. "M., you're a right villain, you know that?"

"No," Marcella said. "If I were a right villain, I would have blown up the house with her in it, faking my own death in the process. Though, I might still. Who knows?"

A knock came at the door. "That'll be Aoife," I said and went to open it. "You missed it," I said with a smirk.

"Yeah, for sure," Aoife responded, stroking Fiona's fur as the little purple lemur cooed quietly on her shoulder. "But I just couldn't watch Marina die again. Sorry."

I tugged her inside. "It's okay. I understand. I couldn't watch it again, either. We're almost ready. Is the car loaded?"

Aoife nodded. "Jeep's loaded. The batteries are charged. I put a fifteen-gallon jerry can in the back. Are you sure you want to bring Leah?"

I nodded. "If anyone can get through to Cait, it's her." Reaching down, I picked up the cat carrier to Jabba's many protests. "Here, add this to the collection." Turning toward the rest of the apartment, I called, "Come on, children, time to go."

"Finally," Katie bitched, but Leah came running out of the tiny bedroom she shared with Katie.

Grabbing a few sundries, a cooler full of blood, and the tablets, we made our way out, Marcella in tow. On the street, we said our goodbyes to M. and climbed into the Jeep. Jabba meowed plaintively from the back but quieted down when Fiona hopped over the seat to peek in at him.

"Aww," Katie said as Fiona reached in and scratched behind Jabba's ear.

"Can you do this?" I called to Aoife.

"I think so. I've visited the gate chamber now, and I've practiced the spell a few times." She raised her arms and said a few words. A portal opened, and the gaping maw of the black gate stood in front of us.

Aoife hopped in, and we drove through, bouncing up the ramp into the fog of Shaddan beyond. A hard left turn took us what we'd figured out was south, toward the ruined city of Nochtanmore, the Vermillion Palace, and my wife—at least, I hoped.

GLOSSARY

Ánámensí (os. [aːˈnaːmɛn.siː]) Matron of one of the remaining thirty-seven high houses of the city of Işir on the world of Óşen.

Bethad (be. [ˈbeɪ.haːd]) The land of the Light Fay. The word itself means "life" in many languages, including many human languages.

Brellis (br. [ˈbrɛl.ɪs]) The homeworld of the Brellians, one of the signatories of the Covenant of the Gates. Brellis is a lush, temperate world celebrated for its fertile lands and advanced agricultural practices, particularly its renowned vineyards and exquisite wines. Brellian wines are highly sought after across the ten known worlds and form a cornerstone of their trade agreements through the inter-dimensional gates.

Centrus (unk. [ˈsɛn.trəs]) City that serves as a hub for the currently open inter-dimensional gates, including, most notably, the Kaushkari, Óşeni, and Niatamo gates.

Déra (os. [ˈdeɪ.raː]) Uncommon Óşeni female name. Most famously, the appellation of a former guard captain of Işir, who vanished following the defeat of Avra in the Cycle of Our Lady 6998.

Earth (unk. [ɜːrθ]) One of the ten known worlds connected by the inter-dimensional gates. Earth is currently interdicted under the Covenant of the Gates, a pact among the Brellians, Kyliri, Centrusians, and Óşeni that governs trade and gate usage. The reasons for Earth's interdiction are related to the maturity of human culture, though speculation abounds among the other worlds. Earth's absence from gate commerce has left it isolated, with little influence on inter-world relations.

Emisai (os. [ˈɛ.mɪ.saɪ]) Construct of Mother Darkness, this creature is bipedal but has no head or obvious sensing organs. Only black-steel as constructed by the Óşeni scholars of Mens-Dhe can harm them. Other metals without magical construction will leave no long-term injury.

Euphoris Flower (be. [ˈjuː.fɔː.rɪs ˈflaʊ.ɚ]) A mesmerizing flower native to Bethad, the Euphoris Flower is renowned for its radiant, rainbow-iridescent petals that shimmer hypnotically, captivating all who gaze upon it. This flower possesses a potent magical essence, capable of inducing vivid, addictive dreams—either of euphoric pleasure or harrowing nightmares—depending on how it is brewed.

Féagharach (sh. [ˈfeɪ.haː.rɑk]) The island that sits at the center of Lindon Danu, north of the Heroes' Field in Shaddan. At one time, it was a hill from which a branch of Crann Bethad grew before the sundering of Shaddan and Bethad.

Işir (os. [ˈɪʃ.ɪr]) Primary city of the world of Óşen. The city is ruled by a matriarchal priestess caste. Males are considered second-class citizens having fewer rights.

Karanite (sh. [ˈkær.ə.naɪt]) A mineral used to make the hardest known alloy of steel. It possesses magical properties and, when properly worked, can suppress Shaddani magic.

Kaushkar (ka. [ˈkaʊʃ.kar]) Kaushkar is a world of humanoid beings whose nobility are renowned as the most powerful magic users among the ten known worlds. Their leader, Dommus—also known as Dyeuspater—rules with an iron will, embodying the Kaushkari traits of arrogance and martial prowess. The Kaushkari are considered warlike and domineering by the signatories of the Covenant of the Gates, often posing a persistent threat to inter-world stability. Their society values strength, both in combat and magical aptitude, and their nobility wield immense influence, both politically and militarily. Kaushkar's history is marked by conflicts with other worlds, further cementing their reputation as a proud and aggressive people.

Koşant (os. [ˈkoʊ.ʃaːnt]) Bipedal demon-like creature with

razor-sharp claws, roughly man-shaped and covered in mottled insectile chitin. It has a triangular, mantis-like face with a beak-like mouth.

Kylr (ky. [ˈkaɪ.lə-]) Single-sex, bipedal humanoid species that is the dominant life form of the world known only as the Kylr Plain. At death, their corpse transforms into a worm-like second stage, carrying a parasitic animal that preserves the deceased Kylr's memories until introduced to a new host, where it assumes control.

Luminara (be. [ˌluː.mɪn.ˈɑː.rə]) The shining palace of Bethad and counterpart to the Vermillion Palace of Shaddan. It is the seat of power for the Bethadi Summer Queen.

Maigh Tuireadh (ga. [ˌmaɪ ˈtɪərə]) A legendary battlefield in Irish mythology, Maigh Tuireadh (meaning "Plain of Pillars") is the site of two great battles fought by the Tuatha Dé Danann. In the First Battle of Maigh Tuireadh, the Tuatha Dé Danann defeated the Fir Bolg to claim Ireland as their own. The Second Battle, fought against the Fomori, was a decisive and brutal conflict in which the Tuatha Dé Danann secured their place as the dominant force in Irish myth. This location symbolizes the enduring struggle between light and darkness, chaos and order, with the gods and heroes of the Tuatha Dé Danann triumphing through courage, cunning, and sacrifice. Maigh Tuireadh remains a potent symbol of resilience and the fight against overwhelming odds in Irish folklore.

Mirgan (br. [ˈmɪr.gən]) A species native to Brellis. Mirgans are distinguished by their bald heads, entirely black eyes, heavily muscled builds, and three-fingered hands and three-toed feet. Known for their physical strength and resilience, they often serve as soldiers or laborers in Brellian society. Mirgans are notable for their loyalty and discipline, often forming the backbone of Brellian endeavors requiring brute strength or endurance. Currently subjugated by the human population of Brellis.

Óşen (os. [ˈoʊ.ʃɛn]) One of the ten known worlds containing

gates to Centrus, the core city of the ancients who constructed the first gates. It is populated by a dioecious species known locally as the Óşeni.

Óşeni (os. [ˈoʊ.ʃɛn.iː]) Bipedal humanoid species populating the world of Óşen. They typically stand 2–2.1 meters tall, with lustrous gray skin, thick silver hair, and muscular frames. Scholars believe they inspired certain depictions of elves due to their pointed ears.

Shaddan (sh. [ˈʃæd.æn]) The homeworld of the Dark Fae, Shaddan is a devastated wasteland, its once-majestic dark forests and obsidian mountains reduced to barren ruins. As the dwelling of Mother Darkness, Shaddan remains steeped in shadow and legend, feared and reviled by the signatories of the Covenant of the Gates. Considered a place of evil, Shaddan is currently interdicted, cut off from inter-dimensional trade and gate travel. Its desolation is a grim testament to past cataclysms, and its feared reputation lingers despite its shattered state. A single well-guarded gate remains in Óşen which no mage has managed to close.

Spley Flower (sh. [ˈsplɛɪ ˈflaʊ.ɚ]) A rare and hallucinogenic plant native to Shaddan, the Spley Flower is poisonous to all but the High Shaddani Royalty. It is a key ingredient in "The Blood of Shaddan," a ceremonial potion integral to the rite of passage for Shaddani Royalty. Little is known of the details of these rites, as the knowledge has been lost among the signatories of the Covenant of the Gates. The Spley Flower's vivid, otherworldly blooms are said to hold visions of Shaddan's past and a connection to Mother Darkness herself, deepening its mystique.

Swasarí (os. [ˈswɑː.sɑː.riː]) The Swasarí are the Óşeni soldier corps, celebrated across the ten known worlds as the finest close-combat fighters in existence. Trained in a relentless regimen that hones both body and mind, the Swasarí are masters of melee combat, capable of overwhelming opponents with speed, precision, and unmatched discipline. Equipped with traditional

Óșeni weapons—typically sword and shield or spear and shield—they excel in formation tactics as well as individual combat. Their reputation stems not only from their prowess on the battlefield but also from their strict adherence to honor and loyalty, making them the backbone of the Óșeni military. To face the Swasarí in combat is to encounter a relentless and perfectly coordinated force, feared even by the most seasoned warriors of other worlds.

Xharpras (os. [ˈxɑr.prɑːs]) A stringed instrument of the Óșeni similar to a harp. The black-steel strings and unusual tunings create secondary thematic elements in music, such as the sounds of waves or wind. It is considered one of the most difficult instruments to play in the ten known worlds.

Umbrá (os. [ˈʌm.brɑː]) Uncommon Óșeni female name. Most famously, the appellation of a Kylr slave who was responsible or the downfall of Avra following the Dark Invasion in the Cycle of Our Lady 6998.

Umbryss (sh. [ˈʌm.brɪs]) The greatest of the Shaddani dragons, sworn to Badb and her successors. It is said that the fire of Umbryss can melt karanite stone, believed to be indestructible by almost any other means.

Valtárí (os. [ˈvɑːl.tɑː.riː]) The Valtárí are the elite warrior corps of the Óșeni, renowned for their exceptional combat skills and unwavering discipline. Unlike standard Óșeni soldiers, who typically wield sword and shield or spear and shield, the Valtárí are uniquely armed with a bóllom, a curved, single-edged sword designed for precise and devastating strikes, and a nisís, a finely crafted dagger ideal for close-quarters combat or finishing blows.

About the Author

Aoibh Wood lives in New England with her wife and their wonderful orange Tabby, who may or may not resemble an intergalactic gangster of some notoriety. She enjoys writing, playing guitar, and the occasional game or two.

Other books by Aoibh Wood

THE SENATOR'S WIDOW
THE SENATOR'S CHILD (COMING 2025)

THE LENA-VERSE

BUT I'M NOT A SUPERVILLAIN!!
EDEN BLOOM (COMING 2025)

Printed in Great Britain
by Amazon